Thirty-Eight
REASONS

Thirty-Eight
REASONS

INTERNATIONAL BESTSELLING AUTHOR
LEN WEBSTER

Published: Len Webster 2014
author.lennwebster@hotmail.com
Editing: Christina @ Black Firefly
www.blackfirefly.com
Proofreading: Jenny Sims
www.editing4indies.com
Cover design: Najla Qamber Designs
www.najlaqamberdesigns.com
Formatting: E.M. Tippetts Book Designs

emtippettsbookdesigns.com

Books By
LEN WEBSTER

Sometimes Moments

Thirty-Eight Series

Forever Starts Today (Thirty Eight #.5) Coming Soon
Thirty-Eight Days (Thirty Eight #1)
Thirty-Eight Reasons (Thirty Eight #2)
What We'll Leave Behind (Thirty Eight #2.5)
What You Left Behind (Thirty Eight #3)
All We Have (Thirty Eight #4) Coming 2016

The Ribbon Duology

The Ribbon Chasers: a short story (Ribbon #0.5)
The Ribbon Catchers: (Ribbon #1) Coming Soon
The Ribbon Release: (Ribbon #2) Coming Soon

Happiness in marriage is entirely a matter of chance.
  Jane Austen, *Pride and Prejudice*

For my readers.
My reason for writing. My reason for continuing. My reason for
feeling so blessed.
You've blessed my life with your love and loyalty.
I love you all.

Prologue

Clara

A little ways down the road.

*A*ll she saw was white, the reflection too beautiful to be her own. Her body succumbed to her nervous trembles. Clara bit the inside of her cheek and stared at the mirror. Her dangling teardrop diamond earrings glittered against the sunlight, and her loose curls rested on the side of her face.

Clara's eyes travelled down and looked at the reflection of her white tulle wedding dress. It was beautiful. A smile spread across her face. *It was time.* She was finally getting married. The nerves that ravaged her system were purely due to her impatience. Clara wanted nothing more than to hear the sound of soft violins as she took her first steps down the aisle.

She glanced down at the engagement ring on her right hand. A pinch of sadness crept into her heart, but all she could do was push it away. Today was not the day to be sad. She left that part of her behind and now she was onto a new chapter in her life. Soon, a wedding band would join her beautiful diamond engagement ring. By the end of the night, she would have a new name. She smiled and thanked the heavens for him.

It wasn't easy. Not when Clara's past put up a fight. She was close to losing her engagement, her brother, and even herself. But in the end, she chose what was right, and in the end, that was what made her happy.

"It's time, Clara."

She turned away from the mirror to see her maid of honour holding up a bouquet of tulips. Clara looked up at Stevie and gave her a reassuring smile. They had both heard the sound of a soft knock before as her brother, Alex, walked into the bridal room.

"I've never seen such a beautiful bride in all my life, Clara. He's one lucky man," Alex said as he walked over to Clara and placed a kiss on her cheek.

Her heart tugged slightly and she looked at the tulips. Even when she was a little girl, they were the flowers she had imagined at her wedding.

"Do you think I made the right choice?" she asked as she looked up at her brother.

A slight frown had appeared before Alex smiled and placed his hands on Clara's shoulders.

"Clara, you know I'm not impartial. I'm just happy that you're happy." After everything they had been through, she was happy. Her life felt complete the moment she had said *yes*.

"*He's* there, right, Alex?" Clara asked. She needed to know that he would be there the moment she stepped into the aisle.

"Clara, Liam isn't doing a runner. It's *you* we're all worried about."

She closed her eyes and took a deep breath. With her brother walking her down the aisle to the person she would and could love forever, Clara knew she'd made the right choice.

"I'm not running, Alex. I'm staying. It was always him. He's the reason for this all."

Chapter ONE

Noel

*N*oel stared at the ceiling vents and let out a frustrated sigh. He leant into his leather office chair and focused on the white paint. July in Boston was hot, but it held nothing to the Australian heat. Australia's temperatures almost doubled what Massachusetts could reach. But in the eight months since his return, Noel had adjusted to life back in the U.S.

He never liked to think about *her*. Sometimes he couldn't help himself and sometimes he'd find himself frustrated and angry. That was when Noel would mindlessly be at the gym or at a bar. He needed a way of release. She still had a hold on his heart. He tried desperately to sever it, but nothing could erase the memories of her. So instead, Noel kept focused on Andrea.

Andrea had been his antidepressant. She took away the pain. Noel refused to call her *Andy*. Not when her full name suited her and separated her from the male dominance of G&MC. Something about her had attracted him the moment he saw her. Noel knew it was her headstrong attitude and her willpower to obtain what she wanted.

Andrea was essentially the complete opposite of the woman

3

who broke his heart all those months ago. Noel tapped his fingers on the leather arms of his chair and swivelled it around until he faced the large office view of the Boston skyline. In the months since his return, Noel had secured three important accounts as well as improving his chances of becoming a senior executive at the office. Long ago, all that didn't matter. Now, it was the centre of his universe. The more consumed he was with work and Andrea meant less time remembering.

"Noel, you busy?"

Turning his chair around, he saw Damien from Marketing standing at his door. Damien's dark hair was almost black and his tanned skin looked darker against the light grey suit he wore. Noel had found a mate in Damien now that he no longer had Rob or Max by his side. Noel couldn't speak so openly around Alex when it came to her. With Damien, it was different. He had no connection to her at all.

"Nah. I've finished with these accounts for the day. Gregson's had me checking the balances and making sure they add up," Noel replied as he leant forward and placed his arms on the cherry oak desk.

"Thought I'd come by and see how you and Andy were getting along for the move? Need an extra hand on Sunday?" Damien asked as he stepped into Noel's office.

Noel reached over, closed the folder in front of him, and stacked it on top of the pile he had formed on his desk. "Yeah. Come by whenever it suits you. Andrea has some furniture coming from her old place."

"You made room for her stuff?" Damien took the seat in front of Noel.

"My apartment has minimal furniture. You've been over."

"Yeah, but what about all her law books and her desk?"

Noel shrugged and started to unroll the sleeves of his white business shirt.

"I've got a spare room that's gone unused. It can be Andrea's office. Should be big enough," Noel said as he buttoned both of his cuffs.

There was silence between them until Damien breathed out and looked at Noel. "Listen, are you sure you're ready to have Andy move in?"

"Why?" Noel asked curiously as he reached behind the

4

back of his chair for his jacket.

"I don't know. But last night you weren't as excited as you led on to believe. Could it be..."

Don't say her name.

"Clara?"

Just her name made him freeze. He tried so desperately to forget her name. Damien saying it out loud brought all the pain crashing back down on him. Noel took two deep breaths and had to remember that he was the one to confide in Damien when he couldn't talk to Alex.

"She means nothing to me. You don't even know her!" Noel growled.

"Then why can't you say her name?"

Noel looked away and stared at his hands. "Does it even matter? I told you all that shit because I had a few beers."

Damien nodded twice and rose from his seat. "No. You told me all that shit because you needed to tell someone who wasn't Alex. You can try to lie to me all you want, Parker, but at the end of the day, you can't even face the facts. You *still* love Clara." Damien got up from his chair, walked toward the door, and stopped before he faced Noel. "I'll see you on Sunday. Realise that Andy's your girl now. Not Clara." Then he exited Noel's office.

Slamming his fists on the desk, Noel hastily got out of his office chair. Pure frustration and anger coursed through his veins. He knew he was being stupid for being so angry with her. It had been months since he'd last seen Clara Lawrence. Last time he'd checked, she had gone and fallen in love with Liam. Max and Rob never said anything about her when they spoke over the phone or through emails and messages. She was a topic they never discussed. But sometimes, all Noel wanted to do was talk about her and find out what he had missed since their separation. Find out if she ever thought about him.

You're with Andrea now.

He had to stop thinking about Clara. He had Andrea and she had an importance in his life. Noel pulled open the top drawer of his desk and took out his phone and wallet. He needed away from his office. Noel thought Boston, Massachusetts was enough distance from Clara. But no matter how far he was, she still affected his life in some way or another. She was the one who got away. The one who haunted his dreams and the one he didn't want to let go.

Noel pushed thoughts of Clara out of his head and hid the memories of her further into the pits of his closed and darkened heart. He couldn't remember their love; it caused too much pain in his life. Noel unlocked his phone to see a message from his best friend, Alex Lawrence.

> **Alex:** *Coming down to NY this month? Keira wants you and Andy over for dinner.*

Noel felt a sense of guilt. He had neglected his own friendship with Alex since *that* day in New York when Alex had revealed that he knew about him and Clara. Noel knew that Alex was trying hard to make things better between them. It wasn't Alex's fault, but Noel wanted to blame someone and found it easy to direct the blame on him. It was hard to admit the faults he couldn't fix.

> **Noel:** *Yeah, towards the end of the month. Andrea's moving in on Sunday and I want her settled before we head down to NY.*

Noel sent the message, bent down, and picked up his briefcase. Before he even got to the office door, his phone vibrated in his hand. He stopped and read the new message.

> **Alex:** *Andy is moving in?*

Asking Andrea to move in with him was quick and decisive. He didn't want Alex telling him how soon it was or mention Clara's name. Noel took it upon himself to make the decision without Alex's guidance or advice.

> **Noel:** *Asked her over a week ago.*

> **Alex:** *Congrats.*

Noel looked at Alex's instantaneous message. One word and that was 'congrats.'

Noel: *Thanks, man. I appreciate the support.*

He waited a few long minutes, but Alex didn't respond and Noel knew the support wasn't there. Rob's words about Alex entered his thoughts, "*...Once Alex finds out, he won't forgive you.*" Noel's nostrils flared and he shook his head. Alex was fine. He had been fine all those months ago. He was probably just surprised about the news of Andrea moving in. Breathing out heavily, he opened the door and then slammed it shut.

Colleen flinched in her seat. "Mr Parker, are you all right?" she asked. Colleen had been his assistant since he took the position of senior accountant in Boston. She was closing in on fifty. Her crow's feet and wrinkles had started to become noticeable, but they didn't take away from her graceful beauty. Her pink lipstick was spread on in a soft pink tone and her nails matched.

"Sorry, Colleen. Didn't mean to make you jump there. I'm heading home early. Finish up and go home, too. Have a good weekend." Then Noel waved goodbye and made his way towards the elevator.

*P*arking in front of the florist on Federal Street, Noel cut the engine and stared at the flowers displayed on the pavement. Then he opened his car door and walked towards the entrance of the small shop and went inside. Different fragrances engulfed his senses. Noel did a quick scan until he spotted the table of cacti. One particular plant had completely caught his attention. It was in a small brown pot with green prickly cacti and two vibrant flowers blossoming from the plant. Noel picked it up and smiled. This would be his housewarming present for Andrea.

Upon reaching the counter, the back of an elderly man's blue T-shirt greeted him. The old man turned and smiled at him. Noel returned the smile and placed the cactus plant on the glass countertop. Then his eyes fell to the bouquet of orange tulips the shop worker held. All air fled his lungs as he stared at them. All memories of Clara and her favourite flower started to flood his every thought. The pain in him became intolerable and could bring him to his knees. Noel looked up to see the old man's mouth move, but he couldn't hear a single word.

Noel had fumbled with his jacket pocket before he was able to take out his wallet. Opening it, he took out his credit card and handed it to the florist. He breathed in heavily a few times as he glanced down at his wallet. The corners of a picture were visible and his fingers dug into his wallet. The man handed back his credit card, and Noel took one more look at the tulips. Then he took the cactus plant and left the store.

Once inside his car, Noel set Andrea's gift on the floor. With a sigh, he took out his wallet and opened it. He removed the credit card from its slot and placed it in another part of his wallet. Noel gazed at the bent ends poking out. He ran his thumb over it and paused. It had been more than six months since he last saw this picture, but Noel wanted to see it. He didn't care that it would open up the wounds he'd tried so desperately to stitch shut. His heartbeat picked up, his palms sweat, and his hand shook. After another sigh, he took out the picture and his heart collapsed at the sight of it. If he hadn't already prepared himself, he'd cry over it.

Noel sat and continued to run his thumb over her beautiful face and then her long brown curls. His eyes burned slightly and that was when he put the picture back in its slot and covered it with his credit card. For Noel, the picture served as a heartbreaking memory of her. No matter how much he tried to forget her, Clara Lawrence would always break his heart over and over again.

Clara

The sounds of bags being wheeled, heavy conversations, and voices over the PA system screeched in Clara's ear. Her head ached slightly. She never expected to be doing this, but she was. She gripped her phone tightly. Her breathing was heavy and her knuckles turned white. Her other hand trembled on the table where she sat. Clara looked over at her brown wristwatch and bit her bottom lip. The seconds continued to tick by and she fiddled with her boarding pass.

"Clara, relax. You're going to be fine." Stevie's voice grabbed her attention.

"Really? Because *this* is stupid. What the hell am I doing? Liam doesn't deserve this." Guilt washed over her like heavy waves pushing her to the seafloor.

"Liam's a good guy, but..." Annie said.

He is a good guy. A guy I don't deserve at all! What the hell am I doing?

Clara let out a heavy sigh. She gazed up at Annie and then Stevie. Annie had a confused expression on her face whereas Stevie's eyes flashed with understanding. If anyone understood Clara's inner demons, it was Stevie.

"Liam's perfect. Everything he is and does is perfect. But he has one flaw..." Clara paused.

"And that is?" Annie asked as she leant forward and squinted at Clara.

She knew Liam's flaw as she knew the ingredients of her peach and tea cupcakes. It was seared into her memory, never to be forgotten.

"He loves me," Clara simply stated.

"But how is that even a flaw?" Annie asked.

Clara's eyes started to burn. She didn't need this kind of pep talk. Her head fell slightly, and she stared at her hands on the white table.

"That's enough, Annie. Come on, Clara. You'll miss your flight if you listen to this dim head," Stevie said.

Clara balled her fists and swallowed hard to stop any tears from falling. She had to do this. Whether she liked it or not, she had to do it. She stood up from her seat and gripped the handle of her small suitcase. Then they all walked quietly towards airport security and Clara's heart raced. She had talked herself out of this so many times before, but this time she had to go. Liam had suggested she take this trip after working hard at culinary school, her placements, and at the bakery.

When they stood in front of airport security, Clara looked at them both. A sad smile on Stevie's face caused Clara's heart to strain in its beats.

"I'll see you both soon," Clara said as she glanced over at the security guard and then at her friends.

Annie hugged her first before Stevie; the concern on her

face had Clara trying to reassure her with a tight smile. Stevie was the one who understood why she was doing it. She hadn't seen her brother in months, and he needed to hear it from her.

"You can do this," Stevie softly encouraged.

Clara nodded and walked towards the security guard, handing him her passport and boarding pass.

After passing through security and weaving through duty-free, Clara sat at the gate waiting to board her Virgin Australia flight. She pulled out her phone to see a message from Liam. Before she could open the message to read it, a woman sat next to her and nudged her arm. Clara was just able to hold her phone so it wouldn't drop.

"Oh my God! I am so sorry. Are you all right?"

Clara looked to her left to see the woman's horrified expression and gave her a reassuring smile. "I'm fine."

"I'm sorry. My wife is still in the honeymoon mood," a man leant over and said to Clara.

Her stomach churned at the sound of 'honeymoon.'

"Oh, wow. That's an amazing ring. You're engaged?"

Clara glanced at the diamond ring that sparkled on her left hand. She was engaged to Liam and had been for a week. "Yes, I am." Clara smiled. It was a truthful smile. She had fallen in love with Liam and saying yes felt right. Until she thought about what being engaged *really* meant.

"Congratulations. That is a really beautiful ring," the woman complimented.

Clara rang her left thumb over her engagement ring to calm her nerves. She could do a lot worse than Liam O'Connor. In reality, Liam could do a lot better than her.

"Thank you. Start of your honeymoon?" Clara asked to be polite.

"We're just about finished," said the man as his blue eyes sparkled against the redness of his sunburnt face.

"Oh, I'm Lauren and this is my husband, Nicholas. Are you staying in L.A.? You'll love it!" she pepped.

"Oh, no. It's just a stopover," Clara corrected, fiddling with her passport.

"Where are you off to?" Nicholas asked.

The guilt washed over her, again, and she started to tear into her boarding pass, trying to buy herself a few seconds. Before Clara could even stop herself, she answered the truth.

"Boston."

Chapter TWO

Clara

"Tall skinny latte for Clara," the redheaded woman behind the counter called.

Clara picked up her suitcase, walked over to her, and retrieved the coffee cup. The barista smiled as she handed Clara her hot beverage.

"Have a nice day," the young woman chimed and shifted her attention back to the coffee machine.

Clara returned her bubbly smile as best as she could and walked out of Starbucks towards the terminal. She couldn't comprehend the size of LAX. She had been to Heathrow International Airport before and that was large, but LAX overwhelmed her. With her latte in hand, Clara slowly walked towards the domestic terminals. She'd spent most of her sixteen-hour flight from Melbourne to Los Angeles sleeping. Liam had convinced her to upgrade her economy seat to business class after they'd argued over it. In the end, she was grateful Liam won the argument as she got better sleep than she thought.

The closer she got to the terminal, the more intense the heaviness in her chest burned. Clara sipped on her latte as she reached the gate. She looked up to see 'Boston' flashing on the

LCD screen. Clara tightened her grip on her takeout cup and stepped forward to the waiting gate.

Clara took a seat behind a pair of men in business suits, reading *The New York Times*. Clara opened her passport and took out her boarding pass. She ran her fingers over each letter that spelt Boston. Part of her kept telling her to turn back—go back to Melbourne or even to New York. But a bigger part told her that she needed to see him one last time. She was putting everything on the line.

Clara closed her passport and placed it on her lap. She let out a heavy sigh and looked out to see the sun shining through the large glass windows. She glanced down to see the pad of her left thumb running along her engagement ring. She'd found herself doing it relentlessly over the past week. It was a way to calm her nerves, reassure her that Liam was the right choice. She fished out her phone to see her screen lock photo. Stevie had taken the picture of her and Liam. The smile on Liam's face broke Clara's heart. She was betraying him and that left a sour taste in her mouth.

She closed her eyes tightly and tried to relax the nerves the engulfed her. She let out a small groan and unlocked her phone. Clara scrolled her contacts to find Liam's number. She needed to hear his voice and remind herself that Liam loved her and she loved him. That this detour she was taking was to confirm that marrying Liam was her future. Seeing Noel was a way to close a book that kept haunting her for the last six months. It was when Liam was on his business trips that Clara unravelled. The tears would pour out and she couldn't control the aches in her heart. Shaking her head and ignoring the heaviness in her chest, Clara dialled Liam's number.

The phone had rung several times before she heard him pick up.

"Sweetheart, is that you?" Liam asked, tired.

Clara smiled at the sound of his voice and the way he said 'sweetheart' always made her heart flutter.

"It's me. I didn't wake you, did I?"

"No. I've been waiting for your call. Are you all right? Did you have a safe flight?"

Clara let out a soft laugh. "I'm fine, Liam. My flight was long. Are you okay?" It had only been nineteen hours since they last saw each other, but Clara was worried about spending the night without him.

"I miss you. I spoke to the wedding planner. Jo said she'd do as much as she can until you come back. Just two more months."

Clara moved her phone from her left ear to her right, staring at her engagement ring. It felt so right to be Liam's fiancée, but at the same time, it felt so wrong. Clara had only met Jo once, but with her placements for culinary school, they had only exchanged phone calls and emails. In two months' time, she'd be married.

"Are you sure you can handle all the wedding planning without me?" Clara asked in a small voice. She had offloaded her wedding responsibilities and flown to Boston instead of New York. If it were up to Liam, they would be married tomorrow. She asked Liam for two months and he didn't argue.

"Clara, don't worry. I'm sure I can pick ivory from white. Plus, if I have any issues, Ally can help me out."

There was a teasing tone to Liam's voice, and it made Clara giggle. He had a way with her and that just confused Clara even more. Liam brought her out from the shadows and she had a lot to be thankful for. She loved Liam. She would do anything to make him happy. Seeing Noel and saying goodbye would give Liam what he fully deserved — her heart completely.

"I trust you." The sound of the flight attendant starting to make the boarding announcement caught her attention. "My flight's boarding," Clara said quickly.

"Okay, tell Alex I hope he doesn't mind you having my surname."

Her heart stopped at the thought of her having Liam's last name.

Clara O'Connor.

"He'll argue with you. Even try to convince you to take my last name," Clara teased as she picked up her bags, walked towards the bin, and disposed of her takeout cup. "I better go. I'll call you later," Clara said as she stood in line to board her flight.

"Okay. I'm glad you're telling him in person and he doesn't hear it from someone else. I'll mail out the invitations tomorrow. I love you, Clara."

"I love you," Clara replied wholeheartedly. She remembered the first time she had ever said those three words. It was a slip of the tongue, and it even surprised her. But Clara knew it was the truth.

"I'll see you soon, sweetheart."

Clara smiled and then hung up the phone. Calls like those made her sure Liam was the one she was meant to marry. But that nagging feeling in her heart always made her doubt.

Noel.

The taxi ride from the airport to the Financial District had almost sent Clara on an anxiety attack. Every few minutes, she found herself biting her lip or gripping the car door handle for an easy escape. It was late afternoon when she arrived outside of Noel's apartment building. The bright red brick walls caught Clara's eyes. She stood there for a moment and observed the beauty of the apartments. A small portion of the entrance had ivy climbing the brick wall. No one besides Stevie, Annie, and Jarred knew she was in Boston. Stevie had been able to coerce Noel's address out of Rob during a night out.

Clara walked towards the entrance as the doorman opened it for her. She politely thanked the middle-aged man and walked into the large and brightly lit lobby. When she approached the desk, a young man manning it smiled up at her.

"Good afternoon, ma'am. How can I help you today?" he asked.

"I'm here to visit someone, but I, uhh, was wondering if I could leave my suitcase with you for a second?"

"Sure, just come back when you are ready."

Clara didn't have to worry about him snooping through her items; her lock ensured he wouldn't.

"Thank you. I really do appreciate it." Then she headed towards the elevator and pressed the up button once she had reached it. She was potentially throwing away her engagement for a man who broke her heart, and it made her sick inside.

She saw the light above the elevator flash and then the

sound of the doors opened. She stepped inside and pressed floor twelve. Clara breathed in deeply and waited for the doors to close.

"Hold the elevator!" a woman yelled out.

Clara quickly held her arm out to stop it from automatically closing. The woman ran inside with a stack of folders in her arms, her chest heaving.

"Thank you," she breathed out. Her vibrant blue eyes sparkled and Clara smiled; the woman's beauty was truly mesmerising.

"Which floor?" Clara asked.

The woman leant forward and shook her head. "I'm good, thanks," she replied and hugged the folders tighter to her chest.

The elevator closed, Clara's heart pumped harder as she neared, closer and closer to Noel's floor. Her left thumb started to run across her ring finger, but she felt nothing. She looked down to see her finger bare and she frowned. After landing, she slipped off the ring and placed it in her pocket. She didn't realise how much she did that little quirk until now. Instead, Clara gripped the straps of her bag tighter. The nerves and emotions made her head hurt and her stomach churn. Clara felt a heavy weight on her shoulders and in her chest. She had no idea what her first words would be when she saw him. She just hoped they would come to her.

The elevator stopped and then the doors opened wide. The woman had walked out first before she turned and faced Clara. She was beautiful. Her vibrant blue eyes were stunning and her dark brown hair was pulled into a bun.

"Thank you again for holding the lift."

Her smile warmed Clara. "No problem," Clara replied as she reached into the pocket of her jeans and retrieved her phone.

As Clara exited the elevator, she looked to see that she had a missed call from Stevie. She had forgotten to call her when she had landed in L.A. and instead she had called her fiancé. Deciding to call her later, she returned the phone back to her pocket and adjusted the cardigan she wore. She took two steps forward and saw the woman from the elevator placing her key into the apartment door. Clara's eyes then swept the hall, looking for Noel's apartment.

A startled, "Oh," gained her attention. Clara noticed the

woman fumbled backwards.

"You never let me use my key!"

"Shut up and let me kiss you already, Andrea."

Clara froze in her place. Her jaw clenched and she stilled. She watched as Noel stepped out of his apartment, resting both hands on the woman's cheeks and pulling her in for a long and passionate kiss. Clara's heart ached and burned as Noel pulled the woman into his apartment, his head turning towards her direction. Their eyes meet for a second before Clara quickly turned and made her way to the stairwell. Her hand then slipped into her pocket and took out her engagement ring.

I'm too late.

Too much time had passed between them. Through blurry eyes, Clara slid her engagement ring back on her finger where it was always meant to belong.

Noel

"Noel? Is something wrong?" Andrea asked.

Noel blinked rapidly, trying to adjust his eyes. He swore for a second that he saw her standing there. Saw those golden brown eyes and her brown curls. He closed his apartment door and faced Andrea. She had a stack of files held tightly against her chest. Noel shook his head to clear that image of Clara. He was losing it. It was Monday afternoon and he had spent too much of the day locked up in his home office. He saw what he wanted to see; his imagination playing a cruel joke on him.

"Nothing's wrong. I just thought I saw something," Noel replied. He then took the files out of Andrea's hands and kissed her cheek.

Andrea smiled as she shrugged out of her suit jacket and placed it over the kitchen barstool. "I'm going to have a long bath. Want to go to that new Italian restaurant for dinner tonight?"

Noel set Andrea's files on the kitchen countertop and nodded. "Sounds good," he replied once he'd walked over to the fridge and took out a bottle of water, handing it to Andrea.

"Thanks. You can go to the bar with Damien if you want?"

A woman who approved of her partner going to the pub with his mates should have made Noel feel like the luckiest man in the world. But he couldn't stop thinking about what he saw in the hallway moments ago.

"Yeah, I might. You go have your bath and relax. That Kennedy account contract must be driving you crazy?"

"The guy is an arrogant jerk who can't accept the terms of the contract. If you want your accounts done by the best, there are fees and heavy paperwork to sign!" Andrea rolled her eyes and threw her hands in the air.

Noel laughed at her annoyance. Andrea huffed and walked towards the bedroom. It was strange to think that they now shared the apartment. What was his was hers. He liked having her living with him, but it was different to when he had stayed in Melbourne with Clara. The past forty-eight hours had him comparing Andrea to Clara.

Noel walked over to the lounge room and sat on the large leather couch. He mindlessly flicked through channel after channel, nothing taking his mind off those brown eyes. He ran a hand through his hair and groaned out. Those eyes not only haunted his dreams but his reality, too. The sound of his phone rung, and he dug his hand into his pocket and took it out. The name on his caller ID left him stunned. Noel breathed in to ready himself and he pressed the answer button.

"Annie, hey. This is a surprise!"

It was seconds of silence before he heard, "Noel. It's Stevie."

Stevie?

"Oh, ahh... hey, Stevie."

"Yeah, yeah. Listen, Annie told me about her helping you out with Clara when you first got here. I'm not calling to give you shit about it. Now, this is important. You listening?"

The forcefulness of Stevie's voice had Noel sitting up in attention. "Uhh, what's up?"

Stevie breathed in heavily and then there was silence again.

"Clara's in Boston. She was just outside your apartment. You need to go listen to what she has to say, please."

She was really there.

"Clara's..." His body began to shut down. It wasn't a dream or a hallucination. Clara was really there.

"She's there, Noel," Stevie softly said.

His heart swelled as hope filled his system.

"I have to go." Noel quickly hung up his phone and got off the couch. The desperation in him to chase her was consuming. He had to see her. His body was making all the choices before his head could really assess the situation. Noel bolted towards his apartment door. When he gripped the handle, he paused and thought about what he felt towards her. Noel wasn't sure if he was angry that she broke his heart or sad that he'd spent so much time away from her.

For the first time in eight months, Noel admitted to himself his true feelings towards her. Those feelings never went away; they still burned fiercely within him. He was with Andrea now. They lived together. Could he really end things to have Clara back in his arms? Noel didn't have the answers, but all he knew was that he had to see her again. With determination flowing through his veins, Noel opened the front door and ran towards the elevator.

He waited the few seconds for it to open to his floor. Once he stood inside, Noel brought up his phone and dialled Alex's number with no response. He tried two more times but still came to the same outcome. Anxiety reached every inch of his body. He was terrified to see her, no matter how much his heart warmed at the thought of seeing those golden brown eyes again. The elevator doors opened to an empty lobby.

"Fuck!" he growled and he ran out looking around. She wasn't there. Noel walked towards the double door entrance to have Pete open it for him. Noel stepped out onto the sidewalk looking in every direction to spot her. He came up empty. Defeated, Noel went back into the lobby and towards the front desk.

"Yo, what up, Noel," the teenager behind the desk said. Dylan worked the afternoon shifts, his small frame never quite fitting his uniform properly.

"Hey. Listen," Noel panted, his chest rose and fell rapidly. "There was a girl here not too long ago. Did you see where she went?"

"Need more than just a girl came through my lobby, bro."

Noel sighed. "She's got curly brown hair and she's almost my height. She —"

"Noel?"

The soft voice caused him to look away from Dylan and turn to see her standing there as beautiful as ever. The sight of her made his throat feel dry and his eyes start to burn. Just looking at her made his heart break and mend at the same time, feeling like he found his home. But his head kept telling him otherwise.

"Hey," he managed. Noel's feet cemented themselves in place. He didn't trust himself near her—he'd do something stupid. He had to remember that he had a girlfriend now, one who was upstairs taking a bath.

"Hey, yourself." Clara smiled. That was their thing and it was like a punch in his stomach. He missed everything about Clara Lawrence and it hurt him to miss her that much.

"You're... here. You're in Boston?" he breathed out in disbelief. Noel panted, his need for oxygen burning his lungs.

He watched Clara fiddle with her yellow cardigan in her hands. He never imagined she'd be here. Not after the way it had ended the last time.

"I, uhh, yeah. I guess I am." Clara's gaze fell to her cardigan before meeting his. The look in her eyes sent an earth-shattering clench to his heart. Because he knew, as he had always known.

I'd never love anyone as I love her.

Chapter THREE

Noel

Noel swallowed hard, that voice was one he still dreamed and grieved over. His dreams never lived up to the reality of her. Her curls spiralled in their perfect shape; her brown eyes had that shade of gold no words could describe. And the way she smiled was like driving a stake straight through his heart. Clara Lawrence was still every inch of perfection and his vision of heaven.

Oh, fuck.

Noel knew he was in trouble. Just being near Clara had his mind thinking of all the possibilities that were unattainable for them. Clara's eyes didn't match the soft smile on her face and couldn't mask the terrified flash he saw in them. His hands moistened as his heartbeat accelerated. He looked around the lobby to see no one else with her.

"Is Alex here, too?" he asked as his eyes met Clara. He watched her chest rise and then she shook her head.

"No. Alex doesn't know I'm here."

Clara never lies to Alex... only when it came to us.

"She's beautiful, Noel."

He tensed at her words.

It pained him to look at the confusion and hurt in Clara's eyes. He turned his head to see the teenager at the desk checking her out. Noel couldn't blame him. Clara was beautiful and always would be. Noel turned his attention back to her. He wanted to say so much, but words seemed to fail him.

"What are you doing here, Clara?" That question had started eating him alive. He needed a reason. He needed to know why here and why now?

"I... uhh." Clara paused. Her gaze dropped to the yellow cardigan she held over in her left hand. When she looked up, Noel saw her eyes start to water. "I'm not even sure anymore. I guess I just wanted to see you."

Those words she spoke had the hope in him explode throughout his body. But there was something in him that told him to give up that hope. He couldn't go through it all a second time. He loved Andrea. He was with her now.

"How did you know I was here?" she asked.

If things were different, he'd throw his arms around her and promise her the world. It dawned on him that this had to be their final stand. It hurt him to believe it was, but he couldn't live with the thought that she'd end up breaking his heart with a change of her mind.

"Stevie called. She told me you were here."

Clara flinched, her face filled with surprise.

"W-what did she say?"

He noticed her arm tensed as she gripped her cardigan tighter.

"All she said was that you're here."

Clara's face relaxed and she breathed out in relief. "Listen, Noel. I have to tell you that—"

"Stop," he forced out.

Clara winced at his abruptness. Noel ran a hand through his hair and took two steps forward. As much as he wanted to reach over and touch his lips to hers, Noel had to be the one to have a say this time. It would physically and mentally pain him for the rest of his life, but he knew what was right.

"Listen to me, Clara, and listen properly. I'm only going to say this once. Okay?"

The tears started to run down Clara's cheek, and Noel steeled himself. She nodded causing more tears to slowly fall.

"I wanted you forever, but you never gave me the chance. Never gave *us* the chance. Now you're here..." Noel paused and mentally remembered every feature of Clara Lawrence — for the last time. "I got over you, Clara. You broke *my* heart and I got over you. You were right. I should be thanking you for ending us. I'm happier with Andrea. She's everything you couldn't be. She can love me without any complications. Why do you think she moved in with me? I was meant to be with her. You wasted your time coming here. I'm sorry you flew out."

It hurt him to say all those lies. But how could they have a future? They had both been in too much pain to see the sight of forever. Noel knew when it was time to stand back and he had to make sure Clara realised that they had nothing going for them. Clara blinked away a few tears before staring at her hands. This was worse than before. This time would be their last time.

"You should go," Noel breathed out, exaggerating the frustrated tone in his voice.

Clara gave him a strained smile. Then she wiped her cheek with the back of her right hand and faced Dylan behind the desk. "Thank you for holding my things, Dylan."

Dylan had glared at Noel, ready to slug him, before walking around the desk and handing Clara a small suitcase. Noel watched Clara's face for a reaction, but all she did was pull up the handle of her suitcase.

"Take care, Noel. Andrea's beautiful and she seems lovely. I'm happy for you." Clara sounded sincere when she spoke and that only added to the pain he felt.

I'm a bastard. But I'd be even more of a bastard if I beg for her to stay.

Clara smiled at Noel once more before she walked past him towards the exit. He listened to the sound of her short heels click and her suitcase wheels squeak until they stopped.

"Noel."

He closed his eyes to stop the tears that burned. He had to have her hate him in order for her to be happy. Last time he'd checked, she was happy with Liam, and Rob would have told him if they weren't together. He slowly turned around to face her.

"I just have to know one thing."

He nodded for her to continue and Clara sniffed.

"The first time you said you loved me. Remember?"

How could he forget? It was one of his most frequent dreams that woke him in a sweat and caused him to sit at a bar where nobody knew your name. He'd drink Clara and every memory of her away as best as he could.

"What about it?" he asked with as little emotion as he could. The sooner Clara left him, the sooner he could pick up the pieces of what would be a regret.

"Did you mean it? When you told me you loved me, did you mean it then? Did you mean it all the times you said it to me? I-I just need to know," Clara choked out.

Simple questions that brought back the familiar ache in his heart and had him struggling to breathe. Clara Lawrence was his air and he was giving her up in order for them to move forward.

"Clara, I—"

I loved you every day I was with you and even now.

Noel clenched his fists tightly and said the one word that pierced his heart, *"No."*

Clara's lip quivered, and she closed her eyes tightly. Noel felt all air leave him. The burning in his lungs didn't out pain the ache that radiated in his chest.

"I thought I did. But being away from you made me realise that I didn't love you the way I thought I did. I love Andrea, Clara. You being here is what I needed to see that. I was meant to be with her."

Clara's face fell slightly to the left. This time Noel had the last words. It was harder than he imagined lying to her. He wasn't sure if this was what he wanted to live with, but they had spent six months apart, and somewhere, Clara had found happiness with Liam. Her eyes met his and he saw the pain in them, the gold colour had disappeared. Clara breathed in sharply and gave Noel a smile.

"I'm so sorry I came to Boston. It wasn't fair of me to just show up and expect anything. I should have known better. You don't deserve this. I wish you all the best with Andrea. I'm sorry I wasted your time in Melbourne. I guess… I thought more of it than I should have."

Every tear that fell caused Noel to become even more

nauseated.

"Goodbye, Noel. I'm glad to see you so happy. You'll never see me again. I can assure you, I have no business being back in this part of the world." A forced smile had spread across Clara's face before she turned and walked towards the exit.

He watched Clara walk out of his life for the third time, and this time, it had been his words to deal the blows. He couldn't listen to her promise a forever they both couldn't keep.

Clara

*C*lara watched the taxi pull away and drive towards the direction of the city and away from Scarsdale. She took in her surroundings. This was what she wanted when she got married. She wanted the suburban lifestyle, to have the white picket fence and see children run and ride their bikes. Clara bent her knees and took the handle of her suitcase.

As she stood in the driveway of Alex's house, a sense of fear overtook her. Alex had his happily ever after, and she was going to walk in there and ruin it. Clara was Alex's own storm. Just at his brightest, she came crashing in, disrupting his life until she left, feeling like a burden on his life. She had promised Liam she'd tell her brother about their engagement and that was what she came here to do.

Noel was a bump in the road, one that she had overcome and faced. Maybe Noel not giving her the chance to tell him was a blessing. Now he could live his life with no regrets and she would marry Liam. Clara made her way towards the white painted door. Upon reaching it, she knocked three times and waited patiently.

"Just a second," a woman shouted. The voice sounded feminine and she recognised it from Alex's Skype calls. The door unlocked and opened, Clara was met with a light-brown haired woman standing before her.

"Clara?" Keira's dark brown eyes almost looked like charcoal, mysterious and beautiful in their own right.

"Hi, Keira. I know this is unexpected, but is Alex home?" Clara asked nervously. This was the first time she was meeting her brother's girlfriend, and from everything she had heard, she was the woman of Alex's dreams.

"Of course. Come on in. I wasn't expecting to see you until Alex's birthday next month," Keira said as she took Clara's suitcase and handbag from her. Keira straightened and was about to say something, but she paused. Her eyes darkened and Clara knew she had noticed the ring on her finger. "I'm going to go get Alex and then we'll go spend some time together." Keira had smiled before she led Clara into the lounge room.

The wooden floors were polished and the French-inspired furniture looked expensive yet cosy; everything was beautiful and she was proud of her brother.

Clara could just make out Keira's hushed voice and then the sound of Alex yelling out, "She's here?"

Her brother's heavy steps on the wooden floors were loud as he made his way through the house and burst through the door. Alex's eyes had met hers for a second before he brought her into a tight embrace. The memory of Noel's painful rejection made the sobs escape from her. It was never Alex's fault that it had failed between them. It was simply hers.

"Kiddo, what's wrong?" Alex asked as he rubbed her back.

Clara looked up at Alex. He was her parental figure—the mother and father she never had. "I did something stupid," she said between sobs. She was certain she was ruining his white cotton business shirt, but he didn't seem to care.

"Liam didn't get you pregnant, did he?" Alex's arms had tightened around her before he slowly released her.

Clara took a step back and took a deep breath. It was impossible for her to be pregnant. Liam had promised they would stay celibate until their wedding night. He was determined to prove that it was love and not sex. Clara bit the inside of her cheek as the last few tears slid down her face. She realised that Alex hadn't noticed the ring on her finger.

"No. Getting pregnant by Liam wouldn't be stupid, Alex. But that's not what I did." The memories began to resurface and it left Clara breathless as an ache filled her chest.

"I got over you, Clara. You broke my heart and I got over you."

Alex's hands rested on the side of her arms, his eyes succumbing to panic and worry. Clara's heart had throbbed before she spoke.

"I went to Boston to see Noel."

Alex's arms fell to the side of his body and the grief filled his face. "I'm sorry, Clara. I should have told you about her."

She shook her head as a sob formed within her. She tried desperately to suppress it by balling her fists. "I didn't make it to his door. I saw them and then I left. He was in the lobby just as I was about to leave."

"Come here," Alex said as he took Clara's left hand.

She closed her eyes for a long second and held her breath.

"Clara?" Alex's brows met, and she could tell her brother was holding in his anger. "Please tell me that this is Noel's ring. That he broke up with Andy and that you and him finally sorted it all out."

Clara took a deep breath, but it couldn't prepare her for what physically hurt her. "No. It's not Noel's. It's Liam's. I went to Boston because I wanted him to change my mind. Tell me that he wanted me and that we'd find a way. But it didn't happen." Clara twirled her engagement ring around her finger as Alex processed what she had said.

"What the *fuck* is the matter with you two? What did he say, Clara? Tell me."

Clara glanced down at her ring as Alex led her to the couch and wrapped his arm around her. Alex had always picked up her mess, but this time nobody could fix her mistakes.

"He said he got over me and that he loves Andrea. He's... *thankful* that I ended it back in Melbourne. I asked him if he ever loved me..."

Alex's hand gripped her arm tighter. Her tears continued. "What. Did. He. Say?" he asked through clenched teeth.

Her heart became heavy, the weight of it driving her tears into overdrive. The sobs finally escaped her and Clara cried into Alex's chest. "He said he *never* loved me. That he thought he did, but he didn't and doesn't. I'm such an idiot for thinking I could just show up and have him tell me my engagement was a stupid decision. I wanted Noel to tell me that we were always meant to be together, but he didn't even love me, Alex. I broke it off the first time because I loved him too much and now..."

Clara let the thought of Noel not loving her sink in. She gave him everything, her heart and her virginity, and she didn't regret either. It was the thought that Noel regretted them that broke her. She had every hope that they'd find a way, but hope was too much of a beacon that had left her burnt.

"I'm going to kill him."

That warning tone in Alex's voice had Clara pushing herself off him. "Don't, Alex. It's done. Please don't say anything to him."

"I can fix this."

Clara breathed out exhaustedly and got off the couch. Pacing around the room, she tried to stop the hurt from consuming her even further. She had to make it clear to Alex that she'd made her decision.

"You can't fix this, Alex. Stop thinking you can. Noel and I, we are never going to happen ever again." Clara's eyes met her brother. They had the same colour except his were a fraction darker than hers were. The pain in Alex's eyes added to the heaviness in her chest. She needed to kill the idea of her and Noel off — for good. "He's done with me. He loves Andrea. He *never* loved me. I should have known back in Melbourne, but I was too in love with him to see anything else."

Clara covered her face with her hands as she let out another sob. Her mistakes cost her Noel and she had realised them too late. The movement of the couch cushions indicated that Alex had stood up. His protective brotherly arms wrapped around her.

"I can make him change his mind, Clara. I know it. Just let me talk to him," Alex softly said, not processing the fact that it was over.

Clara pushed off his chest and wiped her tears away. She had never once stood up to her brother. It was time she dealt with the consequences of her actions, not him. Straightening her body, she looked at her left hand. She wanted to make herself worthy of Liam, and it meant letting Nolan Parker go. It would be easy now that he'd ripped out the part of her that loved him. The part that overlooked his sleeping with Valerie and came back for him. She'd find a way to unlove him.

"You can't fix my life every time I screw things up, Alex. You need to let me deal with my mistakes. You can't make Noel love me. I don't want him *made* to. That's no good to me. I thought maybe the love he held for me was still there, but I was terribly wrong. I was stupid to think that my future was in Boston when it's always been in Melbourne."

Clara gazed up to see Alex's eyes glistening. Her brother never cried, and it made her sick to see him this way. Her slow heartbeat sent the hot pain through each part of her body.

"But, Clara..." he pleaded, but she only shook her head.

"But nothing, Alex. I appreciate it. I truly do. You should've yelled at me and hated me for being with Noel. But you understood and I didn't want to disappoint you, so I came back for him. I've always loved Noel even when he went back to Boston. But this ending is something that was always set in stone. He's over me, Alex. We both need to understand that."

Alex was silent for a moment before his shoulders slumped and he rubbed his forehead. "What are you going to do?"

A simple question that had endless possible answers, but Clara had already made her choice.

"You don't have to marry him, Clara. You don't."

She let out a soft laugh. "Marrying Liam would be the single most honourable thing I could do with my life. You and I both know that. He chose me, Alex, and I can't forgive myself for what I did... But I do have to ask you something."

Alex's confused eyes stared at her and she could see that he was hurt. He had hoped for something that was never going to happen. Clara smiled and knew even if Alex wasn't happy about it, he'd still give her what she needed—his support.

"Will you walk me down the aisle?"

Alex stepped back in surprise and his jaw dropped slightly. "Are you sure you want *me* to be the one to walk you down the aisle?"

Clara grinned and nodded. "I've never been more sure in my life, Alex."

"Then, hell yeah, I'll walk you down the aisle. As long as you're happy that it's Liam you want to marry, then I'll give you my blessing."

Clara stepped forward and wrapped her arms around her brother. In two months, she'd be Liam's wife and Noel would just be a memory, one that Liam could wipe away.

Chapter
FOUR

Noel

*N*oel rubbed the kink in his shoulder. The strain bugged him more than the messed up report that one of his junior accountants had handed him the day before. Noel threw the folder on his desk and groaned out. The mistakes his junior had made were so simple that Noel couldn't understand such atrocious accounting. He pointed it down to laziness. He would have to spend the next few days rectifying the account before the clients noticed the errors and moved their business to one of G&MC's competitors.

Noel stood up from his chair and picked up his briefcase. Then he placed it on his oak desk and opened it. Picking up the report, Noel threw it in his briefcase and shut it with force. Who was he kidding? The hours spent fixing this account would keep him preoccupied. He needed something to keep him busy. Noel took the handle of his briefcase in his right hand and removed his jacket from behind his chair. Once he'd walked to his office door, he opened it to see Colleen at her desk.

"I'm calling it a day, Colleen. You should, too," Noel said as he closed his office door behind him.

Colleen turned in her chair and looked up at him. "Mr

Parker, it's only two in the afternoon."

"I know, but I'm exhausted. Gregson's in New York for the week, and we don't have him breathing down our necks. I'm calling it early. This report Milligan gave me needs a complete rework. I'll be locked up in my office back home. If you want to stay for the rest of the day, redirect my calls to my home line," Noel said as he folded his suit jacket over his right arm.

"I've got to make those copies for the Lyndon account briefing. I'll stay until then, Mr Parker."

"Damn. I completely forgot. When's the briefing with the client?"

Colleen frowned and gave him her famous expression. It was her disappointed look. Then she huffed and took out her brown leather planner.

"Next Monday. Ten a.m. Mr Mercer is coming in from New York also. Will you be coming in on Friday?"

"Depends on this account. I'll have Watson keep an eye on the other accountants if I can't make it in on Friday. Don't stay too late, Colleen," he said and left his assistant at her desk.

Instead of walking towards the elevator, Noel turned to the hallway on his left and into the legal department. He approached Andrea's office and leant on the doorframe. She had a habit of leaving her office door open and Noel took the opportunity to observe her. Andrea had pulled her straight hair into a low ponytail, and buried her face deep in a contract.

"Want to stop looking at me? You're a total creep, Noel," Andrea said without meeting his eyes, staring at the paperwork in her hands.

"I'm your boyfriend," Noel explained as he pushed off the doorframe.

"And I'm starting to regret dating you," she teased.

He walked over and placed his briefcase on her desk, nudging the contract out of her hand.

"Noel!" She turned and looked at him, the irritation evident on her face.

Noel bent down and placed both hands on her face. He leant in and placed his lips on hers. Andrea's lips didn't move until she burst into a fit of laughter.

"You sure know how to lower a guy's confidence, Andrea," Noel said once he broke away. He straightened up and grabbed the handle of his briefcase.

Andrea's hand covered his and stopped him. "Oh, please don't be like that. This contract has my full attention. I'm sorry. I'll make it up to you. Gregson wants this finalised by tonight."

Noel moved his left hand over Andrea's and moved her hand from his. "I know. Gregson has us all on deadlines. I'm sorry. I shouldn't have barged in like that. I'm heading out early. I'll see you at home?" Noel asked. That small frown on Andrea's face turned upwards. The law department was under constant strain and was the department Gregson meddled with the most.

"I'll see you at home. I hope I won't be long with this contract."

Noel placed a kiss on Andrea's cheek and said, "I'll see you when you get home." He flashed her a smile and turned for her office door.

"Noel."

He spun around to see her biting her lip.

"You're not mad, are you?" she asked.

"Andrea, I get it. Work is stressful for the both of us. I'm heading back to the apartment so I can concentrate on this report. Just don't come home too late. Deadline or not, you're not sleeping in your office."

Andrea grinned, shifted in her chair, and started to pick up the papers of the contract she was working on.

*D*ropping his keys on the hallway table, he walked to his home office and placed his briefcase on the desk. He opened his briefcase, took out the manila folder, and placed it on the desk. Sighing, Noel started to unbutton his cuffs and then the buttons of his shirt. He shook his head and decided that right now the report was not important. Milligan's laziness cost him a few days of reading the accounting reports he was working on.

Noel walked out of his office and towards his bedroom. Stripping the shirt off his back, he dropped it on the bathroom floor before moving his hands to his belt and unfastened it.

Digging his hands into his pockets, he took out his phone and his wallet. He looked at the screen to see missed calls from Max, Stevie, and Rob. They never called—not unless it was about Clara.

Their calls had been frequent in the four days since he'd sent Clara packing. Noel unlocked his phone to see missed calls and messages that simply said, "Call me." He'd had minimal sleep. Every time he closed his eyes, those brown eyes of hers killed him, waking him up every night. He was surprised that Andrea slept through his gasps for air.

Noel ran his hand through his hair, the tightened grip in his chest made him clench his eyes shut. Then he slammed his wallet and phone on the bathroom counter and quickly walked to his dresser. He pulled out the first two drawers and threw them on his bed. Removing the contents, he searched through the drawers. Shirts and briefs thrown on his bed, but he came up with nothing.

"Argh!" Noel groaned out and turned back to his drawer, pulling out the rest of the drawers.

Socks and shirts piled up on his bed as he turned each one upside down and shook the contents out. Noel took out the second last drawer and shook it clear until *it* fell out and landed on the pile of clothes. His knees buckled and he sat on the floor right next to his bed. His breathing heavy and short, Noel steadied himself.

Then he picked it up, his heart squeezing so tight he wasn't sure when his next breath of air would come. He held it in his fingers and examined the crease lines. Slowly and carefully, he opened the piece of paper. Once it was unfolded, Noel smoothed it out and held it tightly, afraid to let it leave his fingertips.

I love you.

Those three words he read over and over again. It was the first time since he'd arrived back in Boston that he'd looked at this piece of paper. Noel's fingertips ran over each letter of her beautiful writing. These three words made him whole. To lie to Clara was the only way she could be happy with Liam.

He didn't want to send her away, but the truth was he needed to. Life without Clara was his future, no matter how much it hurt him to know she was with Liam. Had he never known her the way he did, it wouldn't have hurt him so much. Noel would rather give her up than see her unhappy. He knew he couldn't give her the life and the happiness she deserved. Something would have always stopped them. He'd be lying to himself if he thought otherwise.

The last four days had him holding his passport in his hands, contemplating. He wanted to fly out and chase her, but Andrea had always kept his feet cemented. Noel kept his eyes fixed on the piece of paper. He remembered waking up to it and spending an hour just reading it over and over again. Noel sat on the bed and stared at the note in his hands.

The sound of a heavy knock banged from his front door. Noel glanced at the clock on the bedside table to see that it was almost four. He'd been on the bed for almost an hour, reading Clara's words. Breathing out, Noel carefully folded her note and placed it in his pocket. Grabbing the first shirt that he found on his bed, he pulled it over his head and onto his body. Noel fixed his belt and made his way out of his room and towards the front door. Without bothering to check through the peephole, he opened it.

"Alex?" Noel said in shock. He was not expecting to see his best friend in Boston. Not when Alex had important accounts of his own back in New York that needed assessing. There was no emotion in Alex's eyes; his face seemed tense, almost too controlled.

"I stopped by your office and Colleen told me you went home early. Are you alone?" The tone of Alex's voice held little life and the flare Noel saw from Alex's nostrils should have had him running.

"Uhh… Yeah. Why?"

Alex closed his eyes briefly before exhaling loudly. "Good!" he growled.

Before Noel could prepare himself, Alex's demeanour changed. He never saw it coming. Alex's curled fist slammed into his cheek hard and fast. It felt like a slab of concrete taking him out. Noel stumbled back until he hit the wooden floors of his hallway, hard. Noel's left hand immediately covered his cheek, unable to comprehend what had just happened. Noel felt the immediate swelling and pain of Alex's attack.

"What the fuck?" Noel blurted out.

Alex took two long strides into the apartment and hovered over him. "Stay away from her!"

Alex's demands of fury instantly had Noel frozen. *He knew.* "I mean it, you selfish bastard. You stay the fuck away, Nolan! I should have my hands around your neck, but Clara made me promise not to hurt you. Give me a good reason why I shouldn't break my promise and beat the absolute shit out of you? Best friend or not, you hurt my sister! There was only ever one rule and you broke it!"

Alex grabbed Noel's shirt in his hands and brought him up off the ground. The anger possessed in Alex's eyes had truly frightened him. Noel had never seen Alex this angry in his life, not even remotely close.

"How could you?" Alex yelled, his grip tightened and the shirt dug into Noel's skin.

"Huh? How could you do that to her? You love my sister one minute and then you don't! Why did you do it? You sent her away when all she did was come back for you. She tells you, and you don't give a shit. Why, Noel? Tell me! Why did you break Clara like that?" Alex pushed Noel's chest.

Noel fell backwards hitting the ground. He watched Alex ball his fist, his chest rising up and down. Noel stood up, wincing from the pain. "Because she broke my heart first!" he bit back without thinking.

Alex's eyes flashed with rage and he stepped forward until he was eye to eye with Noel. "Don't you fucking dare! Don't you dare say Clara broke your heart first because I know what you did! I know. You don't think I know about Valerie. You sick son of a bitch. You think you can sleep with my sister and then bed Valerie. I don't even know why she loves you. You betrayed me, Noel. Not because you slept with my little sister but because you had the nerve to break her heart. Why didn't you stop her? She came to you and you let her walk away! You could have made her stay. You were meant to change her mind. And you didn't. You selfish bastard, I trusted you. You had one chance to make her stay!"

Noel shook his head, not knowing what Alex was on about. "Make her stay? What are you talking about?" Noel noticed Alex flinch and took a step back.

"You didn't…" Alex ran his right hand across his forehead. "You didn't let her explain?" Alex yelled out and threw his hands in the air.

"Explain what? There was *nothing* to explain."

"No!" Alex shook his head and grabbed Noel by the shirt again. Noel let him. He deserved it for even getting involved with Clara.

"She came here to make you change her mind. She came back for you and you didn't let her finish. She wanted you to change her mind!"

This time Noel had had enough and pushed Alex off him. Alex had stared at his feet before he looked up at Noel with wet eyes.

"That's my sister, Noel. I'm meant to protect her and I let the one person I trusted the most kill the person she was. She came back to change your bloody mind, don't you get that!"

Noel kept quiet. Clara was the one thing Alex treasured more than his life, but Noel never imagined this kind of reaction. Not when Alex was the gentle one.

"All I've ever done was try to protect Clara, but I couldn't protect her from you. From my own fucking best friend. You don't even deserve to know. I love you like my own brother, but I expected more from you. We have never let a girl get in between us. But that there, that's my sister, and I love her. I don't care how long we've been best friends. I can't look at you without wanting to bash your face in. You want to know what I did yesterday? I put my sister on a plane because *you* broke her heart. I only had three days with her, and for the first day and a half, she cried over you! I came here because I wanted to know why you said you never loved her. Actually—no—it's easier if I didn't hear it." Alex wiped his wet cheek and inspected his right knuckles.

The room was silent. Noel looked over at Alex to see the exhaustion on his face. Noel had never seen Alex cry. The despair on his best friend's face could make him sick.

"Are we going to be okay?" Noel asked.

Alex sighed. "I love my sister and she comes before you. I know when to put someone I love first. As for us, we aren't okay. We'll never be okay. I let my sister down. I let you get to her and you fucked her up. You know what the hardest thing in life is? Seeing my sister after knowing the one person she has ever loved doesn't love her back. It's like having your soul ripped out from you. I'm powerless to make her happy. I was powerless to stop her from you. One day, we might be all right. But it won't be for a long time. You need to understand that."

"When we're okay, can you call me?"

"You might be waiting a long time, Nolan."

"I get it," Noel replied and watched his best friend walk towards the front door.

She came back to change my mind.

"Wait!" Noel yelled.

Alex stopped and then faced him.

"Why did Clara want me to change her mind?"

Alex's body tightened, his jaw clenched. Alex closed his eyes for a brief second before opening them, his pupils dilating. "Clara's *engaged* to Liam. She came to Boston because she wanted you to change her mind. She came here to throw away her engagement for you."

Clara

"Welcome back to Australia," the customs officer said as Clara handed her declaration form to him. For the past four days, her eyes felt permanently stained, but today she didn't shed a tear. Not when she knew Liam would be on the other side of those automatic doors.

She'd spent three days with Alex and Keira. Alex had used up some of his leave and took her around New York City. Clara saw it all—Times Square, the Empire State Building, the Statue of Liberty, and every street corner and avenue Keira could take her to. What Clara loved the most was Scarsdale. It was beautiful and everything she could want out of suburbia. She could see her brother and Keira getting married, having their children grow up in their beautiful house and play near the beautiful parks. It was a dream that she wanted Alex to have.

"Thank you," Clara replied as she pulled her suitcase and walked towards the exit.

She didn't have Alex to hold her hand this time. For the past four days, she felt like a child having Alex comfort her, trying to heal her. There were times when she would have to calm him down when he looked at her ring. She had never seen her brother so angry, but she found a way to calm him. Clara wished she never put Alex through all of this. She had him promise that he wouldn't go after Noel or hurt him. It took a lot of effort, but with the help of Keira, Alex promised never to hurt him. It was the last thing she would do for Noel and that was to protect him from her brother.

The doors opened to the waiting area. She saw faces, but none she recognised. Clara took a few steps forward and did another scan. She saw movement to her left and noticed Liam's ash-blonde hair. He reached the steel barrier and he smiled up at her. That smile was too beautiful and meant only for her. Clara looked down to see Liam holding a sign written in purple crayon.

Mrs Liam O'Connor to be.

Clara covered her mouth to hold back her laughter, but the sign and Liam's boyish grin was too much. She walked over to Liam and stopped in front of him. Then she let go of her suitcase and placed both her hands on the cold steel barrier.

"I like the sign," she commented.

"I had help." Liam winked and he looked down. Clinging to his right leg was a beautiful little girl with curls.

"Hello, Clary."

A smile developed on Clara's face; this little girl owned what was left of her heart. Clara moved her hands off the barrier and placed them on either side of Liam's face. She brought his face towards hers and kissed him with all the love in her. Tears threatened to spill, but she held them back. She would make herself worthy of Liam. As long as he wanted to be with her then she would stay.

"Li, can we have ice cream?"

Liam laughed against her lips and he pulled away. Clara's thumb ran along his cheek before she dropped her hands from him. Clara bent down until she was level with CeCe.

"Hello, pretty girl. How are you?"

"I've missed you, Clary." The sweetness of her voice was too adorable.

"I've missed you too, little one. How about I come around and we go get you some ice cream?"

Those blue eyes twinkled and just the purity of this little girl warmed her. The four-year-old removed her hands from Liam's legs and reached out for her.

"CeCe, Clara has to go around. She'll be a second," Liam said sweetly.

CeCe stared up at Liam with those big blue eyes.

"Ahh, CeCe! Put those eyes away!" Liam folded his makeshift sign and placed it in his back pocket. "You don't mind?"

Clara shook her head. CeCe raised her tiny arms up at Liam and he picked her up.

"Clary!" CeCe giggled as Liam handed her to Clara.

She took CeCe in her arms, her cute little blonde curls bounced as CeCe wrapped her arms tightly around Clara's neck. When she got CeCe secured, Clara grabbed the handle of her suitcase and wheeled it as she walked around the long barrier.

"Clary, Clary, Clary!" the toddler chimed.

Clara kissed CeCe's cheek and the toddler broke into a fit of giggles. When they reached the end of the barrier, Liam stood there already waiting for them.

"There's my two favourite girls. You ready to go get that ice cream?" Liam held his arms out and CeCe went willingly. Liam placed her down, her small red shoes hitting the ground.

CeCe held out her tiny hand and Liam took it. The sight of them could make Clara cry. The way Liam treasured his cousin's daughter as his own was simply beautiful.

That would be him with our children.

She froze. It was the first time she ever thought of their future together. Clara blinked as she envisioned what it would be like to be the mother of his children. She could see their children having Liam's eyes and his beautiful smile, his kindness and his heart. It made her smile. That vision of a house in the suburbs with their beautiful children made her heart warm.

I want that.

Chapter
FIVE

Noel

Engaged? No. She couldn't be. It's Clara... I love her.
    "Don't fuck with me, Alex." Noel shook his head. It couldn't be true.

Clara wouldn't marry Liam. She couldn't. It was some elaborate lie Alex had conjured. His heart cemented itself. Just the thought of it being true was making him delirious. Noel looked at Alex. His best friend's hands were in his pockets and his eyes on the ground.

"Tell me it isn't true, Alex," Noel begged. The pleading mirrored the pleas from the night she had ended them. The despair made him feel so weak. So exposed. Alex's pain-filled eyes quickly met Noel.

"Why do you even care?" Alex asked, his eyebrows meeting.

The disgust in his voice had Noel wincing. It didn't take him a second thought to hold back what he was about to say. "Because I love her, Alex! I love Clara. I love her more than I could ever love another woman."

Alex breathed out before he charged after him, grabbed Noel by the shirt, and pushed him against the wall with force.

"Now you love her! Where was this fucking declaration

four days ago, huh? You're a coward!" Alex yelled, the anger possessing him.

"I know, okay. You think I haven't thought about leaving Andrea and going after her? She can't be engaged, Alex." Noel's head dug into the wall, the pressure Alex was putting on his chest had him pinned.

Alex sighed, appearing almost defeated as he released Noel's shirt from his grasps. "You don't believe me?" He dug into his pocket and shoved an envelope at Noel's chest. "There's your proof."

Noel held and looked at the ivory envelope. Lifting the flap, he removed the ivory embossed card. His muscles tensed automatically.

You are cordially invited to share and witness the union of
Liam Patrick O'Connor
&
Clara Louise Lawrence
In Holy Matrimony on the
23rd of September 2014.

Noel tore his eyes off the invitation. Words had failed him, along with his breathing. It was true. He remembered her yellow cardigan covering her left hand and her promise never to see him again. He could have stopped her, but he hadn't. Noel looked up to see Alex, the concern plastered all over his face. The stinging sensation in his eyes returned, but Noel didn't care. He let her slip away and this time he'd cemented her future with Liam. A warm tear ran down his face. Ignoring the weakness of showing his emotions in front of Alex, Noel shoved the invitation into Alex's chest. Noel didn't say a word as he passed Alex and headed into the kitchen.

When he reached one of the top kitchen cabinets, Noel opened it and took out a bottle of vodka. He moved over to the next cabinet and took out three glasses. He turned and lined the shot glasses on the island counter and unscrewed the cap off the bottle. Noel heard the sound of Alex's heavy footsteps enter the kitchen as he poured the clear alcohol into the glasses. Putting the bottle down, Noel lifted and threw back his first shot, the vodka slightly burning the back of his throat. He slammed it down on the counter before throwing back his second and third in quick succession.

"You willin' to share?" Alex asked as he approached the counter, his palms resting on the edge.

"Thought we weren't friends," Noel muttered as he took the neck of the bottle and started to pour his next three shots.

"No. I said we weren't okay. Didn't say anything about not being friends, Nolan." Alex reached over, took a glass, and threw it back just as quickly as Noel took his fourth.

"I fucked up, Alex. I fucked up, again! You need to beat the shit out of me," Noel pointed out.

"Yes, you did, and I hate the sight of you. My sister is getting married, Noel. And she's not marrying *you*." Alex took the bottle and had placed it on his lips before swallowing back a mouthful. Then Alex wiped his mouth with the back of his hand and walked over to the sink, tipping the bottle upside down and emptying it of its contents.

"Alex!" Noel protested.

"You are going to give me the answers I want. But before that, you are going to listen to me." Alex turned away from the sink and set the bottle on the counter. Alex gave Noel a satisfied nod before sitting on a barstool. "Her mind's made up, Noel. She's marrying him."

Alex looked up and the stern look on his face made Noel flinch.

"You can't go after her, you hear me. I will stop you. I will never let you get that close to Clara again. It's my fault you two got together, and I am going to fix it by making sure you don't ruin her wedding. If you even get close to her, I will take you out myself. I'm going to ignore the fact that I know you. I'm going to look at you like the bastard you are. I want Clara happy, and marrying Liam will make her happy."

"No! Being with me will make her happy!"

I pushed her away. I let this happen. How could I let this happen?

"Really? Because all she does is cry over you. You don't give a shit about her. You take one step in the direction of Melbourne, and I swear to God, Noel, I will kill you myself." Alex's knuckles turned a vibrant white colour. "You love my sister?" Alex asked as he rose from the stool.

He had lied once. He wouldn't lie again. "Yes. I love Clara, but I didn't think she'd marry Liam… or anyone. I thought we still had a chance. I thought that somehow we'd find a way. Why would she say yes… to him?"

"Because you told her you didn't love her. I know about Valerie, Noel. She doesn't know that I do. I know about how you left my sister on her birthday to sleep with your ex-girlfriend, and yet she still fell in love with you. To go through all that and come out loving you, I don't understand. But you pushed her too far, and you can never win her back. I will make sure of that. After all the shit my own parents put her through, Darren, and now you, she deserves to be loved. I've seen the way Liam looks at her, Noel. He's undeniably *in* love with her. You won't stand in the way of that. I came here looking for answers, but now I've realised that I came here with an ultimatum. You willingly let go of Clara or we end everything we have here. The choice is yours."

Noel blinked quickly. He slowly processed Alex's words that sounded more like promised threats. "You're asking me to choose between you or Clara?" he asked in disbelief. He had promised Clara that he would always choose her over Alex, but this time circumstances had changed.

"Even if you choose Clara, you won't win her back. You've already done too much damage. Her future is set. I'm making sure you don't fuck with it. I want my sister's wedding to be perfect, and I don't want you wrecking it."

Noel's jaw clenched. Alex was encouraging Clara to marry the wrong man, and they both knew it. Noel placed his hands on the edge of the countertop and slumped forward. He was the one meant to marry her, he was the one who had the ring first, and he was the one to have loved her first. Noel looked up to see the invitation in Alex's hands and felt his eyes start to burn.

"It's funny…" Alex said as he glanced up at Noel with tears in his own eyes. "I thought you'd make it. I honestly thought you would. I was actually praying you would. When Clara asked me to walk her down the aisle, it was easy to imagine I was giving her away to you, but that's not the case. Do the right thing, Noel. We have to accept it. This is what she wants. You know he'll take care of her."

Noel's hands tightened around the edge.

Liam would take good care of what should have been mine.

"Out of all the women in this world, Noel, I didn't think I'd fight you over Clara. Not my sister. She comes first before either one of us. You and I both know that."

Noel felt the warm tears slide down his face. She was the only woman he had ever cried over and he'd been stupid to let her leave. Noel's head fell slightly as he stared at the marble countertop.

"I love her, Alex. I'll never stop loving her. It hurts to be away from her," Noel confessed in an almost choked up whisper. He removed his hand from the counter and dug into his pocket. He took out Clara's note and opened it, completely ignoring Alex's curious eyes. Noel placed the piece of paper on the counter and read it a few times. With a nod, Noel looked up at Alex. "I want her happy, too..."

It felt like daggers had entered his chest as he breathed out. Tremors attacked his heart as the ache consumed his body. At one stage in their lives, their love was mutual, so close to being eternal. But as Clara said, it wasn't enough to save them.

"Tell her congratulations on her upcoming nuptials. She's going to make a beautiful bride and a breathtaking wife that any man would be privileged to have. Liam's the lucky one. I could only imagine what it would be like to have her as my wife. It was my biggest dream."

Clara

A trip to the nearby park, a round of ice cream, and Clara was exhausted. She watched as Liam started humming in CeCe's ear as she slept in his arms. Clara yawned; she had been up for over twenty-four hours and all she wanted to do was sleep. CeCe would leave for Sydney in a few days and Clara wanted to spend as much time as she could with the little toddler. Liam's sister, Ally, had brought CeCe with her when she came to Melbourne to see her brother and speak to the wedding planner. Whenever Ally came to town, she would stay in Clara's apartment. It gave the eighteen-year-old the freedom she wished for when she came to Melbourne.

"I'm going to put her to bed. I'll just be a second," Liam said quietly as he got off the couch and walked over to Sienna's room. Clara had met Sienna a few times and things had been awkward at the start. Liam explained to her that they hadn't slept with each other and that they were actually best friends. Clara was sceptical at first. That was until she properly met Sienna and realised how similar Liam and she were.

Clara stretched on the couch and leant over to slip off her shoes. She stood up when she heard the sound of Liam closing the bedroom door. It was late afternoon and Clara was too tired to go down the bakery to visit everyone. Instead, she decided that she'd spend the rest of the day with Liam.

"She's sound asleep," Liam said as he walked towards Clara. He wrapped his arms around her waist and pulled her in close.

She'd been away from him for far too long and missed the smell of his citrus cologne. What she'd missed the most was the way he looked at her. Liam kissed Clara's forehead before running his hand down her arms and took her hand in his. Without a word, he led her to the master bedroom.

Clara stepped inside the darkened room as Liam shut the door behind them. He looked at her with a lustful desire that she hadn't seen before. Taking her by surprise, Liam quickly placed both his hands on either side of Clara's face and captured her lips. She held onto Liam's forearms and kissed him just as passionately. Sleep seemed ridiculous when Liam's lips entwined with hers.

His hands moved into Clara's hair as he pushed his body close to hers. A moan escaped her lips and Liam seized the opportunity to explore the inside of her mouth. He licked and sucked expertly as he walked Clara to the edge of the bed. Her heart raced and pounded, the passion completely surprising her. Liam gently lowered her down until Clara sat on the edge of the bed.

Then he removed his hands from Clara's hair and then his lips from hers. Clara was disappointed to end things so quickly. She was about to argue, but the untamed look in Liam's eyes had her breathless. They didn't speak, only stared into each other's eyes. Clara's lips tingled at the sensation of his mouth on hers. Liam breathed out and returned his hands to Clara's cheeks.

"I love you, Clara," he whispered as if they were in a crowded room, only enough for them to hear.

Her heart expanded with warmth and she placed her right hand over Liam's. "I love you," she said softly.

Liam had kissed her forehead before placing a chaste kiss on Clara's lips. Moving down, he ghosted kisses along her jaw and then her neck.

Her breathing hitched and her heart rate spiked. Each kiss and feel of his lips on her skin had her closing her eyes and letting a moan slip. Liam's hands brush against the skin that exposed by her raised shirt. She arched her back to offer more of her neck to him and felt her knees weaken. She mentally thanked the heavens that she was already sitting and not standing.

Liam trailed kisses up and down her neck before he stood back. He panted heavily as her own breathing outweighed the erratic beats of her heart. Then Liam stepped forward and bent his knees slightly, ensuring his eyes levelled hers. Clara smiled and ran her hand through his hair.

His lips had pressed on Clara's before touching the exposed skin of her collarbone. Without taking his eyes off hers, he reached over to the button of her blouse. Liam held his breath and popped loose the first. His eyes asking for permission to continue and Clara didn't oppose. She wanted to be intimate with Liam. She wanted to know what it would be like to finally make love to her fiancé.

Liam slowly unbuttoned her blouse until she sat waiting for his next move. The anticipation in her caused her breathing to catch in her throat and feel wasteful. He steadied himself for a second and Clara felt his fingers lightly trail the skin near her bra straps as he slowly removed the shirt from her shoulders. Liam threw the top on the floor and took in her body. He made her feel confident in her body as if she was the most beautiful artefact rather than just another woman he'd bed.

His fingers traced the outline of her bra as his hands made their way down to her toned stomach and to the edge of her jeans. All breath left her as he reached the top of her jeans, pausing for a moment before he unbuttoned them. Clara bit her bottom lip as Liam found the zip and slowly pulled it down. His eyes never leaving hers as she lifted her hips off the bed.

Liam pulled her jeans down her legs and off her body, discarding them as he had her shirt. Clara swallowed hard as he stood up, his hand running up her leg, past her hips and up to her cheeks. This time Clara couldn't help herself as she pulled him down to her, their lips meeting only added to the fire her body created and got consumed in.

Widening her legs and aware that this was as close as their bodies had ever been without their clothes, Clara leant back onto the bed, taking Liam with her. She loved the feel of his body on top of hers and she felt his groan against her mouth as he kissed her hungrily. Clara's hands found the collar of his shirt as she kissed him hard and desperately. Liam's hands made their way to the back of her head as she reached the button of his shirt. Her hands shook in anticipation as she slowly mirrored Liam's moves and started to remove his shirt. When she reached the end, Liam's hands left the back of her head and quickly disposed of his shirt without his lips leaving hers.

Clara's fingers ran down his hard chest and his back as he kissed her harder and faster, causing her to breathe out heavily. Her hands skimmed down the defined lines of his abs as she reached the button of his jeans. Then Liam's hand instantly covered hers and she opened her eyes in surprise, his lips breaking away from hers. Clara saw the conflict in his eyes. He was either going to let them make love for the first time or uphold his vow and wait until they said, "I do."

Liam removed his hand from Clara and placed it next to her head, propping himself up from her body. He kissed the corners of her eyes and nodded the approval she was waiting for. With a deep breath, Clara unsnapped his jeans then slid down the zipper, her heart stopped for a moment.

"Are you sure?" she asked as she searched his eyes.

"No," Liam replied.

Clara's hands reached up and held his tensed face. She had smoothed out the lines across his forehead with her thumbs before propping herself up and placing a kiss there. Liam sighed out heavily and rolled off her. Clara sat up on her elbows and looked at him with a confused frown.

As if he knew the questions she had compiled in her thoughts, Liam pulled her into his lap. Clara wrapped her arms around his neck and she could see the control on his face.

"You're in your underwear... this isn't, ahh, going to work, sweetheart."

Clara shook her head and tightened her grip around his neck and watched him breath heavily before a groan escaped him.

"Clara, I've never..." He breathed out before he quickly pressed his lips to hers. His breath hit her lips with every kiss and Liam pushed her onto her back. He broke their kiss and stared at her.

"If you tell me you're a virgin, then I'm going to question what those girls did when they came over," Clara teased and Liam tensed in her arms.

"Clara, listen to me. This is going to sound stupid, but I've..." Liam paused again as he softly ran his fingers along her cheekbones. "I've never had sex with someone I love before. I've never not known a one-night stand."

She knew the surprise of what he'd said took hold of her face — she felt it. Liam let out a laugh before he kissed the tip of her nose.

"I'd be lying if I said I'm not jealous of your one-night stands," Clara confessed, her eyes averting his.

Liam moved his finger under her chin and lifted her eyes to his. "You don't need to be jealous of them, Clara. I'm marrying *you*. I love *you*. I've never loved any of them. I didn't know a future until I saw *you*. They had no meaning, it was just sex. I want you to know that you'll be the last woman I'll ever be intimate with. I want to touch you, Clara. Really badly. I've lasted eight months and I can wait a little longer. But I think it's that ring that has me losing all sense of control. To know that you'll let me call you *my* wife just triggered something. Sweetheart, please let me put some clothes on you. I can't have you making me want to break my promise."

Clara nodded, unable to help the tears that ran down her face. Then Liam kissed away her tears and she hopped off his lap. He got up from the bed and walked over to the walk-in-robe and returned with a *Beatles* shirt. Liam climbed onto the bed and took Clara's left hand. He brought it to his lips and kissed the engagement ring on her finger. When he let go of her hand and Clara raised her arms up, Liam pulled his large shirt over her body. She smiled brightly when he moved her messy curls out of her face. Then Liam got off the bed and shimmied out of his jeans.

"Do I need to wear pants?" he asked, and she shook her head. He already owned her heart, owning her body was of little importance. Not when he loved her so much.

Chapter
SIX

Noel

"*Y*ou sure Andrea's going to be okay with me staying?" Alex asked.

Noel kept his eyes on Clara's note. He would be living a life of self-harm if he kept it, but he didn't have the will to throw it away. This was his link to her. There was a moment in their lives when they had loved so purely that nothing mattered. But nothing ever stayed pure for long.

"You're my family, Alex. I couldn't turn you away, even if I wanted to. The spare room has your name written all over it. I've got to work on a report one of my juniors fucked up. So, my office down at work is free to use," Noel replied as he glanced up from Clara's note. Whether he looked at it or not, those words would forever be burned into his existence.

"She doesn't know about Clara, does she?" Alex asked.

Noel swallowed hard and took the piece of paper off the counter and returned it to his pocket. He shook his head and Alex gave him a firm stare.

"Don't give me a reason to hate her, Noel. She's a nice girl. But she has what my sister wanted and I don't want to hate her."

That beg from Alex had Noel snapping out of his thoughts. He loved Andrea; he wasn't sure how or when, but he did.

Not the way I love Clara.

Noel let out a sigh as the realisation started to set in. She was right there waiting for him and he'd sent her away. He let her believe that he never loved her when the truth was he'd always loved her.

"I'm sorry, Noel. I didn't mean to lose control over my emotions. I just get… it's Clara. I don't think I need to explain myself."

"No, I'll be 'right," Noel replied. He didn't want to feel, not for a while. He already pictured where he wanted to be in an hour's time. That shady bar where he could get drunk and cry without judgment.

I lost the love of my life. I'm never getting her back.

"I have a meeting with Winters in an hour. Mind if I get ready? Mercer's in Boston, too, for the Lyndon account. He wants to go over the details before the Monday briefing. I won't be back until late. You don't mind?"

Noel knew it was code for 'I give you permission to get laid while I'm gone.' They were roommates in college and during Noel's time in New York, he knew this code very well.

"Where are your bags?" Noel wondered. He remembered Alex laying a fist on his face before he could even comprehend his visit.

Alex let out a short laugh and leant on the barstool. "Left it just by the door before I pummelled your ass," Alex said like the confident bastard Noel knew he was.

"Don't be a dick. You caught me off guard." Noel placed his hand on his cheek and the throbbing caused him to cringe. But as sad as it was, he enjoyed the pain. He'd rather the physical pain over the mental and emotional one he felt scratching to be freed.

"I could take you out completely," Alex stated, and Noel didn't argue.

All he knew was he never wanted to see that side of Alex Lawrence again. And he knew his trigger…

Clara.

*T*he folders on his desk had remained untouched for the past hour. He stared at them, but he couldn't will his body to respond to the demands his brain was giving. He heard and counted the ticks of the old clock on the wall. Nothing stopped him from thinking about her.

She's engaged, my — Liam's — Clara, engaged.

In the protectiveness of his loneliness, he allowed his heart to collapse. His eyes glazing over with unshed tears. All he had to do was give her the chance to explain, and he didn't. He let his pride win and his pride cost him Clara.

He reached back into his pocket and took out the small piece of paper. Noel held it like it was his lifeline. He ran his fingers over the creases of the paper and over those three words.

I love you.

He still loved Clara. But he loved her more to give her the chance to be happy and *in* love. Liam would do right by her and Noel believed so. If anyone was worthy of Clara, it was Liam. Noel stood up from his chair and exited the home office heading towards his bedroom. Flicking on the light, he walked over to the walk-in-robe closet. Reaching up to the top shelves, he moved boxes out of the way until he found the small one he needed.

He left the closet and sat on his bed. Mountains of clothes were still sprawled on top of the mattress, but he didn't care. With a heavy sigh, Noel steadied himself. Lifting the lid and placing it next to him, Noel took out the small velvet box and opened it. Then he ran his thumb over the 'N' and a sob formed in his chest.

He took out the silver locket from the box and held it carefully in his hands. He meant the locket to be a sign of forever. He gave it to Clara when she was a baby, only for her to give it back when she was eight and then he returned it to her on *that* night. The night she relinquished her virginity and he gave her his heart. Somewhere and somehow, they took a wrong turn and ended up further apart.

Noel sat and looked at Clara's locket. It should be fastened around her neck and not in his hands. He held back the pain of losing her as he stood up from the edge of the bed and sat on the ground near the bedside table. Wrapping the locket's chain around his hand, Noel took out Clara's note and started to rip it.

It pained him. But in order to move on, it had to happen. It was the only way. When he was satisfied with the destruction of Clara's declaration of love, he took the piece that held those three words. Those words remained unharmed, but instead, it was a smaller size.

Noel stared at those three words and his heart clenched tightly. This time it had been with more force and made the breath in him flee. He reached up and took hold of the pen on the bedside table. He flipped the paper over and breathed in before writing down all the things he couldn't say and all the things he wished he had said.

No amount of time will account for the days that I've missed you and should have loved you. I will always love you, Clara Louise Lawrence. Always.

Noel folded his confession and his chest continued to burn, desperately seeking to be relieved. Unwrapping Clara's chain from his hand, he opened the locket and placed the folded piece of paper inside. He stared at how well it fit inside. Noel couldn't help but wish that he was the piece of paper and Clara's heart was the locket. Together and perfectly secure.

He brushed his thumb against the note before shutting the locket with force and ensuring that some of the paper got caught. Noel tried opening the Celtic knot locket again but found it difficult. The locket was jammed, keeping his love for Clara Lawrence a secret, forever. A warm tear rolled down the side of his face. Ignoring it, Noel returned the locket back in the velvet box. He looked at it one more time before he shut it. The sound confirming the end of what should have been forever.

He placed the small box back inside the larger one, ensuring it lay hidden under papers before he placed it on the top shelf of the closet. Moving the other boxes and items in front of it and ensuring it remained hidden. A piece of him felt lost as he realised the extent of his actions. She'd be a memory for him. She'd have a new name in two months and the thought made his heart throb.

Clara O'Connor.

It felt like a long time ago that he had hopes of asking her to marry him. He had it all planned — from quitting his job in Boston to moving back to Melbourne. Plans were made but never followed, and promises made but broken.

It should have been me. It should be Clara Parker.

Noel shook his head as the force of the thought slammed into his chest. He had to stop. She was long gone and he couldn't alter it. With her locket and note hidden, it was time he let go of her completely. No matter how much he knew it was impossible, he'd have to find a way. Alex would stop him. There was no point in fighting for her.

Once he'd moved out of the closet, he approached the bed. He picked up one of the drawers and started to return his clothes back to where they belonged. Ten minutes later and just as he closed the last drawer, Noel heard the sound of the front door open before Andrea came rushing in.

"Noel, I saw Alex and…" She paused as she covered her mouth with her hand.

Noel stood up properly and walked over to her. His arms locked around her waist as he held her tightly. In his arms was his future. He couldn't forget how far he and Andrea had come. There was no denying she made him happy and that was enough for him to push the thought of Clara away.

"Your face. What happened?" she asked against his chest.

Noel removed one of his hands from her waist and placed it on the back of her head. "Nothing, it was an accident. Don't worry about me." They stood still for a moment as Noel closed his eyes tightly and remembered that this was his future.

"I want you," Andrea softly said. She moved slightly in his hold and gazed up at him.

He saw the desire in her blue eyes. Noel moved his hands up to her cheeks and held her. "Gregson's deadline?" he asked.

Andrea bit down on her bottom lip and shook her head. Then she released her lip. "I don't care right now. I've been horrible towards you. Let me make it up to you."

She batted her dark lashes, and if Noel hadn't been in need of some sort of release, he'd laugh. He didn't hesitate as he pressed his mouth hard on Andrea's. There was a sense of possessiveness that Andrea could be the one he'd call his without any hidden obstacles.

Noel's hands ran down the side of Andrea's body until his palms rested on her hips. His tongue met hers as he explored the inside of her mouth, Andrea's hands running up and down his chest. He felt the tug of his shirt and pulled his mouth away from hers as she helped remove the material from his body. He groaned as Andrea's lips met the soft spot below his ear. He needed her and badly. He needed to forget.

He broke the connection of their lips and quickly disposed of the tight skirt she wore until she stood in her black lacy underwear. She stepped out of her black high heels and Noel lifted her by the hips. Andrea wrapped her legs around his waist, and they both let out a heavy sigh.

Noel returned his focus and his mouth to Andrea's jaw and then her neck. Her hot and heavy breaths hit his skin as she pressed her body hard against him. His kisses turned frantic as he walked them over to the bed.

"Please, Noel," she softly moaned.

Noel lowered Andrea until her back hit the comforter and he hovered over her. She didn't waste any time as she wrapped her legs tighter around his waist and ran her mouth along his neck several times before she met his lips. He held Andrea's face tighter in his hands and deepened the rough rhythm of his mouth against hers. She let out a moan and dug her nails into his back. It felt off. There wasn't that balance between pain and pleasure. It wasn't how *Clara* did it. Andrea's nails dug too deep. Instead of being pleasurable, it was painful.

He thought back to the times Clara had breathed out his name and made him lose all sense of control. The way her nails dug perfectly into his skin and the way her coconut shampoo and floral perfume heightened his need for her. He missed the way she made him feel.

Oh God, Clara, I love you.

"Damn it!" Noel growled against Andrea's lips. He moved off her body and put space between them.

"Did I do something?"

The worry in Andrea's voice had the guilt in him rising. Noel sat on the edge of the bed and ran a hand through his hair.

"Don't do that, Andrea, please."

"Do what?"

Noel turned to see her sitting up on the pillows. There was a confused look on her face, and he understood it. It wasn't Andrea's fault that he couldn't let go of Clara.

"The nail digging. I don't enjoy it," he confessed. Andrea winced. The hurt had consumed her face and her eyes. The fact was, he did enjoy it, but not the way Andrea did it.

Noel had registered a heavy sigh before he climbed back in bed and lay next to Andrea. He was conflicted and every time he looked at her, it was made worse. He brought her in his arms and held her tight against his chest.

"I'm sorry, Andrea. I didn't mean to be an asshole."

Andrea's fingers traced lazy circles on his chest before she gazed up and said, "I know you didn't. Want to watch TV and order Chinese?"

Noel smiled and rubbed his hand along her arm. "I'd love that."

Clara

Running her finger along the glossy page, Clara found the step she was up to and read the instructions that were next. It had been three days since she had landed back in Melbourne and she'd spent those days giving Liam and CeCe her undivided attention. The sound of the front door opening and closing had her lifting her head up from the recipe book's page.

"Hey," she greeted once Liam walked into the large kitchen.

He approached the bench and then set his keys on the countertop with a heavy sigh. "Doesn't get any harder than that."

A frown developed on her face as she stirred the eggs into the batter. "She cried?" Clara questioned as she reached for the orange and started to zest the peel into the mixture.

"Hysterically. I told her we'd be in Sydney soon, but she

still cried. Ally was scared by the looks she was getting from other passengers. CeCe was reaching out for me and searching for her 'Clary.'"

Liam shook his head and walked around the island bench. He leant over and placed a kiss on Clara's cheek before swiping the bag of chocolate chips she was about to use.

"Hey!" she protested out loud, but he ignored her.

With a satisfied smile, Liam poured himself a handful and began to eat a single chocolate chip at a time. Clara shook her head and let out a short laugh.

"You're such a child."

"And you're marrying me. Sorry, sweetheart, looks like you're in trouble." He grinned.

Clara rolled her eyes. When she reached over to take the bag of chocolate chips, Liam grabbed her hand and stopped her. Clara looked up to see his playful mood change. The expression on his face was one she knew well. It was his 'this is seriously important and we need to talk' look. Clara held her breath as she waited for him to continue.

"When you said you needed to get fresh clothes this morning, did you get them?"

It was something she had said earlier. Clara noted her need to do laundry and get more clothes from her apartment downstairs. She didn't think he'd thought so much of it. It was a simple statement—nothing worthy of a serious talk.

Clara gazed up at him, puzzled, but she just nodded. She wasn't sure what the deal was. They had done it a million times in the space of their relationship. She mostly stayed in his apartment, and when she ran out of clean clothes or needed something, she'd pick it up from her apartment downstairs. They were both quiet for a moment before Liam removed his hands from Clara and pulled her into his arms.

"Clara, I need you to move in with me."

Clara had blinked at him before she frowned. "Uhh, Liam, I have moved in with you," she pointed out.

Liam's tensed jaw didn't disappear. He let out a small laugh before he tightened his arms around her waist. "I don't like you having to go back and forth from my apartment to yours. We're getting married, Clara. I need your clothes to fill those drawers permanently, your dresses hanging up next to my suits, and have those adorable shoes of yours lined up next to mine. I need your things in this apartment, Clara. I need you to make this a home. *Our* home."

Clara felt the burning in her lungs as she momentarily forgot to breathe. Taking in heavy breaths of air, she stared at Liam in shock. His request made their engagement and their future together more real.

"Our home?"

"What's mine is yours."

Clara smiled at his reply. Liam never hid how he felt towards her. It felt empowering to know that she was his first choice.

"All right," Clara agreed.

"All right?"

"We're getting married, Liam. I'm not sure why I haven't packed everything in boxes and moved in sooner."

He broke into a beautiful smile, and Clara felt the satisfaction sweep her system. She liked to make Liam happy.

"I'll call Stevie over after lunch and we'll start," Clara said as she squeezed his arm.

Liam dipped his head into the curve of her neck and whispered, "Have I told you lately how much I love you?"

Clara had smiled before she whispered, "It doesn't hurt to remind me."

"I love you, Clara. I can't wait until you become Clara O'Connor, my wife."

She swallowed the lump in her throat and stared at the stainless steel fridge to her left. "Me, too."

"*I* regret helping you. You have all these clothes that I want but could never pull off. Sweet and floral does not suit me. Damn you, Clara Lawrence!" Stevie complained as she placed what looked like several of Clara's skirts in a plastic bag.

"I said I was shouting you drinks, didn't I?" Clara raised an eyebrow and watched Stevie let go of the plastic bag with a huff.

"Why isn't Saint Annie here?"

"I didn't want a lecture on why I'm marrying Liam," Clara said as she placed a pair of flats in a large box and picked up another pair of shoes.

"Can we speed this up? I'm meeting Rob soon."

Clara dropped a pair of heels and quickly turned to look at Stevie. "What?" she asked in disbelief.

"I'm. Meeting. Rob," Stevie said slowly for Clara to comprehend.

They haven't... have they?

Clara blinked quickly, and her shoulders sagged. "You aren't sleeping with Rob, are you, Stevie?"

"Oh, Clara, you've been in Liam's bed too long and don't get out much. We're making that Jewel bitch jealous."

Clara breathed out in relief and went to pick up the shoes she'd dropped.

"Besides, I wouldn't do that to you. Not after what happened in Boston. You don't need Rob around to remind you."

Clara's heart ached at the thought of what had happened in Boston. The worst decision she'd ever made in her life was to return to *him*, hoping. The day after Clara returned, Stevie noticed Liam's ring and didn't ask for more.

"Stevie, if you like Rob and want to be with him, I don't mind. I wasn't in love with him. It was —" Clara stopped herself. His name wasn't one she would allow herself to say out loud anymore. It was too difficult. The past had to stay the past.

"I'm sorry. Rob didn't tell me he was seeing someone."

Clara willed a smile and faced Stevie. "I think I have some things in the spare room that I should bring," she said as she stepped over the bags of clothes that lay on the floor. Clara had almost made it to the door of her old bedroom before Stevie stopped her.

"Clara, I think I need to speak up. I've been quiet because I wanted you to talk to me when you're okay. But you're not. So talk," Stevie demanded.

The ache in her chest became a full-frontal inferno. "I'm fine. I'm getting married, Stevie. My mind is all over the place with flowers and guest invitations coming in," Clara lied as she pushed past her best friend and walked towards the room down the hall.

Clara stood in front of what used to be *his* room. She had

never stepped foot in it and now, months later, she would. Clara remembered the days after he left. Her brother, Alex, snuck into the room, changed the bed sheets, and aired out the room. He thought she hadn't noticed, but she had. She'd spent many days staring at that door, hoping for his return. But he didn't, and she moved on.

The airing out of her guest room was no use when her bedroom smelt like him. It took a week for his smell to completely disappear. Clara summoned the courage and placed a hand on the door handle. She wasn't sure what she was looking for, but she felt like something important lay in the room. Even if she found nothing, she just wanted to feel connected to him in some way.

Clara opened the door and found the room as basic as it was before he came. She looked around and found nothing out of place. It was as if he was never here. She found it incredibly hard to breathe. They'd both moved on with their lives and nothing bound them together anymore.

When she reached the tallboy, Clara ran her fingers over the wood and closed her eyes tightly. Flashes of their times filled her thoughts.

"Noel," she painfully whispered.

It was the first time she'd said his name since she'd arrived back in Melbourne and it was like the dams breaking. Intense pain filled her chest and Clara felt the burning sensation start to consume her. She needed to leave the room and this apartment. This apartment held the memories she'd tried to run from. As much as she loved her place, she'd rather watch it burn. Before Clara left, she did a quick check of the room to make sure she didn't need anything. She pulled the top left drawer open. Looking down, she saw a single envelope sitting in the drawer.

Curious, she picked it up and then sat on the edge of the bed. Taking a deep breath, she lifted the flap. Pulling out the contents, she instantly regretted what she found.

Just the sight of the first photo had brought tears falling. The smile on both their faces induced simultaneous tremors to her heart and Clara couldn't contain the sobs. It served as a reminder and it hurt her more than it should have. Her hands shook as she looked at the next photo: one of her kissing his cheek. Clara placed the pictures down on the bed and covered her face with her hands.

"I intend on making you happy for the rest of your days."

She felt the full force of another slam of her heart as she remembered every second of that day at the beach. As hard as she tried, she couldn't stop the tears. She couldn't stop the pain that never went away.

All it took was one photo and she remembered all the reasons why she still loved Nolan Parker. Reasons that could undoubtedly end her engagement and the future she had pictured with Liam. It seemed unfair that he still held her heart. Not when Liam offered her the world and beyond.

"I didn't love you the way I thought I did."

"Clara," she heard Stevie say, but she didn't look up. Those photos were the connection, and they proved that she loved him more than he could have ever loved her. The mattress dipped and Stevie took Clara's hand away from her face.

"Clara, what did Noel say to you?" Stevie asked.

Tears continued to fall down her face as she looked at the photos Stevie now held. The pain in her chest made it hard to breathe or speak.

Clara shook her head and wiped her tears. "Why won't it stop, Stevie? Why won't it just go away? It hurts to live like this. I look at Liam and all I feel is guilt. I shouldn't have gone to Boston. I should have just gone straight to New York. I shouldn't have seen him. Then I wouldn't know that he never loved me. Then it wouldn't hurt this much to see those photos. Why would someone like Liam love me? He deserves so much better. I want to be good for him, Stevie, but I'm scared I never will."

Stevie held her hand and squeezed it. "It's meant to hurt. That's the only way to know whether your love for Noel was real. And it was real, Clara."

She let her head fall on Stevie's shoulder as the beating pain in her chest continued. She looked down at the ring and reminded herself that those photos couldn't have the power to break her.

I'm marrying someone far too good for me. I have to be worthy of Liam. I can't cry over Noel. Not anymore.

"Do you regret him?" Stevie asked.

Clara stared at the pictures. That day, she knew she loved

Noel, and she could never regret how she felt for him. "No. I don't regret Noel. I have Liam because of him," Clara said as she stood up. The back of her hands quickly wiped her tears away as she looked at Stevie's concerned eyes. "Burn those photos for me, Stevie. I can't have them reminding me of what I had. I can't let Noel stop me from being happy. I never want to see them again."

She'd find the happiness she knew Liam could give her.

I will marry Liam.

Chapter SEVEN

Noel

Max: *Rob and I are coming up to New York for Alex's birthday. Guess who is also coming?*

Noel looked at the message and his brows creased. Then he squinted at the mirror and tried to style his hair with his fingers. When he couldn't get it the way he wanted without product, he gave up and returned his attention to Max's message.

Noel: *Who?*

Max: *The other Moors brother!*

Noel read it again. He couldn't believe what he was reading. Noel had taken Julian under his wing when they were in high school. They were very much alike. Back in high school, their group of Alex, Rob, Julian, Max and himself were practically brothers. Nothing got in the way of their tight group. Not until Noel and Alex went to Stanford and Julian disappeared shortly after his trip to Thailand. Even though they were apart, they were all still brothers.

Noel: *Julian? Well, fuck me! It'll be good to see him. Glad you lot are coming to the States. I'll see you in NY!*

Max: *Yeah, that son of a bitch, right? Rob's pretty stoked about it. Catch ya there!*

Noel shoved his phone in his pocket and started to button the cuffs of his light green dress shirt. He took one more look in the mirror, and with a satisfied nod at his reflection, he walked out of his bedroom. He made his way over to the kitchen to see his best friend nursing a beer. Alex had his iPad sitting on the countertop as his eyes kept focus on his phone. Until his business with the Boston office was over, Alex had been staying at Noel's.

"Heard the news?" Noel asked as he made his way to the fridge. Opening it, he took out a bottle of water. He wasn't quite ready to drink alcohol. He'd save it for when they got to the club.

"What's that?" Alex asked not taking his eyes off his phone.

"Julian's coming to your birthday in a fortnight's time," he replied.

Alex let out a grunt as he kept his eyes locked on his phone. Besides the fact that his shirt was unbuttoned, Alex looked ready to go out. But the face he pulled told Noel that tonight might be cancelled. It was Saturday night, and they had plans to leave the apartment by seven. He only had an hour to change his best friend's mood.

Noel thought the past few days would be hard considering what he had been through. It was even more painful considering Alex never mentioned Clara's name. When Andrea fell asleep next to him, he'd roll onto his back and stare at the ceiling, wondering. That was all he could do with his life now. Just wonder how she was doing and what she was thinking.

"Alex, mate, what is with you?" Noel asked as he walked over to the island bench and leant on it. Alex remained silent as he continued to look at his phone and then at his iPad.

"Alex?" Noel had asked again before the sounds from his iPad started ringing.

"Shh!" Alex grabbed his iPad and took a deep breath. "You. Stay!" he demanded.

Noel let out an annoyed sigh. "Why?" he asked as he looked at Alex's clenched fists.

"Just stay quiet," Alex replied, and he swiped the screen.

Noel saw the *Skype* icon appear before Alex brought the iPad close to his face. Alex never Skyped anyone—except his sister. Noel fiddled with the label of the water bottle. There was silence before Clara's face appeared on the screen. Noel knew she couldn't see him, but he saw her. And there was no doubt that her beauty still left him speechless.

Aw, shit.

Noel could see that her hair was tied back, and he knew she was at the bakery. He felt the need to leave, but the need to stay was greater, causing his feet to cement themselves to the kitchen floor.

"Clara, you sounded frantic. Are you at the bakery? Can we talk?" Alex asked.

Noel's stomach formed tight knots at the sound of her name. Clara came in close and stared into the camera before she let out an exasperated sigh.

"You're not in New York, are you?" she asked and Alex's head fell slightly. "You broke your promise, Alex. You said you wouldn't."

Promise?

"Clara, I'm not in Boston because—"

"I told you not to hurt him. You can't fix what ended. Is he… with you?"

Noel tensed at her mention of him.

"No. He's with Andrea. I'm in Boston for a meeting with Gregson and Mercer on an account. Since that Owens case, I've been getting the big clients." Alex's eyes kept focused on the screen of his iPad.

Alex never lies to Clara. What the hell is going on?

"Are you at the bakery?" Alex asked as he twirled the beer bottle.

Noel contemplated leaving, but he was scared he'd make a noise so he stood still, staring at the counter.

"Just got some cupcakes in the oven. It's only eight here."

Noel looked up to see Alex nod his head and he could hear the weariness in Clara's voice. For a long moment, there was nothing said between them and all he heard was the sound of the kitchen clock tick and the faint music from Clara's end.

"Kiddo, please tell me what's wrong," Alex asked softly. He always pulled the 'kiddo' card when he wanted something out of Clara.

Noel steeled himself to hear the news he'd rather not hear.

I don't think I can take hearing about her wedding.

"I packed up my apartment, Alex. Besides the furniture, it's kind of empty," she explained.

Noel's mouth made a fine line as he tried to control the raw emotions that ran through his veins.

"You want to sell the apartment?" Alex asked a little astonished.

Noel's jaw dropped.

Not the apartment!

That apartment held all their memories. He'd rather she killed him with her words than get rid of their once safe haven. When he thought of their good times, his mind wandered back to that little apartment in Melbourne.

"No. I don't want to sell it. I love that apartment. I'm going to ask Stevie if she wants to live there after the wedding. I think she's tired of living with her dad and stepmother."

Alex and Noel both breathed out in relief. Clara still loved that apartment enough not to sell it, and Noel felt at peace with the thought.

"What's wrong, Clara? You never call this early unless something's troubling you." Alex's body was strung up tight, and his knuckles had turned white.

Noel was anxious to know what troubled her, too.

"I don't know how to tell him, Alex. What do I say to him about something like this?" Clara's voice broke, and he knew she was on the verge of crying.

"Clara, has it got to do with... Mum and Dad?" Alex asked and Clara sniffled. It was a topic Clara never wanted to speak about, and she only did so with Alex, never with Noel.

"They checked 'No' on the wedding invitation, Alex. They checked 'No.'" Clara was quiet for a moment and then Noel heard that familiar bell ring.

Why would they say no? It's her wedding!

"I'll be back in a second, Alex. Danny wants to have a talk with me. I'll call you back later, okay?" Clara's voice was small.

Noel felt the tightening in his chest.

"Sure thing, kiddo. We'll talk about it later. I love you, Clara. Don't forget that."

"I know. I love you, too, Alex. I'm sorry. Forget what I said about Mum and Dad. I thought since I was getting married things would change... I was wrong." There was a deflated sigh from Clara and Noel could see the sheer rage in Alex's eyes.

"I swear, Clara, I will fix this!" Alex had promised before he hung up. He then slammed the iPad on the counter. Alex's chest heaved and the anger in his eyes had Noel straightening his spine. Alex quickly grabbed his phone and unlocked it.

"Alex, what's wrong? Is Clara okay?" He cared more than he should.

Alex's head quickly snapped over in Noel's direction. "You heard, didn't you? My fucked-up parents said no to Clara's wedding invitation." There was a hint of hate in Alex's voice and Noel knew this was too personal for Alex.

"I just want to know if she's okay,"

"No." Alex sighed. "I can't believe they would do this to her. She's getting married. You'd think they'd put all this shit behind them and be there. It's their daughter, for God's sake!" Alex's resilience started to crack.

Noel played with the water bottle until he pushed it away from him. "We can cancel tonight. I'll call Andrea and she can just have a girls' night. We'll order a pizza and have some cold beers. What do you say?"

"Don't. When I'm done dealing with this, I'm going to need alcohol. I'm going to handle this motherfucking mess!" Alex roared as he pushed off the barstool, the loud scratching sound made Noel wince. Then Alex stormed off to the guest room.

If only I could help her.

Noel shook his head. There was no denying the need for him to help Clara, but he couldn't. He hoped time would catch up with him and erase her from his conscience. Stopped him from loving her.

Noel heard the muffled shouts of Alex's voice in the distance. His legs had him moving before he could stop himself. Alex and Clara's parents had been a topic he always wondered about. From the surface, they seemed perfect... towards Alex. At a young age, Noel had noticed the drifting of Clara from her mother and father; it was something he had never really thought about. Noel stood by the guest bedroom door and listened carefully.

"Listen to me, old man! That's your daughter. How could you check 'no'? It's her wedding day... That's not okay... *You're* meant to walk her down the aisle. Not me! All you've done is be there for Mum... All I've done is raise her because you couldn't give a shit about her... You're a sad excuse for a father... I hope you regret it. It's a fucking privilege to walk Clara down the aisle!"

Noel heard the sounds of Alex hanging up, and he stood straight. Alex opened the door. There was no point in pretending that he hadn't heard. By the tired expression on Alex's face, he needed to finally get it off his chest.

"You promise not to tell anyone?" Alex sighed as he returned his phone in his pocket and stepped into the hallway with Noel.

Noel shrugged. "Who am I going to tell?"

"Clara," Alex said matter-of-factly.

Just her name broke through his walls and made his breathing feel inadequate and intolerable. Noel balled his fist tight and focused on his attempts at breathing properly.

"I ran her out of my life, Alex. There's no reason to tell her any of this. We don't belong in each other's lives anymore," he confessed, and Noel felt the breaking of his heart once more.

The truth hurts.

Alex — understanding the underlying message of his response — patted Noel's shoulder and led them to the living room. Alex had paced in front of the leather couch before he sat on it with a heavy sigh. Noel sat on the armchair next to him.

"Well, I've been dealing with this shit my entire life, Noel. I just need someone else to know, and I'm probably telling the wrong person, given your history with my sister. You know her more *intimately*, albeit more than I would have liked. But you love her enough to care and telling someone is going to stop me from doing some pretty fucked-up shit."

Intimately.

Noel kept quiet and thought back to all the times he'd made love to her. The first time was perfect and that connection he shared with her was one he missed. Worshiping her with all his love was what he had intended to do for the rest of his life. But life had other plans.

Noel's jaw clenched, and he stopped remembering; it was too painful. His gaze shifted over to Alex, whose eyes had softened with a sadness Noel had never seen. He was curious to know the secrets of Clara's life. He'd never tell her he knew. It didn't seem to matter anymore. He would have waited until she told him. He'd have waited forever for her. If she had let him.

"This stays between us. Got it?"

"Yeah, Alex. Just us," Noel replied.

Alex sat forward and rested his palms on his knees. "Remember, what I tell you will change your perspective of my parents. They aren't what you've grown up to believe they are. My mother is a selfish bitch, and my father is a boneless bastard, but yet they love me more than Clara. She was always innocent, but they made her the problem. They blamed her for their problems." Alex stopped for a minute before he locked eyes on Noel.

Why would they blame her?

"Before my parents found out about Clara, my mother was having an affair with some man she'd met before my dad. She would leave during the night and meet up with him, leaving my dad and me at home. Looking back, I think he ignored her cheating. He just refused to believe it. Six months into the affair, my mother found out she was pregnant with Clara. Dad caught her sleeping with that man two weeks after she had told him she was pregnant. I didn't think she ever loved my dad because she had kept the affair going. My mother was adamant it was the other man's baby. She rubbed it in his face that she got away with the affair and she planned on divorcing him. After Clara was born, they had a paternity test…"

Fuck.

"Alex, Clara's your half-sister, isn't she?" he asked in disbelief. Noel now understood Alex's need to protect Clara from her mother, and why he stepped in as her father figure.

Alex gave Noel a sad smile and shook his head. "She's every inch my sister, Noel. Blood and all. She's my father's biological daughter. Whether she was my half-sister or not, I'd always love her more than what our parents could give her. My mother ended up with postnatal depression after Clara's birth. She's been blaming Clara for not being with the love of her life. My mother hates Clara with more venom than anything I have ever seen. It's a hate I don't understand.

"The man she was having an affair with refused to be with her because she had another kid. My dad took her back with open arms because he was blindly in love with her. First, he loved Clara, but then my mother started to see the love and got possessive. In the end, Dad chose my mother and Clara had to fend for herself. That's why I protect her as much as I can. Got her that apartment in the city, paid the bills, and gave her everything so she wouldn't have to struggle and live with them. Clara never once asked for their love, but she wanted it. Now they've continued their streak and aren't attending her wedding."

Noel sat speechless. He had known James and Gillian Lawrence all his life and had never once imagined that Gillian could have an affair. What shocked him most was that James had taken her back and had spent the last nineteen years loving a cheat. He just assumed Clara and Gillian had a falling out over things a mother and daughter fought over—the choice of boyfriends or clothes. But he had never expected this.

"I'm sorry." It was all he could say. Clara had grown up lonely without her parents' love. Had he known then he might have never treated her as he had, but he couldn't alter the past.

"It's not me you should be sorry for. It's Clara. Why do you think I do what I do for her? She's only got me, Noel. When I realised something was going on between the two of you, I hated your guts. But then I saw the way she looked at you and I was happy because I knew you could love her and give her what she needed. It's what she deserved after everything she's been through." Alex paused and then exhaled heavily. "You want to know something. The night we went to that club with Max and Rob, Clara left early with Stevie. Well, when I got home, I found her curled up asleep on the couch. I heard her stir and I went to wake her up. I called out her name and do you want to know what happened?"

The pain sliced him as he held his breath and waited.

"She said *your* name as she slept, Noel. She said your name. That was when I knew she loved you. The next day you left and it was all over. Then she lost you, too."

His stomach and his heart twisted, the searing ache taking over his body.

She whispered my name as she slept.

"I lost her, too, Alex."

Clara

"Clara, I think you should consider it." A smile touched Danny's lips and Clara couldn't shake off the shock in her system. He leant over his desk and eyed her. "Just think about it. That's all I'm asking. When you're ready, we'll talk."

"But—" Clara began to say, but she couldn't form words. She tucked a loose strand of her curly hair behind her ear and gaped at her boss. "You're going to San Francisco to be a head chef, Danny."

"And I want you to think about taking over the ownership of the bakery. I was going to put it up for public sale since it's hot property, but I want someone who loves this place to own it. I know you have your wedding and then your apprenticeship, but I won't be going to California until late October. I want to have this place running properly and in safe hands before I go. If you let me, I'd like to be a silent investor. I know you can make this place a hit and I'd be stupid not to invest. I know you think you can't do it, but I believe in you, Clara. The bakery is yours to take, and I won't put it up for sale until you decide."

Danny handed Clara a folder and she opened it. Inside, she found a contract of sale and her heart stopped.

He wants to sell me the bakery.

"I wouldn't know how to run a bakery, Danny. I don't know how to be a boss," she replied as she flicked through the contract.

"I have a cousin of mine. He's willing to be your financial advisor and since he loves your white chocolate cupcakes, he's willing to do it for practically nothing. I'll stay as your mentor and your investor, but I want you to get full credit for where you take this bakery. You can expand and make those pastries you've been trying and make cakes. It's yours to do as you please."

Her eyes dropped down at her name on the contract. It was real and legal and it scared her. She recognised that this could be her future. She'd be the owner of the bakery she loved more than anything.

"I'll think about it," Clara promised as the bakery doorbell rung. Resting the folder against her chest and wrapping her arms around it, Clara walked out of Danny's office and to the counter. She instantly smelt the fresh Sunday cupcakes that were in the oven. A batch of one hundred was waiting to be cooked for morning tea for the local church down the road. Besides the big order of assorted, it was business as usual.

Dropping the folder on the counter and grabbing her apron, Clara tied it around her waist and walked up to the front counter. When she reached it, she looked up and flinched in surprise.

"Good morning, Clara." Those dark eyes seemed kinder, more heartfelt than she had previously known.

"Darren," Clara breathed and gazed him over. To his left was a pram and in his arms was a baby boy of several months. "What are you doing here?"

"I came by to see how you're going. And well, I wanted you to meet *my* son, Flynn." The smile on Darren's face had Clara's hate for him fading. It seemed he'd turned his cheating ways around and was now a proud father. The beautiful boy in her ex-boyfriend's arms had her forgetting about the situation with her parents.

"He's beautiful. Congratulations, Darren. You have no idea how proud I am to see you with your son."

Darren beamed at her. "Thanks, Clara. I was hoping Flynn would be my secret weapon for being here."

Clara glanced down to see Flynn's small hands move as his eyelids started to fall. "What do you mean?" she asked.

"Mind if we sit? He can get a little restless in my arms."

She nodded as she walked over to a table near the window. Sitting on the metal seat, Clara couldn't take her eyes off Flynn.

Flynn is the most adorable little boy.

"I came here to apologise. It's over a year too late, but I am terribly sorry for being such a dick. I just wanted sex, and I didn't appreciate you. I thought you were teasing, but I realised that you wanted it to be for love. I couldn't love you because I wasn't capable of loving you. I didn't respect you enough. Being a dad has really opened up my eyes. I don't want Flynn to do what I did. I don't want my son to treat women like shit. What I'm saying is that I'm incredibly sorry for being the dick that I was. I don't expect you to forgive me, but just know that I'm sorry." Darren gave her a smile and took one of Flynn's small curled hands and kissed it.

This was all I ever wanted — an apology that actually means something to him.

"I heard you and Noel are engaged. Congratulations, Clara. He'll treat you right. After what I saw that night, no one can deny the love he has for you."

Clara felt the sudden collapse of her heart. All the pain she kept hidden in a box burst open and tears demanded to be shed. Clara balled her fists and bit the inside of her cheek in an attempt to not break down. "I... uhh, I'm not engaged to Noel," Clara clarified as she peeked down at her engagement ring.

"Shit, sorry, Clara. Elizabeth and I have been on Flynn duties. All we heard was that you were engaged. So, who's the lucky guy?"

Clara took her eyes off the ring and directed them back to Darren. "Liam O'Connor," she simply stated.

Darren's forehead creased as he began to mull over Liam's name until his eyes went wide. "The guy who lives in your building? Clara, you do know what kind of guy he is, right? He sleeps with a lot of women."

She let out a short laugh. "If you can completely change, then so can Liam. Trust me, he's different. He is with me," Clara explained.

Darren nodded. "And Noel?"

"Over before anything could happen." Clara felt the sharp pains of mentioning the end of what she had with Noel burn through her. It had hurt and left her breathless.

"As long as you're happy, Clara." Darren slowly stood from his chair and walked over to the pram, carefully placing Flynn in. "You should come over next fortnight. We're having a small party for Flynn, and Elizabeth asked me if I'd come by and invite you."

The sincerity had Clara at a disadvantage. He was so

different and she knew that Flynn was the reason. Clara mentally calculated the dates and let out a sigh. "I'd love to, but I'm going to New York that weekend for Alex's birthday. I'm sorry, Darren."

He gave her a carefree shrug. "No worries. Next time. Well, I have to take Flynn down to the zoo with my parents. I'll catch you around, Clara." Darren walked around to the handle of the pram and gave Clara a smile and then he started to push it towards the exit.

Darren… a father.

"Darren, wait!" Clara yelled out and watched him halt. "I forgive you. I don't hate you or anything because your actions gave you that little boy. So, we can start fresh." Peace had been settled. Now that she thought about it, she was relieved Darren had cheated on her. She wasn't sure how she pictured a future with him. In some way, they were just in a relationship for the hell of it.

"Thanks, Clara. I was one shitty boyfriend, and if marrying Liam is going to make you happy, then I'm happy. Flynn and I will stop by again. He's got to try the famous cupcakes by Clara Lawrence." There was the playful side to him that she had once fallen for and she let out an honest laugh. Darren had changed and he had a reason to.

The bakery and the wedding were the only things that ran through her mind constantly. Between meeting Jo for decisions on the colour scheme of the reception and meeting with her lawyer over the sale of the bakery, Clara was tired. Buying the bakery wasn't something she could afford. She had a significant amount saved, but it was to repay her brother for the apartment. So when Liam found out about the opportunity for her to own the bakery, he had the money in her account the next day.

Clara refused the money and spent the rest of the weekend fighting him over it. In the end, she had agreed, but only if it meant he became an investor and her advisor. It was hard to say no to Liam when he put on those hazel eyes and pouted.

It was even harder to refuse his money when he had used the 'what's mine is yours' card on her. What Clara didn't know was she was marrying into a family with several multi-million dollar companies. Buying the small bakery was like spending a penny for Liam. It put neither a dent in his wallet nor his overall finances.

When Liam had agreed to buy the bakery, Clara decided that she wanted the contract changed to his name rather than hers. It would be one of the many investments he had going, and his portfolio would increase ten-fold. What she had noticed a few days after getting the contract off Danny was that life continued to take her further away from Noel. It hurt to realise how far apart they were, but it was for the best. They never really belonged in each other's lives. They had been brought together by circumstances and convenience.

Two weeks after receiving the bakery contract, Clara stood by the table of finger foods and scanned them. She picked up a small piece of bruschetta and ate it. She looked over the hall and at her brother, Keira wrapped up in his arms, and Clara smiled. They were happy together. After everything her brother had done to protect her, it was time he let go of his little sister and focused on his future with Keira.

Clara fiddled with the ring on her finger and let out a sigh. She was anxious because she knew the inevitable was coming. Soon enough, Noel and Andrea would walk through those doors, and she would have to pretend like it wouldn't hurt. As much as she was adamant about marrying Liam, parts of her still yearned for a life with Noel.

It's pointless and unattainable. I've made a mess of everything.

One thing she didn't want to do was come to New York alone, but she had. Clara had tried hard to get Liam to take a break from the company, but a deal in Singapore was an opportunity that couldn't be missed. He promised that it would be his last before the wedding, and his friend, Adam, would take over. Clara had met Adam several times. The first time was the night of her nineteenth birthday and he had insisted she let Liam take her home. Adam liked to believe he got them together.

Not that Clara was alone. She ended up on the same flight as her brother's best friends, Rob and Max. But she couldn't look at Rob. It wasn't his fault that things ended so wrong for her and Noel, but he served as a reminder. She just had to prepare herself to see him with Andrea. If she could handle seeing them together, then she knew she'd be okay.

Between the fairy lights and live band, Keira had gone all out for Alex's twenty-fifth birthday. He deserved to celebrate. When she broke the news about their parents refusing to attend the wedding, Alex looked ready to explode. Clara hid the RSVP card her parents had sent. Liam had been looking forward to meeting them, but Clara knew that no matter how many times she called to ask, she'd always be greeted by their answering machine.

"If it isn't my favourite Lawrence offspring."

Taking her eyes off her engagement ring and her thoughts on her relationship with her parents, Clara turned around. She couldn't believe her eyes and she found herself blinking rapidly to ensure she didn't see things. Clara let out a laugh and then she playfully smacked his shoulder and pulled an exaggerated frown. He pulled her into his arms with a chuckle and gave Clara a long overdue embrace. There were memories they shared from when they were younger that flashed before her, and she smiled and untangled herself from his body.

"Julian Moors, if you weren't standing before my very eyes, I wouldn't believe it. You've been gone for far too long. You left without even a goodbye to *me*."

Julian's mouth pressed into a hard line and an apologetic expression washed over his face. "Sorry, Clars. You know how much I love you, kiddo. I just needed to get far away. If I told people I was leaving, then they would have tried to stop me. I couldn't miss the opportunity in Sydney." There was a sad smile on his face, and she could tell he remembered what caused him to run to another state. "Well, look at you, Clars. Aren't you just a beauty! But first, is it true? Is our little girl getting married? Did he pass the big brother test or is Alex silently waiting for the fiancé to have an *accident?*" he asked.

Clara giggled. "It's true, I'm getting married. I have an invitation for you, but I had no idea where to send it since you disappeared. And yes, Liam passed all of Alex's tests. Trust me, Alex would have stopped this if he thought Liam wasn't good enough."

There was a 'you're right' nod from Julian, and she smiled. Julian was a year younger than her brother. He had the same brown hair as she remembered and those pale blue eyes were as stunning as ever. When she was seventeen, they had plans to go to the movies, but he had never showed. That night she found out that he had moved away. Clara was hurt that her friend never showed, but Rob had taken his spot and sat through an entire movie and lunch with her.

It was a memory Clara had forgotten about, and she looked over at Rob. His eyes were on Julian before he met hers. There was so much she had to be thankful for with him, but she never once showed him her gratitude. Rob kept the secret of her and Noel and made it his own. But she couldn't look at him. He was too much of a reminder of Noel.

"Want to dance?" Julian asked.

She turned to see the smirk painted on his face. "Only if you behave yourself. I know you, Julian Moors, and I should remind you that I'm engaged." She held up her left hand to him and wiggled her fingers.

"Clara, I can't lie to you. If you'd let me, I'd make sure that engagement was called off tonight." He gave her a wink and she let out a laugh. Julian was attractive and those eyes of his could be a girl's undoing. But no matter how much he charmed her, he didn't have the power to make her heart race. And from the look in his eyes, he was fighting his own demons.

"You're like lightning."

His eyes lit up. "How so, beautiful?"

"When you roll into town, just the sight of you is beautiful, but when someone gets too close, you're dangerous. You could make girls go through hell trying to chase lightning. I know you, Julian, and frankly, I'm glad I've got this ring on my finger. I can assure you, you don't make my heart melt like you want it to."

Julian appeared to think about what Clara had said and then he shrugged. He leant forward, his mouth close to her ear. "See, if I were Noel, I wouldn't have let someone like you go, Clars."

Clara swallowed the lump in her throat and found it difficult to breathe. Julian stepped back and eyed her for a reaction.

Julian knows.

"And if I were Liam, I'd lock you away and make sure no man gets close to you. I'd marry you as soon as you said 'yes.' But the feeling is mutual. As hot as you are, Clara, you are very much my little sister. Unlike Noel, I'm not going to risk the wrath of Alex."

Clara stood there shocked. She shook her head in disbelief as the heaviness in her chest returned. She fought hard against the tears and knew if he continued, she'd need to leave. She came to New York for her brother's birthday and a week away from the wedding and the bakery. Now, Julian was digging up her past, and it was something she didn't want to relive.

"Rob told me." Julian pointed over at his brother. "Sorry it didn't happen for you and Noel. He must have really loved you if he was willing to go behind Alex's back."

Rob stared at her until she looked away.

Noel didn't love me. He said so himself.

"Julian, how about this. We stop talking about Noel and I won't bring up the fact that I know you left Melbourne because of a girl. I know something happened and I know how to make you talk. What's it going to be?"

Panic flashed in Julian's eyes before a grin appeared. "I can see why Noel couldn't resist you, Clars. I like a challenge. Consider him not conversation worthy. That dance?" Julian offered his hand.

Clara let out a laugh knowing he accepted the terms of their agreement. Julian wouldn't talk about Noel, and Clara wouldn't talk about that girl. But unlike Julian, the man she didn't want to discuss would walk through those double doors any second, and Clara would have to face him... and his girlfriend.

Chapter
EIGHT

Noel

"Are you sure I'm dressed okay?" Andrea asked as she stepped out of the taxi. After landing, they had stopped by Alex's house and freshened up before making their way to the party. Noel had used the spare key Alex gave him and claimed one of the guest rooms for him and Andrea.

"Andrea, you look beautiful. You don't need to worry," he assured and kissed her cheek.

"But it's *your* friends. The ones you've grown up with. I want them to like me." Andrea adjusted the jacket she wore over her bright pink dress before fiddling with her hair.

"Andrea, it's just the guys. Alex likes you, and if he likes you, then they'll all like you." Noel took her hand in his and ran his thumb over her knuckles. "Ready to go in?"

Andrea smiled brightly and nodded her head. He placed his hand on the small of her back and led her to the double doors of the hall. Pushing them open, he held them for Andrea as she stepped inside. The old hall was one of the oldest buildings in Scarsdale. Inside, old vintage wooden panels lined the hallways and a large chandelier made out of delicate glass provided light.

"I'm going to the bathroom and I'll find somewhere to put my jacket. You go inside and I'll meet you in a second," Andrea said and then kissed Noel's cheek.

Noel stepped towards the main hall's doors and pushed them open. He walked through and stood at the top of the small steps that led to the dance floor. Scanning the room, he spotted his group of friends near the bar. From across the room, close to the food table, stood Clara and Keira. He watched a smile on Clara's face develop and felt a lump form in his throat. Clara's curls were more like waves that graced the light blue dress she wore.

His eyes fixed on her, he heard no music as he made his way towards her. He ignored the fact that he had passed his friends and kept walking until he stopped in front of Clara and Keira.

"Hello, Clara," he said as he looked into those brown eyes. His heart thumped for her like it always had. "Hey, Keira." Noel did a quick look at Keira to see a smile on her face before returning to Clara. There was a sense of fear radiating from her, and he knew she was terrified to see him. He understood why she feared him. He deserved it.

"Hello, Nolan," she finally said. There was no smile or anger. Her face was almost emotionless.

I'm Nolan to her.

"Can we —" he had said before a hand rested on his shoulder, stopping him. He turned slightly to see Andrea next to him.

Andrea gazed at Clara and then smiled. "You must be Clara. Alex's little sister, right?"

Clara had blinked once before she gave Andrea a smile. "Yeah, that's me. You must be Noel's g-girlfriend." It was clear that Clara had struggled to say that word, but she composed herself quickly.

"That's me. I'm Andrea," she said, putting forward her hand.

Clara put her hand in Andrea's, and that was when Noel took sight of her engagement ring. That large diamond made him nauseated and his head spun.

God, it's real.

Clara's eyes met his. He saw the unspoken apology in them and he was in disbelief. The invitation and hearing about her engagement was one thing, but seeing Liam's ring on her finger was another. It broke his heart.

"Wow, that's a beautiful ring. I didn't know you were engaged," Andrea said.

Clara took her eyes off of Noel and peeked at her ring. Then she smiled. "Just recently engaged."

"Is he here? We'd love to meet him, wouldn't we, Noel?"

He couldn't find the words to speak. His heart was crumbling to dust and he wasn't sure how to deal with it.

"No, he couldn't come to New York. He's got an investment deal he's working on," Clara said as she released her hand from Andrea's and started to fiddle with her engagement ring.

"That's a shame. So, Noel tells me you're a business student. What are you majoring in?"

Clara's posture tensed and he could sense that she was getting uncomfortable, but he couldn't make Andrea stop. He wanted to hear more. Clara had smiled before she looked at him. Her eyes couldn't hide the hurt and the pain.

"Actually, I deferred my business degree. I'm a culinary apprentice chef and I own The Little Bakery on Little Collins Street back in Melbourne."

Noel looked at Clara in surprise. He didn't know any of this. She had literally lived a life away from him. "What?" he asked as all three women look at him. Keira appeared nervous and Clara looked frightened. He didn't look at Andrea, only staring at Clara.

"You own the bakery? I didn't even know you were in culinary school."

"Things have changed since I last spoke to you. I've almost finished culinary school. I'm just doing my apprenticeship. But yes, I now own the bakery." Just hearing her voice directed to him made his knees weak. He wanted to grab her and share an embrace that proved his love for her.

"You're so young. How do you afford a bakery?" Andrea asked and slipped her hand in Noel's.

Clara stared at their linked hands before she glanced at Noel and gave him a forced smile. "I don't. When I got the offer to buy out the bakery from my boss, I was about to say no because I didn't have the finances. But my fiancé runs the Melbourne office of his family's investment company. He bought it for me."

He bought her the bakery.

"Wow. He bought you a bakery? He sounds wonderful and that ring is beautiful," Andrea said.

Clara smiled. "Thank you and that's a beautiful..." Her smile faded as she stared at Andrea and Noel noticed Clara swallow hard. He could see her eyes start to water, but she quickly blinked them away.

She looks like she's about to have a breakdown. I want to hold her and make those tears go away. I want to make her happy again.

"Locket," Clara breathed out and her gaze returned to his.

The look of betrayal in her eyes sliced him and his eyebrows met. Noel's eyes travelled the direction Clara's had made and gazed at Andrea's neckline. He stared for a long second before he looked at Clara.

Clara's locket. Oh God, no. How did Andrea even find it?

"It really *is* beautiful... If you'll excuse me, I promised I'd dance with Julian. It was lovely meeting you, Andrea," Clara said then she smiled pleasantly. He knew it was forced.

"Oh, you, too," Andrea replied in a sweet voice.

Clara and Keira exchanged looks before Clara excused herself and walked away. Clara and Julian said few words before Julian touched her arm and then glared at Noel.

"Noel, I think Alex wants a word," Keira said carefully as she pointed Noel in the direction of his best friend, who stood with Rob and Max.

He glanced at Keira and then nodded. Noel knew that Alex would have told her about Clara, but if he hadn't, then Keira had figured it out for herself.

"Ready to meet the guys?" he asked Andrea, and she nodded. He walked over to his friends, all the while wanting to turn around and see if Clara was okay.

He stopped in front of his best friends, ignoring the dirty look Alex was giving him. "Andrea, this is Rob Moors," Noel said as Andrea and Rob shook hands. Rob wasn't as welcoming as Noel thought he would have been. "And this is Max Sheridan. Max, this is my girlfriend, Andrea."

Max's eyes roamed Andrea's body before he looked up and smiled at her. "So this is Andrea," Max said without taking his eyes off her.

"I hear you're also a corporate lawyer," Andrea said.

Noel turned slightly and scanned the room to see Julian

alone by the finger foods. He looked around again to see Clara was gone. Before he could take a step away to find her, a firm hand was on his shoulder. It was Rob's. He pulled Noel off to the side and glared at him.

"She's engaged," Rob warned.

"She came to Boston and I sent her away before she could tell me. I just need to talk to her, Rob," he said in a whisper. Noel looked to see Max and Andrea still talking while Alex had wandered off to be by Keira's side.

"I know, Noel. Stevie told me. I don't want to see her hurt. Stevie had me promise to look out for Clara. Just realise that what you did in Boston is still fresh for her. You made it easy for her to continue to be engaged to *him*," Rob said before he stared at Julian.

He promised Stevie?

"Rob, are you into Stevie?" Noel raised his eyebrow.

"She's different, okay," Rob said as he brought his beer to his lips, sipped and then he shrugged.

"Are you sleeping with her?"

Rob shook his head. "Nah. We haven't slept together, but we kissed one night to make Jewel jealous, and I don't know, it did something to me."

"Must have been one hell of a kiss."

"Fuckin' keeps me up at night, Noel. I swear I don't know what to do about her. When I think we can be something, she seems to shut off. I don't think she's over an ex or something." Rob's face saddened and Noel felt for him. He knew what those kinds of kisses were like. Since Clara, it hadn't been the same for him.

"Give her some time and hang out with Julian. Look at him, he's striking out with every girl he tries. Help your brother out," Noel suggested.

"He's different, you know. He's not the same Julian he was before he went away. I've tried to get him to talk, but he doesn't want to and we were close. He left and now he's back. I don't get it. That girl did a number on him. I want him home with Dad and me, but I can't convince him. He just needs a reason to come home."

Noel looked over at Julian and saw the loneliness in his eyes. Rob was right. Julian was no longer Julian. No longer cheerful and carefree. He looked guarded and empty.

"You need one, too, Noel. I like Andrea, she seems nice, but your reason is Clara. You need to come home as well. Just don't make her cry or hurt her. Stevie will have my balls if she finds out. Good luck," Rob said before he walked away and towards his brother.

Noel peeked over to see Andrea and Max still wrapped up in their conversation and Alex was whispering in Keira's ear. This was his chance. Heading for the back doors of the hall, he knew Clara would try to get as far away as possible without leaving the party.

He stepped onto the paved patio and appreciated the cool breeze. It didn't take him long to find her leaning against the stone barrier that separated the patio from the garden. The fairy lights provided the brightness he needed to see her and he took her in. She was still so beautiful. He stood there for a moment and then he cleared his throat.

"Clara."

She didn't turn. There was a lot he had to say, but he didn't know where to start.

Andrea would be a start.

"I'm sorry."

Clara pushed off the stone barrier then turned to look at him. He could see the tears in her eyes, and he felt the guilt. He closed the distance until he was only a foot or so away from her.

"Don't be. There's nothing to be sorry about. It was never really my locket. I gave it back to you so you're not in the wrong." Her voice was shaky and she looked him straight in the eyes.

"There's more I'm sorry about, Clara, so much more."

She shook her head as a few tears slid down her face. He didn't care what the repercussions of his actions would be, but he stepped forward and held her face in his hands. Clara flinched. He went against his better judgement and wiped her tears away, relishing the feel of her soft skin.

"Back in Boston, I didn't know. God, Clara, I didn't know. If I had, I would have taken you back, I would have... I would have made you stay."

Two more tears hit his hands. The tears she shed made him believe she felt the pain he was going through.

I miss you. I've been missing you.

"You didn't want to listen to me," she explained.

His heart squeezed at her words. They were the truth. "I know," he said as he ran his thumbs along her cheeks. "Clara, if I had listened to you. If I had just swallowed my pride and listened, would we be together right now? Would that ring still be on your finger? Would it be me you made love to every night and not him? Would I have been the one you woke up to every morning and slept next to every night? Would it have been me you came to this party with? Would it be *me* you were marrying instead of him?"

Clara's eyes widened in shock; they filled with tears and her lips parted slightly. "You told me you never loved me, Noel. You got over me."

I hurt her. Why did I say it? Why couldn't I just listen? We could have been happy.

"I know, but..." He wasn't sure how to explain. His actions that afternoon never had an explanation.

"No, you don't understand. I never, not once, told you I didn't love you. If anything, I loved you *more* and I saw my mistake and came back for you. But you said it so easily, like what you were saying was nothing. How could you just tell me you never loved me? I believed you loved me in some way. I felt it when we were together, Noel. But to hear you never did destroyed me. That night, when you told me to tell you that I didn't love you, I couldn't. I couldn't tell you a lie. I wouldn't lie about my love for you because I cared, Noel. I cared! I gave you up so you could be happy, but I was dying inside because I wasn't with you. When I said yes to marrying Liam, I thought of you and the mistake I made. I wanted you to change your mind and pick me!" Clara placed her hands on his chest and for a moment he felt whole again. Then the moment fled him as she put distance between them.

"You ended us and moved on with Liam," he said.

Clara took a few steps back. "You broke my heart that night, and I realised I wasn't going to make you happy. I loved you, Noel," she softly cried.

Those brown eyes pierced him and he felt his own tears start to burn. "Past tense. You *loved* me, Clara. Past as in you're over me." His eyes met the ground and the despair in him spread through his veins.

"How could you doubt my love for you, Noel?"

He faced Clara and her look of pain was now replaced with disbelief. "What?"

"I told you, I never said I didn't love you. That was you. Not me. I loved you enough to risk my engagement to be with you. And that meant nothing to you. Whether or not I love you right now doesn't matter. You said it yourself, I broke your heart and you got over me. You never loved me the way you thought you did. Everything we had is *gone*. She's wearing the locket and I know what that symbolises for you, Noel."

No. It can't be this way.

"I don't know how she found it, Clara. I hid it away because it hurt to see it not around your neck, where it belongs. It has always belonged to you. You're wrong. I lied, Clara, I still—"

"Clara?"

Her name had stopped him from confessing that he still loved her. Noel watched as Clara quickly wiped the tears from her eyes.

"You out here, sweetheart?"

Noel shook his head. *He* couldn't be here. This was his time to win Clara back.

"Liam," she breathed out, almost sounding relieved to have had him interrupt them.

Clara stepped around Noel, but he couldn't turn around. He couldn't see them together with Liam's ring on her finger. But he forced himself to turn. Before this week was over, he'd find a way to win her back. Noel felt the guilt twist in his stomach. He had a girlfriend and Clara had a fiancé. He was considering hurting Andrea to be with Clara, and she didn't deserve that.

"What are you doing here?" she asked before Liam pulled her in and kissed her passionately.

Noel felt the anger in him rise. It was the ugly kind of anger, the type that had him wanting to pull Clara from Liam's arms and stake his claim on her heart.

It should be me. I should be the one she loves.

"Told the board of directories that if they wanted me to invest then I was going to New York to be with my fiancée. Did I surprise you?" Liam asked as he held Clara's face in his hands.

His fiancée…

Noel balled his fists as he concentrated on getting his emotions under control.

"Have you been crying, Clara? What's wrong?" The genuine worry in Liam's voice was one Noel despised. Liam truly loved Clara, and Noel wished he didn't.

"I, uhh…" Clara started to say, but Noel knew she didn't have an explanation for her tears.

"Sorry, that was my fault. I told her some news about my gran and she didn't take it very well," Noel interrupted.

Clara turned and eyed him, seeing straight through the lie.

"Is your gran okay?" Liam asked.

"She's all right. She's been feeling ill lately. Clara was close to Gran when she was a kid," Noel said. It wasn't quite the lie. His gran had called to tell him that she had recently been having fainting spells whenever she visited the vineyards near her house. "She's okay. I tried to tell Clara that, but—I am so sorry, Clara." He let that apology hold a hidden message that Liam wouldn't get.

"It's okay. Umm…" Clara said as she stepped away from Liam. "Nolan Parker, this is my fiancé, Liam O'Connor. Liam, this is Noel, Alex's best friend," Clara introduced.

Noel took a step forward and reached out his hand to Liam.

"I remember you. I met you outside of *our* apartment last year, yeah?" Liam asked as they shook hands.

Noel didn't like the way Liam emphasised 'our' when he spoke. There was a hint of possessiveness in his voice that only Noel had picked up on. But it could just be Liam illuminating the fact that he was proud to live with her. If Noel were Liam, he'd be proud, too. He'd climb on top of mountains and beat his chest, screaming his love for her.

He remembers me.

"Yeah, I was visiting Alex," Noel replied.

Their hands parted and Liam took Clara's left hand. She didn't look at Noel and he knew this was uncomfortable for her.

She loved me first.

"Well, any friend of Clara's is a friend of mine. It was nice seeing you again. You don't mind if I borrow Clara for a minute… that is, if you're finished talking. I can wait inside."

Clara's right hand touched Liam's arm, and she shook her

head. "We're *finished*, aren't we, Noel?"

He knew the real meaning of Clara's response, and he shook his head. "No. We're not. But I can wait for you until you're free," Noel replied.

Clara flinched slightly and she breathed in sharply. "Well, I don't think you should wait. You have fun tonight. I'm glad Granny Parker is fine. I knew she always would be," she said before she walked in the direction of the hall.

He waited to see if Clara would turn back and look at him, but she didn't. Instead, she placed a kiss on Liam's cheek and smiled. Noel stood alone in the night. It was hard to see her with Liam. It was hard to know that Liam had her, got that ring on her finger, and made love to her. He felt sick at the thought. The thought of Liam touching what he had first made him insane beyond thought.

I was her first.

He took deep breaths, but the anger in him lingered. He had no reason to be so angry; he had been with Andrea since Clara. It would be hypocritical of him to judge her. Noel shook his head and tried to forget the pain that radiated from his chest. Walking into the hall and towards the dance floor, he spotted them.

A smile on Clara's face as Liam spoke to her, then she laughed and rested her head on Liam's chest as they swayed to the song the jazz band was playing. Noel stood by the edge of the dance floor and watched them. That diamond ring was all he could look at. He had been so close to asking her and so close to having *his* ring on her finger. Noel clenched his jaw to control himself. All he wanted to do was walk over there and rip Liam's hands off her.

Noel peeked to see Julian standing next to him as he, too, looked at Clara. Then Julian asked, "What's the plan to ruin that engagement of hers?"

Clara

" can't believe you're here," she said once the song had finished and they stopped dancing. Things with Noel were getting too personal and she was thankful for Liam's arrival. There were so many things unsaid that it hurt to bring them up. Her reason for being in Boston was explained, but it still tore a hole right through her chest.

She thought she'd be okay when she saw them together, but seeing the locket she used to call hers was hard. The moment she left Noel with Andrea, she had walked over to Julian. He was her source of comfort in a hall full of strangers until she needed to be alone with her thoughts. Clara was relieved that Liam had come. It meant she wouldn't do something crazy in the week she'd be in New York with Noel.

"I felt guilty that I keep putting work first. Being here is important to you and spending time with Alex is something I want to do."

Clara got on her tippy toes and kissed Liam's cheek. "You're amazing. You have no idea how thankful I am to have you here." She was relieved that she wasn't in the presence of those green eyes. If she had been for any longer, she would have confessed that she still loved him. Clara loved Liam, but the love she felt for Noel wouldn't leave her. It had to. It wasn't fair if it stayed and lingered.

I don't ever want to hurt Liam.

"Clara, we're just about to make speeches. You're after Noel. Is that okay?" her brother's girlfriend asked.

Clara turned to see Keira eyeing the sight of Liam holding her hand.

Oh, God. I have to make a speech.

"Okay," Clara said as she gave Liam a quick kiss on his cheek and followed Keira towards the stage.

As she climbed the steps she could see Noel holding the microphone as he waited for her. Keira walked past Noel and returned to Alex's arms. Clara looked out at the guests to see Liam next to Rob and Julian, and Max and Andrea smiled up at her. Clara's eyes found the locket on Andrea's neckline and she quickly looked away.

"Are you okay?" Noel whispered.

No.

"Yes," she lied as she tried to control her breathing. Public speaking was something she didn't do well and the shakes started to control her body.

"Hey, everyone. I'm Noel. A lot of you know me since I

worked with most of you while I was in New York. For those of you who don't know, I'm Alex's best friend. We have been since we were kids. What can I say... Only that I love him. Alex and I have been through everything and I owe him so much. The past year... Has tested us. I did things that he wasn't happy about, and I knew I might lose him as my brother. He supported me even when I didn't deserve it. He's the best man I know. But just know that I never regretted what I did." Noel stopped and looked her right in the eyes. "*Ever.*" He gave her a sad smile. "Because we became even tighter. We share each other's pain and joy. He showed me what a better man was like."

Clara stunned, looked away from him and at Alex, who only gave her a nod to the pleas she had silently made. She started to feel a little lightheaded and decided that not looking at Noel was her safest bet.

"Happy birthday, Alex. I speak for everyone when I say you deserve a happy life with Keira. I'll pass it over to Clara." Her name on his lips woke her from her thoughts. Noel handed her the microphone, and she took it. His fingers brushed over hers, and the tingling sensation had her heart clenching. Their eyes met and she knew he felt it, too. Their mutual attraction hadn't been lost. Something was *still* there.

"Alex, umm, uhh..." Clara began to say but once she stared at the crowd, she felt slightly nauseated. She searched the crowd of guests but couldn't find Liam. She was frantic. He was the person she would focus on, but he was gone.

I can't do this. I can't speak in front of all these people.

"It's okay, Clara. Stay with me. You're okay. Just breathe," his voice whispered in her ear.

She felt his hands on her shoulders and her heart expanded. Closing her eyes, she breathed in deeply and faced him. His eyes searched hers, but they said nothing.

I miss what we had. I miss being what made him happy. I miss him loving me... and I miss loving him. I gave him that nothingness in his eyes. I gave him pain. I don't deserve him.

"Thanks for that, Noel. I appreciate it," Liam said, interrupting them.

Clara shook her head until she felt Liam's hands entwine with hers.

"You've got this, sweetheart," he whispered reassuringly.

Clara felt the difference. Liam's whispers didn't make her heart hurt in such want and need as Noel's did. She smiled and squeezed Liam's hand. His whispers were more supportive... like a crutch. Clara frowned.

Is Liam my crutch?

Now's not the time, Clara.

Concentrate.

"I'm sorry. I'm not really into speaking in public. Alex, you are the most amazing person in this world. It is such an honour to be your little sister. I know we haven't had it easy, but I love you and I am so proud to see all your friends here and your life in New York. There is no one on this Earth I look up to more than you. I am who I am because of you and your love. Happy birthday, Alex!" Clara wished with adoration in her voice.

Alex had kissed Keira's head before he walked over to Clara. Liam let go of her hand as her brother wrapped his arms around her. "I love you, Clara. Don't think for a minute you've ever hurt me. No matter what happened or what will happen, you will always be my first priority. I will always protect you."

Clara let a sob escape her. They were words her father should have said to her. But, instead, it was her brother. She held him tighter. "I love you, too, Alex," she whispered back. "I can never repay you for what you've done for me."

Alex let go of her, put his hands on her arms, and looked her straight in the eye. "Just be happy, Clara."

Just be happy.

Before she could ask what he meant, Alex took the microphone from her hand. He stepped slightly to the left and Liam took her hand again. She gazed up at Liam and smiled, forgetting the fact she didn't yearn for his whispers. He made her happy. Was that the happiness her brother meant? Clara shook her head. She was analysing it too much.

"Thank you all for coming here tonight to celebrate with me. First off, I need to thank this special woman. Darling, you've made me a better man, and I love you. The boys from Melbourne, nice having you lot here. Noel, you've had my back since day one, you get to live," Alex joked and the hall filled with laughs. "And my little sister. I love you, Clara. I will *always* protect you and you are more important to me than you think."

Clara smiled at Alex's acknowledgement.

"Right, before we all get that wasted, we aren't only here to celebrate my birthday... my little sister is getting married to this man right here! I couldn't be happier. So, glasses up everyone. Congratulations, Clara and Liam, on your engagement. And to my brother-in-law-to-be, welcome to the family! You treat my sister wrong in any way, be sure to find me ripping your balls—"

"Okay, that's enough from you," Keira said taking the microphone. "Congratulations, Clara and Liam. We wish you a long and happy marriage together."

A round of applause had echoed before a set of cheers, and Clara's face started to turn bright red. The cheers increased when Alex pulled Keira in for a very steamy and public kiss in front of the crowd. That was when Clara realised just how much Alex had to drink.

"Did your brother accept our engagement and then threaten me?" Liam asked as he walked Clara down the stage steps.

"Yes, I believe he did." Clara let out a laugh and so did Liam. She noticed Noel walk past them, and the pang of guilt erupted inside her. One she didn't understand.

"I better thank him," Clara said.

Liam let go of her hand and nodded. "I'll go speak to your brother and convince him that no ball ripping is necessary." He winked and walked towards her brother.

Clara approached the bar that Noel leant on. He had a beer in his hand, staring at it. She breathed in sharply as he straightened his posture and his green eyes met hers.

"I just wanted to say thank you for back there on the stage. I appreciate you calming me down." Clara waited for Noel to say something, but he kept his eyes focused on her hand.

"Can I see that ring?"

Unsure of his motives, Clara raised her left hand up to Noel. He surprised her by taking her hand in his and inspected the engagement ring on her finger. Instead of letting go, his fingertips slowly ran across her knuckles and then her ring finger. She held her breath as Noel touched her, leaving her with wanting a little more than the trailing of his finger.

"You and I both know this ring doesn't belong on that finger." Noel dropped her hand and it fell beside her. He leant in close, his lips almost touching her right ear.

His hot breath had her heart accelerating and her breathing heaved.

"If you feel the way I do, Clara, then we both know what's going to happen. You'll be getting married... but it won't be to Liam. I'll make sure of that."

Chapter
NINE

Noel

*H*er wide eyes spoke the words that failed to come out of her mouth. She wasn't expecting him to declare his intentions, and truth be told, he wasn't either. But the sight of Liam holding her was enough for him to lose his composure. That moment on the stage, that was his, and Liam could never take it away. It was a risky move to whisper in her ear and touch her. But his body and his heart had controlled his actions.

She loved me first. I have to believe she loves me more.

The disbelief in Clara's face was evident. Her face went pale and she blinked at him. Over nine months apart and still she had the power to send him to his knees. Somehow, he needed this week to work. He needed to figure out where he stood with Clara. He needed to make sure Clara understood his true intentions.

"If you think I'm letting you get away this time, then you're wrong, Clara. I'm not over us. You can try and run, and try and forget, but you and I both know it's *still* there." He let that sink in for a moment before he quickly scanned the room to ensure they were out of sight and then Noel took her hand. "I'm determined to show you just how right we were together. We weren't wrong for each other. We are, should be, and always will be right for each other." Noel ran his fingers over the knuckles of her right hand. If he tried her left, he'd take that ring off her finger and hand it back to Liam.

He noticed Clara's chest heave and he could see the conflicted emotions in her eyes. He entwined his fingers with hers and squeezed her hand gently.

"Remember me. Remember us. Remember how perfect we are together." It was selfish of him, but he couldn't help himself, not when it came to Clara.

That moment before she pulled away was bliss. Clara took a step back and separated them. She shook her head and her eyes searched his.

"Don't," she softly pleaded. "Don't do this to me, Noel."

He took a step closer, which was met with Clara taking one back.

"Why are you doing this? You can't give me words of hope and expect me to fall into your arms. I'm engaged and too much time has come between us. Don't ruin this night for Alex. Please, don't do this." Clara's eyes watered and he felt the guilt. He was being too forward, but it was the only way.

"Clara."

"It's too late, Noel." Her eyes fell to the floor. It didn't hit his heart as he had expected. He knew for himself that it wasn't too late. She hadn't said 'I do' to Liam. There was a small glimmer of hope.

When Clara's eyes met his, all he saw was the sadness that succumbed her. Then Noel noticed Liam walking towards them and he pressed his lips tightly together. Liam approached them and then wrapped his arm around Clara's waist. Her eyes left his and met Liam's. That smile that developed on Clara's face was honest and sliced his heart open. He wasn't expecting that loving look on her face towards Liam.

"Clara, I need a little backup with your brother. He doesn't like the fact that you'll be an O'Connor soon. Do you mind settling him down a little? I think you were right when you said Alex would want me to be a Lawrence."

The hate in Noel grew. His hand immediately returned to his beer bottle, and he held it tight.

Just the idea of her having his name…

"I warned you, Liam. I knew this topic would come up eventually. Thanks again, Noel. Have a good night," Clara said sweetly as she stepped out of Liam's hold and took his hand. Noel could tell she wasn't doing it on purpose, but the sight of them together was destroying him.

For all the shit I've done to Clara, I deserve that.

Noel leant on the bar and watched as Clara and Liam walked towards the end of the hall. Clara didn't look back at him, and he felt the anger in him settle. The smile on Liam's face had Noel seething. They seemed happy and that killed him inside.

"Nice work. You caught her off guard."

He turned slightly to see Julian nodding his head in approval. "What if I'm hurting her more by doing this? I pretty much just declared to her that I have every intention of ruining her engagement. I'm a selfish asshole." Noel shook his head and brought his beer up to his lips and drank the bottle empty.

"Sure, you'll confuse her, but maybe it's what she needs. I see the uncertainty in her eyes. I don't have to know much to see it. You should have seen her when I mentioned your name. It was like that little twinkle in her eye faded away and I could see how much she is hurting over you. If you want my honest opinion, Noel…"

They both looked over at Clara as Liam bent down and whispered in her ear, a blush became visible on her cheeks.

Fuck. That hurt.

Julian took a step in front of Noel and looked him straight in the eye, blocking his view of Clara and Liam.

"I say you fight for her. Don't go to the extremes where she cheats on Liam to be with you but make her second-guess whether marrying him is what she wants. Remind her of how good you guys had it, before Alex and all that shit happened." The concern in Julian's eyes was evident; he understood more than anyone else in this room.

Noel took one more look at Clara as Liam kissed her forehead. Ignoring the clench of his chest, Noel turned around and ordered another drink. "What happened to you, Julian?" Noel asked as he took the shot glass in his hand and threw back the whiskey. The burning sensation in the back of his throat was a relief. He needed strong alcohol. He needed it to hide behind all the regret he was living.

"What do you mean?"

The weariness in Julian's voice had Noel facing him with a raised eyebrow. "Come on, Julian. You know about the shit I'm going through. We told each other everything. Even when you told me about how you lost your virginity to your neighbour's niece."

Julian let out a burst of laughter. "And how she laughed after we had sex. Probably the worst way to lose your virginity, but hey, I was one horny teenager."

Noel set the shot glass on the bar and laughed along.

"I told you everything, didn't I?"

Noel pressed his lips together and nodded.

Julian ran his hand through his hair and let out a heavy groan. "Don't tell Rob, okay?"

"Promise."

"I moved because I didn't want to tell Rob that I fell in love. He'd call me a fucking pussy, but she ripped out my heart and left me. We spent this unforgettable week together in Thailand and I took her virginity. I wasn't expecting it, but I felt grateful that she could trust me. I had this plan to tell her everything about me and have her tell me where she came from. I wanted to know everything about her. I woke up the next morning and she was gone. I thought she went to the beach but nothing. I know nothing about her." Julian's voice went soft as he stared at the wood of the bar. "Want to know something crazy?" Julian asked as he looked up and pushed off the counter.

"Yeah."

"I've spent three years looking for her. All I have is her first name and this old book she left behind. I think I've read it a million times. I know every little note written, every stain, and every creased page. I ran because, well, I was confused. I never had a woman just leave me after sex before, especially not one that I fell in love with. When I was with her, she made me forget about the pressure of being Rob's brother. She made me forget about life back home. She gave me this taste of freedom and it was like she saw something good in me. She just wanted to be around me. And no one has looked at me the way she did since. She's unforgettable."

"Shit. I'm sorry, man. For what it's worth, I understand

what you're going through. There's hope. You just have to find her," Noel said.

Julian let out a short laugh and shook his head. "I think it's time I gave up. It's been years, Noel. Who knows, she's probably forgotten about me. Got some sort of fairy tale life. Guess her book is just a memento for me."

Before Noel could offer his support, Andrea approached them both with a smile.

"Hi, you must be Julian," she said and put her hand forward.

Julian stared at Andrea's hand before he looked across the room at Clara. There was a forced smile on Julian's face before he placed his hand in hers and said, "Yeah, and you're Andrea."

"You're Rob's brother, right?" Andrea asked.

Noel glanced at the locket. He thought he had hidden it, and seeing it around her neck made his stomach drop.

It looks wrong around Andrea's neck.

"Yeah, I'm related to that kid, unfortunately. Which reminds me, I need a word with him. It was lovely meeting you, Andrea. Looking forward to getting to know you." Then Julian left.

Andrea turned to face Noel and then her smile began to fade. He couldn't take his eyes off Clara's locket. He stepped closer to her and traced the locket that clasped around her neck.

"Andrea, where did you find this?" he asked, his eyes darting up to hers. He thought he'd never see that locket again.

If she tried to open the locket, she'd find my note to Clara.

"You don't remember?" she asked astonished.

"What do you mean?" Noel's fingers left the locket and ran them through his hair.

Remember? What the hell did I do?

"Noel, you *gave* me this locket. You and Alex went out drinking one night when he was in Boston. You came back, tore apart our bedroom, and told me to hold on to it. You said it was someone's you lost and loved. I asked you, but you wouldn't say. You asked me to wear it."

Noel's mouth dropped. He knew of the exact night Andrea referred. The night Alex had found out his parents wouldn't be attending Clara's wedding.

I keep fucking up!

Noel covered both hands over his face and stifled the roar that rumbled in his chest. Andrea's fingers wrapped around his wrists and pulled his hands from his face. That sad look in her eyes had him frowning. She raised her hands around her neck and unclasped the locket. She held Noel's hand out and then placed the locket in his palm.

"I'm sorry, I shouldn't have worn something that didn't belong to me. You were drunk. I shouldn't have taken advantage of that. That person you lost, who was she?" Andrea asked as she closed Noel's hand. Those blue eyes were curious and beautiful.

"Someone from long ago," he replied softly. Noel opened his hand and stared at the locket. He'd find a way to return it to Clara. He couldn't be like Julian and hold on to it for years, waiting. Andrea understood, and he felt guilty for what he was doing to her.

She took the locket from Noel's hand, smiled, and placed it in his jacket pocket. Her hands reached for the back of his head and lowered his mouth to hers. Her lips didn't have the effect they once did. He hoped with each movement of her mouth, that burst of emotions would happen. But it never occurred. Noel placed his hands on Andrea's cheeks, pulled her back, and looked her straight in the eye. She loved him. Those blue eyes couldn't deny it.

"I'm sorry, Andrea," Noel said as he pulled her in and held her tightly in his arms. He wasn't sure what he was apologising for exactly, but he was sorry. As he held Andrea tightly, he looked up. He saw Clara standing alone near the exit watching them and his eyes met hers. The pain in Clara's eyes tore right through him. He wanted to run to her and be the one to kiss her. He would if he knew it wouldn't hurt her more.

He unwrapped his arms from Andrea and straightened his body. He watched Clara look down at the floor and then up to her left. Noel's eyes followed to see Liam offering her his jacket. Clara smiled and placed her arms through the sleeves. Liam adjusted the large jacket on her before he whispered in her ear. Clara nodded, her gaze meeting Noel's one last time before she turned and left through the double doors.

"Clara's really beautiful. She'll make a beautiful bride, Noel."

Noel watched the doors swing close. He looked at Andrea and nodded his head. "She would make a beautiful wife."

To hear those words mended her, but to see them kiss only moments later broke that mend. She was used to disappointment, but this time those words were the words that brought with it hope.

I shouldn't hold on to hope. After everything, there's no such thing. I already hurt Noel. I can't hurt Liam.

"You all right, Clara?" Liam stood in front of his rental car and stared at her.

She smiled to reassure him. "Yeah, I'm okay."

Liam stepped in front of Clara and took both her hands in his. His fingers traced the ring. She peeked up to see the sorrow in Liam's hazel eyes, confusing her.

"I'm sorry, Clara. I should have come to New York when you did. I shouldn't have let you come alone. I let Dad suck me into another investment deal. I should have said no—"

Clara moved her hands from his and rested them on his cheeks, stopping him from continuing. "You have nothing to be sorry about, Liam. I've told you this. I'm glad you're here. You shouldn't have left in the middle of the deal. Are you sure they're going to be okay?" Clara asked worriedly. She didn't want to be the reason for the company to lose an important investment.

"They need me more than I need them, Clara. Expanding investments to Asia was Dad's idea. My portfolio is profitable. Money isn't important, not when I have you."

Clara laughed lightly. "You can be so cheesy sometimes. You know that, right?"

He nodded. Suddenly, the cool wind hit her skin and she shivered. Liam reached for his suit jacket that she wore and buttoned it. He ran his hand along her right arm until he entwined his fingers with hers.

"Clara, hey! Wait up a sec."

She craned her neck to see Julian running up to the rental car, his eyes immediately taking in the image of Clara and Liam holding hands. He stared for a moment before he looked up at them both.

Julian dug his hands into his pockets and cleared his throat.

"Ahh, are you guys heading off to Alex's? Or have you got a room booked in a hotel or something?"

Clara quickly looked at Liam, arching her brow.

"Unless Clara opposes, I'd like to stay with her, if that's okay?" Liam asked, hopefully.

Clara let out a laugh at his innocent question. "I'd be offended if you got a hotel room."

Liam smiled largely at her and then squeezed her hand. "Well, we're off to Alex's. You want a lift, Julian?" Liam asked. Clara watched the surprise take Julian's face. She was sure he hadn't expected Liam to be so friendly.

"Sure, thanks, mate. I was expecting to be turned down. Thought you wanted some alone time with the fiancée." Julian wiggled his eyebrows at them.

Clara annoyingly shook her head. "Get in the car, Julian! Before I decide to revoke Liam's offer and make you walk."

That pout and eye roll he pulled were a Julian Moors trademark. One Clara knew well. Liam laughed as he released Clara's hand and held open the car door for her.

"You're a pain in the ass, Julian Moors," Clara said as she got into the car.

"Yeah, yeah. You've missed me," he stated.

*L*iam parked the car on the side of the road, leaving room for Keira to park in the driveway. It was close to one in the morning. As tired as she felt, too much had happened at the party for her to find any sleep. She was sure she'd be staring at the ceiling, thinking about the promise Noel had made to get in the way of her wedding to Liam.

"I'll get my bags, Clara. I'll meet you inside," Liam said once he'd opened the passenger side door for her. Clara got out of the car and nodded. She heard the sound of the passenger door open and close. She turned to see Julian standing there, observing them.

He didn't want just a ride, did he?

Clara opened her small clutch and took out Keira's house key. The wind picked up and pierced her exposed skin. She walked around the rental car and up to the front door of her brother's house. Then she put the key in the lock and opened the door.

She walked into the hallway and placed the house keys on the long table against the wall. With a sigh, she turned around to see Julian with his hands in his pockets. Being so connected with every one of her brother's best friends was tough. She couldn't escape them or Noel. Their lives entwined with hers. She'd tried to forget, but it was impossible.

She casually shrugged at him, fiddling with the clasp of the clutch. Clara pressed her lips together and looked down at her engagement ring. She breathed in sharply and looked up at Julian's needy eyes. He wanted an explanation. He'd been asking 'why?' the whole time they were at the party.

"Look, I know you don't like that I'm getting married to him, but he makes me happy. It's different with Liam. I don't have to compete with his past or anyone. I can honestly love him and not be afraid that someone or something will take him away from me. I need him. I know it's not the same as Noel, but it's real. I love Liam, and I'm proud to be his fiancée. He made the pain go away."

Clara twisted the platinum ring around her finger and watched as Julian carefully processed what she had said. He frowned and removed his hands from his pockets.

"I get it. Too much time has passed for you and Noel. You have the fairy tale ending…"

That smile of his assured her that he understood and Clara let out a sigh of relief. Julian walked towards the stairs that led to the guest rooms. He started to climb the steps until he paused and turned to face her.

"But is this *your* fairy tale ending, Clara? Are you sure you aren't taking someone else's ending?" Julian asked.

All the air left her lungs; she was shocked and unsure how to respond. With a satisfied nod, Julian walked upstairs. The thumps of her heart had Clara breathless.

Could I really be taking someone else's ending?

*C*lara lay on her back as she stared at the ceiling. She fell asleep for a little while, but a dream of Noel woke her. The dream had him at the end of the altar waiting for her. Alex was his best man and Liam sat with the guests, holding hands with a woman she couldn't see. When it came time to speak now, the room was quiet, no one objected, and those green eyes started to water. That first kiss as Noel's wife never happened as Clara woke up from her dream, gasping.

She never fell back asleep. Instead, she looked up at the ceiling and waited for time to pass. Clara let Liam sleep since he was exhausted from travelling from Singapore to New York to attend her brother's birthday party. She looked at the alarm clock and breathed out. The sun would be rising soon, and watching the display of the morning sun was something she liked to do when she was in New York. The sunrises were different from back home in Melbourne.

Clara lifted Liam's arm off her stomach and rested it on the bed. She loved to watch him sleep. When Liam was asleep, he looked at peace and free. He didn't have to worry about his family's company or the wedding. Those constant worry lines never appeared when he slept next to her.

She walked over to the small armchair in the corner of the room and placed Liam's hoodie over her. It would be warmer during the day, but the early morning winds were harsh. Then she tiptoed out of the bedroom and carefully closed the door behind her. Clara knew everyone got home much later than Liam and she did, so she was careful not to make noise. A house full of hungover men was something she didn't want to mess with. She walked down the stairs and to the double doors that led out to the patio.

Closing them behind her, Clara walked towards the edge of the porch, the cold wind hitting her exposed legs. She cursed herself for wearing a short nightdress instead of pyjama pants. But she was thankful to have Liam's hoodie on her as she hugged herself and smelt that familiar citrus fragrance of him.

Liam's safe.

103

Alex's backyard was larger than the one they grew up with back home in Australia. She could see it; her future nieces and nephews running around with her brother and Keira. The house filled with the sounds of tiny footsteps every moment of the day. She wanted it for Alex and hoped she'd have it herself one day. The sun started to poke through the spaces the tree branches made. The sight was utterly beautiful. The shades of orange and yellow that displayed before her eyes were stunning.

"Clara."

The voice called to her heart, making it dance and ache inside of her chest. Clara bit the inside of her cheek, trying to fight against the feelings that came rising when he spoke her name. Her fingers automatically found the strings of the hoodie and she fiddled with them. After a deep breath, she turned to see him.

"Good morning, Noel," she said sweetly. It didn't help that she dreamt of those green eyes, but her memories didn't do him justice. He was as beautiful as ever.

I had a dream of marrying you.

Her eyes refused to look at the engagement ring on her finger. Instead, she kept them focused on those green eyes. The same green that made her believe he had loved her at one point.

"What are you doing up so early?" Clara assumed he'd be hungover like the rest of the boys.

"Couldn't sleep, really. I heard a sound outside and looked out the window to see you out here. I thought you could use some company." His voice was mixed with caution and hope.

She should go inside and go back to bed. But that dream and what he had said at the party had her confused and willing to have him join her. Common sense, however, told her to think it through. Clara stared at the two mugs in his hand and then looked up to see a sweet smile on his face.

Why does he have to make it so hard?

"Noel, I don't think you should be sneaking out of her bed to join me. I just needed air."

He stepped forward and handed her a hot mug. Clara wrapped her fingers around the handle as he looked at her. Those green eyes held every inch of sadness she felt.

"I don't want to miss a moment with you. All I have is now, Clara. And I'm afraid that's all I'll ever have. My best days were the ones I spent with you. If standing next to you while you get some air is all I'm going to get, then I'll take it. I'll always meet you on this porch at sunrise if you'll let me."

Surprise registered on her face, and she was momentarily out of breath.

I want those sunrises together.

Chapter TEN

Noel

*L*ittle by little he hoped somehow she'd let him in. The way the rising sun hit her skin and her messy curls had him remembering the times he woke up with her in his arms. The way the light radiated from her as she slept was a memory he reflected upon frequently. What he didn't like was the way Liam's hoodie kept her warm from the morning chill. The sudden urge to lift that hoodie off her was animalistic. Noel watched as a shy smile appeared on Clara's beautiful face.

God, I miss that smile.

"Okay," she breathed out.

Noel stared at Clara as she tucked her hair behind her ear and smiled again.

"Okay?" he asked, unbelievably.

Clara had moved the cup from one hand to the other before she looked up at him. Those big brown eyes still had their way with him. "We'll have the sunrise together, Noel…"

His breath caught in his throat and a need to throw his arms around her strengthened. He just needed her in his life again.

"But only in the most platonic of ways."

For now, it would be enough. He knew she wouldn't be

willing to offer more, not just yet. He'd find a way for them both to have *more*.

"Right, you and me, platonic. Got it." He winked. Noel stepped around Clara, ensuring his hand brushed against hers. Clara tensed at his touch.

There's no way I'm going to let us stay platonic. It's impossible.

Noel walked across the porch and sat on the step that led down to the paved path. He set his ceramic mug down next to him as he watched the sun rise above the tall trees. He didn't hear a sound behind him, and he feared she had snuck back inside. Noel turned to see Clara staring at her cup with that little frown.

"Thought we were watching the sunrise together, Clara?"

She glanced up and her frown disappeared. Instead, a sweet smile replaced it.

"We are," she said. Clara wrapped both hands around the mug, walked over to the step, and sat next to him, her body close. The temptation to wrap his arm around her filled his system. If it had been different, he imagined Clara resting her head on his shoulder and telling him that he was what she needed.

Clara brought the mug to her lips and sipped on the tea. She didn't say anything to him as she continued to watch the sun start to climb. The way she looked at the sky with such wonder reminded him of the first time he watched her make cupcakes. The inspired expression on her face was truly beautiful.

"Noel." She breathed out his name, and her eyes met his. He noticed a slight pink colour tint her cheeks. Clara placed her cup between them and squinted at him. "Stop staring at me. The sun is that way." She pointed out with a raised eyebrow.

Noel let out a chuckle and watched as Clara's hair untangled from behind her ear. Leaning forward, he brushed her loose lock out of her face and tucked it behind her ear again. Clara's eyes widened. Noel settled the palm of his hand on her right cheek. The contact of his skin on her warm cheek had his heart clenching.

This moment is ours.

Noel looked straight in Clara's eyes. He expected her to pull away, but all she did was stare at him. At that moment, he was very aware of how much he loved her.

"You're my sun, Clara. When I see you, I am always drawn

to you. And when you go away, you take my heart with you."
All he had was the truth to give, and with such circumstances
against them, the truth was all that mattered.

Clara's lips made a fine line and her eyes fell to the ground
for a moment before she looked back up at him. "Noel, you
promised we'd be platonic." Her brown eyes glazed over with
unshed tears.

"You didn't define what kind of platonic relationship we'd
have together," he stated as he placed his right hand on her
cheek and brought her face close to his.

Clara blinked and her lips parted slightly. "The one where
all we have is a friendship."

She pulled back, to his disappointment, and placed her
hands on her lap. He noticed Clara fiddle with her engagement
ring. The large oval diamond surrounded by smaller ones had
him lifting his eyes, not wanting a reminder of what he didn't
get the chance to do.

Noel didn't reply. He didn't know how to form the words
to respond. His heart dipped. The concept of friendship with
her was more than he deserved, but it wasn't enough for him.

"Noel, say something." Clara's voice sounded small and
fragile. Noel noticed that her fingers now fiddling with the
strings of Liam's hoodie, and he forced a smile.

*I don't want to be her friend. I want to be Liam. I want to have
her and hold her. I want to be what she needs, not what makes her run
away.*

"You don't want to be friends. I get it." The shakiness in her
voice caused his chest to tighten. Clara stood up, leaving her
cup behind.

He watched those toned legs start to walk away. The same
pair that he'd once had wrapped around his waist as they made
love. The fear of losing her had him on his feet and taking her
by the hand, stopping her. Noel stepped in front of Clara and
held her right hand firmly in his.

Breathing in deeply, he took Clara's left hand and entwined
their fingers together. He brought their hands up to her face,
and Clara looked at them intently.

"This is how perfect we are together, Clara," he said, placing
her palm flat on his chest, over his heart. "The way my heart
beats for you is the same as it did back in Melbourne. When you

came to Boston, did you come for me?"

Clara kept her hand on his chest for a long moment and then pulled away. She looked around their surroundings before she ran her hand through her curls and breathed out. "I—" was all she got out before the sound of the doors leading onto the porch opened and silenced her.

"Good morning, Noel." He heard a sweet voice behind him.

Clara dug her hands into the pocket of the hoodie she wore. Noel turned around to see Keira stepping onto the porch. She stilled the moment she took in the sight of Clara next to him.

"And Clara!" The glee was evident in Keira's eyes at the fact that she had caught them together.

Damn it, Keira!

"How's Alex going?" Clara asked.

Noel knew that their discussion had ended. Until the next sunrise, he wouldn't have her alone again. Keira's gaze met Noel's before moving to Clara. He saw the apology in her eyes, and Noel balled his fists, his opportunity lost.

"He's going to be very hungover. I think the other boys, too. You guys want breakfast?" Keira asked as she knotted the ties of her dressing gown.

"Thanks, Keira, but I'm going back to bed. I didn't get much sleep. I think I'll go lie down for a little while," Clara said as she walked past Noel.

"Oh, all right then, Clara," Keira replied.

Clara walked past Keira and entered the house. Once he couldn't see her through the glass panels of the door, Noel walked up to Keira. She had her hands up to stop him.

"I'm sorry. I had no idea that you two were alone. I wouldn't have disturbed you both," she apologised.

Noel shrugged. "Your timing is awful, Keira." He laughed and Keira raised an eyebrow.

"*My* timing is awful? Noel, I think that title goes to you. Look, I love Alex but what you do to Clara affects him and, therefore, me. I love Clara like a sister, and I don't want to see her hurt but…" Keira stopped and stepped towards him. "Let's take a walk around the garden together. I don't want someone accidentally overhearing us. What do you say?"

He nodded. "Lead the way."

*T*wo sunrises passed since their first together. The topic of 'them' was off-limits. When they spoke, it was minimal. He was losing time, but he couldn't push her further into the arms of Liam. Noel would walk onto the porch and see Clara already sitting on the step as the sun started to rise. He'd sit next to her until she got up after the sun had risen brightly and returned inside the house and to her room.

It was late afternoon when he walked into the kitchen to the smell of cinnamon and apple in the air. The first thing he noticed was Clara's hair tied up in a high ponytail as she sliced an apple. She hadn't noticed him, and he took this moment to watch her, to immortalise her in his memory.

Clara stopped chopping, and she looked up from the cutting board. She ran the knife under the apple slices and used the blade to lift the slices and place them in a bowl. Clara placed the knife down and reached for the tea towel.

"Hey," she said softly as she wiped her hands on the towel. Clara's eyes didn't meet his as she smiled.

"What smells nice?"

Noel turned to see Liam entering the kitchen from the other entry. His head nodded Noel's way in acknowledgement as he walked over to Clara and gave her a kiss on the cheek. Noel realised it was Liam she was speaking to and the disappointment settled in his veins.

"Keira's favourite. Want to help?" she asked Liam and handed him an apple.

"Love to. I just got off the phone with Ally. She says she'll call you later to see if you were coming up to Sydney to go dress shopping or if she had to come down to Melbourne." Liam reached over, took the knife, and started to peel the apple.

Clara's gaze met Noel's and he saw the confusion in those brown eyes. Clara closed her eyes tightly for a second before she turned to face Liam. "Ask her if she's okay with coming down to Melbourne. Stevie and Annie want to come as well and it'll work out better that way."

Clara's voice didn't sound convincing, but it was enough to

make Noel turn and walk out of the kitchen. The thought of her trying on wedding dresses made him sick.

Walking towards the doors that led to the garden, he could see the boys kicking the football on the grass. Only two days ago, he had walked through the garden with Keira. She had explained that the first time she'd met Clara in person was the first time Alex found out about his sister's engagement and her time in Boston. Hearing that Clara had cried in Alex's arms over him not letting her explain caused the guilt in Noel to well up. His chest burned and screamed for him to fix the mess they were both in.

Noel walked over to the step and sat down on it. He watched as Julian complained to Max about Rob's awful kick. The brothers argued as Max stood in the middle trying to keep the peace. Alex was to the side laughing until he spotted Noel. Alex didn't say anything as he walked away from the others and joined him on the step.

"Where are the girls?" Noel asked as he scanned the garden for Keira and Andrea.

"Went down to DeCicco's to grab stuff for tea," Alex replied.

They watched Rob put Julian in a headlock before Max pulled Rob off Julian. Noel and Alex sat there watching them as they returned to kicking the football back and forth.

"How you holding up?"

Noel turned to see Alex staring at their friends. "What do you mean?"

There was a short laugh from Alex before he turned to face Noel. "How are you doing with Liam being here *with* Clara?"

Noel breathed out and stared back out at the garden. "I can't take seeing him with her. I hate knowing that when she goes to sleep, she's in his arms. I hate the idea of her marrying him. I heard her talking about her wedding dress."

"You know it's a two-way street, right?"

Noel knew what Alex meant and he nodded.

"Whatever you say won't mean anything to Clara, not when you're still with Andrea. If I had it my way, you'd be with my sister and all of this wouldn't be happening, but shit happened. You don't want to hear what I'm about to say, but I like Liam marrying my sister. He doesn't hurt her, and he makes her happy. He can provide for her and give her a happy life in Melbourne. Them getting married makes sense."

Noel's eye fell to his hands. He definitely didn't want to hear Alex's approval. "It doesn't make sense to me, Alex. Clara's meant to be with me. I shouldn't have lost her when I did."

Clara

*C*lara heard the soft sound of her alarm ringing. She opened her eyes and reached for her phone to turn it off. Then she rubbed her eyes as she placed it back on the bedside table.

"Clara," Liam mumbled.

She turned on her side and placed her hand on his naked chest. "Go back to sleep, Liam," she softly said and kissed his cheek.

He moved and wrapped his arms around her. "I love you," he mumbled still asleep.

Clara closed her eyes tightly at his words. "I love you, too," she whispered back.

The words didn't feel right, and it made her feel guilty. She shouldn't have come back to the States. She ended up more confused about her engagement than ever. Liam was her source of comfort, and their time baking Keira's cupcakes made her very aware of her love for him.

However, Clara knew her love for Liam differed from the love she had for Noel. She wanted to make Liam happy and that drove her to make the decisions she had. The minutes ticked by as she watched him sleep. With Liam, it was easy; she didn't have to worry about whether he'd hurt her. She didn't have to compete with his past.

When Liam's arms started to loosen around her, Clara stayed. She didn't immediately get up from the bed. Instead, she lay and studied his features. To be his wife and the mother of his children someday would be an honour. But as much as it was a future she felt she could live with, what Julian had said the night of Alex's party haunted her.

Am I really taking some other woman's happy ending with Liam? And am I also taking away Liam's true happiness by staying with him?

She closed her eyes and pushed the thought away. Liam

was sure his future was with Clara and that was more than enough for her. When she returned to Melbourne, she'd find her wedding dress and she'd say 'I do.' Opening her eyes, Clara slowly lifted Liam's arm off her. She silently got out of bed and placed the covers over him properly.

Clara turned to the small chair in the corner and saw the hoodie of Liam's she had worn the mornings before. She walked over to it and held it in her hands. A sense of sadness overwhelmed her, and she put it down. Instead, she turned and picked up a woollen cardigan that hung on the hook behind the door. She fed her arms through the sleeves and reached for the door handle. She turned to see Liam still asleep and the sight had her almost removing the cardigan and returning to bed.

Noel will be meeting me on the porch soon.

The sudden burst of her heart had Clara gripping the handle and she twisted it. Her heart needed to see him even though she knew it was making it harder for her to marry Liam. Clara closed the door behind her and walked silently down the steps. When she reached the double doors that led to the porch, she was surprised to see Noel leaning on the pillar. She smiled at the sight of him, ignoring the way her heart violently clenched. She breathed deeply to calm the butterflies she felt and raised her shaky hands on the handle to open the door.

"Noel," she said.

He turned around at the sound of her voice and the smile that developed on his face had her breathless. Those green eyes were gentle and beautiful, and for a moment, she believed he only had eyes for her.

"I didn't think you'd show."

"I slept through my alarm," she lied.

Before she could even step towards him and sit on the step, Noel walked to her and took her hand in his. Jolts of emotions caused her heart to stop. She looked at their hands and then at Noel, seeing a smile so sincere and loving that she didn't pull away. He walked her to the step and they sat next to each other, never letting her go.

"You should let go of my hand, Noel. It isn't very platonic."

He let out a light laugh and squeezed her hand. "Clara, I told you. I don't have any intentions of being platonic."

Her heart and body betrayed her; those words had her

breathless and speechless, and she knew her cheeks started to turn red.

Noel's hand reached up and cupped her face. "I need to hear you say it, Clara. Did you come to Boston to throw away your engagement?" His thumbs ran across her cheeks and sent her heart fluttering.

I should lie. I have to tell him no.

"*Yes.*" The word came out without a proper thought.

The truth was out and the heaviness in her heart started to disappear. Noel's other hand reached her face as he held her.

"That's all I've ever wanted to hear, Clara." He slowly breathed out her name as his face inched closer to hers.

Her eyes fluttered close as his lips came close to touching hers.

"Clara!" someone yelled.

She quickly opened her eyes and noticed her hands on Noel's arms, her engagement ring glittering from the sun's rays.

"Oh, my God," she breathed out in disbelief.

Noel's hands disappeared from her face, and she felt the emptiness in her heart. Her eyes searched Noel's to try to find an explanation, but she couldn't come up with one. Clara quickly stood up and looked down at him. The sadness in his eyes tore a hole in her heart.

"I'm sorry, I shouldn't have—" A tightening in her chest returned as she tried to apologise, but she stopped, unsure what to say. She turned away from the one person she had ever *truly* loved, and her eyes met her brother. The shock on his face had Clara feeling sick. "I'm sorry, Alex. It won't happen again."

Her brother's nostrils flared. "Get inside, Clara. Go back to your *fiancé.*"

Fiancé.

The word drove a stake through her heart, and Clara nodded. She didn't say another word as she walked to the door and into the house. Clara paused and was tempted to turn around, but the sight of her engagement ring stopped her. She could hear the sounds of Alex's voice but couldn't make out the words. Clara climbed the steps up to her room.

Once she opened the bedroom door, she noticed that Liam was still asleep in their bed. A lump in her throat formed as she stepped foot into the room and closed the door behind her. She approached her side of the bed and looked at him.

I wanted Noel to kiss me.

She knew she couldn't hurt Liam, but it was killing her to have feelings for Noel, feelings that wouldn't go away. Clara turned from the bed and made her way over to the armchair by the corner. She removed her woollen cardigan and let it fall to the floor. Then she picked up Liam's hoodie and slipped it on.

Clara settled in the chair and wrapped her arms around herself. She was torn between what she knew was right and what her heart had yearned for. The smell of Liam's cologne reminded her of the times they had shared together. She closed her eyes and tried to forget the feeling of Noel's touch and the way he looked at her. That moment today on the steps would not make her end her engagement.

*P*lacing her MacBook on the kitchen counter, Clara sat on the barstool. She typed in her password and brought up her emails. She looked at the long list of unread emails from her wedding planner. Clara scrolled down until she reached the oldest message. Opening it up, she quickly read that she had to finalise the flower arrangement choices.

Clara clicked the link to the page of flowers to choose. This morning's sunrise was the first since her almost kiss with Noel. They never spoke. Instead, she kept her eyes on the rising sun. She shouldn't have come out and continued watching with him, but she couldn't stop herself. No other words were spoken except for 'good morning.' She had ignored the pain in her heart and his stares. Clara stopped scrolling down and brushed her curls over her shoulders and onto her back.

After the sun had risen, Clara had returned to the house and found Liam on the bed, looking at the guest list. She sat with him and went through those they invited to the wedding. Once they got to her parents' name, Clara quickly changed the topic to Ally visiting Melbourne when they returned home. She wasn't sure when she'd come clean, but right now wasn't the time. Liam would undoubtedly ask questions and she didn't want the truth of her mother's hate for her to be revealed. Clara winced at the thought. Liam wouldn't understand, and she wasn't sure if she did herself.

"Hey, Clara."

She looked up from her laptop to see Andrea walking into the kitchen with a smile on her face.

"What are you doing?" Andrea asked as she sat on the barstool next to Clara.

"Oh, umm, my wedding planner wants flower choices for the centrepieces. I've kinda been ignoring her emails."

The confidence shone through Andrea's smile and Clara felt small in comparison to her. The way she carried herself and treated Noel made Clara realise that Andrea deserved him. Something she hated to admit.

The only way to forget about Noel is to submerge myself in my wedding. I can't ruin what he has with Andrea. It's not fair for anyone.

"Want some help? I know I'm not one of your bridesmaids, but another opinion could help you out." The genuine friendliness in Andrea's eyes had the guilt erupt in her chest.

I'm in love with your boyfriend.

The thought had Clara quickly turning away. She swallowed the large lump in her throat and blinked the threatening tears away. Admitting to herself that she was still in love with Noel was painful. Clara faced Andrea and smiled as convincingly as she could.

This woman deserves him.

"Sure, I'd like that," Clara replied. She moved her laptop so Andrea could see the pictures of the bouquets on the screen.

Andrea was kind and honest, and it made the guilt in her grow. If Clara were to be with Noel, then she'd hurt Andrea, and the thought made her heart sink. Andrea gave her opinion of every piece they looked at, and Clara found herself laughing at the jokes she'd made. As they clicked on the next page, Julian walked into the kitchen, dragging his feet and mumbling under his breath. Clara turned away from Andrea and looked up at him. The obvious frown Julian wore had her almost leaping from her chair.

"You okay?" Clara asked.

"Fuckin' peachy, kiddo. Rob's an ass. Won't get off the phone," Julian said once he leant on the bench, staring at Andrea and then at her. "What are you girls up to?"

"My wedding planner emailed me some flower arrangements. You want to help choose? I mean, it's really girly, but—"

"Please." He cut her off, grabbed the laptop, and then walked around the bench until he sat on the barstool next to Clara. "This flower choosing has more balls than Rob. I've never seen a man work so hard for a bang. My brother is so whipped it makes my balls hurt. This *Stevie*—or whatever her name is—has him wrapped around her little finger. Rob is such a dumb shit!"

Clara wasn't sure if she should laugh or frown at Julian's rant. His annoyance merely masked his jealousy. It seemed that things between Rob and Stevie were progressing, and Clara smiled at the idea.

"Stevie is a lovely person, Julian. I think they'd be happy together. Don't you want that?"

Julian stopped scrolling through the flower choices and glared at her. Andrea stared at Julian as they both waited for his reply.

He let out a sigh. "Sure. Of course, I want that, but with someone named *Stevie*? She sounds more manly than Rob, and that's a little sickening to imagine."

Clara shook her head at him. "Julian, I should remind you that you packed your bags over a girl. You can't judge Rob. He's making an effort," she scolded.

"You left over a girl?" Andrea asked.

Julian shot Clara an icy stare. "Long story, Andrea. Not even worth the mention." He waved the comment off.

"Jul—" Before Clara could continue with her scolding, her phone lit up and rang.

"Who's Ally?" He tilted his head and arched his brow up at Clara.

"Liam's younger sister," she replied. A little glint appeared in Julian's eyes, and she and Andrea both laughed at his excitement. "She lives in Sydney, by the way." With that one sentence, Clara knew she had him.

"Sydney, hey?" The fascination in Julian's voice seemed to indicate he was seriously considering the thought of Ally.

Clara didn't swipe her phone in time to answer, missing Ally's call. "I know what you're thinking and stop that! She's going to be my sister-in-law."

Clara quickly sent Ally a message and looked back at her laptop. Julian and Andrea debated over their preferred choice when she heard her brother's voice. Clara watched as he walked into the kitchen with Noel, his eyes meeting hers before turning to Andrea. Rob, Max, Keira, and Liam walked into the kitchen moments later.

Liam rounded the bench and stood behind Clara. He let out a laugh and whispered, "Got Jo's messages, I see," and then kissed her cheek.

Clara's eyes never left Noel's as she noticed him ball his fists.

"We're hitting the golf course. You guys want to come?" Alex asked.

Andrea hopped off the barstool, walked over to Noel, and took his hand. "I'm a pro at golf. Practically grew up on the green," she revealed.

"Andrea's on my team. I'm not losing to Rob at anything ever again. Not after that race we had on the Yarra last week." Max winked at Andrea, and she let out a laugh.

"Coming, Clara?" Noel asked.

It was the first proper thing he had said to her in a day, but she shook her head. "I suck at golf, and I have a lot of stuff to do and emails to answer. You guys have fun. Liam, you go, too. I know how much you wanted to try out the course."

Liam swivelled Clara around until she faced him. "You sure?" he asked.

Clara nodded. "I'm sure."

"Don't worry, Liam. I'm staying with Clara. We can have that Clara and Keira day I've been waiting for," Keira cheered and gave Alex a quick kiss. Then she made her way around the bench and sat on the stool next to Clara.

"Well, we better get going. We'll take my car and Noel can take Keira's. Liam can come with me. I think it's time we had some time together since you'll be my brother-in-law soon," Alex said.

Fear flashed in Liam's eyes, and Clara laughed at how cute he looked when he was terrified. She placed both hands on Liam's cheeks. "Alex is not going to hurt you. Are you, Alex?" she asked over her shoulder.

"I make no promises, Clara," Alex answered.

She turned and glared at her brother. His face was tense, but no matter how much of a serious act Alex would pull, he wouldn't hurt Liam. He meant too much to Clara.

"You are going to be fine, Liam," she assured.

Liam kissed her forehead and walked towards the others. They had all said bye to Clara and Keira before they walked out of the kitchen. Clara didn't look in Noel's direction. Instead, she stared down at the bench. Once she heard the door close, she let out a sigh.

"Thank you," she whispered to Keira, who took Clara's hand and squeezed it.

"Alex told me about yesterday. How about we forget about those boys and have an afternoon together. Have you chosen a bouquet yet?"

Clara smiled and was thankful for her brother's girlfriend.

"Yes, I've chosen white tulips."

Chapter
ELEVEN

Noel

"Where'd you pull that shot?" Julian asked, astonished.

Noel looked at him and shrugged. "I have no clue. Fluke shot." He walked out of the bunker and stood next to Julian.

"We're so shit that everyone's three holes ahead of us. Andrea wasn't lying when she said she was a pro. Look at her," Julian said.

Noel gazed out into the distance to see Andrea swing her club and hit the ball expertly. It only took her one swing to hit the green, only just missing the hole.

"Her dad owns a golf club in Phoenix. I don't think she's been on a golf course since she moved to Boston." Noel placed his club into the hired golf bag and then made his way to the cart.

Once he reached the golf cart, he loaded it up with his bag and then Julian's. Noel reached for his bottle of water on the seat, uncapped it, then brought it to his lips and drank.

"What are you going to do about Andrea?" Julian asked as he leant on the cart and crossed his arms over his chest.

Noel capped the bottle and placed it back on the seat. Then he ran his hand through his hair and groaned. "I don't know. Each time I'm with Clara, I feel myself falling out of love with Andrea. I care about her. But I keep remembering why I love Clara each time I'm near her. I almost kissed her yesterday."

The surprise flashed in Julian's eyes as he pushed off the cart. "Almost?"

"Alex caught us. You should have seen her. She was horrified when she realised what was happening. I was so close, but then again, I'm kind of glad Alex caught us. I don't want her to hate me if I did kiss her."

Julian scratched his head. "You need to work this out, Noel. You don't have a lot of time left. Andrea was helping Clara choose flowers for the tables. I helped so I could see what she was up to. Heard her the other day with Liam talking about a guest list and a registry. This wedding is happening, and you need to quickly make up your mind to stop her."

Damn. I'm running out of time!

"Don't look now but Alex is coming. Guy looks ready to run you down with his golf cart," Julian warned.

Noel turned to see Alex drive his golf cart over the hill and stop in front of them. Alex then removed the keys from the ignition and got out of the cart. He took his phone out of his pocket as he frowned at Noel. That concerned expression of his had Noel tensing.

Something's wrong. Clara has to be okay.

"Alex, what's up with you?" Julian asked.

Alex glanced up and his jaw clenched. "Julian, take the cart up to the others. Noel and I will meet you guys a little later. They know that we'll meet you at the club bar."

Noel's eyebrows met, and he stared at Alex. "What's going on, Alex?" Noel asked, fearful of what he'd say.

Alex placed his phone in his pocket and shook his head. "The Lyndon account is collapsing. Your junior fucked up. Mercer and Gregson want a conference call. Now!"

Noel froze. He'd spent hours fixing the mistakes his junior had made. The idiot needed to be fired because that was what HR had hired. An idiot. "Are you fucking kidding me? What the hell did Milligan do now? I haven't been gone a week. Why didn't Colleen call me?" Noel reached into his pocket and retrieved his phone.

"Mercer just told me and he's got a video call set up for us. We have to go now. You'll be 'right, Julian?"

Noel handed Julian the cart's keys as he tried to figure out what Milligan could have done. His promotion and his job were on the line if it was that bad.

"We'll see you later, Julian," Noel said as he followed Alex to his golf cart.

"You're the worst golf partner, Noel. With you gone maybe I can actually win. Good luck, boys."

"Not with Andrea and Max as a team. Liam's pretty good and Rob's been awful. Must run in the Moors genes to be that shit at golf!" Alex shouted as he climbed into the cart.

Noel followed and let out a laugh.

"You're so funny, Alex. I hope you get fired, you bastard!" Julian yelled as he kicked the grass.

*A*lex cut the engine and they sat in the car for a moment. Noel knew they were both worrying about their futures at G&MC. Alex unbuckled his seat belt and looked at Noel. The smile on his face confused Noel.

"Relax, Noel," Alex instructed.

"Relax? Are you kidding me? Milligan has probably fucked us both over with his laziness." Noel unbuckled his seat belt and glared at him

"Milligan didn't fuck us over. I *lied*."

Noel stared at his best friend in disbelief. Alex was never the type to lie. "You what?"

Alex had chuckled before he tensed and a stern expression consumed his face. "Yesterday, when I caught you, I didn't want to catch you. But I didn't want Clara to feel awful about kissing you, so that's why I stopped you. Not because I didn't want it to happen. I didn't want Clara to feel like she became Darren. I lied about the conference call so that you and Clara could have a moment together. No interruptions from any of us. This is your chance. I was probably the reason why you guys ended in the first place, and I want to fix that. If Clara says no, then you need to let her go, okay?"

Noel couldn't believe what he was hearing. The thumps in his chest intensified and his heart rattled against his ribcage. "You did this for me?"

Alex nodded his head. "You're my best mate, Noel. I want you to have every bit of happiness that I have with Keira, and well... you love my sister. The way she looks at you is enough for me. She's just really confused. All she needs is time but give her a reason."

I have one chance. Alex is giving me one chance with Clara.

Noel had opened and shut the car door behind him before he walked up the path to the double story house. He didn't bother knocking as he entered the house and made his way towards the living room. He stood by the doorway as Keira and Clara's backs faced him, sitting on the white, French-inspired couch.

"I don't know, Keira. I'm so lost. There's this big part of me that tells me that marrying Liam is the right thing to do. But there's a bigger, more needier part that wants Noel," Clara said in a tight voice.

His heart throbbed with an intense pain and pleasure. A part of her still wanted him, one that outweighed her need to marry Liam. There was still hope.

"I can't forget him because he's the first man I've ever loved. When we were together, I was happy, and it felt incredible and right to be with him. I never knew that feeling with my ex. I never had sex with Darren. All he was after was my virginity and then Noel..." Clara's voice went ever smaller, almost a whisper, as Keira's hand moved to Clara's shoulder.

"Did you lose your virginity to Noel?"

Clara sniffed. "Yes, just don't tell Alex. If he found out, he'd think the worst of it all. It wasn't like that."

The memories of their first date flooded his thoughts, and his heart squeezed in both pain and relief. Every cell in him wanted her, needed her, and most importantly, missed her.

I fell in love with her that night.

"You and me. Outside. *Now!*"

Noel heard Alex's growl behind him. He had closed his eyes tightly before he turned around. Noel knew what was coming, and he would take it.

He nodded. "Okay."

Alex pushed past him and stalked through the living room, surprising Keira and Clara.

"What's going on?" Keira asked, startled.

Noel followed Alex, his eyes meeting Clara's fearful gaze as he walked towards the porch. He didn't say anything to her as he exited the house and went down the steps to the garden where Alex waited.

Alex balled his fists, his nostrils flared, and Noel could see the rage flash brightly in his eyes. Noel raised his hands up at Alex to signal he had no intentions of fighting. Noel heard the sound of rushing footsteps behind him and the panic began to rise.

"If you are going to hit me, then do it now." He didn't want either Keira or Clara to stop Alex.

"You... took..." Alex shook his head. Noel could tell he couldn't get a grip on the concept of him being Clara's first.

"Clara lost her virginity to *me*."

That was all it took. The pure anger had been evident in Alex's eyes before his fist made contact with Noel's cheek.

"*Noel!*" Clara shrieked.

His skin broke as blood started to seep out. Noel took two steps back as he recovered from Alex's punch, his hand touching the open wound.

Clara was in his sights in seconds, and he noticed Keira by Alex. There were tears in her eyes as she held onto his wrists. The blood dripped from his face and onto her hand, but she hadn't notice.

"I'm so sorry," she whispered as she let go of his wrist. Clara spun away from him and looked at her brother. "Alex, what are you doing?"

"Step away from him, Clara."

Clara shook her head. Noel stepped forward and took her hand.

"No!" she said firmly.

Alex didn't flinch. His nostrils flared at her defiance. "Now, Clara! Step away from him. I will make you."

"Al—"

Noel stepped forward, stopping Clara from continuing. "Don't, Clara. I deserve it. It's been a long time coming," he explained.

Clara gazed up at him and she shook her head, causing tears to slide down her face. If he didn't have his left hand covering his cheek, he would have brushed them away.

"He knows we slept together. I don't understand why he has to punch you."

He squeezed her hand. "Clara, he wasn't expecting that *I* would be the one to take *your* virginity."

Clara's brown eyes glimmered. Then she let go of his hand and faced her brother. "Noel didn't *take* my virginity. I gave it to him—willingly—I might add. I fell in love with Noel. It wasn't just sex, believe me. I was the one who asked for it to happen, Alex. Don't blame Noel. I asked for him to be my first. I don't regret losing my virginity to him. I could have done a lot worse. Darren could have been my first."

Just the mention of Darren's name had Alex unclenching his fists. "You're right," he said, conceding defeat. Alex stepped away from Keira and closed the distance between them. "I'm sorry, Noel. I didn't expect you'd be the one to... You never want to know that your best friend deflowe—you know. For a second, I saw you as the guy I went to Stanford with. The guy who treated women like they were dispensable. I know you're not that guy anymore." He gave Noel an apologetic-yet-strained smile. Alex held out his hand, and Noel shook it with his blood-free one.

Clara had stepped between them before she took Noel's hand. Her touch caused the warmth to return to his chest. "Come with me," she instructed to Noel.

Noel wiped the blood off his cheek and followed Clara into the house. She led him upstairs and to the first bathroom to their right. Noel walked into the middle of the light blue painted room. He turned to see Clara lock the door without any hesitation.

"I'm so sorry. Did he hurt you when he was in Boston?"

Noel stepped towards her, took her hands, and shook his head. Clara smiled up at him, and his heart stretched.

I love her smile.

"Sit on the bathtub and I'll clean you up."

Noel followed her instructions and sat on the edge of the tub. Clara then began to search through the cabinet under the sink. Moments later, she stood up and had a bottle of rubbing alcohol in one hand and a bag of cotton balls in the other. She studied him and frowned at the sight of the blood on his face.

Clara set the bottle and the bag on the counter. He smelt the strong rubbing alcohol as she poured it onto a cotton ball. His eyes never left those lips that formed a frown. She held the soaked cotton up to his cheek. Noel didn't care that it would burn like hell. He finally had her alone. Taking the opportunity that had presented itself, he waited until her soft hand rested on his cheek, steadying his face. Before she was able to place the rubbing alcohol on his face, Noel raised his hand up to Clara's face and ran his fingertips along her cheeks several times. Feeling her heavy breaths hit his skin, he had a realisation.

I can't let her go.

"I'm leaving her," he announced. He watched the surprise take hold every inch of her face.

Clara's hands left his face, and she put distance between them. "You're what?"

"I'm leaving Andrea, Clara. And I need you to do the same. I need you to leave him."

Clara

*H*er breathing came out in gasps as she quickly blinked at him. Clara's lips parted, as she tried to comprehend what he had just said. She turned and placed the cotton ball on the counter. Noel stood up from the bathtub and she noticed droplets of blood hit the tiled floor.

"Clara, say something."

She faced him properly and shook her head. "You want me to leave Liam?" It sounded unbelievable coming from her mouth.

"Yes," he said as he took her hand. Noel's thumbs softly ran across her knuckles and causing the increasing spikes in her heartbeat.

Clara took back her hand and gazed down at her engagement ring. The pounding in her chest made its way to her eardrums. She closed her eyes tightly, trying to comprehend it all. With an exasperated sigh, she looked at Noel through blurry eyes.

"You want to leave Andrea?" she asked, needing him to

repeat his intentions out loud.

"Yes, I want to be with *you*. I've only ever wanted to be with you, Clara." The begging in his voice had her heart breaking.

Could I really just call off my engagement?

Clara glanced at her engagement ring and then at Noel. He wanted her to make a choice, but she couldn't. "You have no idea how selfish you sound," she cried. The tears started to fall as she realised just how hard this was for her.

"I know, but I can't do it anymore, Clara. I can't keep watching you be with him. And the idea of you marrying him. It's wrong. Your forever was always meant to be with me."

His words pierced her chest and she took a step back.

My forever... with Noel?

"You love Andrea. You wouldn't have sent me away the first time if you didn't. You wouldn't have been with her all this time or had her move in. You love Andrea. Please don't hurt her."

Noel stepped forward, placed his hands on her hips and held her close to his body. His touch made her want to weep. "We're hurting everyone by denying each other this. Choose me, Clara. Choose *us*," he begged.

I've spent ten months being Liam's. I can't break his heart.

"I—" she stuttered. "I need time, Noel. You're asking a lot from me. I'm throwing away not only an engagement but also a marriage and a future. You can't expect an answer from me right now."

Clara pushed off his body. There was too much to consider. The idea of a future with Noel gave her heart a burst of life, but the reality of the idea sent it plunging.

Too many people will get hurt. I'll lose everything: Liam, Ally, CeCe, and the bakery. I'll lose them all.

"I can't give you an answer. I need time to think about this all. I'm supposed to be getting married. You have to understand why this is so hard for me."

Noel's green eyes dulled as pain consumed his face. "I know. I'll be waiting for you." It sounded like a promise.

Clara swallowed hard. She didn't enjoy seeing Noel broken. She pressed her lips firmly together and turned for the bathroom door. Clara resisted looking over her shoulder. She unlocked the door and exited the bathroom.

I have to make a decision.

After Noel's declaration, Clara hid away in her bedroom. She had run through the pros and cons of leaving Liam and the only pro she could come up with was that she'd finally be with Noel. There was no Stevie or Annie to turn to for advice. Her calls to her best friends went unanswered. When she had left the bathroom, she heard nothing until the bathroom door closed and then the sound of Alex's car driving away. The only thing Clara heard next was Keira knocking on her door moments later. Keira had wrapped her arms around Clara and hugged her while she silently cried.

It had been an hour since Keira had left Clara alone. The sunset's rays pierced through the sheer curtains. She looked up at the ceiling as she lay in bed. She brought up her left hand and stared at her engagement ring. The way the diamonds sparkled in the sunlight reminded Clara of the moment he had proposed. Liam's smile as he asked her to marry him and the beautiful sunset.

The bedroom door opened and Clara quickly propped herself up onto her elbows. Liam entered the room with a frown on his face. When he reached her, he climbed into the bed and sat in front of her. Then he kissed her forehead softly and it made her smile. His lips were delicate against her skin. The little things he did made her fall in love with him.

"Did you see Noel's face?"

Clara nodded and he took her hands.

"Apparently, one of his junior accountants screwed up one of Alex's accounts. Noel hadn't looked over the account or something and your brother punched him in the face." Liam tensed once he spoke of her brother's violent side.

Clara moved forward, removed her hands from his, and placed them on his cheeks. "My brother takes his job seriously. He isn't going to punch you in the face because he knows it'll upset me."

Liam's hands covered hers. "He might when I tell you some news."

Clara's left eyebrow shot upwards.

"I have to leave for Singapore tomorrow."

Her hands moved from Liam's face, and she got off the bed. "Tomorrow?" she breathed.

"I'm sorry, Clara, but they're impatient now, and I want this deal wrapped up before the wedding," he explained.

Liam moved towards the end of the bed, and he held her hands in his. Clara was disappointed; she wanted more time with Liam. If she were to go back to Melbourne, their time together before the wedding would be limited. His thumb ran across her engagement ring and she smiled.

He's loved me unconditionally for far longer than I've loved him.

"Come with me?" Liam asked.

Clara's smile widened. It was the first time he had ever asked her to join him.

This will give me time.

"Okay. I've never been to Singapore before."

The surprise on Liam's face had Clara kissing the tip of his nose.

"You really want to come? What about Alex?"

Clara untangled their hands and wrapped her arms around his neck. "I want to go with you. You're my fiancé and Alex will be fine."

The smile on Liam's face had every doubt of hers fade away.

I want to make Liam happy.

"I'll book the tickets after I have a shower. I had no idea golf could be that difficult." Liam's lips found hers and she realised that she could be happy with Liam for the rest of her life. As long as she made him happy, she would be content.

*

Every time she felt those green eyes glare at her, all she wanted to do was slip off her engagement ring and throw her arms around him. But that smile on Andrea's face as they held hands or kissed at the table had Clara stopping herself. So she kept her head down and her eyes away. It was better that way.

Seeing Noel every morning on that porch with a smile on his face broke her heart again and again. Clara looked up at the ceiling and closed her eyes tightly and imagined a life where Valerie or Sarah had never got in the way. It was a life she wanted but was too scared to go out and fight for.

This time it wasn't just Alex she'd hurt if she pursued her feelings, it would be Liam and Andrea. Her eyes watered and she opened them to blink the tears away. Liam's fingers moved across her stomach and she turned her head to face him. There was so much guilt welled up inside her; the constant pressure overtook her body, making it hard to think clearly. A pressure that made it hard for her to breathe and hard to fight back the tears. Liam would die trying to make her happy.

Whatever I feel for Noel is the result of the memory of us. They're just memories.

Clara turned her head to the right and saw the time on the clock. The sun was starting to rise and she could see the sky lighten through the thin shades of the window. As another minute ticked over, Clara held her breath.

This would be a sunrise she'd miss with Noel. Yesterday was their last; she just never expected that she'd end what she felt like she needed. She rolled onto her side and ran her fingers along Liam's cheek. There was something making her stay.

The sound of footsteps outside the bedroom door had Clara's fingers stopping. The pacing stopped. She sat up and looked at the small gap the bottom of the door made. She saw the shadow of two feet and her stomach formed knots.

"Don't do this, Clara. Don't take this away from me. I'm sorry. I am so sorry. Dammit. If I have to break down this door and drag you out, then I will. You can't give me those mornings and take them away so suddenly. I need you, Clara."

The begging in his voice had her pulling over the covers and walking towards the door. They weren't the three words she was hoping for, but it still made her heart dance. She still had to make a decision. Swallowing hard, Clara opened the door to find Noel standing there, his eyes watery with a sad heartbreaking smile. In his hand he held a single purple tulip.

"I love you, Clara Louise Lawrence. I love you."

Chapter TWELVE

Noel

Memories were the underlying demons of his soul. Every memory he ever had of Clara he cherished, but they were also his kryptonite. Nothing could ever hurt him the way she could. But nothing could ever mend him the way she could, too. Noel had never known such heartache and loneliness until she walked away all those days and all those nights ago; days that had turned into weeks and then months.

Noel stood at Clara's bedroom door and stared at her as he waited for her to speak. The pain in her eyes reminded him of the night of his brother's wedding. It was the night Clara had given him back her locket and said goodbye.

Clara had glanced over her shoulder before she faced him. "Noel, please keep your voice down."

"I love you," he said in soft voice.

They weren't the words she wanted to hear, but I'll be damned if I don't fight this one last time.

Her quick blinks and heavy breathing didn't stop him. Noel stepped forward and wondered if there was ever a chance left for them. Noel looked down at the purple tulip he had picked from Keira's garden. The small tulip was his symbol of hope. The innocent flower symbolised every ounce and every inch of his love for her.

A soft sigh from Clara had his eyes meeting hers. After a deep breath, she asked, "You love me?"

His heart beat out of sync as he remembered Clara's reaction to the first time he had declared his love. His eyes never left hers as he cupped her face with his right hand.

All I have left is the truth. All we have that's stopped us is the truth. The truth is both our beginning and our ending.

"Clara, I *never*, not once, stopped loving you. I lied to you. I shouldn't have back in Boston, but I wanted you to be happy. I should have gone on my knees and I should have promised myself to you, forever. You, Clara Louise Lawrence, are the love of my life. You were then, and you are now until forever. I've only ever loved you, and I've been lying to myself by pretending that I don't. I can't love anyone else because letting you go haunts me. Letting you go was the worst decision I have ever made."

Tears ran down Clara's beautiful face. The burning in his chest intensified the moment her hand covered his. Clara's lips formed a fine line as she closed her eyes tightly for a second. When she opened them, her beautiful golden brown eyes saddened before him. Tears brimmed Clara's eyes as she placed her right hand on Noel's cheek. Her touch brought the tremors back, and he couldn't control his own tears from forming.

For now, I have to believe she still loves me. I have to help her find a way back to where she belongs, with me.

Clara's thumb caressed his cheek, and for the first time in a long time, he had her back. Her beautiful brown eyes spoke the words she couldn't. This moment was theirs. Their past and their current circumstances didn't stop this moment.

After a period of undeniable bliss, Clara let out a sigh and whispered, "You have the worst timing, Nolan Parker."

Disappointment inflamed him as Clara's touch left his. She looked into his eyes as that hint of love slowly vanished behind a wall he knew she had built and guarded. Clara crossed her arms protectively over her chest. The apologetic smile that formed on her lips had Noel wincing. She took a small step to her left and leant on the door, allowing him to peek into her room.

The first thing he noticed was Liam sleeping between Clara's sheets and then he saw the suitcases at the foot of the bed. Noel's teeth clenched at the sight of her bags. He stared at the pain that consumed her facial expression. She was still as beautiful as ever, but the torment in her eyes certainly broke his heart.

"You're leaving?" he asked once he'd formed words. He balled his right fist, but not his left for fear of crushing the delicate purple tulip.

Clara's gaze fell to the floor for a second before she looked up at him and whispered, "Yes."

Noel blinked to spare him some time to come up with a response. Clara watched him as Noel glanced at the tulip.

When will we find our ending together? Is there one?

"The week's not over!" He raised his voice slightly higher than he should have.

Clara's head quickly turned as she looked over at the bed. Noel peered past her to see Liam move slightly before his body relaxed.

She let out a sigh. "I don't want to wake him. Maybe we should talk… later? He might hear or see us."

Knowing that his time with her was ending before it would begin, Noel took a step forward, unlinked Clara's arms and took her left hand in his.

"I don't really care," he confessed.

Clara's eyes met their linked hands before she whispered his name, "Noel."

He stepped closer to her as Clara lifted her chin to meet his eyes. He discovered a hint of hope shimmering through and he believed they were possible. But Noel knew what he had to do; he couldn't rush her. Not this time.

"I love you," he whispered.

Instead of Clara rejecting his love, she smiled lightly.

"Just give me today's sunrise, please, Clara." No words were said as he held Clara's hand just that little bit tighter. He needed that reassurance of her touch as he pulled her in the direction of the stairs.

Clara stopped after a few steps and looked at him. She let go of his hand and he instantly felt the yearning for her touch again. Clara's thumb ran across her engagement ring, and Noel knew she was walking away. She let out a heavy sigh as she turned around without another word. The twisting pain in his heart had the power to bring him to his knees. Memories of the first time he had watched her walk away mirrored this exact moment for him.

He counted the three steps she took until she reached the bedroom door. Three steps that ensured him that he had finally lost her. Noel didn't blink. He forced his eyes to witness this moment. She reached for the door handle and it was as if the story of them was ending. Noel's eyes fell to the floor.

I deserve this. I never deserved her love in the first place.

The sound of the bedroom door shutting had him lifting his head. His heart relaxed in relief when his eyes found her standing there, holding the door handle for a moment, before turning around. Her soft and beautiful smile was the only incentive he needed to walk towards her and take her hand. The feeling of home overtook his entire system, and for the first time in a long time, he felt whole.

Noel didn't waste any time as he led Clara down the stairs, through the double doors, and to their step. He never let go of her hand as they sat down to the sight of the rising sun. Their arms touching as Clara placed her right hand over their entwined hands. He craned his neck to the right as Clara's head rested on his arm. Everything he ever wished for was currently his reality. He finally had Clara; not in the way he would have liked, but it would be as close as he would get.

The smell of her floral perfume was one he craved, and at that moment, he let himself get delirious. Noel peeked down at the purple tulip he still held and twirled it in his fingers.

"You can't leave me, Clara," he softly said after they shared the silence.

Clara tensed. She let out a heavy sigh before she untangled her hands from his and faced him. Sadness consumed not only her eyes but also every aspect of her beautiful face. Her lips formed a frown and her forehead slightly creased. Noel shifted his body to mirror the way Clara sat.

"I have to go home sometime, Noel. I don't belong here in the States. My life is back in Melbourne. You know that." Clara had tucked her loose curl behind her ear before her fingers fiddled with each other in her lap.

He reached out and rested his right hand on Clara's left cheek. He held the tulip in front of her. She looked at it with a pained expression as she accepted and held it. Noel's left hand held Clara's right. It was too early for anyone to catch them, and honestly, he didn't care if anyone did.

"Do you believe me?" he asked.

Clara's eyes widened at his question and then searched his for the truth of his love. Her lips parted slightly as she nodded. "I do, but you were really convincing back in Boston. How could I not believe you then?" The guilt hit him like a concrete block falling on top of him. Swift and unexpected. His hands left the touch of Clara's, and he splayed them flat on the wooden step.

"Clara, I could only ever love you. I was willing to lose everything with Alex to be with you. I'm sorry I turned you away. I thought it was better for us that way. I couldn't go through all that pain of losing you again because it scared me to hell. But I will go through it all again if it means I have a slim chance of being yours. I just need a chance, Clara. Just one. I know I don't deserve it when you have someone like Liam. But it's *us*, Clara. It's you and me. It's always been you and me."

He never noticed his tears until Clara brushed them away. The touch of her fingertips sent his heart soaring. He'd only ever love her; it was that clear. He only ever wanted to be worthy of her. Before she could move her hand away from his cheek, his hand covered hers to stop her. For a second, his thumb brushed the back of her hand. If there were any time to kiss her, it would be this moment. His eyes met Clara's for a long second before he looked down at her pink lips.

The idea of Liam proposing first stopped him. She was engaged. They'd have a moment in time, but right now wasn't it. Noel removed his hand from hers, and she leant back, creating a small distance between them. Clara cleared her throat as she placed the purple tulip on the wooden step below them.

"Do you remember when I was four? I fell in your garden and scraped my knee. That was the day you gave me a purple tulip, remember?"

The corners of his mouth rose, and he smiled at her. A memory and a point in their lives that they had shared together; an innocent moment that had led them to being something more at one stage. That purple tulip started *their* story.

I unknowingly loved her as a child, and I've loved her every day since our paths crossed once again.

Clara ran her fingers through her hair as a sad smile developed on her face. "That day I fell, you told me scrapes like the one on my knee would heal with time. You said the pain would go away, and it would be all right in time."

The break in her voice caused an immediate and violent squeeze of his heart. She paused for a moment and took his hands in hers before she looked into his eyes.

"Please don't hate me, Noel. But unlike when I was four, these scrapes aren't just breaks in my skin. They're deep and open. I've had time, and the pain hasn't gone away. You broke my heart, Nolan. Shattered it, completely. I thought Liam could fix me, but he just masks the real pain. The pain I feel isn't small breaks in the skin, it's much worse. I need time. More time than it takes to heal a scraped knee. I need you to give me enough to heal and enough to figure this all out. I need this distance from you. That's all I ask, time and distance. Just please don't hate me."

The begging in Clara's voice had him quickly brushing away her tears. What she'd said was heartfelt and honest. He quickly wrapped his arms around her and held her close. His face in her hair and the smell of coconut filled his senses. He loved her enough to give her this.

"I could never hate you, Clara. God, I love you. I can only ever love you," he whispered in her ear. He held her tightly, afraid to let her go. She stayed in his arms for a long while, his heart yearning for more. "Two weeks, Clara. I'm giving you two weeks, and then I'm coming after you. You hear me? Two weeks."

She nodded into his shoulder. He hoped that would be enough time for her to find her way back to him. Clara hadn't clarified whether she still loved him, but he had hopes that she still did.

"Thank you," she whispered.

He held the love of his life in a moment where time and place didn't matter. She offered him a chance. He would have waited forever for this chance. When Clara moved out of their embrace, he saw the relief in her golden brown eyes. The relief masked what he hoped was the look of her love for him. He would have to be patient. It was about her needs and not his own.

She'll be leaving soon. I'll be here, and she'll be on the other side of the world.

"Clara," he softly said. His eyes never left hers. He had and always would see forever in her beautiful eyes.

"Yes."

Noel reached forward and tucked back the loose curl behind her ear. "I can't watch you walk away. I'd only stop you, and you want time. I wouldn't be able to stop myself. I don't want you to leave."

Clara's eyes watered as she scooted forward and set her hand on his left cheek. Her soft thumb ran along his cheeks as she looked into his eyes and whispered, "Close your eyes, Nolan Parker."

He searched Clara's eyes to read the emotions, but his mind went blank the moment she placed her other hand on his right cheek.

"Close your eyes and count down from ten," she instructed.

His eyes willingly closed.

"Ten... nine...eight..." he slowly breathed out the numbers.

Clara's thumbs continued to softly and slowly drag themselves across his cheeks. Noel raised his hands and held onto her wrists.

"Seven...six... five..."

Clara's fingers stopped their slow movements.

"Four..." He paused his count, his heart beating too fast and too loud.

"Three..." Clara whispered as she continued the count for him.

"Two..." he breathed, knowing that once he said 'one' their time together would be over for now.

"One..." Clara said.

His heart stopped at that last number. Noel was about to open his eyes and protest when her breath fluttered over his lips. His heart burned and then it stopped again. He kept his eyes closed as he felt Clara's soft lips graze his. One sweet moment of their lips touching had his breath catching. The short touch of her lips reminding him how much he loved her.

"I believe you," she whispered.

The moment she spoke those words, Noel felt her hands move from his face. He kept his eyelids clenched shut as he took in the feel of Clara's soft lips and the sheer pleasure it brought him moments before. He heard the sound of footsteps, and then the door opening and closing.

He slowly opened his eyes to find Clara gone. Noel turned to the right to see her approaching the stairs, through the glass panels. He ran his hand through his short hair and exhaled. She had kissed him, and even if it was for a short second, it was still the most amazing moment of his life. Noel looked down at the bottom step to see the purple tulip was gone.

Clara

I shouldn't have done that.

The same thought continued to run through her mind. A need in her controlled her actions. The temptation to kiss Noel had been strong and evident since the first sunrise. The slight touch of his lips and she had almost broken down and deepened the kiss. It was a test to see what his lips could do to her. The slight contact of his mouth brought back every blissful memory. That kiss only strengthened the thought she tried to suppress.

I'm still in love with Nolan Parker.

It was wrong to have her lips touch his, but the rightness of it made the guilt in her grow. Nolan Parker was a danger to her engagement. In a strange way, she liked the danger, but then again, it frightened her. Liam deserved her heart completely and that was what she wanted. She wanted someone who could love him without any faults. And for almost ten months, Clara believed she was that someone.

I was that someone until he proposed.

Clara glanced down at her engagement ring and felt the heaviness of it. The day Liam proposed had awakened the suppressed emotions. It had awakened her second-guessing and the reality of her true emotions. And the touch of Noel's lips felt like home. There was no doubt she loved Liam. Before Noel had walked back into her life, Liam was what she wanted.

Clara groaned as she fell back on the bed. The sound of the shower running didn't ease her thoughts.

After walking away from Noel, Clara had returned to find Liam still asleep in their bed. She placed the purple tulip on the bedside table and lay next to her fiancé. She had to remember that as long as Liam's engagement ring sat on Clara's finger, she was still his. She had watched as he woke up to the brushes of her fingertips across the side of his face. Liam's unconditional love for her was evident in his just-woken eyes. She'd be happy to marry him, but Clara knew he deserved more. She had two weeks to make a decision that would impact everyone's lives.

Clara's wet hair had soaked the sheets beneath her, but she didn't care. As she focused on the ceiling, she couldn't help but wonder when she'd have a happily ever after. She wasn't even sure if she deserved one, but she held hope. Clara heard the sound of the shower shutting off, but she didn't move. Two weeks from today, she'd have to make the ultimate choice.

Noel or Liam? Forever or always? For now or for eternity? I have to choose one.

The bathroom door opening had Clara on her elbows. Liam ran a white cotton towel through his wet hair and Clara let out an anguished sigh. The devilish smirk on his face had her biting her bottom lip. He dropped the towel he'd held and walked around the bed. Her eyes travelled down his naked defined body until she took sight of the towel wrapped around his waist. She mentally groaned at the thought of betraying the perfection that stood in front of her.

The thought vanishing the moment Liam's hands cupped her face and his soft and warm lips pressed against hers. The movement of his lips had Clara sighing and bringing him down on top of her. The deeper the kiss, the more urgency for her to forget occurred. Clara wasn't sure what exactly she needed to forget, but the thought was there. Her hands gripped Liam's hair; she was afraid he would leave her and witness the monster she truly was.

"I haven't packed yet," he whispered against her lips.

Liam's hot breath was enough to make her sigh. Clara rolled them over until Liam was on his back and she was on top.

She panted heavily as she hovered over Liam's lips. Those hazel eyes were soft and full of love. One day Liam would see just how undeserving she was of him. In time, he'd realise and leave her. It was a fear she had. She needed him as her sense of direction. In the months since Noel had broken her heart, he had been the one to try to mend the pieces together.

Her hands moved from his hard chest to his face. Clara ran her fingers along his cheeks and then his jaw. Liam's hand stopped the movement of Clara's left hand. He brought the engagement ring to his lips and kissed the large diamond. Like a Super 8 camera projecting the last ten months they'd spent together, Clara watched the moments flash before her. The last memory was on that winter day back in July. Liam on one knee as the sun set to her left with the same diamond ring sparkling before her.

Clara leant forward, her lips close to contact with Liam's when the door burst open.

"Clara, I—Jesus!" Julian shouted. She and Liam stilled at their intruder's voice.

"Oh my God, Julian! Get out!" she yelled.

Liam cheeks turned pink. He gave her a grin before he wrapped his arms around her back and sat them up. Clara quickly turned to see Julian's hands over his eyes.

"Clara, you're practically my little sister, I really don't need to see you straddling your fiancé like that!"

"Who barges into someone else's room? God, Julian. People with common sense knock on doors." Clara shook her head. She gave Liam a quick kiss, hopped off him, and then smoothed her light blue baby doll dress.

"Well, I didn't think, okay! Do you want me to come back? When you two are, uh… done?"

"You ruin romance, Moors," Clara said. "You can move your hands now."

Julian dropped his hands and rolled his eyes at her. "Please, you kids know *nothing* about romance."

"If you say so. Care to explain this visit of yours?"

"Heard you're leaving today. We've barely had any time together. Reckon I can steal you away from your morning sex and be a bit of a cock block? I suggest a walk. What do you say? If that's okay with Liam."

Clara turned and raised her eyebrow at Liam.

Liam chuckled. "I still have to pack and get dressed before

we take the hire car back to the airport. Spend some time with Julian before we leave, Clara."

She turned back to Julian and smiled. "I'm all yours, Julian Moors."

He smirked. "Ah, yes, as it should be, Clara Lawrence."

*C*lara and Julian had walked the lonely and quiet streets until they reached the village. The beautiful and ornate clock stood in the middle of the roundabout, a park a short distance away, and empty car spaces lined the front of the closed stores. She would be happy to live in Scarsdale. It would mean a beautiful suburbia life and being in the same country as her brother.

The sun had started to warm her skin. They hadn't spoke as they made the short walk from her brother's house to the bench in the park. Clara sat down to see it shaded by tall, slim trees with branches that contained dry leaves. She closed her eyes, and for a moment, peace settled within her. When this was over, she hoped both Liam and Noel ended up happy. Her own happiness didn't matter.

"Noel told me what happened this morning," Julian said softly.

Clara opened her eyes at the sound of his name. She leant forward, placed her palms on her knees, and stared at the empty road. She let out a sigh. If there was a way to quicken the pain to overcome it, she would.

"I'm glad he's given you some time to think about your choice. Just before, the way you looked at Liam, Clara, I don't doubt your love for him. But I don't envy the position you're in. It must be tough to choose one love out of two. Before my mother married my dad, she went through something similar. She prayed to God for answers, but He never listened. Maybe He just wanted her to listen to her own thoughts and her own heart. In time, she found one quote by James C. Dobson that made her realise her choice."

Clara leant back into the wooden bench and tilted her head at Julian. She saw the sadness in those beautiful blue eyes. His untold story had her curious and weary. One day, she would ask him, and one day, she hoped the truth would set him free. Clara's hand settled on Julian's thigh, and she nodded for him to continue.

Julian breathed in deeply, his hand covered hers, and he said, *"Don't marry the person you think you can live with; marry only the individual you think you can't live without."*

The quote he recited had Clara's heart stopping. The honesty in those simple words had her eyes focused on her engagement ring. Once upon a time ago, his mother was in her position. Clara was too afraid to ask Julian about his mother's choice, but from what Clara remembered of her, she had loved her husband.

"Clara," he softly said, her name settling in the silent village before vanishing into the atmosphere. "My mother loved my father. She chose the only man she would ever love and the only man she couldn't live without. My mother died loving my father until her very last breath, and knowing that woman, she'll love him to eternity. You owe yourself some happiness. Let it be with the person you choose to spend the rest of your life with. Forget that I'm friends with Noel. Right here, right now, I'm your friend. Be strong and brave enough to choose the person you can't live without. As my friend, Clara, promise me that you'll do this for me."

Marry only the individual you think you can't live without.

The quote ran through her mind on a continuous loop. The one she couldn't live without would be the one she'd married. She had hopes that this one quote would lead her in the right direction. The same quote that had guided Julian's mother to his father.

"Thank you, Julian."

"I'm your friend, too, Clara. I don't like seeing you so conflicted. When you make a choice then tell the person you don't choose goodbye." The look of utter pain engulfed his eyes, and she knew he was talking about his own personal experiences. "I know it'll be hard, but say goodbye to the one you don't choose. Goodbyes are hard. But never getting one is worse. It leaves open a door that should have been bolted shut. It makes you believe and hope for things you shouldn't. Goodbyes let a person know that you are never coming back for them. Goodbyes put people out of their misery, no matter how much it hurts. Goodbye means you don't have to wait anymore." Julian's fists clenched so tight that she saw his knuckles turn a violent and bright white colour.

Julian never got his goodbye… I can't do that to either Noel or Liam.

Clara reached over and unclenched Julian's fist. She entwined her fingers with his and squeezed his calloused hand. He'll always be the foolish boy she once grew up with, not the heartbroken man who tried not to cry in her presence.

"I promise I'll give him a goodbye. Whomever I don't choose will get a proper goodbye. It's what he deserves."

Chapter THIRTEEN

Noel

*E*ight days had passed since he felt those lips touch his ever so slightly. August had quickly passed and September twenty-third was fast approaching. Three weeks and four days until her wedding. Clara had six more days before he'd demand an answer. Back in New York, he never said goodbye to her when she left with Liam. Goodbye meant the end, and Noel was sure they hadn't reached that yet.

The moment he'd returned from New York, things felt almost stale. His relationship had faltered and the heavy workload assigned by Gregson added to the strain. Both he and Andrea had senior management conducting performance reviews. He was waiting for word on whether he'd make it as a senior executive, and Andrea was waiting to hear if she had made it as the accounting firm's senior lawyer. Later nights at the office meant little time with each other.

In some way, Noel had appreciated the distractions that came with their performance reviews. The more he focused on meeting deadlines and efficiency levels, the less he thought about Clara's impending decision. As for intimacy, he had only gone as far as kissing Andrea. Every time they got close to having sex, a phone call from work would interrupt them or a flash of Clara's smile would break through. He was slowly pulling away from Andrea in hopes of something with Clara.

He loved Andrea, cared for her enough to have her move in. If things had been different and Noel had never returned to Melbourne, he'd spend forever with her. But the universe was funny like that. The universe seemed to decide how he'd love and whom he'd love. It was no longer a matter of choice anymore. His love for Clara burned through the iron gates that had once guarded his heart. After Valerie, he promised himself to no other until Clara entered his life and slammed that door in his face. *Twice.*

He remembered the last time he saw Valerie, even the last words he spoke to her. Throughout high school, he believed he'd marry her. Little did he know that the love he needed was the love hidden before his very own eyes. Clara Lawrence, little sister of his best friend. Noel wished that as a teenager he had once taken better care of her. But he didn't. The moment he left with Alex for the U.S., Noel felt free of Alex's clingy little sister.

That was before he knew of Clara's actual life. The loneliness behind those hopeful young eyes was a projection of deception. Noel played a part in her loneliness and leaving her unprotected from her parents. He was the one who deprived Clara of her brother's love. The selfish little things he did to keep Alex from leaving the U.S. had an effect on Clara, one that he didn't realise.

I'd take it all back, but it would mean I'd never have what I did with her. I'd rather live with the regret of losing her than never being able to love her.

He leant into the leather chair and breathed out. If he knew he'd come out loving Clara, he wouldn't have treated her so wrong. But those memories brought them together: the locket, the tulip, and the toucans. He believed they were *made* for each other. It just took them growing up to see that. Moving the reports aside, Noel looked at his surroundings. He was working towards a promotion he was going to give up for her.

I'd give this all up, just like last time.

He didn't want the large office, the view of the city, or even the high-end pay. He just wanted Clara. Noel spent his nights hoping that her time in Singapore didn't have her falling back in love with Liam. He should have stopped her, but he had to be selfless and let her go this time. He wanted Clara's choice to be the one she chose willingly and not the one he convinced her to make. He didn't want her to be convinced. Noel wanted Clara to know without a single hint of hesitation that it was him she spent forever with.

"Noel."

He glanced up to see Andrea by the door. The exhaustion on her face had him frowning. She walked into his office and sat on a chair in front of his desk.

Before he could ask her what was wrong, Andrea sighed out and announced, "I didn't make senior lawyer."

"Then who did? No one has more experience than you do. This is ridiculous. I'll go speak to Gregson myself."

Andrea let out a short laugh and shook her head. "Michael got the position. Jerk-bag got up in Gregson's daughter, and he got it. You don't need to do that, Noel. It'll ruin your chances of becoming a senior executive. I know how hard you've worked." She removed her jacket and placed it on the desk. "I'm going back to Phoenix tonight."

Noel flinched, surprised by what she had said.

"I hate this company, Noel. I hate Gregson, too. Dad has a few contracts lined up and wants me to have a look at them. I haven't been home since before I came here from D.C. I need a break from this place, and I need to see my family. I'd like you to come, but I don't want to risk your chances of that promotion. I'll only be gone a few weeks. Once I get back, we can celebrate you being an executive." Andrea stood up from the chair and picked up her jacket.

Noel stood up and went around the desk. He knew she was escaping because she'd missed the senior position. "Andrea, I'm sorry," he said and pulled her into his arms.

"You don't need to be. I'll be okay. Some time off is what I need. HR has been threatening me to take my vacation, so why not now. I had two contracts to draft up, and now that I'm on vacation, Michael's going to have a hell of a time replacing me for these contracts." The humour that glimmered in her eyes indicated that she seemed pleased with herself.

"You want me to take you to the airport? I can pack this all up and do it from home," Noel asked. Her blue eyes were clear and beautiful, but they weren't the eyes he longed for.

"Not necessary. I'm going to take a nice long hot bath before I catch my flight. I'm sorry that I'm leaving you here on your own. I know things between us have changed since we got back from New York, but I swear, I'm all yours once I get back from Phoenix." Andrea's love was one he didn't deserve. Not when he loved Clara more than life itself.

When she comes back, I'll end things, even if Clara doesn't choose me.

fter a visit to the bar down the block, Noel unlocked his front door to a quiet apartment. Andrea had called him after he left the office shortly after nine p.m. She had arrived safely in Arizona and Noel had found himself in a bar. The moment he entered his apartment, he dropped his briefcase and removed his tie to join his briefcase on the floor. He walked to the fridge, opened it, and took out a cold beer.

Then Noel settled into the couch in the lounge room and decided to continue where he left off after he left the bar, and that was to continue drinking. Noel pulled out his phone and stared at the screen. He did nothing but keep an eye on his phone since Clara had left New York. Unlocking it, he pulled up her messages. Once she had made a decision, she would find her way to him, but he heard nothing from her. Noel saw the last message he ever sent Clara.

Noel: *I'll always love you, Clara. Always.*

And that promise went fulfilled. He still loved her and would always love her. It was a matter of her heart. Her heart's choice. Liam offered her a marriage, money, and a life in Melbourne. Noel could only offer Clara his love and a life together. He'd leave Boston for her; that had always been his intentions. He didn't have millions like Liam, but he made enough to provide for her.

I can make her happy. I did once.

Noel placed his untouched beer on the coffee table and let

the alcohol already in his system do the talking.

Noel: *Please find your way back to me, Clara. I love you.*

After he pressed send, Noel reached for his beer and chugged it down. He wasn't going to expect a reply. He knew he was making it harder for her, but he felt like she needed a reminder. Noel wanted to talk. His first instinct was Alex, but he never felt comfortable talking about Clara to him. He thought of his co-worker, Damien, but he had moved out to the Florida office. Noel knew he could turn to the one person who had helped him and Clara last year.

He searched through his contacts until he got to Rob's number. Noel leant into the leather couch as he waited for Rob to pick up but was only met with the voicemail. Noel tried once more but had the same outcome. He looked at the clock to see it was one a.m. in Boston and only five thirty p.m. back in Melbourne. Sighing, he went back into his contacts and decided to call someone else. He needed to hear from one of his childhood friends. He listened to the phone ring until he picked up.

"Noel?"

He heard heavy pants on the other end. "Max, what's up?"

"Not a good time, man!" Max let out a groan, and Noel rolled his eyes.

"Babe, stop. I'm on the phone," Max breathed out.

Noel shook his head and pulled his feet up on the coffee table. "Dude, isn't it like five o'clock there? You want me to call back when you're finished?"

He heard movement until Max said, "Nah, you never call me. It must be important. I'll, uhh, get back to her in a minute. We needed a break anyway."

"You sure? I don't want to be a cock block. If you need this lay, then hang up," Noel said.

Max laughed. "I mean, you are being one, but when my best friend needs me, I'm there. We made that pact when we started kindergarten, so what's—"

"Max, do you want anything to eat?" the female's voice asked, cutting off Max.

Noel tensed.

That voice.

The line went quiet and Noel was in disbelief. He sat up from the couch and shook his head. He ran his fingers through his hair, and he couldn't understand what would make Max run to her.

"Noel, listen, I can explain," Max quickly said.

"What the fuck, Max? *Her.* Really?" Noel heard the disbelief in his own voice.

"Don't tell Alex, please!"

The plea in Max's voice had Noel wincing. He didn't want to be stuck in the middle, but he understood that this was most likely Rob and Max's position when he was with Clara. But these circumstances were different. It was *her.*

"Seriously, Max. What the hell happened to bros before hoes?" Noel lectured as he stood up from the couch and walked to the kitchen for another beer. Max was quiet. Noel opened his fridge and took out the remaining beers of the six-pack.

"Yeah? What about bros before their little sisters? Double *fucking* standard, Noel!" Max yelled back.

Noel slammed the beer on the counter. "Don't you fucking say that, you asshole! Clara is not a ho. It's different and you know it. Don't you fucking even put Clara close to *that.* What I had with Clara is nothing compared to what you have with her, not even close. Don't you remember what she did? To Alex, to all of us! She's bloody trouble, and you know it. Let me remind you what she did. She faked a pregnancy to keep Alex. She cheated on him and manipulated him into thinking she was pregnant. She even claimed she had a miscarriage when Alex started asking to go to her ultrasounds. How could you sleep with that? All she does is ruin people's lives!"

The memories of their final year of high school flashed before him. The pain Alex went through. The nights Noel spent making sure his best friend didn't do anything stupid.

Sarah ruined our lives back in high school. The amount of times she'd tried to end my relationship with Valerie. Yet Val stayed best friends with her. I'll never understand.

"You want to know why I fell in love with Clara? Because she isn't manipulative. She loves and cares, she is selfless, and she has the power to make me whole with just her damn smile. Clara has this kindness and she makes me want to be a better man. Tell me Sarah does that to you, and then we'll be on the same page. I came out being *in* love with Clara. I came out wanting to throw it all away for her. I came out prepared to propose to her!" Noel confessed. The stings in his eyes burned as he remembered the night he was going to propose and promise Clara forever.

"You were going to propose?" The disbelief in Max's voice confirmed that Rob had kept Noel's secret.

"The night of your cousin's birthday. I had the ring and then Clara ended it before I could ask." His heart constricted as memories of the worst night of his life enveloped him.

"I had no idea. Does Alex know how serious you were about Clara?" Max asked.

"No, he doesn't. It was meant to be the night I finally got to call Clara *mine* so freely. It was meant to be the night Clara and I started a life together." He balled his fist tightly, ignoring the stinging in his eyes.

"I'm sorry, Noel. Jesus, I had no idea you wanted to marry her and that you had a ring. Clara is no way like Sarah. I shouldn't have compared them. I caved in and acted on my childhood feelings for her. You know how much I've liked Sarah. But Alex got to her first. I just see more to her than everyone else. You're right. It's nothing like what you and Clara have. You both love each other. Sarah and I are just fuck buddies. But don't tell Alex. I'll tell him. Working for Dad's law firm sent me to a dark place, Noel. Sarah was there and I let her in."

There was exhaustion laced in Max's voice, and Noel knew the pressures of his job in the family business had driven Max into Sarah's evil grasps.

"Just don't get attached, Max. The moment you start falling for her, remember what she can do. She's trouble. I know you've liked her since we were kids, but she has venom running that cold heart of hers. I don't want you to go through what Alex did. She causes too much pain in people's lives. Just be careful." As mad as Noel was at Max for even comparing their situations, he wasn't one to judge. They both went behind Alex's back.

"Just make sure you tell him, Max. He's in love with Keira. He'll be okay just—" The beeps of another call coming through interrupted him. Noel looked to see Alex's name flash on his screen. "Speaking of Alex, he's calling. I had better get this. He never calls me this late. Be careful with Sarah, Max. I love you, man, but I don't want what she did to Alex to happen to you. She almost destroyed him. Don't get attached. Let it just be sex between the two of you." Noel hoped his warning would burn itself into Max's brain.

"Will do. Thanks, Noel. I'll tell Alex. I'm sorry that I said that stuff about Clara. I want that one day. The love you have for her. I want that," Max said.

Noel smiled. Loving Clara was the best of him. "I'll see you, Max."

"Wait!" Max said, stopping Noel from hanging up. "Why'd you call? Must have been important."

Noel picked up a beer and sighed. "Just needed advice. I'm breaking up with Andrea when she comes back from Arizona."

The line went quiet once more.

"You're breaking up with Andrea? What? Why? Really?" Max asked in disbelief, and he almost sounded relieved. "Are you sure? I mean, if I were you, I wouldn't... Andrea's lovely... *seems* lovely."

Noel noticed the nervousness in Max's voice as he uncapped his beer. "I'm sure, Max. Whether Clara chooses me or not, Andrea deserves someone who loves her without a hint of hesitation. I love only Clara. Andrea needs a man who will love her, and I can't be that man, Max." No truer words were said. His mind was made, and he would let go of Andrea. Noel heard the beeps of Alex's call, and he knew it had to be urgent. "Got to run, Max," Noel said and hung up before Max could say goodbye.

Max's nervousness and interest in his impending breakup with Andrea had him curious, but he dropped it. Noel walked over to his couch and sat on the slightly warm cushion. He saw that he had several missed calls from Alex and quickly called him back. Alex picked up the call in a few rings, and Noel could hear him instructing Keira.

"Noel! I've been trying to call you!" Alex sounded irritated and flustered.

"Sorry, I was on the phone to Max. What's up?" he asked as he settled properly into the couch. Noel wasn't going to be the one to tell Alex about Max and Sarah. Alex deserved to hear it from Max.

"I just got off the phone with Clara."

Alex's words had Noel's heart stopping. His grip on the beer bottle tightened as he held his breath.

"She's got cold feet, Noel. She called me hysterically, and she was mumbling about how she doesn't think she can go through with the wedding. She didn't tell me everything. Instead, she wanted to speak to Keira. The next thing I know, Keira's in tears and demanding I take her to Boston tonight. I couldn't get flights for tonight considering it's almost two in the morning. We're driving up now. Put the kettle on and we'll see you in three or so hours."

Clara

She read his messages over and over again until she fell asleep. The first thing she did this morning was to check that the message Noel had sent her was actually real. Getting it was something she hadn't expected. Especially while out celebrating dinner with Liam and his co-workers. Even though she saw little of Liam in Singapore, he managed to secure the new investment contract. By the time he got his signature on the dotted line, their stay in Singapore was over. Clara sat in the hotel room waiting more than she had explored Singapore. The only time she'd managed to see the beautiful country was when they were leaving it. Sighing, Clara looked down at her phone.

Noel: *I'll always love you, Clara. Always*

Noel: *Please find your way back to me, Clara. I love you.*

She had never deleted his final message. The same message he had sent her before he left Melbourne. She didn't have the heart to. Clara left it on her phone and as time and new messages passed, it moved to the bottom of her inbox. Noel's message last night had her heart stopping. She had to excuse herself in the middle of dinner and rush to the ladies' room. She had never expected those words.

Find my way back to Noel?

When she checked Boston's time, she saw it was one a.m. and put it down to him being drunk. But something in her heart told her that he spoke the truth when he was intoxicated. The next thing she did was call Alex. She couldn't walk back into the restaurant and bottle up Noel's words. His words had her doubt going through with her wedding. Her wedding plans were submerging her and making it difficult to breathe. She was having second thoughts when it came to marrying Liam. Clara told Keira of Noel's message and her cold feet. Keira's soft and understanding voice calmed her enough to sit through the rest of Liam's dinner.

Clara glanced to her left to see Violetta's Bridal Boutique, one of Melbourne's most prestigious bridal boutiques on Hoddle Street. Somehow, Jo managed a private wedding dress consultation, and Clara knew the prices of the dresses Violetta's was offering. From Alex Perry to Lusan Mandongus and Vera Wang, Violetta's had every famous brand, and if they didn't, they would order it. Clara didn't need an expensive dress. When she was a little girl, a small local bridal shop in the Berwick Village always had her hopeful.

Removing the keys from the ignition, Clara opened the driver's side door then walked around the car and stepped onto the concrete footpath, locking her car behind her. She peered into the windows of the cream painted store. Inside and already looking at dresses were Stevie, Annie, and Ally — three of her five bridesmaids. Josie had work and couldn't make it, and Keira was in New York. When she opened the boutique door, the bell rang and all her friends had turned and smile at her. It was early in the morning, but she had to do the consultation before she met up with Liam at the church.

Jo's constant messages and calls had Clara reaching her limit. She knew how behind she was on flowers, the seating arrangements, the choice in music… the entire wedding. Noel gave her time to decide, but the choice in happily ever after played heavy on her heart. It wasn't a choice she wanted to make, but her deadline was fast approaching.

She would be losing someone. It was a matter of whom. Exhausted over the meticulous dealings that came with Jo and her wedding, Clara turned off her phone. Getting married was meant to be a happy time in her life, yet it felt like a chore. One she didn't fault Liam for but herself instead. Clara dropped her phone in her handbag and shook her head. She needed to concentrate, and she needed to focus. The choice she was about to make would be easier than the decision Noel wanted from her.

"Ready to try on wedding dresses?" Annie asked with an excited smile.

Clara's mouth twitched as she managed a controlled smile. She noticed that Stevie, Annie, and Ally all held champagne glasses in their hands.

"I need champagne and cake first. More champagne than cake... actually just the champagne." Clara hadn't missed the glare Stevie shot her, but she only shook her head and reached for the glass Ally handed her.

"Thanks," Clara muttered and downed it in one go.

"Whoa, tough night?" Ally asked with a raised eyebrow.

Clara held it out for another glassful, and Ally poured it willingly. "You could say that. Liam's dinner was filled with so much investment jargon that I started to get a headache trying to keep up."

Ally let out a laugh. "Yeah, family dinner is worse. When you get Dad and Liam talking about the family business, I get this insane urge to shoot them both."

Clara nodded her head in agreement as she remembered the first time she had met Liam and Ally's parents. David O'Connor was quite the business mogul and where Liam got his looks. Though Liam lacked the Irish accent from growing up in Australia, his father had a noticeable one. Ally got her looks from their beautiful English mother, Imogen. Besides the fact that David shoved the idea of offspring down her throat, Clara loved them both. They were what she imagined parents were like.

"Are you bringing a date for the wedding, Ally?" Annie asked.

Clara squinted at her sister-in-law-to-be.

Ally sighed. "Sadly, no."

"That has got to be a joke, right?" Clara asked, bewildered.

"Girls, Sydney's not what you believe it to be. The Cross is a hell hole, and Bondi is fresh out of talent. Take me back to Spain where the men were actually men. How about you, Stevie?"

Ally asked dodging further questions.

"She's bringing Rob!" Annie gleefully said.

"Who's Rob?" Ally asked as she sliced a piece of cake.

Clara raised her brow at Stevie for a 'please explain.' "My brother's best friend. Stevie's just afraid to admit she's interested. Ask him to be your date for my wedding, Stevie. If you don't, you can't come," she warned.

Well, Rob and Alex are best friends. It's safer if I didn't mention Noel.

"Drop it, Clara. Rob and I are not happening."

Before Clara could say more, she heard the sound of heels down the stairs.

"You must be Clara." A woman in her early thirties interrupted them with a smile as she held out her hand. Her black curls were pinned back and her blouse tucked into her black pencil skirt.

"Yes, that's me. Thank you for agreeing to a private consultation. I know how far in advance you need to book to even step foot in your store." Clara shook her hand.

"Not every day an O'Connor gets engaged. When the news broke out that it happened, trust me, every bridal shop has been trying to secure you. Lucky I grew up in Sydney and I personally know Jo. So, the honour is all mine. I'm Violetta."

*V*ioletta had lined up a freestanding rail of wedding dresses in the dressing room. Clara sat on the small seat as her eyes swept over them. The large curtained off dress room felt small around her. It was fun going through them while they were on hangers, but now that she had to try them all, the doubt in her grew. She couldn't stop thinking of the one person she shouldn't be thinking of. Clara couldn't control the gasps she took as the air failed to reach her lungs.

"Clara," Stevie said softly as she peered into the dressing room. "Are you okay?"

Clara stared at the wedding dresses and shook her head. "Stevie—"

"I sent the other girls to check out bridesmaid dresses. I told them Josie would sue our asses once she becomes a practiced lawyer if we chose orange. Let's talk. The moment I saw you, I knew something happened." Stevie sat next to Clara on the small seat and took in the wedding dresses with her.

"Noel texted me last night during my dinner with Liam. It's messed me up. I called Alex and spoke to Keira and… I'm having doubts. I don't know if I should marry Liam, but I want to. I don't know what to do. I love Liam but Noel—"

"Rob and I kissed," Stevie announced.

"What?" Clara exclaimed with a grin on her face. She knew Stevie was distracting her.

It happened!

"There. I knew that would get a smile on your face." A pleased smile overtook Stevie's face.

"How? What? When?"

Stevie laughed at Clara's eagerness. "We were making Jewel jealous at PJ's and I lost at darts. The next thing I know, we're kissing and we left the pub…" Stevie trailed off.

Clara was in shock. "You guys had sex?"

"No." Stevie laughed. "I mean I wanted to. I got him almost naked, but I kept having flashes of Thailand, and I had to stop myself. I've never had this problem before. Something about Rob brings it all back and it's scary."

Clara grabbed Stevie's hands in hers and squeezed it to reassure her.

"How about this. You'll try on dresses and I'll try to make things work with Rob. What do you say? Forget that you're marrying Liam and just try on all these dresses." Stevie got up and ran her fingers along the hangers of the dresses.

"Stevie, wait." Clara stood up. "I want you to be my maid of honour."

Stevie froze and turned to her, the shock on her face had Clara smiling. "You want *me* to be *your* maid of honour? But Annie is more qualified than I am."

Clara shook her head. "Stevie, you've been there for me for everything, including the saddest parts of my life. But this time, I want you to be there when I get married. I've never had a best friend like you. You know my struggles and you know my pain. You are more than qualified to be my maid of honour. I want you there in my bridal suit to hand me those tulips just before I walk down the aisle."

Tears pooled Stevie's eyes, and she pulled Clara into her arms. "I would absolutely love to be your maid of honour."

Clara smiled knowing she'd made the right decision.

Then Annie and Ally walked into the dressing room holding up bridesmaid dresses. "Let's get you into some dresses, Clara," Ally beamed.

Clara parked her Audi just in front of *St. Ignatius Church*. She'd sold her Lexus when the engine blew and Liam convinced Alex that she needed an upgrade. The sale from her beloved Lexus added to the account she had for Alex. Her brother had argued, but Liam won once he'd said it was his turn to provide for her.

Stepping out of her new car, Clara smiled at herself. She did it; she chose her wedding dress and she had a maid of honour. Cementing plans for her wedding had her leaning towards Liam, but she hadn't made a proper decision. She couldn't rush her choice. The few hours spent trying dresses was enough for the one glass of champagne she did drink to leave her body. Clara locked her car and started to walk up to one of Australia's oldest churches. It was like a fairy tale to see the church.

Liam had wanted a traditional wedding and she would have loved a wedding out in a beautiful garden, but seeing the church for herself, she was glad she hadn't argued. The church was breathtaking. She could see herself running down the few steps with Liam holding her hand. She was starting to envision more and more of her wedding with Liam. It frightened her slightly, but she was starting to move on from her second-guessing.

Clara noticed Liam and the minister at the top of the small steps by the large wooden doors. The grin on Liam's face was blissful, and Clara found herself smiling at him. She looked at her engagement ring and felt the warmth in her chest. Clara made her way towards them while they spoke. She was only metres from the steps when her phone vibrated in her hand. She peeked down to see Noel's name appear on the screen.

Clara stopped and her heart ached at his name. She peered up to see Liam laughing with the minister. Closing her eyes tightly, she swiped across the screen and answered his call.

"Noel, this is not a great time," Clara said, trying to control the imbalance in her voice.

"Clara, you *need* to come back to the U.S." The begging in his voice had Clara's chest burning in pain.

"What?" Clara breathed out.

Liam's eyes met hers. As she listened to Noel's reason for her return, she couldn't stop the tears from falling. Her heart broke as she heard Noel's own cries. Clara hung up the phone the moment Liam was by her side.

"Sweetheart, what's wrong?" The worry in his voice made the ache in her worse.

"I'm sorry, Liam. I-I have to go back to the U.S. I'm *so* sorry."

Chapter
FOURTEEN

Noel

It had been over a day since he had called Clara, begging her to come back to the States. The moment he'd heard her voice, he had pleaded for her return before he even said anything. Noel looked at his phone and knew she'd be here soon. He wanted to be there when she landed, but he couldn't get himself to a cab. He was a wreck, and he couldn't stop the pain he was in. He couldn't leave where he sat.

The last thirty-six hours had been hell. No matter how much he wished he could make the sounds stop, he couldn't. Those beeps wouldn't go away; even when he slept, they seemed louder, almost mocking him. The constant noise reminded him that it should have been him. He wanted a trade with the universe. He wanted it to be different. Those beeps mocked him and ridiculed him. They tortured him.

As much as I hate the sound, they're keeping Alex alive.

Noel glanced at the monitor as it continued to signal the heart's activity for Alex. Each spike made him hopeful, but with every hour that passed, he wanted to grab Alex by the hospital gown and beg him to wake up. Noel needed him; they were brothers, and he couldn't imagine life without Alex. The idea hurt him as much as the idea of living a life without Clara. They were a package deal.

"You better wake up, you weak shit! Or I swear to you, Alex, I'm going to kill you myself. You aren't leaving me here, and you sure as hell aren't leaving Clara and Keira. If you're taking a break from life, well, break time's fucking over. We need you, Alex!" The stinging in his eyes returned.

Fuck!

"Jesus Christ, you don't deserve this! Neither of you deserves this. If I hadn't sent her that message, then you'd be getting ready for work. Just wake up, Alex. Just wake up!" Noel begged, but the constant beeps from the heart monitor machine was the only answer he received. He leapt out of the visitor's seat and paced around Alex's ICU room.

Noel stood by the bed and looked at his best friend. Alex had a bandage wrapped around his head from the doctors opening up his skull to relieve the swelling of his brain. Besides a few cuts and internal bleeding, the doctors had said he'd be okay. But through the night, Alex's heart had started to beat erratically. The swelling in the brain was too much for Alex's body, and the doctors had placed him in a medically-induced coma to help his body mend itself. It was temporary, and the doctors told Noel that when the swelling went down, they'd wake him up.

If I had told them to wait until morning, they wouldn't be out that late. That drunk driver wouldn't have gone through that red light. Alex wouldn't be in a goddamn coma.

He placed the blame on himself. It all started with that intoxicated and truthful message to Clara. The moment he got off the phone with Alex, Noel drank. He had beer after beer waiting for them. He'd passed out and woke up late afternoon to see calls from the Emergency Room of Yale-New Haven Hospital. Alex and Keira had just made it to New Haven when a drunk driver had hit Alex's side. The driver was lucky and only suffered a broken nose, whiplash, and some other gashes. After being hit, Alex's car veered off and hit a pole on Keira's side. Keira was lucky that the pole had hit the back of the car, but she was badly broken.

They made it to Connecticut. They made it sixty miles. I should have told them not to come. I should have told them that it didn't matter, but I wanted them to come. I was selfish, and it came with consequences.

The moment Noel got the voicemails, he had gotten into his car and drove down to New Haven. The hospital had called the last number Alex had dialled and that was Noel. He wished he hadn't gotten so drunk that he slept until the afternoon. But what good would it have done if he were still drunk. He ignored going to work and drove to Connecticut, a state he had never visited. Noel paced around Alex's bed and kept his eyes on the machine. No slight changes but he had to remind himself that a constant and levelled heart rate was good.

"I'm sorry, Alex. I'm sorry you're lying here when God knows you don't deserve it. I should be lying in that bed. I should be the one in a fucking coma. All our lives, you've put me before yourself. I swear it won't be like that anymore. Wake up and let me be the one to look out for you this time." Noel breathed out and ran his hand through his messy hair. He glanced at the drip before he looked down at Alex's unconscious body.

"I'm sorry I hurt Clara. I *never* wanted to. I'm sorry I couldn't keep her happy. I'm sorry I couldn't stop her. I'm sorry I never got the chance to be the one to look out for her. I'm so sorry, Alex. Wake up and let me have the chance to one day ask you for permission to marry her if she chooses me. Just give me a chance to make up for all the wrongs I've done to you, Alex. I can't lose you, not after I already lost her." Noel wiped the tear from his cheek and silently prayed that God offered Alex a chance at the happy life he deserved.

*A*lex never moved. Not a single twitch or stir. All Noel saw him do was breathe and that was only from the ventilator. He checked his phone and knew he would have to leave to see Keira soon. She would want to know of Alex's condition. The doctors made sure to stress that Keira needed to stay in bed and her parents were determined to keep her in it. They didn't want Keira to panic or open up her stitches when she saw Alex.

He checked his phone and hoped Clara would call him.

Their phone call was brief, and she was silent. Noel cried over her voice and then he broke down when he told her of Alex and Keira's car accident. Noel knew a nurse on duty, and she had agreed to make an exception for him and Clara to stay past visiting hours. The nurse on duty was the wife of one of his clients. Noel would go back to his hotel room and shower before grabbing food and returning to the visitor's chair he had claimed. He had made the calls back to Melbourne to tell everyone of the accident. When Noel looked up at the freshly changed drip, he heard the sound of heels stop outside the room and he turned around.

Clara.

The first thing he had noticed were her red eyes laced in disbelief. Those eyes locked on his and his heart began to break. He looked down to see a small suitcase in her hand. Clara peered over at Alex. The moment she saw Alex linked up to the machines and in the bed, she dropped her suitcase. Clara sobbed and Noel ran to her. He wrapped his arms around her and tried to hold back his own cries. Clara's arms wound tightly around his waist as she cried into his chest. Each cry pierced his heart, and he let his own tears run freely.

I need to pull myself together. I have to be strong for her.

"This can't be real, Noel," Clara whispered; the devastation was clear in her voice.

He only held her tighter. He couldn't face this alone. They stood there in the doorway of the hospital room, crying. He would have liked to have Clara back in his arms under better circumstances, but he needed her. Noel couldn't lose them both.

Just as he was about to unwrap his arms from around her body, Clara held him even tighter. "Don't let me go, Noel. Not yet. If you leave me, I'll break down. I won't be able to pick myself up. I need you right now. I need you to tell me he's going to be okay and that this is just some sick joke to get me back."

Noel blinked away the tears and his throat tightened as he tried to form words. "I wish it was, Clara. I wish this were a fucking ruse to get you back, baby. I wish it was."

*N*oel held Clara's tea in his hand. The coffee machine was down the hall and he had to leave her sitting on the white visitor's chair next to Alex. Clara didn't say much. Instead, she just cried and held Noel's hand. The way she touched him made him hopeful, but it was under the wrong circumstances. She needed support and that was what he would give her.

"Noel, how's she doing?" Morgan, the night duty nurse, asked.

He stared at the takeout cup and sighed. "She won't talk much, but it's better than what I thought would happen. Alex is all she has and..." Noel trailed off and Morgan gave him a smile.

"The doctors say he'll wake up, Noel. It's medically induced, remember?" Morgan placed her hand on his arm, and he nodded.

"I know," he replied and then left her to return to her duties.

Noel walked up to Alex's room and noticed Clara standing next to the bed, her hands entwined with Alex's fingers. He leant on the doorframe and watched her.

"Please don't leave me, Alex. I know I've been a heavy burden on your life, but I need you and I love you. If you go... if you leave me here... I have *nothing*." Clara's choked sobs caused his tears to fall and his throat tightened again.

"I know I've made you unhappy. I make stupid choices and you always have to pick up my mess. You've been more of a father than a big brother, but I need you to be both in my life. I need you to wake up and tell me you're proud of me, that you love me, and I need you to call me 'kiddo' again. I want to hear your voice, I want to feel you hug me, and I want to hear your laugh. Please wake up. I can't do this without you. I can't live a life without you. *Please.*"

The begging in Clara's whispers had the tears running down Noel's face. It was breaking his heart to see her so broken. He pushed off the doorframe and entered the room. Clara turned around at the sound of his footsteps. The tears that ran down her cheeks pained him. She let go of Alex's hand and walked into Noel's arms, crying. She clung to him. He held her for a minute, careful not to spill tea down her back. Noel's left hand stroked the back of Clara's head. He'd hold her for as long as she needed him.

Clara removed her head from his chest and looked up at him with those sad eyes that told him she was broken. She sniffed and closed her eyes tightly. When she opened them, her shiny eyes were set on his. Noel moved his left hand from the back of her head to her cheek, wiping her tears away.

"I can't lose him, Noel. I can't lose Alex, not after I lost you. I can't lose everyone I've *ever* loved." Her words made his heart ache for her. She spoke of how she lost him when he lost her.

Noel bent down, placed a kiss on her forehead, and wrapped his arms back around her. "I'm not going anywhere, Clara. You'll *never* lose me again. I promise. I'm here to stay. I'm not ever letting you go, baby. Never again."

*B*y the time he had another cup of tea in his hand and returned to the room, Clara was asleep in the chair next to Alex's bed. She had moved it as close to the bed as possible. Her head rested on Alex's hand as she slept.

I need to get her in a proper bed.

He looked at the time on his phone and it was just after twelve p.m., but Clara would be jet lagged considering it was four in the morning back in Melbourne. Noel crouched down next to her and smiled at the sight of her. She looked at peace when she slept and that was what he had loved waking up to. Noel set his palm on Clara's cheek and let his thumb stroke her soft skin. She snuggled into his touch and he sighed.

"Clara," he said softly.

She opened her eyes and looked up at him. He saw the exhaustion on her face. He removed his hand from her cheek and then took her hand.

"Come on, I want you in a bed to rest up. You've had a long day, and you need to sleep."

Clara squeezed his hand and sat up, rubbing her eye with

her free hand. "I don't want to leave him," she said looking at Alex. Noel didn't want to either, but he needed a shower and Clara needed to rest.

"I know, but he wouldn't want you sleeping on that chair. Come, I have a hotel room. You can take a nap, and when you wake up, I'll take you back."

Clara's head fell as she sighed out. "Okay, just promise me we're coming back the moment I wake up."

Noel kissed her temple and said, "Of course."

Setting down Clara's suitcase in the carpeted hallway, Noel dug into his pocket for the key to his hotel suite. His hand never left Clara's as they entered the foyer of Omni New Haven Hotel. Noel inserted the card into the electronic reader until he heard the door unlock. Then he placed the key between his lips as he bent down and picked up Clara's small suitcase.

"Noel, you don't know where that's been," Clara lectured.

He turned to see a slight smile on her face. It was the first since she had arrived in Connecticut. "I live on the wild side, Clara," he said trying not to drop the keycard from his mouth.

Clara giggled, and it was music to his ears. "Don't try to sell me that. I know you. You may be an asshole, but you'll always be the boy who gave me that tulip." Clara smiled and took the key card from his mouth. "Don't be anyone but you. That's who I once fell in love with."

Her words gave him hope. He smiled and pushed the door open. He tugged Clara into the hotel room and closed the door behind him. He set Clara's suitcase by the door and watched her take in the large hotel room. A large king-size bed sat in the middle of the room against the wall; a large LCD TV was on the wall opposite the bed and the curtains were drawn back. Clara walked up to the large windows and gazed out.

Noel made his way behind her and wrapped his arms around her waist. Clara didn't push him away as she took in the view of New Haven.

"See those Gothic buildings over there?" he asked as he removed one hand from her body and pointed.

"Yeah," she said.

The wonder in her voice had him smiling. "That's Yale University."

Clara smiled at the sight of the large campus. "It's beautiful," she breathed.

Not as beautiful as you are.

Clara spun around in his arms and kept her eyes on his chest. She breathed out and Noel tensed as her hands gripped his forearms.

"Look at me," he instructed.

Her watery eyes met his as a clenching sensation heated his chest at the sight.

"He's going to be okay. It's Alex, Clara. He won't give up," Noel said to reassure her.

Clara nodded and stepped out of his touch as she approached the couch.

"What are you doing?" he asked, raising a brow at her.

Clara ignored him and took off her shoes. She then sat on the couch before she lay on it.

"Uh-uh, Clara, you are not sleeping on that couch." He made his way to her, but she had already closed her eyes.

"This is *your* hotel room, Noel. You paid for that bed, not me. Tomorrow I'll get a room for myself. Let me just nap on the couch, please." Her voice had softened as she finished her sentence. He knew she was quickly succumbing to exhaustion.

Noel sighed knowing that he shouldn't wake her. Instead, he sat down on the floor next to the couch.

I'll be here the moment she wakes.

Clara

The warmth she felt had Clara opening her eyes to find a blanket wrapped around her. Rubbing at her face, she stared at the blanket and let out a yawn.

"Mornin'," Noel greeted.

Clara sat up and looked around the hotel room. She felt horrible, but that was the best sleep she'd had in the last forty-eight hours. Her gaze landed on the couch to her right.

"Why am I in your bed?" Clara asked as she threw back the

quilt.

"Because I refuse to let you sleep on that couch." Noel smiled and sat on the mattress. He took her hand in his and she let him. His touch told her that she could overcome the pain of Alex's accident.

"Noel," she said annoyed that she hadn't woken up on the couch.

"Clara, you're staying in this room with me. I want to make sure that I'm here when you need me because I need you here. I'm not okay, and I'm trying to be strong for you, but I can't. I'm going to break down. I need you with me to bring me back, Clara. I can't do this alone."

She melted at his words.

"Just let me have the couch then," she said.

Noel shook his head. "Absolutely not. That is non-negotiable. You are sleeping in this bed. I'll be on the couch."

Clara huffed out and nodded her head in agreement. "Wait! Did you say it was morning?" She glared at him.

"Uhh, yeah. I let you sleep because I saw how exhausted you were. I had Morgan, the night duty nurse, keep an eye on Alex. I know you wanted to nap, but it's better if you had some proper sleep," he explained.

Clara ran her hand through her tangled curls and gave up. She should be angry because she needed to be with Alex, but she finally had decent sleep.

"I must look horrendous," she said matter-of-factly.

Noel placed both hands on her cheeks and brought her face close to his. Her eyes widened in surprise.

"You look beautiful, Clara," he said softly before his hands left her face and swept her hair away.

He's only called me beautiful once before, and that was after I lost my virginity to him.

"Take me to the hospital please, Noel. I need to be with Alex."

He nodded. Clara got off the bed and walked over to the bathroom.

"You've always been beautiful, Clara. I never said it enough and I should have," Noel said regretfully.

Clara tried to block his words from entering her heart, but it was a failed attempt. So, instead, she didn't reply.

They took a detour to Starbucks and had their coffees and muffins to go. Clara had kept quiet in the car as they drove to Yale-New Haven Hospital. She sent a message to Liam telling him that she was safe and apologised for her abrupt leaving. Liam understood and asked her if she wanted him there, but Clara had refused. She wanted him to focus on the wedding and on the company. Part of her didn't want the drama of having Noel and Liam in the same state again, and another part of her wanted to be alone with Noel.

Noel's phone call tore apart the world she once knew. Alex and Keira's car accident was her fault. If she hadn't called them about Noel's message, they would have been safe. They'd both be home and not in hospital. Stepping out of the elevator, Noel took her hand. She didn't pull away; she felt connected to her brother through him. Her eyes stared at their hands, and she remembered how perfect she felt being with him back in Melbourne. Once upon a time, Noel was her world.

I gave him up.

Clara swallowed the large lump in her throat. Noel sensed her hesitation and he stopped them by the nurse's desk.

"You okay?" he asked worriedly. The sight of her brother in that bed made her sick, but she had to visit him. She wanted to be there when he woke, and she wanted to see Keira, too.

"Yeah, I'm just not used to seeing Alex like this. He's always smiling and calling me 'kiddo' and —" Clara stopped as the tears came back. The pain hit her so fast that all air left her lungs.

"Hey," Noel said as he stepped in front of her and cupped her face in his hands. "He's going to wake up, Clara. We need to just give him time."

For a second, his eyes claimed hers. The deep, beautiful green had her momentarily breathless. The sound of a squeaking gurney broke that trance, and she nodded at him. Noel took her hand and led her to Alex's room.

Clara watched their feet walk in sync, perfectly in time with each other's. They were just outside her brother's room when

Noel squeezed her hand.

"*YOU!*"

Clara's head snapped up when she heard the voice yell and Noel's hand tightened around hers. The moment they entered Alex's room Clara couldn't breathe.

Oh, God, no.

"You did this! This is all *your* fault!"

Clara closed her eyes as the screamed words dug dip into her chest.

"Gillian, please lower your voice."

She opened her eyes at the low voice she had only really known in her childhood.

"You did this. Because of you, *my* son is in this hospital bed! If you weren't such trouble, he wouldn't be hooked up to all these machines. All you've done is ruin our lives and now look at what you've done."

Noel tensed beneath her touch, and she let go of his hand. Her father looked at them and blinked.

"I don't want you here! Get out!" her mother yelled.

Clara winced.

"Gillian, I called you to see your son *not* to yell at Clara." There was a warning in Noel's voice, and Clara felt his protectiveness.

"No, Noel. She's right. This is *my* fault. I'm the reason why Alex is in that bed," Clara said. She didn't dare look at her mother. Instead, she focused on her father. This man had once loved her before he left her, too.

Her father looked away with the same expression he had given her throughout the years until she had moved out. He was ashamed of her.

"Let me say goodbye to Alex. I won't be here when you're here. I'll let you have your time with him," Clara said to her father, trying to hold back her sobs.

"Gillian, let's go outside for a minute," her father said.

They walked past Alex's bed until Clara's mother looked her in the eye. Gillian glanced at Noel before she returned her attention back to Clara. The hate in her mother's eyes always made her flinch.

I'll never have her love.

Gillian took a deep breath. "I wish you were *never* born.

This wouldn't have happened, and I'd have my son back. We'd all be happy and you wouldn't be running around ruining people's lives."

Clara winced. It hurt her more than she was willing to admit. It wasn't new, but this time she was laying on the malice thick. Clara didn't respond. She feared she'd cry and look weak.

"Gillian," Noel warned.

He seemed to know more than he should, and Clara ignored it. Her mother walked past her, and her father stood in front of her. Clara waited. She still hoped he'd love her, but as he stood there, the disappointment was clear in his eyes.

I'll never win back his love.

"It's time you say goodbye to your brother," her father announced.

It felt like they were taking Alex from her. They wouldn't let her see him after this, and Clara knew it. Alex couldn't fight them this time, and they were taking advantage of it. Her father exited the room, and she breathed out. The white walls of the room started to encroach, and she felt ill at the thought of them taking Alex from her.

No. I need more. I haven't waited two years to see them for this!

Clara ignored the words Noel was saying and walked out of Alex's room. She could see her father's back as he made his way towards the elevator. Determination fuelled her courage and Clara needed answers.

"Daddy!" she yelled.

He stopped in his tracks and stood there for a second. Clara halted just near the nurse's desk. He turned around and the agony filled his brown eyes. He resembled Alex and that hurt her the most about the man who stood in front of her. His love for Clara hardly reflected his son's. And that was what differed between her father and her brother—only one willingly and unconditionally loved her.

"Why?" Clara cried out.

He looked at her, and she felt Noel's hand in hers. She didn't need Noel for this. Years of neglect came to this moment, but she appreciated his support.

"Why won't you come to my wedding?" It was all she could ask. Noel flinched, but she ignored him and took her hand away from his. She took a step closer to the man who had been a stranger in her life.

"Clara, it's not what your mother wants."

"But what about *my* wants? I'm getting married, Daddy. Does that mean nothing to you? Don't you even want to walk me down the aisle?"

He had closed his eyes tightly as if it pained him before he opened them and stared at her. "I'm sorry, Clara. I don't want that."

A blunt knife slowly made its way through her chest and into her heart.

"You're missing out, James."

Clara turned around to see the fury in Noel's eyes.

He has no idea what he's talking about.

Noel stood in front of her. Her eyes planted on his back.

"You're missing out on a big part of her life. You've spent years neglecting her. When she needed you, you weren't there. Alex was. Don't you or Gillian ever try to separate them. If Alex were awake, he'd never let you or Gillian speak to Clara like that so I won't either. As for walking her down the aisle? That will be *your* regret. Your daughter..." Noel stopped and faced her.

Clara hadn't realised the tears that formed from his words until he was a blurry vision.

"...is memorable. To watch her walk down the aisle would be an honour and to actually walk her down would be one of life's greatest treasures. I had the chance to love your daughter, and I screwed it up. I fucked up badly. That's *my* regret. Clara is beyond beautiful, and I was lucky enough to have her love me back, even if it was for a little while. Liam is the luckiest man on Earth to be able to keep her. Your daughter is the most amazing person to have ever graced my life. I love your daughter more than I could ever comprehend. My biggest regret is never loving her the way she deserved."

Her chest rose and fell heavily as his words burned her heart. The tears wouldn't stop. Back in Melbourne, those words would have stopped her from walking away. But she had decided that when it came time to choosing, it was her he didn't choose.

"Noel," she breathed out.

"I love you, Clara Louise Lawrence."

I love you, too, Nolan James Parker.

But Clara kept it to herself. Those words were hers to hold. Instead, Clara gave him the best smile she could muster under the circumstances. She stepped around Noel to see her father's surprised expression.

I will not let my parents ruin Noel's confession.

"Am I even your daughter?" Clara asked.

Her father flinched. "Biologically," he stated and Clara knew then that it was time she said goodbye to this man.

It's time I stop hoping.

"That's not enough for me. Biologically, I am your daughter, but I need more than that. I needed your love. I've waited for it. *She* hates me and I've accepted that, but I hoped more from you. I had hopes that you would come back to me and love me the way you love Alex. I've *needed* your love for the last fourteen years. But seeing you, I don't want it. I shouldn't have to work so hard for it. It shouldn't to be like that. A father should love his daughter unconditionally, but there are too many conditions for us. All I've ever needed was my father and you weren't up to standard." Clara stopped. Her heart broke at all the wasted tears, hopes and wants she had for him.

"Don't come between Alex and me. Don't you ever! I've been patient, I've taken her blows, and I've blamed myself for you both not loving me. Alex is all I've ever had. You've put yourself first every time. I'm *never* someone's first choice, but I am to Alex. When I was six, I had Parents' Day and *you* didn't show. Neither of you did. I was the only child without a parent. But Alex knocked on my classroom door and said he was *my* parent. He ditched school for something you should have attended. It was then that I knew you never loved me, and it was then that I never wanted to let Alex go. Alex is mine and will always be mine. Alex is my family."

It was the first time she ever saw tears fill James Lawrence's eyes. It hurt to remember the years of neglect, but she needed to let go. Clara turned away from the man she had once wanted to love her and be proud of her.

Alex is the only one who's ever been proud of me.

Clara stopped the moment she looked at Noel. She smiled at him and she knew his words were enough. She had relaxed her shoulders before she turned to her father, knowing it was time to say goodbye to the hope she had held since she was six.

"James," she said.

His wounded expression was one she had to ignore. She wasn't the hopeful six-year-old anymore. Breathing in and clenching her fists, Clara knew it was time.

"If you haven't done so already, remove my name from your will."

Pain and grief filled James' eyes.

I never needed him because I've always had Alex. He's the unconditional love I want and need. God, please let him wake up.

Chapter
FIFTEEN

❦

Noel

Watching Clara stand up for herself against her neglectful father had Noel in awe. The only other time she had left him so amazed was when she had confessed that she loved him, too. James Lawrence looked at the daughter he forgot and the regret consumed his brown eyes. His eyes matched Clara's, but unlike hers, years of unspoken words and unvoiced love filled James'.

"Clara," James quietly said.

Noel noticed Clara balling her fist just like when her ex-boyfriend, Darren, had begged for her forgiveness and attention.

"You should speak to Mr Rawlings and get your will redrafted and resigned. I don't want your money. I never needed it. I needed a father and I never got one. Money won't buy back the childhood I lived without you." Clara unclenched her fists and relaxed her body. "I don't want any of my trust funds. Let the money just sit there. I do not intend to ever collect it when I turn twenty-one. I'll hire Max. I won't need Mr Rawlings as my lawyer anymore. I'll see if I can get the money returned to you and Gillian."

Noel knew Clara chose her words carefully. She had

carefully constructed her response to formulate a goodbye without the possibility of a hello. She was cutting her ties.

"Your trust funds are yours to use as you wish, Clara."

James gave her a sad smile and Noel looked at Clara. She seemed to be questioning his response, but she shook her head.

"Thank you, but I don't want them," she replied without hesitation.

"You're just going to turn your back on trust funds that are worth almost two million dollars each?"

Noel was surprised. He knew Clara's family was rich. They were both raised in one of the richer areas of the southeastern suburbs. His family was well off too, but Clara having three trust funds with that much money confirmed that the Lawrence's were way past well off.

"To be honest, James, I've never once thought about them. I've grown up fortunate, and I still turned out unhappy," she confessed.

"You don't care about money? You're marrying an O'Connor. Liam's portfolio almost doubles the millions I made selling the real estate empire."

Liam's that rich. Before tax, I barely made anything close to a million.

Clara let out a laugh and shook her head in disbelief. "I don't want millions. I never have. I just want someone to love *me* and put me first. See me for me rather than want another woman. Liam makes me feel special. I never knew how much money he made until *after* I said yes to his proposal. His money means nothing to me. I fell in love with him because he makes me happy. I'm more than happy to sign a prenup that gives me nothing out of the marriage. I'm not in it for money. I never have. For richer or poorer, I want love, just love."

She wants to be loved and Liam made her feel like that and more.

Noel gazed down at his feet. He realised he had never made Clara feel that sure of his love for her. It ended all too quickly before he had the chance to. He knew Clara wasn't in it for money. That was Gillian Lawrence. Had he had the chance, Noel would have bought Clara the bakery. With it being in the heart of the city, he'd never afford it like Liam did, but Noel would have worked numerous accounts and taken out loans for that bakery on Little Collins Street.

"I need to be by Alex's side. Gillian will be back and I'll have to leave. Goodbye, James." Clara spun around, and without another word, she took Noel's hand and walked towards Alex's room. He couldn't help but feel inferior to Liam. He offered Clara the security Noel couldn't.

I live in Boston and Liam lives in Melbourne. I can't offer her the things she needs.

Noel stopped Clara just outside of Alex's door. He watched the surprise consume her face and he looked at her. He was proud that she stood up to her father, but he realised he didn't measure up to Liam. He'd hurt Clara too many times.

"Clara." He brought his hands to her cheeks and breathed out.

"Yes, Noel."

"I can't offer you the same things as Liam. I can only offer you the person I am. I don't have millions and you know that."

Clara tilted her head at him, her lips pressed together tightly and her brows knitted. "I just need the promise of forever, the promise of eternal love and commitment. I need someone to love *only* me. I'm not the easiest person to love. I'm doubtful and scared. I'm not perfect. I need someone to hold my hand while I contemplate my life and bring me back when I lose the sense of direction. I just need love, Noel."

Her wants and needs burned through his heart. "I can offer all of that and more, Clara." Noel's thumbs softly stroked her cheeks.

"Are you still with Andrea?"

He stilled instantly. That wasn't the response he had expected. He couldn't lie. He promised himself that he was done with lies when it came to Clara.

"Yes," he answered truthfully.

Clara gave him a tight smile before she shook her head. "Then I don't think you can, Noel." Clara gripped his wrists and then moved his hands from her cheeks. She took a step back and looked at him. "I believed you could have."

Clara bit her bottom lip and the sad gleam in her eyes tore into his chest.

"Then, I'll just have to prove that I can this time."

Clara blinked, the confusion on her face was clear. Determination filled his body. He knew this would be the last time he could prove that he was *her* forever.

She breathed out and tucked her loose curls behind her right ear. "Then prove to me that you'll only ever love me. Convince me. You were so sure last time, but you deceived me. Show me forever isn't just a dream for *us*. That I'm the one you want in your life and I'm *your* future." Clara gave him a tight smile before she entered Alex's room and stood by her brother's bed, holding his hand.

I need to prove my love. I have to prove that my heart belongs to her. Only her.

*M*oel sat in the visitor's chair as he watched Clara speak to her unconscious brother. The stories she told of their childhood had him smiling. Every time she mentioned the three of them, she'd look at Noel and smile. The way her lips curved had always been his undoing. He just needed a way to prove his love.

"Remember the time when Alex almost got busted sneaking out to meet Sarah?" Clara asked him.

He heard the slight hesitation when she said Sarah's name.

He grinned. "The idiot couldn't shimmy down the pipe and got stuck. I had to sneak out of bed and find a ladder. You stood guard for us that night," Noel said, reminiscing.

Clara laughed at her brother's expense. She looked over at Alex and sighed. "I'm glad he never ended up with her," she confessed.

"You don't like Sarah?" Noel got up from the visitor's chair and stood next to her.

She stared at her brother. Clara's silence made the sounds of the heart monitor machine seem louder. Then she faced him, her eyes searching his. She had blinked twice before she shook her head. "She's not my favourite person in the world, Noel. I'm just glad Alex left her." She swallowed hard and tears brimmed her eyes. He wasn't sure why she was so upset, but he knew it had to do with Alex's ex-girlfriend.

He stepped forward and took both her hands. "Did Sarah hurt you?" he asked concerned. He knew Sarah was dangerous.

She had the ability to ruin lives. The thought that someone so evil got close to someone like Clara made his heart ache.

Tears ran down Clara's face and she stared at him as if he should know why.

"Clara, what did Sarah do?" he demanded.

The hurt in her eyes replaced the beautiful gold colour. She let go of his hands and wiped her tears away. It was as if the life in her had vanished at his question. Noel moved his hands to cup her face.

"What did she do?" he asked desperately.

Clara shook her head at him.

"Why are you protecting her? Please, Clara, tell me what she did to you."

If Sarah did something to Clara, my friendship with Max is over. Clara comes first.

"I'm not protecting her. I'm protecting *you.*"

"Me?" he let out, surprised. "Why me?"

"Because you don't want to know and neither does Alex. It's in the past. It's not something I want to talk about, especially with you and not around Alex. Coma or not. Just trust me. I'm protecting you both. She's someone I don't want to talk about right now."

Whatever Clara was hiding, he'd find out. He wasn't going to let her keep this from him. For now, he'd drop it, but when they were alone, he'd make her talk.

Sarah hurt Clara. I have to make sure Max doesn't fall in love with that bitch!

"You'll tell me what she did, Clara." It wasn't a request.

"I promise I will. Just not right now." Clara's voice sounded regretful, and she placed her hands over his. She looked defeated, as if she was ready to give up what she was fighting.

"I'll get you some tea. Sit down and I'll be back in a minute," he said. Clara nodded and sat in the chair. He crouched in front of her and set his hand on her knee. "She hurt you and I'll make sure she never hurts you again. Don't believe whatever she said, Clara. She's manipulative and has a personal vendetta against me and Alex."

Clara's face went blank, and she only managed a nod. He stood up and placed a kiss on her head.

"You have to be believe me, Clara. I'll *never* let anyone hurt you ever again."

$\mathcal{I}$nstead of going to the coffee machine at the end of the hall, Noel took the elevator down to the cafeteria. When he'd first arrived at the hospital, he had concluded that he'd stick with coffee from the machine. It was flavourless, but he didn't want to leave Alex alone for long periods of time.

Noel stood in line as he examined the food. He reached for a tray and stared at what he could get for Clara. She was probably hungry. A small snack would do until he took her somewhere away from the hospital for lunch. Noel reached over for an apple when someone stood next to him.

"How long have you been in love with *my* daughter?" he asked as Noel picked up the red apple and placed it on a tray.

Noel sighed. "Your daughter? Last time I checked, you didn't claim her as yours for the last fourteen years," he stated and moved along in the line.

"I'm serious, Nolan."

Noel turned at the sound of his full name. He was about to tell James to stick it where the sun don't shine, but James' tired and defeated expression stopped him.

"Can we talk for a second?" James asked.

"You're not distracting me so Gillian can get Clara alone, are you?" Noel held the tray tightly in his hand.

"She's gone back to the hotel. I just want to talk."

Noel stared at James and nodded his head. He set the tray down on the counter and walked towards an empty seat in the middle of the cafeteria. The table they sat at wobbled.

"I don't want to leave Clara alone for very long. So talk, James."

He wasn't going to beat around the bush. James had five minutes and then Noel was leaving. James leant back in his seat and Noel raised an eyebrow at him.

"My daughter loves you," James pointed out.

Noel swallowed hard.

What would he know?

"I'd love that to be true, James."

"Well, I see it. Not even a blind man could miss it. Look, I've been a terrible father to Clara, but I've done it all to protect her from Gillian. I love my wife and my daughter, but Gillian wouldn't let me love both. She got jealous and that's when she started to withdraw. Her depression got worse and she started to blame Clara. When I realised how out of love Gillian was with me, it was too late. Clara had grown up hating me, and I'd neglected my own daughter. To stop Gillian from throwing her out, I stayed away. Alex went to college in the States and that was the only way I could protect her. You have to believe me. All I want is to walk her down the aisle. But I don't deserve that honour," James said as his eyes watered.

"So, you're telling me you ignored Clara to *protect* her." Noel let out an exaggerated laugh. "Why don't I believe you?"

"You don't have to believe me. I may not have shown her love, but Clara is *my* daughter and I have protected her the best way that I can… from a distance. I keep my tabs on her. I'm damn proud of her for deferring her degree and starting culinary school. Back when she was a kid, she loved watching your grandmother cook. It's better off if she hates me, but I'm not changing my will. Alex and Clara are my children and I am proud of how close they are. They don't need a father like me." James clenched his fists until his knuckles turned white. "You mind doing me a favour?"

"Depends." Noel shrugged.

"You win her back."

James's request surprised him. Noel's eyes widened and his lips parted.

"I see the way my daughter looks at you, and it's *you* she loves. She's been infatuated with you since you were kids. You both have obstacles, but you can overcome them. Just be patient with her. She's been waiting a long time for you, Nolan. Whether she realises it or not." There was a firm nod from James and then he stood up from his seat. "Just promise you'll love her. Clara deserves that. I know her fiancé can but it's not the love her heart needs. It's what her head wants. Make my daughter happy," James said with a sad smile.

"I've unknowingly loved your daughter my entire life, James. I'll find a way back into her heart and make myself worthy of her love." They were promises he'd fulfil and never break. He was sure of it.

"Then I know she's in safe hands." James nodded and then walked towards the exit. Noel sat there stunned. James Lawrence was not the man Noel had believed him to be. He loved his daughter and wanted her happy.

I'll find a way to make her happy. I just need to make this chance count.

oel held a small plastic bag of chips and fruit in one hand and Clara's tea in the other. He stood in the elevator alone as it moved up the levels of the hospital. Noel had James' blessing to love his daughter. Although he didn't like that James was not open about his love for his daughter, Noel understood. Gillian was not a woman to displease, but he wished James would leave his wife.

Just as he stepped out of the elevator, his phone vibrated in his pocket. Noel juggled the tea in one hand as he fished for his phone. He continued to walk until he was near Alex's room and pulled it out. He looked at his caller ID and frowned. The guilt in him burned as he pressed answer.

"Andrea, hey," he greeted as best as he could.

"I've been trying to call you for days. Is everything okay?" she asked worriedly.

Noel realised that in his haste to get to the hospital, he had never told Andrea where he was going. Sighing, he gripped the phone tighter. "I'm in New Haven," he said.

"What are you doing in Connecticut?" He heard the surprise in her voice.

"Alex and Keira were on their way to Boston when..." Noel stopped. The anger in him started to burn his eyes. They didn't deserve to be in those hospital beds.

She gasped. "Oh my God, no!"

"Alex is in a coma, and Keira is broken up."

"Do you need me to be there?" Andrea asked.

"No, stay with your family. Listen, Andrea, we need—" The sounds of loud frantic beats caught his attention. He looked around and noticed nurses running towards him. He stepped towards Alex's door and saw the machines flash.

"Alex!" Clara shrieked. The beeps grew louder as nurses entered the room. "No, please! I can't leave him!" A nurse tried to pull Clara away from the bed.

"You need to leave, please, Miss Lawrence," the nurse begged.

"Noel!" she cried out for him, and it hit him hard.

His feet were running to her before he could process another thought. "Jesus. Clara!" His heart constricted at the sound of her begs and pleas to the nurses.

"Noel, what's going on?" Andrea's voice didn't stop him.

"I'm sorry, Andy. Clara needs me." Then he hung up and ran to Clara.

"Code Blue. South Pavilion, fifth floor, room two," paged throughout the hospital and a cardiac arrest team entered the room.

Noel wrapped his arms around Clara as she tried to hold on to Alex's hand; her cries drowned by the beeping of the machines.

"No. Let me go, Noel. Let me go! Al-Alex. Save him! Please save him!" Clara cried.

"Noel, get her out of here!" Morgan yelled out.

He nodded.

"No! I'm not leaving him. I won't leave him, please. Please, Noel. Let me stay. Alex, wake up! Wake up!" Clara screamed and thrashed.

"Not responsive," a doctor announced. "Get me the defibrillator, two hundred joules," he instructed the nurse, and she wheeled the defibrillator to the bed.

Morgan took the bag and takeout cup from Noel's hand and he lifted the thrashing Clara in his arms and out of the ICU room.

"Alex, you can't leave me! You can't leave me!" Clara cried as he carried her out of the room.

When the door closed behind him and the curtain covered the glass window, he set Clara down.

"I hate you," Clara screamed and punched his chest. "I hate you so much!"

Tears roll down his face as he heard the doctor yell, "Clear!"

Before Clara could land another fist on his chest, he brought her in and wrapped his arms around her. She clung on to his chest and cried. He held her tightly, wishing he could take away her pain.

"He's going to be okay," he tried to assure her.

Noel held her tightly, afraid to let her go and afraid that she'd see the fear he was trying to hide. The longer they waited, the more Clara clutched him and cried in to his chest. After some time, the noise in Alex's room silenced and the sound of Alex's door closing had Clara pulling away from him. She rushed over to the doctor, who had a grim expression on his face, and Noel followed her. He was scared for her and terrified of what the doctor would reveal to them.

"Your brother is stable for now. His heart went into cardiac arrest. We'll need to do some scans immediately. We need to make sure the swelling is down. Be mindful that Alex's injuries are severe. The next twenty-four hours are crucial. The nurse will tell you when you can see him, but right now we need to run the test," the doctor said.

The sheer relief of the doctor's words was liberating. He hadn't realised it, but Noel had managed to finally breathe. His best friend was stable, and he mentally thanked any and every higher power that would appreciate his gratitude.

Noel took Clara's hand in his. He needed to feel her touch again. He looked up to see Clara nodding as the tears slid down her face.

"Thank you, doctor. Is Keira okay?" Clara asked.

The doctor rubbed his forehead with his hands and let out a sigh. "She's better than she was yesterday. If you'll excuse me, I need to prep your brother's cardiac CT. We'll know more once we run the test."

"Thank you," they both said.

Alex's doctor walked past them and Noel stared at the door. Inside, his best friend lay, and he would do anything to trade places with him. Noel would give anything for Clara to have her brother back.

"I can't lose him. Why couldn't it be me, Noel? Why can't it be me! I deserve it more than he does. Why can't it be me instead?" Clara asked.

Noel let go of Clara's hand and faced her. The defeated glaze in her eyes made his stomach churn. His hands were on her arms, ensuring she kept her eyes on his. The thought of Clara being in that bed made him sick and angry.

Never Clara.

"Don't you *ever* say that, Clara! Don't you fucking dare! I'd trade my life for yours and so would Alex. I'd be dying inside if it were you. I'm hurting that it's Alex, but if it were you, Clara, I couldn't live with myself. Right now, my life is empty without you. If you died, there would be no life without you. I love you more than life. Alex is going to be okay. Don't you ever think like that again! I love you, for God's sake!" The ache in his chest made its way to his throat, making it impossible to breathe.

Tears slid down her face. "It should be me, Noel. I—"

Noel quickly cupped her face and his lips found hers, silencing her and pouring his love and absolute soul into hers. His heart could take no more at the thought of a life without her on this Earth, even if she chose Liam. Earth was heaven when Clara's life graced its surface. He let impulse take over and the only way to shut her up was just like their first kiss. He hoped his kiss would remove at least a single inch of pain from her heart.

His chest imploded at the feel of her lips moving against his. It was beautiful, heartbreakingly sad, and moving. These lips were the pair he loved more than any other. He kissed her for dear life and waited for her to pull away. Instead, Clara brought her hands to his waist and depended their kiss. Each movement of her mouth mended and broke his heart, feeling every inch of sadness and pain. Their tongues found each other in a familiar dance of need and desire. He savoured the soft moan that escaped her as his heart beat violently against his ribcage. *More.* He wanted more. He wanted to make love to her. Keep her in his arms until the last star in the universe burned out.

I can't have her. She's Liam. She's hurt. I can't have her this way.

Clara's tears hit his hand, and Noel regretfully pulled back. The moment her lips left his, he already missed them. His hands never left Clara's face as his thumbs brushed her tears away. That one heartbreaking kiss confirmed it all. She was the *only* one he'd love. No one else mattered. He just hoped Clara came to the same conclusion.

"I can't imagine a life without your smile, whether it's

directed at me or not. I will never know a greater love than the love I've held for you. It'll never change. My love for you is eternal and forever, without the concept of time or place. It's you, Clara. It's *always* been you," he whispered and rested his forehead against hers.

Clara's eyes fluttered close and she wrapped her arms around his waist.

At this moment, I'm hers again.

Clara

I love you.

Three words she wanted to say but they weren't the right circumstances for it to be said out loud. The reality was that she wasn't sure how she felt. His lips were perfect and made her heart burn with such passion it terrified her. His words sliced her heart open, leaving her to bleed. Noel ran his thumb along her bottom lip as she opened her eyes and stared into his green eyes, hoping they'd offer a way into his thoughts.

"That can't happen again, Noel." As much as she wanted it to, it couldn't. The moment got to them both, and he had acted on impulse. A kiss she dreamed of. But inside her heart screamed *'yes'* while her head screamed *'cheater.'*

Noel had kissed her, but she hadn't stopped him. The instant their lips touched, unanswered emotions stopped her from pulling away. She was confused. She was losing her brother, and she'd accepted Noel's kiss. Her heart yearned for more, but she was dying at the idea of losing her brother.

"I know." He sighed as he brushed her hair back. "But I can't ignore that it happened," he added.

Noel wrapped his arms around her and pulled her back into his hard chest. Clara's heart stretched painfully. She had gotten the kiss she had dreamed of, the mouth she yearned for, and the touch her heart craved for. His lips made her feel like forever was possible for them. Her heart didn't want him to stop. It had been waiting almost a year for him.

Clara stepped out of his arms. She breathed out to calm her erratic heartbeats and looked up at him. His green eyes were like emeralds submerged in water. Those were the eyes she had once wanted to look into when she walked down the aisle.

Why can't this be easy? Why am I so confused when it comes to him?

"If I choose you..." Hope sparkled in his eyes and for a second she had closed hers tightly before she looked back to see Noel's frown. "I lose Liam," she breathed out.

"You lose him," Noel agreed.

"And if I choose Liam, I lose you. I don't want to make a choice when I know it hurts someone I love. I'm not prepared to lose you again, but the thought of losing Liam kills me. I'm a terrible person for what I'm doing. I'm a horrible fiancée to him. If you had never walked in to my life, I'd be marrying the most wonderful person in the world. Why can't I let you go?" she cried. It was a question she had asked herself many times since she ended them. "It's not meant to break my heart every time I see you. It's not meant to be this hard. I'm meant to be okay. I'm meant to be over you!"

The frustration in her voice surprised her. He didn't say anything. Clara noticed the hurt flash in his eyes, and she blinked away her tears.

Noel exhaled. "You choose him and you lose me for good, Clara."

I lose him forever.

"I'm sorry," she whispered out. "I didn't—"

Noel stopped her by stepping forward and taking her hands. "I'm sorry, too," he said and pressed a kiss on her forehead. The contact of his lips on her skin sent a tremor to her heart. When Noel pulled back, he cupped her face and searched her eyes. "I keep hurting you and I don't want that. I'm trying to win you back, but I'm doing it unfairly."

I'm the one being unfair to him.

Clara held the small bundle of daisies she had picked from the small store near the cafeteria. Noel had led her there to get a bottle of water, and they had drawn her attention; the same flowers were displayed on Keira's dining table.

The vibrating in her pocket had Clara stopping. She pulled

it out to see Liam's face on her screen. She ignored the way Noel winced next to her. After taking a deep breath, Clara answered her phone.

"Hey," Clara greeted cautiously, afraid that she'd confess that she had kissed Noel.

"Hey, sweetheart. How's Alex?" Liam asked.

Clara swallowed hard. "He went into cardiac arrest earlier."

"Shit, Clara! I can't take being here and not being able to do anything. I'm coming to Connecticut. I need to be with you. I don't want you to be lonely," Liam said.

The concern and love in his voice had the guilt in Clara welling. She was selfish. She didn't want Liam in the U.S. She wanted to be around Noel for as long as she could. She wanted to know the extent of how she felt towards him.

"You have work and the wedding. I'm okay here, Liam. I'm not lonely. I'm with—" She paused and glanced up at Noel.

I'm a terrible person.

"Keira," she breathed out.

The line was silent. Liam didn't say anything as Clara kept her eyes on the frown Noel had made.

"You don't want me there?"

Liam's question tore her heart apart. He was the last person she wanted to hurt, but she was being selfish in order to have Noel in her life for just a little longer.

"Liam," she breathed out. "I want you here, but..."

"But this is about you and your brother. I know how important he is to you. The moment you need me there, call me. I'll take the company plane to you." He didn't seem angry. He should be, and she didn't get it.

"You're not mad?" she asked.

"Should I be mad?"

"Yes. I'm a terrible fiancée to you," she confessed, looking away from Noel.

"No, you're not, Clara. It's just an emotional time. I get it if you want some time alone. All you have to do is tell me and I'll be there," Liam said.

Her heart twisted in her chest. He didn't argue or fight her. She didn't deserve him. Not his love or his devotion.

"It's getting late. Call me if you need anything, sweetheart. My phone will be next to me. I love you, Clara."

Clara sighed. She would never understand how someone like Liam O'Connor could love her. "I love you, Liam," she said before she hung up the phone and returned it to her pocket.

Clara lifted her chin to see the hurt expression on Noel's face. She hated what she did to both men but hated what she did to Noel more. He was aware of her conflicted heart, and Liam wasn't.

"Come on. Let's go see Keira," Noel said.

She nodded, knowing that he didn't want to discuss Liam or the fact that she had said that she loved her fiancé. He turned and they walked down the hall silently.

Ignoring the large knot in the pit of her stomach, Clara knocked on the door. Keira turned her head to see them and a beautiful yet sad smile developed on her face. The way her eyes held no blame allowed Clara to feel free from the guilt—but only slightly. The reason they were in the hospital was because of her.

"Clara, you're here in the States," Keira said before she winced.

Clara entered the room and sat in the chair next to the hospital bed, and Noel stood next to her. She handed the daisies over to her brother's girlfriend and said, "I'm sorry, Keira. This is all my fault."

Keira immediately frowned. "Thank you. They're beautiful. And this is *not* your fault, Clara. You didn't make that man run a red light. It was an accident and I don't blame anyone, not even the driver of the other car. I want to. I want him to stand in front of me and makes him listen to what I have to say. I've thought about it, but I can't form words. I want to blame him, I do. But I can't. I'm not a hateful person, even when he could be the reason why I lose Alex." The choked sobs and pain in Keira's voice caused Clara's chest to ache.

Keira sniffed and placed the daisies in her lap. "I knew it was bad when Alex didn't open his eyes. The car stopped moving, and he didn't say a word. I begged him to wake up, but he didn't. The next thing I know, I'm being pulled out first and Alex still had his eyes closed. They won't let me see him. Is he okay?"

Noel reassuringly placed his hand on Clara's shoulder. His support gave her the strength to shake her head. "He went into cardiac arrest just before. They said he's stable," Clara said in a small voice.

Keira let out a sob. It was painful and heartbreaking to see. If Clara ever doubted Keira's love for Alex, she'd be proven wrong. It was evident that Keira loved Alex more than life itself.

"But he's going to be okay, right?" Keira's empty eyes pierced Clara's heart. She had no idea what to say. She didn't know what Alex's scans would reveal.

The thought of losing Alex forever devastated Clara. He was her rock, but he was Keira's life. She didn't want Keira to know the pain of losing someone you love. She had lost Noel so many times, and it still pained her.

"Keira, Alex's fighting to see you again. He's the strongest man I have ever met. He'll find his way to you," Noel said as he took hold of Clara's hand.

Keira's eyes fell to their linked hands and smiled. "Alex would be happy with what I'm seeing right now. He never wanted you two to end. The day he landed, he called me and said he had suspected something. I could hear the protectiveness in his voice, but he was honestly happy. He loves you both so much." Tears ran down Keira's face and Clara felt her own fall. "He never once thought either of you betrayed him. Alex just wanted you both to be happy."

The large lump in Clara's throat almost choked her. She saw the sadness in Noel's eyes. She wanted to take it away, but she knew it would come at a cost.

After chatting for as long as Keira could stay awake, Noel and Clara left. Noel's hand parted from hers. When they stopped by the nurse's station, Morgan assured them both that she'd keep an eye on Alex and would call if she heard anything from the doctor. Once they reached the elevator, Clara stared up at him. His green eyes were, just like the rest of him, as beautiful as the first day he had walked back into her life.

I have to go back to where we started.

"Question five," she announced.

Noel's eyes darted to her and he knitted his brows. "What?"

"Twenty-one questions, Nolan Parker. I'm asking you number five."

Noel turned to her and said, "Okay."

It started with one game of twenty-one questions. Our game went unfinished.

"Say we got to the part where we told Alex. Before we went to that club, before Katie's birthday and before that night. Would we have made it? Would we have been happy together?"

Noel breathed out and gave her a heartbreaking frown. "*Yes.* We would have made it, Clara. I would have made sure we did. I had our future together planned out. I would have followed you to the ends of the Earth just to be with you. We would have been happy. I would have spent my life making sure you were."

The elevator dinged and the doors opened. Noel stepped inside and Clara looked at him. Regret flowed through her veins and entered her heart.

"I'm sorry, Noel. I'm so very sorry."

Chapter
SIXTEEN

Noel

"I was scared," Clara whispered. Her eyes fell to the floor and her shoulders dropped. Noel stood in the elevator and watched her. A small sob escaped her lips just as the doors started to close. He quickly held out his arm to stop them from automatically shutting.

"Clara," he breathed as he stepped out of the elevator and pulled her into his arms.

Those were the words he had hoped for, all those months ago. But even hearing them now didn't heal the pain that tormented his heart. The same torment that made a mess of his life. Her fear sent her running. He'd known that, but he couldn't blame her. He should have gone against what she had said and he should have proved to her that fear couldn't rule their lives.

I should have stayed in Melbourne. I should have fought for her.

"I'm sorry, I—" She sobbed into his chest, and he held her tighter.

"No, not yet, Clara. I understand. I do. You ended us for a reason and as much as I want to know, I'm scared to hear it. I did something and I'm scared that by knowing, it'll open up all our wounds again. I'd only push you further away." He knew he'd regret the words that came out of his mouth. But Noel knew the circumstances they were in had them in a moment of regret. Things between them had gone wrong and Alex's accident was driving them back together again. He wanted her to be honest because she wanted to be, not because he pressured her to.

"I don't deserve him. I shouldn't have gone to him. I should have never been the one he fell in love with." Clara had sniffed before letting go of his waist and stepping out of his arms.

Noel swallowed the lump in his throat. "I-I…" he began to say, but he closed his mouth.

Clara's gaze fell to her engagement ring and his eyes followed.

"You do deserve him, Clara."

Her eyes shot up and she blinked at him in surprise. "No. I don't. I *never* deserved Liam. Not even after things ended with Darren. He deserves so much better than me. His biggest flaw and biggest mistake was choosing to fall in love with me." Turmoil filled Clara's brown eyes, and he felt her anguish.

"Clara, choosing to fall in love with you isn't a mistake someone makes. It's a privilege. His biggest flaw would be *not* falling in love with you."

My biggest mistake was losing her.

The saddest smile he had ever seen developed on Clara's face. "I'm sorry I walked away, Noel. I should have stayed, and forgot what was said and done. I shouldn't have been so scared. I didn't want you to lose Alex, but look how far it got us. We might be losing him, and this time, we wouldn't be getting him back. I was so scared that you'd end up regretting us and hating me." Clara's hands covered her face and she let out a frustrated sigh.

He took a step forward and his fingers curved around her wrist, pulling her hands away from her face. Those brown eyes still sparkled even though he could see the sadness that projected through.

"I would have *never* regretted or hated you, Clara. That's impossible. I wanted…" He removed his hands from her wrists and kept them by the side of his body.

To marry you.

But Noel kept that to himself. He didn't want her to know that just yet. If he had a chance of Clara choosing him, then the first time he wanted her to know his intentions of marriage was when he was on one knee. So, instead, he said, "To keep you forever."

"Forever?" Clara looked surprised by his response.

For Noel, forever meant marriage. He stepped forward and cradled Clara's beautiful face in his palms. "I did promise you forever." He thought back to the moments after she had told him that she loved him, too.

"Then love me forever."

Those were the words that had him willing to promise forever. They only had that one night, and then it all had started to end. Clara smiled and he saw the hope radiate from her eyes. That smile gave him something to believe in.

"Come on. Let's go find a place to eat and we'll come back and be with Alex." He didn't ask for her hand, he took it.

Clara peered down and then closed her hand around his. The security of her touch could break his heart. He was in too deep. She had the ability to break his heart with a simple word. But, for now, he hoped that the possibility of more was in *their* future.

*H*e found himself loving the sounds of those once annoying beeps from the heart monitor. He feared a loud erratic noise from the machine but was more terrified to hear it emit silence. Silence meant no heartbeat and that was a noise he never wanted to experience. Noel needed the beeps. He needed them like he needed air and Clara's touch.

Alex's chest rose and fell with the assistance of a respiratory ventilator. Clara's hands had left his an hour ago and held on to Alex's. She didn't say word. She only looked at her brother and silently prayed. Every time he looked at Alex, Noel felt the guilt rise from his stomach and attach itself to his heart. Alex was in that bed because he stupidly sent Clara that message. He wished he hadn't sent it to her because it would mean his best friend would be going about his life.

After lunch at a small Italian restaurant near the hospital, Noel and Clara stopped by to see Keira, but she was still asleep.

She was better than the first time Noel saw her, but he knew Keira was heartbroken; she was sheltering the blame and guilt, too. He begged her to forgive him, but she had fought him and said that none of it was his fault. He knew it was a lie. It would always be his fault.

A soft knock had Noel turning. He swallowed hard at the sight and instantly stood up. The frown on her face and the sadness in her eyes had Noel's stomach dipping.

"Andrea," he breathed. He met her blue eyes before he looked down at Clara.

"How is he?" Andrea asked as she took a step into the room.

Clara turned around and gave Andrea an appreciative smile. "I think he's okay," she replied.

Noel watched as Clara's eyes started to water. She quickly wiped her face and turned to face Alex.

"I told you—"

Andrea shook her head, cutting him off. "I couldn't stay in Phoenix, not when Alex and Keira are in hospital." Her blue eyes darkened, and she seemed guarded. "Can we talk outside?" she asked, her eyes focused on Clara.

He realised that in a room with both women, his heart was still set on Clara. Noel nodded, followed Andrea out of the room, and walked down the hallway, away from Alex's room.

Andrea stopped and leant on the white wall, her head dropped forward and her fingers twiddled. Noel dug his hands into his pockets unsure of where this would take him. He loved Andrea, but he wasn't *in* love with her. He knew what being in love was like and he wanted that, even though he knew how much being in love physically hurt him.

"It's *her*, isn't it?" Andrea peeked up at him.

The hurt in her eyes made his stomach flip. "What do you mean?"

"The one you loved and you lost, Noel. It's Clara, isn't it?" There was no hint of betrayal in Andrea's voice. "You don't love me like you love her," she said once Noel didn't respond.

He stood there, speechless, and watched Andrea push off the wall. She turned and faced him. Her eyes shone with unshed tears.

She knows about Clara.

"How'd you…" he started to ask.

Andrea breathed out and shook her head. "You called me *Andy*. You've never once called me Andy. That's when I knew. I had this feeling back in New York, but I ignored it. I should have known the moment she saw that locket. The way she looks at you and the way you look at her. I knew, but I didn't want to believe it. I started to realise it all when we got back from New York and then your phone call. The way you said her name like you were scared to death of losing her. It was heartbreaking to hear you love someone that much. I'm no longer Andrea to you, I'm Andy."

Tears slid down Andrea's face and he stepped forward and took her hands. Andrea squeezed his hands, her eyes never leaving his.

This is my chance to do the honest thing.

"I'm sorry, Andrea. I tried. I tried to get over her, but I couldn't. I'm sorry, but Clara's…"

Andrea let go of his hands and placed hers on his cheeks. "The One. Clara's the one for you," she whispered.

Noel nodded his head. She smiled and blinked her tears away.

"Then win her back," she said as she stepped back, creating space between them.

"You're not mad?" he asked in disbelief.

Andrea shook her head. "No. I'm not. I'm hurt, but I'm not mad, Noel. You don't love me, and I can't make you change your mind. Not when I'm up against someone like Clara. She was before me and she made you fall in love. I can see why you'd fall in love with her. She's beautiful and sweet. It must be real for you both. Even though you're both apart and in two different relationships, I see it. You try not to stare at her, but you do it anyways. I saw it in New York, Noel. You stare at her like she's it, and then you realise you can't have her, so you smile for her being happy. I want that look one day. All this time apart and you're both so in love with each other. It's so clear, but you're both so oblivious to it."

"Andrea," he said.

She stopped him with a firm shake of her head. "I'm going to do you a favour. I'm ending us. I want you to go after her because whatever she did is what I'm doing. As much as I'm going to regret this, I want you happy, Noel. Looking at Clara and the way she looks at you, she did the exact same thing, didn't she? She put your happiness first and you didn't even realise it. Well, I'm putting your happiness first as well. I don't want you to have to be with me if you're in love with someone else. I know you tried hard, but we aren't meant to be together. I want you to try with Clara," Andrea said as she reached into her pocket.

She's ending us.

She pulled out their apartment key and placed it in his hand. "I'm giving you this back."

He looked at it and then at her.

"And this," Andrea said as she reached back into her pocket. She brought out something silver and he squinted his eyes at it. His heart stopped and the air in his lungs evaporated.

Clara's locket.

"You should give it back to her." Andrea placed it in his hand and closed his fingers over the silver locket. "We're over, Noel," she confirmed with a sad smile.

"You'll find someone who deserves you, Andrea. I'm sorry I couldn't be that person. I do love you, just not the way you deserve to be loved. Even if Clara doesn't choose me, you still deserve someone better than I am. He'll be the man I couldn't be. That man has been waiting for us to be over to be with you." Noel stepped forward and pulled her into his arms. Though his heart ached for Andrea, Noel felt it break from its chain. He felt free. Andrea was giving him the chance.

"She'd be stupid to walk away," Andrea mumbled into his chest.

He hugged her tighter and pressed his lips together. "You don't know her like I do, Andrea. Walking away is what we do best. But I'm going to try," he promised. They stood there in an embrace they knew would end. The moment they parted, it was over between them.

It felt like Andrea was savouring him, remembering him for the last time. He knew she'd find someone else. She was any man's vision of perfection, but not for Noel; no one was besides Clara.

Then they separated and stared at each other. Those blue eyes saddened and his heart pained for her. It wasn't the same pain he felt when he lost Clara, but it still hurt. He was losing a wonderful woman in his life, but she deserved to be let go.

"So this is where we end? I just say goodbye to you." Andrea looked away.

"Hey," he said grabbing her attention. "We can still be in each other's lives. I don't want this to be where I never see you again, Andrea. Friends?" he asked holding out his hand.

Andrea looked down and smiled. "Friends," she confirmed and shook his hand. After a few shakes, she let go and pursed her lips.

"Just don't give her a false sense of forever. Don't you ever do that to her because no one deserves that. Keep her forever this time and don't let her go," Andrea said. There was no bitterness or anger. Andrea genuinely wanted him to be happy with Clara.

"It won't be like that. Not this time. Thank you," he said.

She breathed out and looked at him one last time before she turned towards the elevator. Noel gazed at Clara's locket. He found it unclasped with the piece of paper nestled inside. He looked back up to see Andrea enter the elevator. She had read his confession. Noel closed the locket and placed it in his pocket. He said goodbye to Andrea. Now, he just had to wait for Clara.

Breathing out and with the idea of being Clara's future immersing itself in his mind, Noel went back into Alex's room. Clara still sat in her seat. Noel returned to the seat he had vacated and sat down next to her. Clara had kept her eyes focused on Alex before she let go of one of her brother's hands and gripped Noel's. She entwined her fingers with his. Noel glanced down at their linked hands before he looked at her. Their eyes meeting and a soft smile graced her face.

"We're over," he announced.

The surprise enlightened Clara's brown eyes. "Over?" she whispered.

Noel squeezed her hand and smiled. "I'm all yours, Clara."

Clara

Alex, please stay. I need you. Alex, please don't leave me!

"Clara! Wake up, baby. Wake up!"

She opened her eyes and gasped, her heart aching and her breathing faltering. "Noel?"

"Thank God," he breathed. His eyes watered as he pulled her into his arms. "I've never been so scared in my life. You wouldn't wake up. You just kept crying and screaming out Alex's name."

Clara wrapped her arms around Noel's waist and cried. "It felt real. I lost him, Noel. He died and I had to live without him. It felt so real. I can't lose him. I can't. I lost you, and I can't lose him, too." Clara's throat tightened; breathing became difficult as the dream ran cycles through her mind.

"Hey," he softly said.

His voice soothed the tremors that spread through her chest, and Clara looked up at him. Those green eyes sparkled with the tears that brimmed his eyes.

"You're not going to lose Alex. He's fighting. The doctors said he's doing well. You won't lose me. I'm here, baby. I've always been here. Just close your eyes, okay. When you're ready, I'll be there. I've been yours the moment I knocked on your door." He rubbed her back. She missed everything about his touch and the way his arms fit around her.

Clara held him tighter, afraid she'd lose him all over again. The pain in her chest intensified at the reminder that Noel wasn't hers. He was single, but she wasn't. She hadn't made a choice, but her heart struggled to let someone go.

"I-I can't lose you, Noel. You're all I have left."

Noel laid them both down on the bed, her head resting on his chest. The sound of his steady heart called to her as he held her. Tears continued to fall down her face. She missed her brother and Noel was her link to him. Clara settled her hand over his heart and he tensed underneath her touch. She looked up at him, the control evident in his eyes.

After a moment, he let out a heavy sigh. "You'll always have me, Clara. I love you," he softly said.

Her heart squeezed at those three words. The same three

words she longed for. Noel gazed down at her as different tears brimmed her eyes. They weren't tears about losing Alex. They were tears over losing Noel.

"I'll always be yours. I'd wait forever if I have to," Noel said.

She kissed his chest near his heart. It was all she could give him. She couldn't return the words. With the circumstances they were in, it just wasn't fair to him. Noel held her tighter as she snuggled into his chest. Memories of Melbourne and their nights together replaced her dream of losing Alex. Her heart was on fire. Back then she wanted to lay the way they did forever. In those moments, he was hers forever.

She sniffed as the tears returned and she let out a struggled breath. She took in that familiar smell of him: woody and spicy. She smiled at the memories. The ones she had sadly looked back on since she walked away.

"It was just a dream, Clara. Just close your eyes."

Clara's eyes fluttered shut. All she could think of was the last time they were together like this.

The moment after we said I love you to each other. That moment when Noel was once mine.

*T*he sound of her phone vibrating woke her up. Clara sat up to find herself alone in the bed. She rubbed her eyes and noticed that Noel was asleep on the couch. Stretching for her phone, her eyes never left the sight of him. She swiped at the screen and read her unread messages.

Stevie: *How are you, Clara? My thoughts and love are with Alex and Keira.*

Ally: *Your wedding dress is here waiting for you! Bring your brother home with you. We're all worried.*

Julian: *Clara, you call me when he wakes up!*

Jo: *Hello, Clara. I know this is bad timing, but we need* *finalisations on either the harpist or the violinist. – Jo.*

Liam: *Sweetheart, remember, the moment you need me, I'm leaving to be with you. I love you. Call me at anytime.*

Rob: *You take care of Noel, Clara. He's going to need you.*

Clara dropped her phone and left all the messages without a reply. Her chest was still burning. She wanted to forget about her wedding. Alex was in the hospital; getting married was the last thing on her mind. Throwing back the blanket, she walked over to the couch and hovered over Noel. The peace on his face as he slept made her heart melt. Clara brushed his short messy hair away from his forehead, allowing herself to remember the times she used to do it. Just as she was about to move her hand away, Noel grabbed her wrist. His eyes slowly opened. Those beautiful green eyes had her heart stopping.

When he realised it was her, he loosened his grip and smiled up at her. "Good morning, Clara," he said, his voice still heavy from sleep.

He slowly sat up and pulled her into his lap, Clara straddling him. She was shocked as his hands cupped her face. His fingers sent tingles straight to her heart. She couldn't control the smile on her face.

"I woke up and you were on the couch instead of the bed," she pointed out.

He laughed at the way she pouted at him. "Being in bed with you is a temptation, Clara." Noel swept the curls behind her ear. "No matter how much I enjoyed having you sleep in my arms, I had to put some distance between us."

"I'm sorry about last night," Clara said as her eyes set on his naked chest.

Noel crooked a finger under her chin and brought her eyes level to his. "Don't be. You were having a bad dream. I didn't want you alone. You should never be alone, Clara."

Pieces of her dream started to resurface: Clara in her wedding gown; Alex not being there; the picture of Alex's grave. She felt the lump form in her throat.

"Baby, it's going to be okay," Noel assured her. His words

of endearment pierced her heart. She should have felt like he had crossed a line, but he hadn't. He brought her face closer until his soft lips touched her forehead. He let his lips linger for a moment longer.

When his eyes met hers, Clara placed her hands on his cheeks. This was the love she'd walked away from and her heart wanted him back. But her head told her otherwise. Clara's thumbs ran across his cheeks and she smiled up at him.

Noel was once my heart.

Clara's thumbs stopped the moment Noel's hands gripped her hips. He didn't push her closer to him. He simply held her.

"It's not fair, Noel." She breathed in heavily and closed her eyes tightly.

"Hey, talk to me. I'm here."

His words had her opening her eyes. "Why is it him? Why did it have to be my brother? Why is it that the best person in the world is in a coma? Considering there are people who deserve it more... people like me. It's all my fault. It's *always* been my fault. Why couldn't I be stronger? Why did I have to depend on him so much? I'm not losing my brother because of my mistakes. Alex deserves better. He deserves to have anyone else but me as his sister."

Noel squeezed her hips and rested his forehead against hers. "This isn't your fault, Clara. It's mine. I shouldn't have sent you that message. It caused a chain reaction and I'm the reason why Alex is in that bed."

Noel's tears hit her hand and she brought his face up to hers. "No. This started a long time ago, Noel. Long before we fell in love with each other," she explained as her fingers traced the side of his face. Her heart plunged, heavy with sorrow. "Why couldn't my parents love me?" she asked as she looked into his eyes. Clara noticed them darken as the sadness had replaced the shimmer.

"Clara," Noel breathed.

"Why couldn't they? If they had just loved me, Alex wouldn't have had to take care of me. I wouldn't be such a burden in his life. He would have gone to Stanford without worrying about me, and he would have enjoyed college. This—me—all of this wouldn't have happened. This is my fault. Everything is my fault. Your break up with Andrea was my fault, too." It was painful to say, but all the bad times in Noel and Alex's lives were because of her. She had almost ruined their friendship.

Noel's hands left her hips and returned to her face. His eyes darkened and hers widened in surprise. "Nothing is your fault. Nothing is ever your fault. Understand that, Clara. Alex and I, we love you. We make choices *because* we love you. God, I love you. I love you so damn much!" Noel removed his hands from her face and wrapped his arms around Clara's back.

"Noel," she breathed out.

He stood up from the couch holding her. Clara wrapped her legs around his waist as she held his face in her hands. No words were said as he breathed heavily, walking them to the bed. He carefully laid her on the unmade bed. Noel hovered over her as he lowered his body on top of hers. Clara's breathing became shallow as her fingers graced his cheeks.

His breath hit her skin and she closed her eyes tightly as her heart continued to slam itself against her chest. When she opened them Noel's face tensed. He let out an exasperated sigh and rested his forehead back against hers.

"I want to, Clara. God, I would love nothing more than to show you my love. But I can't. Damn it, I can't! I want to make slow and passionate love to you. I want you to remember every bit of pleasure I ever gave to you. I just want to kiss you. But I can't. Not with that ring on your finger. A ring that isn't mine."

All air left her lungs. Noel pushed himself off her and got off the bed. Clara sat up and looked at him.

"What do you mean, Noel?" she asked.

He ran a hand through his messy hair. "Nothing," he mumbled. She could see the frustration on his face and her shoulders sagged. "We better go to the hospital and see Alex. I'm going in the shower. Order room service, whatever you like, Clara." His eyes met hers, and she saw the conflict.

He shook his head as he walked towards the bathroom. He left Clara on the bed to mull over what he had said. She gazed down at her left hand and felt the nagging pain in her heart.

A ring that isn't his?

Chapter SEVENTEEN

Noel

The summer breeze blew as he walked the quiet streets towards the hospital. He had one focus and that was controlling his mouth when it came to Clara. He wanted too much and she hadn't expressed her intentions when it came to *them*. Noel ensured that he'd remained three steps ahead of her. The moment she had walked out of the bathroom in her pale yellow dress, Noel knew that distance was desperately needed.

That pale coloured dress reminded him of their time at Chelsea Beach, and it hurt his heart too much. He said nothing as he led her out of the hotel and towards Yale-New Haven Hospital. The temptation to hold her hand was strong. His hands twitched every time he thought about it, but he had kept space between them. He took the right turn off Temple Street and quickened his steps once he hit George Street, the hospital only minutes away.

"Noel," Clara called out, but he ignored her. "Noel, Stop!" she yelled.

He breathed out, exasperated. He halted at her command and turned. The sadness in her eyes had him balling his fists as he tried to control his erratic heart. "What, Clara?" He exaggerated the forceful tone in his voice.

"What did I do?" she asked, bewildered.

He stared into her eyes one last time before he pivoted and continued stalking down the street, towards the hospital.

"Question six!" she yelled out.

Noel instantly stopped. Breathing in, he spun around and then took long strides until he came close to her.

"No! Don't you dare!" he warned her.

"Twenty-one questions without limits, Nolan Parker! You promised me that, and I'm collecting question six." The way she glared at told him indicated that she wouldn't let it go. He saw the hurt she tried to hide consume her eyes. "What did I do this morning? I said something that made you act this way. I feel like you don't want me here. I'll get another room. Just don't look at me like you hate me, please."

Remorse filled his entire body and he shook his head at his own stupidity.

I want her back and I'm treating her like this. I'm an idiot.

"God, Clara, no," he said, already regretting his behaviour. "You're engaged, for Christ sake's. I can't be doing the shit I'm doing. I'm making you do things you shouldn't because I'm selfish."

"Oh," Clara softly uttered.

"Last night, you said my name when you were in my arms. Do you know what that does to me?"

Clara shook her head at him.

"It gives me hope, Clara. It gives me damn hope. It makes me believe that we can be together, but I look down and you've still got that ring on your finger. How can I win your heart back when you walk around with that ring and the title of someone's fiancée?"

Clara took a step back and she blinked quickly at him.

"Question nine," he had said before she could say anything.

Clara stared at him and only nodded. He looked past the hurt in her eyes and continued on.

"Does he treat you good?"

Noel knew the answer, but he needed to hear it for himself. *She wouldn't have stayed with him this long if he didn't.*

"Yes, he treats me good. He treats me like I'm his world.

Like I mean more than I should. I'm special to him and I matter." Clara's words punched him in the stomach.

Before he could think and take back the words, he yelled out, "And I never did?"

"No, you didn't." She didn't hesitate. The tightening returned to his chest. "For a moment, you did. I believed I mattered to you at one point. But it all changed." Tears slid down Clara's face and she wiped them away with the back of her hand.

"What changed?" he asked.

She glared at him like she didn't understand. His patience snapped and Noel took her hands.

"Question ten. What changed, Clara?" His voice projected more force than he would have liked and he felt her wince.

"You slept with Valerie!" The break in her voice had him faltering for words. Clara pulled her hands from his.

"You're still holding that against me? We *weren't* together!"

He noticed her breathing had hitched as she tried to hold back the tears. He saw the pain etched on her face and then her tears rolled down her cheeks.

She wiped her face and said, "You're right. We were never *really* together. It still broke my heart nonetheless because I cared. Maybe I cared too much. Maybe I loved you more and despite you sleeping with her, I came back for you. I wanted one more chance to redeem myself and be with you. I erased the thought that you slept with someone else. I erased it because I was completely and madly in love with you. That's why I came back. That's why I risked my engagement to be with you. Sleeping with Valerie changed us."

We got past Valerie. We fell in love, we made love, and we were in love. How can she hold Valerie against me? I was only ever hers.

"But I slept with you. I was your first. I thought that meant something to you," Noel uttered out. The burning in his chest brought the stinging to his eyes.

"Is that it? My virginity?"

He looked around to see it was still quiet on the street, too early for people to be roaming around.

"I gave you more than that. I gave you something worth more than my virginity. I gave you my heart, Noel. God! Why is this so hard for us?" She had tilted her head back and stared at the sky before she breathed out.

Noel ran a hand through his hair and sighed. "It's us, Clara. We've always been complicated. It's never been easy for us. Being with you meant more than you think. I fell in love with you the moment you let me in. I chose you over my friendship with Alex. You have to believe me. I was quitting my job to be with you."

"What?" Her eyes widened in surprise.

Noel gently cupped her face and looked into those brown eyes that he wanted forever. "I was giving it all up for you. I was moving back to Melbourne. That was the plan. I made them before I even decided to tell Alex about us. I love you, Clara. You have to believe me. Being with you meant everything to me. I would have promised you the world and fought off every bad dream you had. I would have moved mountains for your happiness." Noel lowered his hands and then took a step back. "Being here with you, it makes me think of all the things we could have been. I want you to choose me because you love me and want to spend your life being with me."

Clara pressed her lips together as she took a step forward and cradled his jaw in her palms. The moment her thumb gently stroked his cheek, he found it difficult to breathe.

"Maybe we weren't meant to cross that line, Noel. Maybe we were just meant to be Alex's best friend and Alex's little sister. Maybe we weren't meant to fall in love with each other. We're destructive when we're together. That line was there for a reason."

His hands gripped her wrists. Clara's thumb instantly stopped its gentle strokes. "Maybe we didn't try hard enough, maybe that's where we got it all wrong," he whispered.

She gave him a tight smile and softly said, "Maybe."

Two had days passed since he found out that his sleeping with Valerie added to Clara's fear and had sent her running. He was sure there was more, but he didn't want to hear it. More added to his frustrations, more showed him he could have easily won her back if he had just stayed.

Noel exited the bathroom to find Clara sitting on the bed with her phone in her hand and a sullen expression on her face. He crouched in front of her and looked up at her.

"You okay?" he asked.

"It's been almost a week since the accident, Noel. He should be awake by now, right?" she asked before her eyes fell back to her phone. He glanced down to see a picture of Clara and her brother. Alex had a large and proud grin on his face as he hugged Clara. The picture was one of Clara in her school uniform. He read the small inscription on the border of photo.

Clara's first day of school.

"Alex wouldn't let me keep the actual picture. He wanted to take it to Scarsdale with him. He sent me a scan of it," Clara said, passing him her phone. Noel sat on the bed and stared at the picture. Clara wore her hair in pigtails that were tied with purple ribbons. His heart broke when he noticed that the inscription was Alex's writing. It was as atrocious now as it was when he was ten.

"Who took this picture?" Noel asked as he passed Clara her phone.

"Max did when he used to walk to school with us." She set the phone on the bed and turned to face him.

Before Alex and Keira's accident, the last time they were in bed together, he had fucked her, letting raw emotion control his body. Had he known then that it was the last time he'd ever be intimate with her, he'd have been passionate. Make love to her and make it so memorable that she'd never want another man but him. But he hadn't made it memorable because Clara found another to make love to and want him so much that she was willing to marry him.

"Noel," Clara said as she took his hand and entwined her fingers with his. He squeezed her hand and Clara smiled at him. "I want you in my life. As hard as it would be, I want you to be there. I can't pretend you don't exist. Not when you're Alex's best friend. Not when you were the one I fell in love with, and you were my once everything."

His stomach dropped. "You're choosing Liam."

She shook her head. "No. I'm not choosing anyone, yet. But

as much as I try to run from you, I find my way back and I feel like I should stop running. My life is entwined with yours. I've tried staying away, but I don't know how to let you go and that's not fair."

He balled his fists to try to prevent the pain from spreading. "I can't pretend like the last ten months have been easy, Clara. I thought about you in some way, every single day we were apart. Even when I was with Andrea, I thought about you. Tell me you thought about me that way. Tell me that you felt a piece of you missing because I wasn't there."

Clara removed her hand from his and scooted forward. "I shouldn't have, but I thought about you. I've always had a piece of me missing since we ended. I have to ask you something."

"Anything."

"If I choose Liam... I want you at my wedding."

What?

"You want me to watch you get married? Clara—"

She stopped him by standing up and facing him. "Noel, I need you there. I need to know that when I get married to Liam, you'll be there supporting my decision. I need you to sit in that church aisle and support me. Promise me a dance at the wedding."

His heart was breaking at the thought that she'd still marry Liam. Noel got up off the bed and stepped in front of Clara. His hands settled on her hips as he brought her close to his body.

"But you haven't chosen him yet?"

If she hasn't, then I have a chance.

"No. This is all a hypothetical scenario. Just promise me you'll be there when I get married and that you'll save me a dance?" she asked hopefully.

Noel closed his eyes tightly for a moment and then he opened them. "I don't want to promise you that. I don't think I could watch you get married."

Clara stepped away from his touch. "Oh," was all she said.

They both fell silent. He noticed Clara fiddling with her engagement ring.

"I'm sorry that was unfair of me to ask. Never mind." She gave him an unnatural smile that he knew was forced.

He sighed. He hated making her unhappy. "Okay. I'll be at your wedding. I want to be in your life, but if you choose Liam, that'll be my closure. Then I know it's over for us, for good. One last dance and we move on with our lives."

"Thank you," Clara said.

The concept of our ending will kill me, but if it makes her happy, I should do it. If her head and her heart is choosing Liam, then I have to let her go.

"I'll drop you off at the hospital before I drive to New York to meet with Mercer and deal with Alex's clients. You'll be okay at the hospital on your own until tonight? Morgan will look out for you," Noel said as he walked past Clara and stood by the door.

"I'll be fine. Just be careful driving, okay? I don't think I could take it if anything happened to you, too."

He tried to build a wall around his heart to stop her words, but it was no use. He hated that she gave him hope with such simple words. "See, you can't say shit like that. You're not making this easy for me. I don't deserve what you're doing to me. I don't want you to act like you care about me and then you marry *him*. Don't give me false hope, Clara. It's not fair."

Clara blinked quickly. "You're right. I'm sorry."

They stood there in silence until he hated the way her anguished expression bore into him. "I wish you had told me how you felt about Valerie. I wish you hadn't run. We could have been happy together for months, Clara." He didn't wait for a response. Instead, he twisted the door handle and held the door open for her.

*L*istening to the sound of smooth jazz playing through the elevator speakers eased Noel's nerves. His meeting with Mercer went as well as it could, considering the circumstances. He and Alex had made a pact when they had first started at G&MC. That if anything happened with either one of their jobs, the other would help out. The first time they went through with the pact was with the Owens account and Noel went to Melbourne. This time, Alex was in a coma and Noel was calming down the worried client. He had discovered that Alex was working on a multi-million dollar account with an advertising company on the West Coast. If the account went through, Alex could become one of the senior accountants of the New York office.

The hour and a half drive back to New Haven had his nerves rising. The tension hit every muscle in his body. He wanted to see Clara. Every moment he was away, he couldn't help but think of a way back to her. His idiotic mistake with Valerie wasn't over for her, and if there was a way back, he'd find it. He stupidly agreed to watch her marry Liam, but that wouldn't be happening. Being in Alex's office and remembering what Alex was doing the night of the accident made Noel realise he wasn't going to show a white flag. He had to win Clara back.

The moment the doors had opened, he quickly walked to Alex's room. His mind had a somewhat speech planned. He knew he wouldn't compose himself; he was sure there would be some begging. All his built-up anger and hurt fled him as soon as his eyes spotted Clara. Her legs were tucked up on the seat as she slept. It was almost six p.m., and he knew how exhausted she was.

Clara had rested her chin in her palm as she slept. He knew she wouldn't be comfortable, but he'd let her sleep. Noel walked up to the bed and took the blanket that was at the end of the mattress. When he reached Clara, he had kissed her head before he covered her lap with the blanket.

"I saw that."

First, his heart stopped and then the rest of his body. He turned around and was in disbelief.

"A-A," he uttered out and took a step towards the bed.

"Keep your voice down. Clara's asleep," Alex said as he sat up on the bed.

I owe you one, Big Man. Thanks for making sure Alex is okay.

"How long have you been awake?" Noel asked.

"'Bout an hour or so. Woke up to a nurse changing my drip. She had a doctor come in and I told them that if they woke up my sister they'd be in a hospital bed. They told me about the accident. I'm just glad Keira's okay. I've been waiting for you. Where've you been?" Alex asked as he fiddled with the drip needle in the back of his hand.

"New York. Spoke to Mercer and your clients," Noel replied as he shrugged out of his suit jacket and set it on the bed.

Alex's brows furrowed. "Should have just concentrated on your own job, Nolan. They would have had to deal with it, but thanks, man. How is she?" he asked nodding over at Clara.

"You scared the hell out of both of us. You're quite the selfish fucker. Don't do that again. We thought we were going to lose you. She's been okay, but it hasn't been easy, especially with your folks."

Alex's jaw clenched and the sounds of the heart monitor hitched for a few beats. "My parents were here? What happened?"

"Wasn't pretty. But she handled herself well. I was actually proud." Noel glanced back at Clara. The way she slept was truly beautiful.

"How are you both?" Alex asked cautiously.

"Are you sure you should be asking so many questions? You were in a coma, Alex."

"I'm fine. I've just got some cuts and bruises, some cracked ribs, and sore legs. You know Keira and I were coming down to convince you to go back to Melbourne, right?"

Noel nodded. "She left me because I slept with Valerie, and she held it against me. She used it as scapegoat, to prevent you and me from hating each other, I suppose."

Alex leant forward and stared at his little sister. "She did it all to make you happy, Noel. You still with Andrea?"

He shook his head. "She broke up with me a few days ago. She realised that I'm in love with Clara." Noel examined his best friend. Besides the bandage around his head and some cuts, Alex looked okay.

"Is she still marrying Liam? Tell me you won her back?"

Noel dug his hands in his pockets and shrugged. "I don't know. I've told her how much I love her, but I don't think it's enough. She asked me to be there when and if she marries Liam."

Clara

A familiar voice had her slowly opening her eyes. Two sets of voices, two that she painfully loved. Clara sat properly and rubbed her eyes. She had spent the entire day at the hospital while Noel was in New York dealing with Alex's work.

"Noel," she said as she stretched. She wasn't sure how long he'd been back, but she had spent her day thinking about him and them.

Noel turned around and smiled at her.

"Listen, about this morning —"

He took a step to her right. The sight instantly had her heart rejoicing and her tears brimming. Before she could even consider the fact that he was hurt, she lunged at Alex and wrapped her arms around him.

"You're awake!" She sobbed and held him tighter. "You're awake, Alex!"

He winced, but she didn't care. He was conscious and he was alive. Alex wrapped his arms around her and rubbed her back. "I'm sorry I scared you, kiddo. I'm here now."

"I thought I lost you," she cried into her brother's chest.

Alex pulled her onto the bed and he held her, their reunion mending her broken heart slightly. "Noel, you mind giving me and Clara some time together?" he asked.

"Of course." Noel nodded and exited the room.

Clara pulled away from her brother. Then she wiped away her tears and from the window, she noticed Noel standing in the hall. She swallowed the lump in her throat. She would have to go back to Melbourne soon. The intensity in her heart increased and she felt a new form of tears fall.

Alex took Clara's hands and she faced her brother. Relief that he was staying in her life flooded every inch of her heart. She smiled at his touch. It wasn't a dream; he was right here with her.

"You told him the reason why you ended it."

Clara nodded and then bit down on her bottom lip as the uncomfortable heat spread through her chest.

"Keira and I were going to Boston to get Noel to come to Melbourne. I know you love Liam, but being with him was making you unhappy, Clara. You keep denying yourself happiness with Noel. Why?"

She crossed her legs, as she got comfortable on her brother's hospital bed. Letting out a huff, she asked, "You think I'm that unhappy with Liam?"

Alex squeezed her hand and then nodded. "I do, kiddo. I know you want to make Liam happy since he was there for you after you and Noel ended. But you got to let him go. For once, you've got to put your happiness first. Don't become like Dad, in it to make Mum happy."

Alex's words left her breathless. She turned and gazed over at Noel. He was leaning on the hallway wall, staring at his feet. The sad expression on his face broke her heart, like he knew their goodbye was fast approaching.

"Clara, I don't really want to go back to Melbourne to watch you marry the wrong man. I'll support you, of course. But I think this time you need to be selfish."

Noel looked up and their eyes met. The hurt in them pained her. She gave him a sad smile and thought about all the times his eyes had radiated with the happiness she had loved.

I fell in love with him the moment he let me in.

"What feels right to you?" Alex asked.

She shifted and faced her brother. The bandage wrapped around his head had her remembering to take life for all it had. She had almost lost her brother for good; she wasn't sure she could handle losing Noel.

"Noel feels right. Noel's my heart's choice. I want to choose him." Clara smiled. The revelation giving her the freedom she had desired.

I want a life with Noel.

The thought eased her heart. Taking a deep breath, Clara craned her neck to see Noel's hands in his pockets, the nervousness clear in his eyes. Clara got off Alex's bed and fiddled with her engagement ring.

"I love Noel. I think I've loved him my whole life."

The joy in Alex's eyes made her heart relax with its choice. "And Liam?"

"I felt like I was taking his happily ever after away from him. I need to figure it all out first before I tell either one of them of my choice. I need to wake up tomorrow and still feel this way before I tell Noel. Hang on, I'll be back in a second."

Clara didn't wait for her brother to reply. Instead, she turned and hurried towards to the door. After opening it, she stepped into the hallway and Noel met her halfway.

"I have to go back to Melbourne."

"Already?" he asked, disheartened.

Clara took his hand and entwined her fingers with his, and softly said, "Yeah."

A few days after Alex had woken up from his coma, Clara found herself sitting in Noel's Camaro heading down Interstate 91 towards Bradley International Airport. Her phone call to Liam didn't make her decision any easier. It only made it tougher. She knew she wanted Noel, but until she faced Liam, she wouldn't know the true meaning of her feelings.

Peeking at Noel every chance she could made her stomach feel light. The last few days had been an emotional roller coaster. Seeing Alex so alive made her appreciate life. Seeing Keira and her brother together made her value their love. That unconditional love in Alex and Keira's eyes was what Clara wanted. She knew Liam had that look in his eyes, but she knew she didn't. It made her feel guilty that she couldn't love Liam like she loved Noel, but she loved him nonetheless.

I want someone to love Liam as he loves me.

Goodbye seemed final once Noel parked the car in short-term parking. They had hardly said anything since they left the hotel. Goodbye was the word she didn't want to use, but for now, it had to be said between them. Just until she knew that her heart's choice wouldn't come with severe consequences.

"I'll get your bag," Noel said. Then he had stared out the windshield and at the parked cars in front of them before he opened the car door. Her heart sank at the sound of it shutting. She worried that it could really be goodbye for them.

Staring at her engagement ring on her finger, Clara felt the pang in her chest hit her hard. She wanted this ring. She wanted the concept of marriage and being someone's wife. But the security of forever meant losing the love of her life. Her side door opened and Noel held it wide for her. Clara unbuckled her seat belt and placed her hand in his. The feeling of his touch always made her a little breathless. The moment she was out of his car, Noel released her hand. The disappointment had left her feeling bitter.

"Here." He held out her small black suitcase.

Clara managed a controlled smile as she took her luggage in her hand. Noel never begged her to stay, never pleaded with her to, but she knew he was giving her what she had wanted — another one of her faults.

"You're going to miss your flight," Noel said in a tight voice. His eyes wandered over to the international departure entry.

"Right," she replied. Instead of turning for the airport, Clara stood there, her feet not wanting to walk away this time.

Please say something.

After a few minutes, she closed her eyes and accepted he wouldn't. She turned and made her way to the departure doors without another word to him.

"Dammit!" Noel growled. "*Clara!*" he yelled out after her.

She stopped and then spun around at the desperation in his voice. Noel stalked towards her until he stood centimetres in front of her. His nostrils flared and she knew he was trying to control his upcoming actions.

"I just need ten seconds of your time, Clara."

"Umm, okay?" She set her suitcase down.

"Ten seconds," he stated.

Clara nodded, unsure of what he meant.

"I just need *you* for ten seconds," he explained before he took her left hand in his.

"Noel," she breathed out.

His fingers grazed over her ring finger and her eyes never left his. He looked up at her for a form of rejection, but the fire in his eyes had her speechless.

Noel's jaw locked as he stared at her left hand. He breathed in sharply as she watched and felt him pull Liam's ring off her finger. She felt free, the burden of the ring was off her shoulders and she gazed up at Noel in bewilderment. Before she could say anything, his hands were on her cheeks bringing his lips to hers.

Finally.

The first brush had her heart stopping. The second had her melting into him. She kissed him back. She poured every inch of love she held for him in that one flawless kiss. His arms were around her lower back, bringing her closer to him. Clara locked her arms around Noel's neck, never wanting to let him go. Just one kiss that broke her heart at the mistakes she had made.

Her head spun at the rightness of this moment. This moment was theirs. No one could tarnish it. She finally had Noel and her heart felt complete. He withdrew his mouth from hers. Her body tingled from the passionate, yet heartbreaking, touch of their lips.

"Ten seconds, huh?" Clara said tightening her arms around him.

"It wasn't enough back in New York. I needed you, the *real* you, for ten seconds," Noel explained. The way his green eyes shone with love had her heart warming.

Clara gave him a slight smile.

"I love you, Clara."

It's time I said it back.

"Noel, I—"

He stopped her with a shake of his head. "Not yet, Clara. I want to hear it, but not yet. I want to hear it the moment you're no longer engaged. I want to know that those three words are honest and true. I want you to go back to Melbourne and make the right choice for you. I gave you two weeks and Alex's accident has placed pressure on you. I want you to make a choice you won't regret. I want you to love me because I'm the one you love and are willing to spend the rest of your life with, without a single ounce of regret. I need you to go back to Melbourne. I want you to decide if what you feel for me now is real or if it's the result of Alex's accident."

Tears instantly brimmed from his words. This man had been the boy she had unknowingly loved her whole life. He was giving her the chance to decide how real her love was.

"Okay," she agreed.

Noel hugged her tightly. "I just hope you find a way back to me, Clara."

I'll find my way back to him.

After a moment of embrace in the middle of the car park, Noel let Clara go. He held out her engagement ring and took her left hand. Breathing out, he slid the ring down Clara's finger. She kept her eyes on him as he did so, imagining the possibility of his ring on her.

The torment that succumbed Noel's eyes had her feeling

discourage. She had hurt him so many times. Once she had said Valerie's name, she no longer held it against him. He was right. Technically, they hadn't been together, but it still hurt her.

"I love you, Clara," Noel softly said.

Letting his words sink deep into her heart, she smiled at him. Though she never said those three words back, she hoped the smile she gave him was enough. Clara bent her knees and picked up her suitcase. She stared at him, remembering this moment—how his eyes filled with sadness and love, how his frown broke her heart, and how the hope that consumed his face had her chest tightening.

She gripped the handle of her luggage tighter and turned for the airport doors. Tears rolled down her face as she took step after step away from him. Once inside, she spun around to see Noel wiping his face.

Noel's my choice.

Chapter EIGHTEEN

Clara

Liam: *Meet me at the bakery.*

There was no *'welcome home'* or *'sweetheart'* message, and Clara felt the worry rise within. Biting her lip, she reread the five-word message again. With no possible clues as to what to expect, she locked her phone and placed it on her lap.

Watching Noel wipe those tears away broke her and wore her down to making a choice. Calling Liam during her stopover in Singapore made that choice redundant. The flight from Sydney to Melbourne had her undecided. Sitting in the back of the taxi, she rubbed her eyes and hoped maybe seeing Liam would finally give her the courage to break someone's heart, even if it meant her own.

When the taxi stopped, she breathed out, knowing she'd have to face Liam.

"Thank you," she said and handed over the fare. Clara opened the taxi door and stepped onto the concrete footpath with her luggage in hand.

Her eyes roamed the white bakery, and she felt the instant bile start to rise. It was a sight she had never expected. It felt like a lifetime ago since she was in front of the bakery, but it had only been just over a week. The grip she had on her suitcase handle loosened and it fell to the ground with a moderate *bang*. There was no temptation to pick it up. Her eyes watered at the sight of her bakery.

Closing her eyes, she had prayed to the universe before opening them again. The sight didn't vanish. Black sheets hung from inside of the bakery, obscuring prying eyes into the once visible shop. Every single window was covered, the flower boxes that once lined the windows were now gone and the outdoor chairs and tables were nowhere to be seen. Looking up at the building, *The Little Bakery* sign was no longer bolted above the door.

"No," she whispered. Swallowing the large lump in her throat, she bent her knees and picked up her suitcase. "It can't be," she chanted several times and shook her head.

Taking a few steps forward, she stopped in front of the once white painted doors to find that the paint had been sanded down. The sign in front of Clara had her blinking several times.

CLOSED UNTIL FURTHER NOTICE.

The struggle to breathe grew fierce as the reality of the sign hit her, completely and utterly surprising Clara. The bakery was closed. The only time it closed was for Christmas and Easter. The removal of the bakery sign and the black sheets covering the windows only confirmed the ache in her heart.

I'm losing the bakery.

It was a concept she didn't want to believe. Liam couldn't have sold the bakery so quickly, but with the lure of such an area, it would sell instantly. Movement caught her eye and she saw the black sheet covering the door move slightly. Liam looked at her; those hazel eyes were darker than she last remembered. Clara took a step back as he opened the door and stepped on the black footpath. He didn't pull her in for a kiss or greet her, his face expressionless. Her eyes roamed the building and then they started to sting.

"I'll buy the bakery from you," she uttered after she placed her suitcase back on the ground.

"Clara." His voice was tight and controlled.

"No, you can't sell it. Please, Liam. I'll pay double what you paid," she begged.

His eyebrows shot up and the surprise succumbed his face. "I paid well over eight hundred thousand," he stated.

Clara did the math in her head; including taxes and transfer fees, it would cost her close to one-point-nine-million-dollars. The total figure sent her heart plunging.

"That's a lot of money," Liam pointed out.

A tear fell and she quickly wiped it away, knowing she'd have to sell her soul for the bakery. She let out a defeated sigh, and instantly regretted what she would say next. "I have that kind of money."

"What?" Liam blurted out.

"I can afford the bakery. Name your price and I'll pay it."

The surprise on his face faded as he frowned. "Almost two million dollars, Clara? How do you have that kind of money?" He sounded hurt.

"I have three trust funds. Two of them have clauses that let me invest the money in projects after I turn eighteen. I can't access the one my father set up until I'm twenty-one. Let me talk to my father's lawyer and have my trust funds looked at. Just please don't sell the bakery. If I can't get my trust money, let me ask the bank. I have enough for a loan, I hope." She was begging and pleading. The bakery was where so many firsts had happened that she couldn't imagine not owning it.

Liam's body stiffened. "You have trust funds? How much money are we talking?"

Averting his stare, she felt her hands sweat and she fiddled with her fingers. "Almost six million dollars," she revealed.

"Six... million... dollars?" Liam uttered out.

"Yes," she confirmed and a smile spread across his face. A cold wind blew and Clara involuntary shivered; it was much cooler in Melbourne than it was in New Haven.

Liam stepped forward, bent down and took her suitcase. His smile confused her and he took her hand. The first thing she noticed was the difference in his touch. Liam felt off and his behaviour with her was unlike him. He led her to the door, set the suitcase down, and with his free hand he opened the bakery doors. The black sheets that covered the windows had made the once bright bakery eerily dark. This wasn't what she had imagined for her bakery; she knew she had to beg Liam to sell it to her.

The moment he let go of her hand, she heard the door close, stopping the small amount of light from entering the bakery. She stood there in the darkness until she heard her suitcase being set down.

"Surprise!" people shouted out loud in unison as bright lights blinded her eyes.

Her hands quickly rose to cover face. Clara heard the sounds of rushing footsteps and then she was being hugged tightly.

"Clara!" Annie squealed.

Clara couldn't move her hands to see her. Arms tighten around her and she felt herself being completely squashed.

"I think we're suffocating her," Jarred pointed out.

Her lips formed a smile at his voice; she'd missed him and realised that she'd spent weeks distancing herself from him. Jarred was there when she had ended it with Noel, his judgment of her was one she valued.

"Please," Clara had choked out before the pressure around her eased. Moving her hands, she took in the air her lungs needed but kept her eyes closed.

"Surprise, sweetheart! Open your eyes," Liam instructed, his arm wrapped around her.

Slowly, she lifted her eyelids. All breath left her as she took in the vision of the bakery. "Oh, my God," she breathed. Clara scanned the shop floor, taking in her surroundings and the familiar faces she could see.

"You like it?" Liam whispered in her ear.

She couldn't respond. She was utterly speechless. "How?"

His touch left her as he stood in front of Clara. His hazel eyes made her realise just how innocent he was. Perfection looked at her and it killed her inside.

"I wanted to surprise you. You left the list of your plans in the study. Your blueprints weren't that hard to find. I asked Danny to close the place down so I could have the tradies come in and renovate. I hope it's everything you ever wanted."

The hope in his voice and face had Clara smiling. The old décor was now replaced with a French theme. Whites and pastel colours filled the shop and she spotted vinyl booths towards the back of the bakery.

"Does that say cakes?" Clara pointed at a glass display. Each display would fit a four-tier cake.

"I told him you'd like that display much better for cakes. The macaron bar was Jarred's idea. But those booths being towards the back was Josie's," Danny, her boss, said as he pointed around the room.

The faces that filled the room made her smile but at the same time there were people missing. "Where are Rob and Max?" she asked.

Behind Liam, she noticed Stevie shaking her head at her question.

"They couldn't make it. Sorry, sweetheart."

I have my dream bakery, but I don't have my two friends… I don't have Noel.

The beaming smile from Liam caused an internal sob. She was in too deep. This surprise party just shot the plan to end her engagement to hell.

"Clary!" a little voice shrieked.

She watched a little blonde girl run to her. Clara bent her knees and scooped CeCe into her arms as the tears that had brimmed her eyes fell. "Hello, pretty girl."

CeCe wrapped her arms around Clara's neck. "I missed you," CeCe said against her neck.

"She's been looking for you," Ally said as she walked over to them.

Clara managed a smile and nodded her head. There were no words she could form. The sight of Liam, Ally, and CeCe reminded her of what made her stay for all those months. Her heart knew that there was no way back to Noel. That idea of leaving Liam came with consequences and it took returning to Melbourne to realise what they were.

"I think it's time we celebrate the fact that my son's finally landed an amazing girl," Liam's father, David, said loudly.

Her eyes couldn't meet David's. There was so much shame that filled Clara's mind and chest. The realisation was making it difficult for her to breathe. Fearful she'd drop CeCe, Clara handed her to Liam. Her head felt incredibly light, and for a second, she thought she'd faint.

"I had no idea your parents were coming this early," she managed to say.

"Oh yeah, they came to surprise you. Mother's been staring at your wedding dress ever since she landed yesterday. Don't worry, I haven't looked." Liam winked.

The thought of her wedding dress made her sick.

"Sienna!" Liam waved her over. It had been months since Clara had seen Liam's best friend.

"Clara, so good to see you. I'm so glad to hear that your brother is doing well. He'll make it to the wedding, right?" Sienna asked as she swirled the straw in her glass.

The wedding.

Countless pairs of eyes met hers, waiting for her answer. Her throat tightened and the room felt small around her. "Yes," she croaked out, instantly regretting the word that had left her mouth. That one word sealed her fate; there would be no future with Nolan Parker.

Clara's eyes met Stevie's, whose brimmed with tears. Because, at that moment, Stevie understood what she had just decided.

*L*ooking at the paper in front of her, she felt pieces of herself start to crumble. A confession of her love written down in words that would never be read. When she stood at the mailbox at the post office, she realised she couldn't mail it. Liam's surprise engagement party had hijacked her. There was no way she could end her engagement in front of all of Liam's family. A room filled with almost a hundred people unnerved her. In comparison to all of Liam's loved ones, Clara had next to none.

In total she had five guests: Stevie, Annie, Jarred, Danny, and Josie. There was no Rob or Max. There was no one else. The realisation had Clara running to Jo for the guest list. Add in her brother and Keira, Clara had seven guests to her own wedding. Her parents had refused to attend, and Max and Rob still hadn't made a choice. She knew their loyalty wasn't hers to claim.

There would be close to two hundred guests and only seven of those were Clara's. Placing the papers down, she picked up Noel's invitation. He promised that if she chose Liam, then he'd attend, but part of her wanted him to come and steal her away. She could run away with Noel, but the unfairness of inviting him had her setting the envelope down. In the two days since her arrival back in Melbourne, Clara had regretted every decision she had made.

She picked up Noel's letter. Having read it one last time, she folded it and placed it in a purple envelope. She leant into the wooden chair of the office Liam had set up while she was away and sighed. There was no doubt that Liam made her happy, but it wasn't the same. It wasn't until Liam spoke of her so fondly and lovingly that she had willingly accepted a life with him. He would be proud of her and she didn't want to be selfish when it would hurt him.

Part of her hated herself but another part told her that she had made her bed long ago and now had to lie in it. She'd have lost the bakery, Liam, Ally, and CeCe. They were as close to a family as it got for her. They took her in and accepted Clara. She could love Liam, but at the same time, she knew it wasn't the love he wanted from her. One week and six days until her wedding. If there was a time to run, it had to be soon. The only problem—for the first time in her life, Clara had no idea how to run.

"You coming to bed?" Liam asked from behind her.

Clara turned and smiled at the sight of him. His shirt was unbuttoned and his hair ruffled. He didn't deserve to have his heart broken. She wouldn't allow herself to do that.

"Yeah," Clara replied. Picking up Noel's envelope, she opened the drawer to her left and slid it under a pile of paper. She closed the drawer and Clara's choice felt cemented. She had no idea if she'd send it, but she'd let Noel know of her choice. It would break her and leave her hollow inside, but Noel deserved someone better than her.

"Are you packed?" Clara asked as she stood up from the chair and walked towards him.

"Yeah. Can't wait to go on this bachelor party; this is going to be insane! You sure you don't want to go to some resort or another country for your bachelorette party?" Liam asked sweetly as he brought her into his arms.

Clara shook her head. "No, I'd rather not. The hot springs is what I want. I wish you'd tell me where you're going."

Liam kissed her cheek and then shook his head. "Sorry, Clara, but this one I'm keeping from you. The boys want this to be a complete bachelor party." There was something off about what he said. He didn't seem as excited as he had tried to project, but she ignored it.

Resting her head against his chest, Liam's heartbeat sounded strong against her ear. He was always the strong one and the one she had depended on. The thought that she could ruin him had her accepting the marriage she would be entering.

"You be good," she teasingly warned.

Liam cupped the back of her head with his palm and held her tighter, his chin resting on the top of her head. "You love me, right?"

She tensed at his innocent question.

Wrapping her arms around his waist, Clara nodded into his chest. "Of course, I do," she replied honestly. It was true, she loved Liam and always would. But the fearlessness that came with loving Noel didn't overtake her when it came to loving Liam.

"I love you, Clara," Liam whispered.

It almost sounded like a goodbye, tainted with so much sadness that Clara's eyes started to sting.

Noel

"The Lyndon account has been secured, and they're open for us to do business with them for the next five years," Gregson stated as he moved his glasses up the bridge of his nose.

Noel nodded and fiddled with his pen, not really bothered to pay proper attention.

"Miss Wallace, I trust you won't let me down and draw up a new contract," Gregson said without looking at Andrea.

Looking at Andrea from across the table, Noel saw the twitch in her lip. He offered a smile, and she relaxed.

"Yes, sir," Andrea said with no arguments.

Gregson glanced up with a raised eyebrow. The smirk on Andrea's face had Noel internally laughing.

The meeting continued to drag on as he sat uncomfortably

in his seat. All the major players in the Boston office of G&MC filled the boardroom. But his head wasn't in it. Instead, he thought about Clara. One week and four days until her wedding, and he still hadn't heard a word from her.

After twenty minutes of the lifeless meeting, he felt his phone vibrate. Not caring about being caught, he took out his phone and his heart stopped mid-beat. Clara's name appeared on the screen. Swiping his thumb across it, he opened her message.

> **Clara:** *I'm sorry, Noel. I don't know how to find a way to you without breaking his heart. I'm so sorry.*

He felt the sudden burst of anger in him. It couldn't be. He shouldn't have let her go without her expressing her love. If she had said those words, she wouldn't be returning to Liam. The pressure in his chest had him out of his seat.

"Mr Parker, where's the emergency?" Gregson's stern voice laid his irritation on thick.

"I'm about to lose the love of my life!" Noel blurted out.

Everyone in the boardroom looked over at Andrea.

Raising her hands, she shook her head and said, "Don't look at me. I'm not the love of his life."

Eyes darted back over to him, and he gave Andrea an appreciative smile.

"We're in a middle of an important meeting, Mr Parker. I suggest you sit down. A senior accountant up for promotion would know better than to leave a meeting like this," Gregson stated. Then he looked down at the file in front of him and continued with the meeting.

Countless pairs of eyes locked on him and Noel shook his head. "Screw the promotion! I couldn't give a shit about it. God knows I wouldn't get it. Give it to someone else and demote me if you like. The woman I love is about to marry some other man, and I've sat back and let it happen. I'm getting her back for good this time." He didn't wait for Gregson to reply. Noel stormed out of the boardroom, unsure if he would have a job when he returned.

He stalked towards the stairwell door, pushed it open, and entered the stairwell. Adrenaline from telling Gregson to shove it coursed through his veins. Noel was stupid for letting her go. Clara was beyond doubtful; one smile from Liam and she would accept his hand in marriage.

Steadying against the metal railing of the stairs, he called Clara. He heard the international dial tone before the regular rings began. With each second that passed, he felt her slipping away.

"Hey, you've reached Clara. Sorry I—" Noel hung up at the sound of her voicemail message.

"No! You can't do this to me, Clara!" he yelled as he redialled her number. Looking at his watch, he knew it was three a.m. back in Melbourne, but he didn't care. He was sick of her games and wanted it to end between them.

He was just about to hang up when he heard her answer.

"Nolan, please—" she began to softly say.

"No, don't *Nolan* me. God, you can't end us and marry him, Clara. You almost told me you loved me less than a week ago. What the hell?" He heard the desperation in his own voice. It made him sound weak, but he was where Clara was concerned.

There was nothing but silence as he ruffled his hair. It was ending, and he didn't want it to be over. This chapter in their complicated story couldn't be their last.

"Don't you want a life with me?" he asked, dejected.

She sniffed. "I'm tired, Noel."

He knew she had meant that the time of their phone call was late for her. But it didn't stop what he was about to say. It was the truth.

"Then stop being what you think Liam needs. It's not the real you and you know it. I get it. You want to be something worthy of him, but you're perfect the way you are. I miss you, Clara. The *real* you. The one that I know is in there, the one that loved me, the Clara that wanted me and had me promise to love her forever. What happened to her?" he asked as his eyes focused on the stairwell door.

"I-I," she stammered out, and then she exhaled heavily.

"I shouldn't have let you get on that damn plane! I should have worn you down and convinced you to stay with me. If I had just let you say those three words then I'd never have let you leave me again," he confessed.

"I regret not saying it to you back in Connecticut. In fact, you're my favourite regret, Nolan Parker. That's the only way I can simply put it. It's three words that meant everything to me. But this time, I don't think I can come back to you. I'm in too deep..." Clara's voice trailed off.

His heart ached for her. He knew how hard of a choice it was for her.

"Please don't come after me. *It's time.*"

He heard her sob and his knees buckled. Noel sat on the concrete stairs, his back against the railing. His heart started to shut down at her words. They sat in silence as the minutes ticked by.

"I wish you a good and happy life, Clara," he said once the silence started to eat him alive. He blinked to let the tears that had brimmed his eyes to fall freely.

"Thank you for loving me the way you did. You gave me a love that no one else has."

He sensed her love in those words. His heart decided that at that moment it wasn't enough for him. Getting up, he held the phone tighter to his ear, savouring her words.

"I chose to love you because my heart wasn't giving me any other option," Noel admitted before he hung up.

He wasn't going to give her a chance to have the last word. Placing his phone in his jacket pocket, Noel opened the door and walked back into the office space. He did not intend to go back into that meeting. Instead, he made his way to his office.

Just shy of his office door, he heard someone calling his name. Turning around, he watched as Andrea ran up to him.

She breathed out and then smiled at him. "I'll make sure you have a job to come back to. I'm pretty sure no one here would like to see you go. Gregson needs you, and he wouldn't fire you. Go get her."

"I will," he promised himself more than he was promising Andrea.

I have to get my passport and get on the next plane to Melbourne.

*W*hen the doors had opened to his floor, Noel exited the elevator, and reached up to his grey tie to loosen the noose he felt around his neck. He had his game plan cemented and memorised. Gregson wasn't happy and Noel walked out of the office with unpaid leave—not that he cared.

He tore his gaze off his shoes and noticed someone leaning on the wall next to his door. Squinting, all air left him. Noel willed his legs to continue the steps needed to get to his apartment door. Their eyes met and he was confused by the happiness he saw in them.

"Hey, Noel."

He blinked several times to make sure he was not hallucinating. "Liam," he said, noticing the surprise in his own voice.

Liam pushed off the wall and held his hand out in front of Noel. Confused for a second, he composed himself enough to shake hands.

"Is… she with you? Is she okay?" Noel asked with much concern.

A sad smile developed on Liam's face. "You love my fiancée *that* much. But no, she's not here, and no, she's not okay." Liam's entire body seemed to lose its strength before Noel's very eyes.

"You know about what happened between Clara and me?" Noel gripped his briefcase tighter.

Liam let out a small laugh and nodded. "I've known about you two for a long time. When you were back in Melbourne, you and Clara were on the balcony, and I saw. What are you doing to her?"

Liam knows.

Noel breathed out. He had and still expected a punch in the face. "What do you mean?"

Liam ran a hand through his ashy blonde hair and shook his head. "You should be with her by now. I thought this time when she came back she'd end it but nope! She's still with me. She's still *my* fiancée. Why didn't you convince her to stay?"

What?

"I don't—" Noel couldn't comprehend Liam's presence let alone what he was saying. "What are you doing in Boston?"

"My bachelor party's in Vegas, and I made a stop to see you," Liam admitted.

"Why?" Noel asked unbelievably. Liam should be angry with him for trying to take away Clara, yet he stood calmly in front of Noel.

"I need to give Clara the choice. If she chooses me, then I know she wants a future with me. Then I know we're meant to be together and we all get our closure. And well, because she loves you. She doesn't love me like she loves you and it kills me that she doesn't. You have to come back and convince her to be with you. I can't do it. I thought about ending it, but I love her too much. I've only ever loved her so it's hard for me to let go. You can understand where I'm coming from, you love her, too," Liam said. The pain in his eyes was one Noel knew well. It was a look he saw in the mirror after Clara had ended them.

"But why would you give me permission to go after *your* fiancée?" Noel asked, bewildered. If it were the other way around, he'd be threatening Liam's life.

"I miss her smile. She doesn't smile the way she used to. I'm in the way of her being happy," Liam confessed. "I need her to smile again, Noel. I need that old Clara back. I need you to save her from a life with me." Liam wiped a tear that escaped him, reached behind him, and pulled out two envelopes. He then handed them to Noel and said, "I need *you* to make her smile again. I need you to love her and make her happy. Her heart doesn't want me and all I've ever wanted was her heart. I couldn't compete with your love. I tried, but I just keep losing."

Noel glanced down at the envelopes and frowned. "What are they?" he asked as his eyes met Liam.

"The ivory one is an invitation to the wedding and the purple one is a letter she wrote you. I need you to stop this and get this idea that I need her out of her head. I don't know how late I am, but I'm hoping I can change your mind. I'm stopping Clara from being happy, and I can't be selfish anymore. If you don't come to the wedding, I'm marrying her without a second thought. But if you do decide to fight one more time, I ask that you come just before the wedding. It'll force her into a final decision, and she'll finally give us her *true* choice."

"You love Clara enough to do this for her?" Noel asked as he held onto the sealed envelopes.

Liam nodded. "Please come back for her. It's *you* she needs, not me. It was never me."

Noel peeked at the envelope and saw his name in her scripted writing.

"Just think about it, okay?"

He nodded and saw a heartbreaking smile on Liam's face. "Thank you," Noel softly said.

"I'm glad I'm losing her to you. She deserves to be happy. But…" Liam put his hands in his pockets and Noel noticed the exhausted expression on his face. Liam then shook his head and asked, "D-did you sleep with her while she was here?"

It would have been the same thought that kept me up at night.

"No. We didn't. But I kissed her and she told me no. It happened a few times and all those times were because of me," Noel honestly confessed.

Liam let out a laugh that confused him. "Yeah, I'd kiss her, too. I should be mad that you made a move on my fiancée, but I honestly don't blame you. Just come back to Melbourne." He didn't let Noel reply as he pushed past him and made his way to the elevator, leaving Noel with two envelopes—one that contained an invitation and one a letter.

Chapter
NINETEEN

Noel

*P*acing in front of the dining table, he kept his eyes on the two envelopes on the glass top. He had never expected Liam to give him permission to have a life with Clara. If it had been Noel, he would never give any man that option. He'd have never let her go. Looking into his eyes, Noel knew Liam loved Clara enough to do this for her. If anyone ever really deserved Clara, it was Liam.

Noel reached into his pocket; he took out and unlocked his phone. Then he dialled Alex's number. Besides a few broken bones and the healing scar on his head, Alex was doing okay. Keira was released a few days ago; she had a few broken ribs and a dislocated arm. Alex was released early yesterday after numerous tests were conducted to ensure no brain damage. The swelling was just that, swelling.

"Hey!" Alex greeted with a chirp, his voice sounded distant.

"Keira only letting you use the speakerphone on all your calls?" Noel asked as he pulled out a dining chair and settled in it.

Alex laughed. "Yeah, she's paranoid that I'll have some sort of brain malfunction if I put my phone close to my head, but I'm good. The doctors said I was good. I got on the plane all right. I'm good."

Noel recognised that Alex had said 'good' one too many times. He knew his best friend was still in pain, and the plane ride back to New York wasn't easy.

"What's up?" Alex asked.

Noel wasn't sure how to go about it. In fact, he couldn't believe what he'd just witnessed. "Liam came to my apartment," Noel stated.

"What?" Alex asked, surprised. "Was Clara with him?"

"No. I spoke to her just before I left the office after telling Gregson that I didn't give a shit about my job. Got to my door to find him there."

"Seriously?"

"Yeah. He told me that he knew about Clara and me. Said that he couldn't make her happy and knew that she was only marrying him to make him happy. He handed me two envelopes, an invitation and a letter from Clara, and told me to stop the wedding because he couldn't." Noel picked up the purple envelope, placed it in front of him, and ran his fingertips over his name. His fingers twitched in anticipation.

"Damn. He's a stand-up guy." Alex sighed.

"Kinda makes you think she really does deserve him instead of me," Noel said honestly.

A familiar hum from Alex told Noel that he was weighing up the options. "Doesn't matter if he is a stand-up guy. You're my best friend and I'm not impartial on this. Do what you got to do."

Tapping his fingers on the glass table, Noel thought about his options. Option one included him being selfish and going after the woman who held his heart. Or option two was to let her marry a man far more deserving than he was. Noel glared at the ivory envelope, and his heart ached at the thought of her being married to anyone other than him. His heart and head united to make a decision. He was going to be selfish.

"When are you going back to Melbourne?"

"Couple days. Keira won't let me go until I have another MRI here in New York. I'm worried about her broken ribs and she's hell-bent on worrying about me instead of herself." Alex proudly exaggerated his annoyance.

"She loves you, you clueless bastard!" Noel chuckled. It was good to have his best friend conscious and talking. He had missed Alex.

They shared a laugh until Alex coughed and composed himself. "Noel, I'm not the clueless one here. Read my sister's letter and read between the lines. The choice is yours to make, but I hope to see you at the wedding."

With a firm nod and the ache of missing her fuelling him, Noel said, "I'll see you in Melbourne," and then hung up.

He placed his phone on the table, took the letter in his hand, and ripped it open. He removed the folded sheets of paper, and the first thing he noticed was her beautiful writing.

Dear Noel,

There's a lot I'm afraid to say and many things I should have done when it came to us. But when it came time to acting, I didn't take the opportunity. There's a lot I am sorry for and more than likely regretful over. If anyone had told me a year ago that I would be falling in love with you, I'd have told them they were crazy. Looking back, I was the crazy one because I did fall in love with you.

I spent my childhood in fear of you because you looked at me with such hate that I never thought you'd let me into your life. Fast forward and it was I who didn't let you in. Walking away from you and the concept of us will always be one of my most regrettable mistakes. If I could go back and have made you stay that night we went to that club, then things for us would have been different. But looking back, I realised that I used you sleeping with Valerie as my escape route. I was scared to love you. I was scared of what would happen if Alex knew and everyone else. I was scared that you wouldn't see me the same and this fairy tale of you loving me would be just that, a fairy tale. Who would have thought that Nolan Parker, the jerk of my childhood, would be the prince I wanted to save me. I've always needed saving. I thought I didn't, but I've always needed someone to catch me each time I fell. Just like how you caught me and helped me with my bloody knee when I was four.

Falling in love with you, I realised that our lives always entwined with each other, but maybe it's time we sever that link between us. I kept thinking I'd never see you again after I walked away the first time. But the truth is my heart kept hoping to see you because my heart will always be drawn to you. I'm going to have to tell my heart that it's time to stop being hopeful of a life with you. It's time we end.

I feel like I ruined your life, inflicted unnecessary pain, and some days, I wish you never loved me. It would have been better between us if you and I hadn't. Those days before you, I thought I was happy, but now I know I was pretending to be happy. I was missing one thing in my life and that was you. Walking away confirmed that piece would always be you. You were the piece of me I've been waiting for. I don't know if either of us knew it, but I think I've been in love with you for far longer than either one of us first believed, far longer than you standing at my door that day in October.

That day changed my life. You changed my life. I can't ever regret what we had. The only thing I can and will always regret is how we ended, and how I didn't try hard enough. I have this firm belief that I'm not the woman you're meant to spend the rest of your life with because, if we removed this façade, I'm still just Alex's little sister. I'm not that strong woman I see you with. I'm just a coward.

I've decided to marry Liam. It might be hard for you to contemplate and you may hate me forever, but I owe him a lot more than just my heart, though you seem to own it. I owe him compassion, I owe him a friendship, and I owe him loyalty. He deserves far better than me, but he chose me. The love in his eyes is hard to say no to and I feel my love for him. It may not terrify me like the love I've held for you, but it's there.

I know it's hard for you, and it's hard for me, too, but I think it's best if you don't come to the wedding. It was an unfair request and I will not hold you to it. You deserve happiness too, and I've done nothing but inflict pain on your heart. I wish I could love him as I loved you, but maybe that's what makes my love for Liam different and worthy of lasting. We built our love on pain and uncertainty; how could that kind of love last forever?

I'm choosing Liam. I hope you live a good and happy life, Nolan. And I hope that the woman who ties you down makes you happy. But I know she will because you will never change your mind about her. You will love her forever, simply forever. I don't know if I'll ever send you this. Maybe I'm writing this to rid my heart of the things I'll never say. The things you deserved, but I'm just too selfish to give you a proper goodbye. Goodbye means I'll never have a chance to be with you and maybe never giving you this letter lets me have some sort of happily ever after. Maybe in another life we could have made it. I'm so sorry I did this to you and to us. I'm so sorry I chose to walk away instead of fighting with you and for you. I'm so sorry you fell in love with me and held on to that love. I'm so sorry I broke your heart and denied you love with Andrea. I'm so sorry, Nolan Parker. I'll never stop being sorry.

I wish you nothing but pure happiness. You deserve it after loving someone like me. Just know that I loved you. With all my heart, I loved you.

Clara.

Chapter
TWENTY

Clara

"Clara, you are going to look absolutely beautiful in your wedding dress," her mother-in-law-to-be, Imogen, commented.

"Thank you, Mrs O'Connor."

Imogen turned around and tilted her head at Clara. "Darling, it's either Mum or Imogen. You're my daughter now, too."

All Clara did was smile back and nod. She took in the sight of the altar. In five days, she would be getting married. Liam had returned from his bachelor trip with a smile, and she was happy to see him. The nervousness in his eyes no longer existed. Instead, he looked content.

At the end of the altar, she watched as Liam spoke to the minister who would marry them. The grin on her fiancé's face made her smile. He was happy, and for the first time since returning from Connecticut, she was, too. The pure joy on Annie's face had Clara raising her eyebrow at Jarred.

He shook his head and chuckled. "She's getting ideas," he said as he walked down the aisle to Clara. "Mrs O'Connor, may I please borrow Clara for a moment?" Jarred asked with such sweetness that it was impossible to say no.

Imogen smiled and nodded her head.

"I'll be back," Clara said. She followed Jarred as they left the altar, walked towards the large wooden doors, and exited the church.

They walked in silence as he led her away from the church and behind a large tree, some distance away. Jarred stopped and then faced her.

"You okay?" he asked.

She hadn't realised how tense she was until she walked out of the church. Looking around and seeing no one around, Clara slipped out of her heels and let the cold tarmac relieve her aching feet.

"I'm good, really good. Absolutely good." She nodded as she wiggled her toes.

"You said 'good' three times, Clara."

"And?"

"You repeat words when you lie," Jarred pointed out and dug his hands into his pockets.

"I do not! I'm good, fine, perfect. I'm happy." Clara threw her hands in the air, exhausted.

"You used far too many words to describe that lie."

The seriousness in Jarred's usual carefree face had her shoulders sagging.

"Jarred, I really don't want to have this discussion with you." Clara fiddled with her engagement ring. There was a sigh from Jarred, and she met his concerned gaze.

"Tough luck. Don't you remember?"

"Remember what?" Clara asked, her eyebrows knitted.

"Almost a year ago, you and Noel ended. Don't you remember how I said I'd have that legal pad with reasons why you made the right choice when you found the one? Well..." Jarred pulled out his right hand and held out a folded piece of yellow lined paper.

She looked down at it and her heart sank. He was there that night she had walked away. In his moment of compassion towards her, he had made her a promise that he now fulfilled.

"Jarred," she softly said.

"I'm your best friend, and I know we've drifted. You have your reasons and I'm always here, but this was a promise I wasn't willing to break. Just read it," Jarred begged with a sad smile.

She took the piece of paper from him. Clara held it tightly in her hand and bit her lip.

"Don't end up like Stevie," Jarred said as he walked past her and made his way back to the church.

When she was sure she was alone, Clara started to unfold the piece of paper. She looked down to see Jarred's writing, and his words instantly brought the fire in her chest and the stinging in her eyes.

> Reasons why I know Clara found the one:
> You've already found him, and he's waiting for you in Boston.
> Noel's the one.
> Because no matter how much you think you love Liam, he's not Noel. You found the one, Clara. You've fought countless battles and you've been through more pain than others have. You will always come out loving him no matter how much you try to tell yourself otherwise. The reason why I know Noel's the one: because your heart won't let him go, even after all this time. You need to let Liam go, Clara. It's time you let your heart win. It's time you won your battles. It's time you let Noel back into your life and willingly into your heart.
> P.S. I'm not good with words; I should have asked Annie for help! But I hope you get what I mean.
> Noel's the one.

Chapter
TWENTY-ONE

Clara

*J*arred's reasons were not her own. Though his words touched her and made her heart ache, it wasn't the driving force. It wasn't enough for Clara to leave Liam. It wasn't enough to will her to end it. She had spent the last two nights reading Jarred's reasons. He said he wasn't good with words, but he had proven himself wrong. That afternoon they spoke in private, and he understood why she couldn't succumb to the piece of paper. In the end, he had her blessing as she had his.

Looking down at the paper in her lap, Clara let out a heavy groan.

"You okay over there, Clara?" Keira asked peeking up from the bridal magazine she was reading.

Clara raised her legs and crossed them on the cream French couch of her Royal Suite at The Hotel Windsor. She gazed over at the French-inspired fireplace to her right and frowned at the extravagance of the her room. Liam had practically booked out floors of one of Melbourne's most prestigious five-star hotels.

Holding up the blank piece of paper in front of her and the end of her pen to her lip, she shook her head. Accepting defeat, she let the paper and pen fall to the ground. "I don't know how to write my vows. I need Google."

Keira laughed as she held the side of her body, trying not to cause discomfort to her ribs. "You don't need Google. These things take time."

Scrunching up her nose, she looked over at Annie, who sat in the armchair in front of her.

Annie pointed at Clara and said, "It should come naturally."

She flinched. Drawing up her knees, Clara wrapped her arms around her legs and rested her chin on her knees. "I know it should," she whispered and closed her eyes.

"No, Clara, I didn't mean it like that. Please don't be upset with me."

Opening her eyes, Clara smiled up at Annie. "I'm not. I just... I don't know with this wedding stuff. Honestly, I never imagined myself getting married. My parents put me off the idea, then Darren and—" Clara stopped herself. It was a lie, she saw herself marrying Noel, but she also saw a life with Liam.

"You're going to be fine." Keira gave her a beaming smile.

"Easy for you to say. You have my brother so in love with you that marriage is around the corner," Clara said as she unwrapped her arms and reached over for the pen and paper on the floor. When she sat back up, Clara saw the contented smile on Keira's face.

"I see myself being Alex's wife. I'd love that honour."

"I'd marry Jarred," Annie joined in.

Clara smiled at Annie's words as she shook her head. "Better not talk about that kind of stuff around Ally and Stevie," Clara said as she tapped the pen on the paper.

I need to write my vows.

Clara gazed down at the paper. She tuned out Annie and Keira's conversation and concentrated on her vows. She didn't really need to hear about how romantic her brother was. It was a little sickening, but she was genuinely happy for Alex and Keira.

Twenty minutes later and she still had no words. She needed inspiration and she needed a certain search engine. Groaning out, Clara scrunched up the unwritten piece of paper and threw it across the room.

"Clara—" Keira had said before her phone beeped and stopped her.

She tilted her head at her brother's girlfriend. "Yeah?"

"Maybe something's stopping you from writing your vows. Annie and I will leave you to it." Keira walked over to Annie and pulled her out from the chair.

"Hey—Oh!" Annie said as she caught a glimpse of Keira's phone.

"You two are up to something. Oh, my God! If a stripper comes, then I'm going to be furious. Is that why Ally and Stevie went out to get *food*?" Clara raised her brow at them.

They were sharing a secret, and Clara wanted in but with everything Jo had wanted finished, she had no time for silly secrets. Getting up from the couch, she approached the small table next to the window and unplugged her laptop from its charger.

"If it's a stripper, then you're all in trouble! We agreed no strippers!" Clara called out as Annie and Keira giggled until they left the room.

After scrolling down the fourth website for hints on wedding vows, Clara rubbed her eyes. The screen brightness made them feel dry. The only words she was able to write on a new piece of paper was 'I promise…'

She never realised how hard it was to write vows until she had to write her own. A knock on the door was an answer to her prayers. She needed a distraction, and she knew Stevie was on her way up to Clara's suite.

"Stevie, use your key!" she yelled out, scrolling through another lot of example vows.

"Clara."

The voice made it difficult to breathe. Clara shifted her focus towards the door. Then she shook her head slightly at her guest.

"What are you doing here? I thought I told you not to come for me?" Her lip quivered, and her heart succumbed to a heavy pain at the sight of him.

He's really here.

"How did you know I was here?"

"I texted Keira and she gave me your room key. Listen, baby, you've got to put a stop to all of this," he begged.

Those green eyes made her tremble. The tiredness in Noel's eyes had her moving the laptop off her lap and standing. He almost ran to her and his hands were on her waist before she could refuse.

"I'm writing my vows."

His eyes saddened, and she placed her hands on his chest.

"I told you, Noel, I'm in too deep. I can't—"

Noel brought her closer, removed his hands from her hips and cupped her face. *"I was scared that you won't see me the same and this fairy tale of you loving me would be just that, a fairy tale. Who would have thought that Nolan Parker, the jerk of my childhood, would be the prince I wanted to save me."*

Her heart stopped.

"I was missing one thing in my life and that was you… You were the piece of me I've been waiting for…" he continued.

Clara blinked in shock. "How—" she struggled out.

His hold on her tightened as if he knew she would back away. "It's *me* who needs saving, Clara. It wasn't a fairy tale. It was real, more real than anything I've ever felt or experienced. There is more than just one piece of me that's missing since you left. My entire being. I need you for the rest of my life."

He ran his right thumb along her cheek before he let go of her face. Then Noel took a step back and reached into his back pocket. The butterflies that he always gave her resurfaced, and she bit her bottom lip to contain the flutter.

Clara looked at him confused as he pulled out his wallet. He stared up at her and gave her a delicate smile. He wasn't giving her any clues. Noel flipped open his wallet and took something out from the slot.

"I never expected to fall in love with you. Not because you're Alex's little sister but because I neglected to see that the opportunity to fall in love was before me my entire life. If I never get the opportunity to say it tomorrow or the next day, then I love you, Clara Louise Lawrence. I love you. I've unknowingly loved you my entire life."

They're the words.

Noel stepped forward and handed her what he took out of his wallet. The air caught in her throat as she looked at the picture he gave her. It was a photo of them. The exact photo she'd had Stevie burn. Clara ran her fingers over their faces. Tears ran down her face as she looked at the love in his eyes as she kissed him in the photo.

"You kept this?" she asked unbelievably.

"I couldn't get rid of it. My heart wouldn't let me. My heart won't let you go."

This one photo had her believing. She wiped her tears and looked at him. The words he spoke were familiar, almost word-for-word. Staring at the picture of them one last time, she handed it back to him. Noel had stared at the picture for a moment before he put it in his pocket.

"How do you know what I said about you being my missing piece and saving me?" she asked.

Noel tensed and reached back into his pocket and held out the pieces of paper she recognised.

"Oh my God," she breathed out.

"*Just know that I loved you, with all my heart, I loved you,*" he recited to her.

She felt a pain in her heart that she didn't know very well; someone betrayed her. He had the letter she'd hidden away.

"How did you find that?" she asked, completely shocked at what he held.

"Liam gave it to me."

"What?" she breathed out.

Liam. No. He wouldn't. He couldn't.

"He stopped by Boston not too long ago and told me to come and change your mind."

Clara shook her head. "No, he wouldn't do that. He doesn't know about you. How could he?"

"Clara, he's known a long time." The hope in his eyes had her conflicted.

Liam doesn't want to marry me? He gave Noel my letter.

"He also gave me this," Noel said and took out the invitation she had never sent him from underneath a piece of paper.

"He came to Boston to give you all this?" Clara asked as she fiddled with her ring. Then it made sense. It all clicked.

"*You love me, right?*"

Another tear rolled down her face. Liam knew. Clara took a step forward and took her letter and invitation out of Noel's hands. She looked up and met Noel's eyes. The fear of rejection was clear, but she walked past him and bolted out of the suite.

I need to see Liam.

Running down the grand staircase of The Hotel Windsor, she didn't stop. She clutched the letter as if it was a lifeline. One act of selflessness and Clara was running. Halfway down the stairs, she felt a stitch but she pushed through it. She passed wedding guests who were staying at the hotel, but she had ignored them.

Entering the grand ballroom, she noticed Liam speaking to a worker, pointing at the lights. As if she was naturally drawn to him, Liam turned and smiled at her. He glanced down at her hands and his smile instantly vanished. He excused himself and the male hotel worker left the ballroom from the rear exit.

"Clara." Liam's voice sounded like he was trying to calm her before he even knew what she'd say.

Her chest rose and fell heavily as she panted. "What the hell is this?" she asked furiously and threw her letter and invitation at his chest.

Liam didn't say anything as they experienced their first argument. The sad frown broke her heart. She wasn't sure why she was hurt. Whether it was because Liam had betrayed her or if he was willing to lose her for her to be happy.

"I had to do it, Clara. I can't let you marry me if I'm not who you want to be with. I knew about you and Noel, and I still went after you. I didn't let you get over him, and I selfishly took you before you were ready to open up your heart to anyone else. I couldn't live with myself if I'm somehow forcing you to marry me."

She stepped forward and cupped his face. Clara breathed out and gazed deep into his hazel eyes. "Why are you doing this?"

His hands covered hers. "When you smile at me, it's a little off. Like you're saving your best smile for someone else. Like you've been saving your heart and your beautiful smile for Noel. Clara, your heart won't let me in because you're still in love with him."

Liam's words stilled her. "You love me enough to let Noel come between us?"

"It's not fair to me to be married to you if you're not really in love with me, Clara. I love you enough to know that I'm in the way of you being happy. Your happiness means more to me than you know. I need you to make your choice based on your wants and needs. I'll be all right. If you still want to marry me, I'll be here. But I won't be mad if you leave me for him."

His hands left hers as he took a step back and picked up her letter and the invitation. Her heart swelled for him. Liam was sacrificing it all for her. He found Noel and was selfless enough to bring him to her.

"Liam."

"Yeah," he said once he stood straight.

Taking the papers from his hand, she placed them on the white-clothed table to her right and took his hands, entwining their fingers together. She looked around the ballroom and smiled at him.

It would be a shame to break Liam O'Connor's heart.

Noel

*C*lara didn't say anything. She took off like the wind and fled the suite, leaving him alone and hoping she'd come back. But the realisation in her golden brown eyes had him concerned. Looking around the large suite, he knew Liam could offer her these things so generously. Though it was expensive, Clara didn't enjoy luxury. That he knew.

The sound of the key card in the lock had him standing straight. When the door opened, he felt the disappointment settle in his heart.

"Noel, what are you doing here?" Stevie asked as she closed the door. She walked over to him, placed the bags on the couch, and pulled him into a tight embrace. After a quick hug, she stepped back and looked him over. "I don't care. I'm happy you're here. She's struggling, and she's very close to breaking. I'm glad Liam found his way to Boston."

"That was you?" He stared at her, his mouth gaping.

Stevie nodded. "Yeah. Liam threw Clara this surprise engagement party at the bakery, and I could see it in his eyes that he wasn't expecting her back with that ring. Once he drank,

I got him talking, and he's known about you guys for a really long time. I convinced him that it was time you two had a talk, and I'm glad he went to Boston before Vegas."

"You did this? Why?"

Sighing, Stevie sat on the couch and ran her fingers through her straight blonde hair. "Look, I feel awful about going behind her back, but I couldn't take it anymore. I know she's doing this because Liam loves her, but she needs some perspective. It's frustrating to see her in so much pain. I know she's better than this, but she's messed up when it comes to being in love. She doesn't want to be selfish."

Stevie took the bags off the couch and patted the free spot for him. Sitting down, he saw the sadness in Stevie's eyes.

"I know she's making a mistake, and I've tried to get her to go back to you. I knew about the letter because I was the one who convinced her to write it. I've had this plan in motion for a little while. It's going to suck not being her maid of honour, but this wedding can't happen. You've got three days, Noel."

"I know. I just have to find a way to her." He reached into his pocket and felt the locket touch his fingers.

"She doesn't want to give up the idea of a family. Liam, Ally, CeCe, and even Mr and Mrs O'Connor have taken her in as their own. You need to make her realise that they'll be okay without her. But she won't be okay without you. She tries to hide that sad smile she puts on, but I see right through it. I know that smile well. I'm an expert at it. It's the rehearsal dinner tonight. Don't do anything till after, okay? Let her have tonight and then go after her. Liam won't let her go because he loves her too much, but he's given you his blessing. He'll marry her if she chooses him. One last fight before we end this story. What do you say?"

"No," he said, his eyes never leaving Stevie's. He knew she wasn't expecting that reply. Noel stood up from the couch and glanced down at her. "One fight is not enough. For the rest of my life, I'll fight for her. Our story is entwined, forever. Clara is my life, and until I know she couldn't possibly love me for the rest of our days, then it's not over."

Stevie stood up and then hugged him. "If this isn't true love then I don't know what is. You two are so frustrating that it makes you realise just how much love is only for the lucky."

When Stevie's arms let go of his body, Noel smiled down at her. "Love is for everyone. It's just about finding the right one."

Chapter
TWENTY-TWO

Noel

Three days had quickly passed and in those three days, he had stayed at Max's. Noel never got her alone. Clara would always have to make decisions on the final touches of the wedding or have breakfast, lunch, or dinner with Liam's relatives from Ireland. Every time he went to her door, she wasn't there. The last time he had checked, there was an emergency with her dress.

He missed Clara's apartment. It had a cosy feel to it and Max's had little life at all. The day after the rehearsal dinner, Noel had walked out of the guest room to find Sarah in the kitchen. He had gagged at the sight of her and said nothing as he walked out the door. Noel was hoping to see Rob's brother, Julian, at the rehearsal dinner, but he couldn't get out of Milan in time for the wedding. Rob was annoyed, but the moment a woman with ash blonde hair walked into the room, he never mentioned his brother again.

Noel stood outside of Clara's suite. Alex had told him she would be there for some time before she finished getting ready in the bridal suite of the church.

Maybe telling her that Liam gave me the letter made her realise that she loves him more.

Pushing the thought away, he knocked on Clara's door. He didn't wait for her to reply. He used the key card and opened the door. His heart was too impatient to wait for her reply. Bursting into the room, he watched Clara jump off the couch. She placed her hand on her chest. The first thing he noticed was the white dress she wore, tight and so unlike her. She left him breathless and in awe at the sight of her.

"You scared me. You need to give me that key card. I could have been naked!" Clara huffed and picked up the piece of paper she'd dropped.

Walking into the sitting area of the suite, he stopped in front of her. It broke his heart to see her in white. "Not like I haven't seen you naked before," he stated.

Clara's cheeks reddened at his honesty. "Yes, well... that was a long time ago."

"Not long enough if I can still make you blush. Tell me no one's here," he said softly.

Those golden brown eyes still held a grip on his heart and Clara shook her head. "No one's here. I sent them away so I could read my vows."

"What are we doing, Clara?" he asked exhausted.

"I'm getting married."

"Why?"

Clara looked at the piece of paper and placed it on the coffee table behind her. Walking over to the window, she stood there for a moment. She was stunning in white, but the sadness in her eyes didn't match the smile she projected. Clara turned and looked at him. The sun radiated through the windows and hit her skin perfectly, reminding him of the mornings he'd woken up next to her.

"I love him, Noel. I didn't realise how much until he was willing to let me go. You read my letter. I owe him a lot more than just my love."

Taking long strides, he stood in front of her and took her hands. "You owe no one anything. The only person you owe is yourself. You have to be selfish and leave him. I came here to ruin your engagement. That's the kind of selfish man I'm being. I let you get away, and I shouldn't have. I should have been selfish the first time so we could have avoided all this. I love you and I want to love you forever. You have to know that I don't regret ever coming back to Melbourne. That one decision changed my life. Had I known that I'd be so in love with you then, I wouldn't have fought so hard against it—"

"Noel," she said stopping him.

He let go of her hand and placed his hands on her neck, feeling her pulse on his skin. "Don't stop me yet. I need to finish what I came here to say. I'm hopelessly in love with you that the idea of you marrying someone else kills me. And someone so deserving of your love, like Liam, it's destroying me. For so long, I've stopped myself from flying back home to beg for you back. But every time I try, I think of how happy you are. That ring on your finger deserves to be there. The life Liam offers you is one you deserve, but I need to plead one more time. I need to make one last attempt at your heart. I love you, Clara, and I want to be with you for the rest of my life."

The tears in her eyes had him believing. Without letting her say another word, Noel brought her lips to his and kissed her. Her lips sweeter than he remembered and the way they felt against his was perfection. Clara's hands were in his hair, tangled and controlling the depths of this one kiss. A small moan from her had him eager to explore her mouth, but he controlled the urge and savoured the feel of her lips.

He reluctantly separated his mouth from Clara. Those brown eyes would always have a pull on him. He would always long for that colour.

"Are you showing me what I'm going to miss?" Clara asked. He heard the hurt in her voice.

"No. I want you to remember our good times. I want you to remember me and us for the good times we had and the love we once shared. For me, the idea of loving another woman was over the moment I kissed you. And it would be forever over the moment I made love to you. You need to realise that you are the best thing that has ever happened to me. But if I'm not what you need for the rest of your life, then I'll do it."

Clara's hands wrapped around his wrists and she blinked away a tear. "Do what?"

An honest smile developed on Noel's face. "I'll watch you marry Liam. It will kill me inside knowing that there isn't a chance, but I love you too much to make you unhappy. I'm done hurting you because it hurts me, too. I'm tired of knowing that I've made you cry and hurt inside. I'll dance with you one more time. But if it's me you choose, I'll be there waiting for you."

Taking a step back, Noel reached into the jacket pocket of his suit and took out Clara's locket. Taking her left hand, he placed the silver locket in her hand and closed her fingers over the Celtic knot. He smiled at his engraved initial. It was as if Fate had always had their lives entwined from the very start.

"Your name will forever be the one my heart yearns for." He didn't say anything else. He took one last glimpse of Clara and then walked out of the suite with much struggle. His heart already regretted the words he spoke, but he was happy with what he'd said. He was happy with the look in her eyes and he was happy that she had *her* locket back.

After entering the hotel bar, Noel took a seat next to Max. He let out a heavy groan and settled onto the stool next to his best friend.

"Did you hear that Val's in town?" Max asked.

Noel shook his head. "Nah, I'd rather not hear it. Val and I ended on good terms. I don't need Clara seeing me with her. It'll only make things worse. How'd you know she's in town?"

Max swirled his scotch and glanced at Noel. "Sarah's with her… I think I love her, Noel."

"What?" Noel blurted out, almost falling out of his stool. He saw the conflict in Max's eyes and knew what his friend had revealed was the truth.

"Listen to me, Max. If you haven't watched the woman you love walk out of your life, watched her love another, begged and pleaded for her love, then you haven't loved as I have. You haven't suffered and had the greatest love. If you're prepared to suffer what I've gone through, then you love her and I hate to say this, but keep her. Only the lucky find their love," Noel enlightened.

Before Max could reply, his phone on the bar counter flashed and Sarah's text message came across the screen. Max sighed and read the message. "I'll be back in a second. Sarah and Val want to talk to me about something."

"Good luck," Noel wished as he signalled the bartender over for a drink.

Clara

*I*t had been over an hour since Noel had left her. Clara ran her fingers across the silver locket. He'd reunited her with a locket that held so many memories for Noel and her. Later in the afternoon, she would be married, but for now, she sat on the couch of her suite staring at the Celtic knot and letting Noel's words sear themselves into her heart. Clara then closed her eyes and gave her heart one more chance at making a decision.

Come on, Clara. Make a choice for you. For your happily ever after.

Opening her eyes, she looked at her surroundings. French wallpaper, hotel suites, trips around the world, and Liam's money. He would buy her the world if it made her happy. But the key to her happiness was never money. The key to her happiness was companionship and love.

"Clara!" Annie squealed as soon as she entered the suite.

Dropping her hands in her lap, Clara smiled at her bridesmaids. "No Ally?" she asked.

Stevie shook her head. "With her parents discussing something about her future. She'll be back soon."

Clara gazed at Annie, Keira, Josie, and Stevie. They all looked beautiful in their peach-coloured bridesmaid's gowns and their hair pulled up in buns. She ignored the chatter as her bridesmaids started to get ready. Josie proved that she was quite the beautician and offered to do their makeup. The engraved 'N' on the locket had Clara thinking of all the moments they had spent together throughout their lives. She noticed the clasp of the locket didn't close properly. Curious, Clara opened the locket to find a piece of paper in it.

Taking out the paper, she placed the locket in her lap. She started to unfold the small piece of paper and smoothed it out. Her heart and breathing stopped as she stared at the worn paper.

I love you

Her heart give way at the sight of those eight letters that formed the most liberating words she had ever known. They were the words she wrote the morning after they had said it to each other. That night they had made love that made her cry at one stage. He held her and whispered those three words until she slept peacefully and happily in his arms.

She noticed the indentation of words on the paper and turned it around to see that there was more. The first thing she noticed was Noel's writing, her fingers running along the words he wrote. Breathing in and steeling herself, Clara read the words he wrote.

No amount of time will account for the days that I've missed you and should have loved you. I will always love you, Clara Louise Lawrence.

"Oh my God," she whispered. Tears rolled down her face. Her heart ached at the declaration Noel had written. The paper looked worn, as if he had written it forever ago. She placed the note in her lap and silently cried into her hands. She was happy she hadn't done her makeup yet. She knew her tears would have ruined it.

"Clara," Keira softly called her.

She wiped her face and turned to see her brother's girlfriend sitting next to her.

"He's loved you a long time," Keira said, her eyes on Noel's note.

Clara sniffed and picked up the small piece of paper. This one note brought back so many memories and love. Carefully, Clara folded it and placed it back in the locket before she snapped it shut. Looking up at Keira, she smiled. Words were not necessary. Keira's eyes had watered before she took Clara's hands.

A knock on the door had Clara peering past Keira to see Annie opening the door. Max stormed into the suite and Clara stood up, locket in hand, to see the grief and apology in his eyes. Before she could ask him any sort of question, the last two people she had ever expected to see walked into the room.

"Tell her!" Max roared and everyone in the room stared at him. Clara had never seen Max like this except for the time he had helped her at that dodgy pub almost a year ago.

"Valerie? S-Sarah? What are you doing here?" Clara asked in disbelief. Gazing up at Valerie, Clara knew she held no hate for her. But when she glanced at Sarah, she saw something in her eyes. Clara looked at Max and then at Sarah.

"Oh my God," she breathed out. The look in Sarah's eyes explained it; she'd fallen in love with Max Sheridan.

"You tell her, Sarah!" Max yelled.

Clara saw the pain on his face. Tears filled Sarah's eyes before they met Clara.

"I'm sorry," Sarah whispered.

The blood drained from Clara's face. The room started to spin, and she felt violently ill. That night at Katie's party, Sarah had told Clara that Noel had slept with Valerie and that Valerie was moving to the U.S. to be with him. Clara had believed Sarah. Believed it when she'd said Noel had stayed at Valerie's and that what Clara and Noel had wasn't love.

"It was a lie?" Clara managed to ask.

Sarah nodded.

"I'm sorry, Clara. I'm so goddamn sorry for doing this to you and Noel," Max said.

Clara walked up to Max and wrapped her arms around him as he repeated his apology numerous times. She hugged him tighter to try to reassure him. "It's not your fault, Max. It was *never* yours. It was mine. It's my fault that I believed her." She stepped out of their embrace and let the peace settle within her.

"Clara, I swear, I never slept with Noel. He came over and gave me advice about moving to Chicago and then he went to Max's. I promise you, it didn't happen. I kissed him, but he told me that he loved you instead," Valerie explained.

"So it was you!" Stevie yelled.

Turning around, she saw Stevie's jaw clenched shut as her nostrils flared. Clara simply shook her head at her best friend.

"Clara, the reason why you, Noel, and Liam have been through so much pain and misery is because of her damn lie!"

Clara handed Keira her locket and looked at every single

person in the room. "No. *I'm* the reason why Noel and Liam have been through so much pain. I'm at fault, no one else."

Focusing on her brother's ex-girlfriend, Clara wasn't sure how she felt towards her. But it surprised her to see such sorrow and regret in Sarah's eyes. Before she could even say any words, Liam opened the door and stepped inside. Annie was by Clara's side covering her up with a silk robe.

"Liam! It's bad luck to see the bride in her dress before the wedding!" Annie scolded.

Liam chuckled. "We aren't very traditional, are we, sweetheart?"

Clara smiled at the wink he sent her way. But she knew tradition meant everything to him. She hadn't seen him in almost a day; he had insisted on staying in his parents' suite last night instead of with her.

"Clara, do you mind coming for a walk with me?"

The sweetness in his voice had Clara removing the silk robe and handing it back to Annie.

"Clara," Max said.

She shook her head at him and slipped on her white high heels that sat next to the couch. Liam held out his hand and Clara took it. Lifting up her long wedding dress, she walked out of the suite.

Liam stopped at the top of the stairwell and looked at Clara, his thumb caressing the back of her hand. Slowly and as silently as they could, they walked down the staircase hand in hand. They managed to dart past most of their wedding guests until they reached the main doors of the hotel. A black Bentley was parked, waiting for them. Liam held her hand a little tighter as he walked her to the passenger door. The doorman opened and held the car door for them. Without any arguments and very curious as to where their walk was taking them, Clara slipped into the back seat, careful not to damage her dress.

Liam sat next to her just as she buckled her seat belt. He took her right hand and kissed her knuckles. Then he had smiled at her before he breathed out and said, "St. Ignatius' Church, please."

Chapter
TWENTY-THREE

Noel

"Noel!" he heard Max yell out his name behind him. The beer Noel had ordered long ago was now warm. The amount of times he thought about drinking it had crossed his mind, but in the end, he knew beer wasn't going to stop the nerves he felt. Turning, he saw Max rush to his side, followed by Sarah and Valerie.

"What the hell are *they* doing here?" Noel asked, irritated.

"I'm sorry, Noel. You warned me and I didn't listen. Believe me, I had no idea."

Max's pleading had Noel confused. "What are you—" He stopped, realisation setting in, and got off the stool.

"Sleeping with Valerie changed us."

"What did you say to her?" Noel raised his voice at Sarah.

She flinched and looked at Max and Valerie for mercy and assistance.

"What the fuck did you do?" He didn't care if he made a scene.

"I-I…" Sarah stuttered.

Valerie stepped in front of Noel, as if she had sensed he'd harm her.

"You knew, Val?" Her hair was much shorter than it used to be, the colour much lighter, no longer the bright crimson tone he remembered.

"Yes."

Noel shook his head in disbelief. He ran both hands through his hair and looked up at Max.

"We tried to tell her, but she didn't say anything. She went off with her fiancé. I swear, Noel. I had no idea that one lie did this to you and Clara. Sarah just told me and I had her tell Max," Valarie explained.

Noel saw the pain in his eyes and knew this hurt him. Max shared a friendship with Clara, and he had indirectly hurt her. He grasped Valerie's arms and then moved her aside, coming face to face with the woman who had destroyed his chance at happiness. He stared into those cold eyes. Noel knew Sarah had never lost the one thing worth living for.

"What did I ever do to you? What did Clara ever do to you? Wasn't it enough, when you cheated on Alex and broke his heart? You've caused so much pain in our lives, and you don't even think of the consequences of your actions. I hope you feel the pain I've gone through when it came to losing Clara because of *you*. I hope you know what it feels like to be unloved. Get out of here! Before Alex finds out what you did. He already hates the sight of you, and if he finds out what you did to Clara, then he'll show a side you've never seen."

He fought back the fire that fuelled his hate for Sarah. She had intentionally sabotaged what he had with Clara and she had succeeded.

"I'm sorry, Noel. I didn't mean —" Sarah started to apologise, but he shook his head at her.

"You don't have a sorry bone in that soulless body of yours —" He stopped the moment he felt his phone vibrate. Ignoring the tears in Sarah's eyes, he reached into his pocket and saw a new message from a number he didn't recognise.

> **Unknown:** *I've taken her to St. Ignatius' Church. Come through the side entry. I have a car waiting for you. We're almost at the church. I'm going to try one last time. – Liam.*

"Noel," Valerie said.

He read the message a second time. He'd have to thank him one day. Liam wanted Clara happy, and he believed Noel would be the one to do so.

"I have to go," he said looking up at Max instead of the women around him.

Max opened his mouth to say something, but Noel stopped him with a shake of his head.

"Don't. Not now, Max. I just... I can't... Look, I have one more shot before I lose her for good. She's more important to me than my friendship with you, and I can't lose her because of this." He didn't wait for a reply. Noel ran towards the entry of the bar only for Alex to stop him.

"Whoa! Where's the fire?" Alex chuckled, blocking Noel's exit.

"Alex, I have to —"

"Is that Valerie and..." Alex squinted and his nostrils automatically flared. His jaw clenched and Noel could see him starting to put it together. "Was it Sarah who got to my sister?"

Noel noticed Alex's clenched fists along with the healing cuts Alex had from the car accident. "Yeah, it was."

"Go find Clara. I'll deal with this. You had better come back with my sister in your arms. Otherwise, you gave Sarah exactly what she wanted." They nodded at each other and at their own personal missions. Frankly, Noel didn't want to be in the same room as Alex and Sarah. It would be messy.

Darting past Alex, Noel ran out of the hotel and towards a black car with a chauffeur standing by the opened car door.

"Mr Parker?" the chauffeur asked.

Noel nodded his head.

"I'll take you to Mr O'Connor and Miss Lawrence. Please," he said, gesturing to the back seat.

Climbing in, he hoped this car ride would lead to his forever. It was a seven-minute drive that seemed to drag into an eternity. Seven minutes and he'd have an answer. As the chauffeur drove down Wellington Parade, he could see himself settling back into Melbourne. He could see himself living in Melbourne. He could see himself living in any city if it meant he'd have Clara by his side.

He recognised the church he had seen plenty of times

during his childhood. The stonework was absolutely beautiful and breathtaking. He could imagine Clara getting married here, but then again, it seemed so traditional and unlike her. The car stopped by the side entry of the church. Giving his quick thanks to the driver, Noel stepped out of the car and noticed the old wooden arched door. Adjusting his tie to calm his nerves, he opened the door.

Stepping into the church, he found himself in a small room that led to the chapel of the church. The door remained open, and Noel walked through it. The first thing he saw was the cathedral style arches and the stain glass windows of Saints. The long benches were empty but flowers and unlit candles lined the aisle. Scanning the large church, he found them standing at the end of the altar. He was close enough to hear them, but he walked forward and stood behind the stone pillar. Noel promised himself that Liam would have his say first.

Peeking around the pillar, he saw Clara's back turned to him and Liam holding her hands. The smile on Liam's face had Noel sweating. His body filled with nerves as he tried to control his breathing. Liam glanced his way, their eyes met, and he gave Noel a slight smile before looking at her.

"Liam, what are we doing at the church? We've just been standing here," Clara said, the worry could be heard in her voice.

Liam let go of one of Clara's hands and turned her so that Noel could see them both. Clara's eyes set on Liam. The sad smile on her face had Noel wanting to go over to her, but instead, he leant on the pillar. Liam would have his chance to say what he needed to.

"Clara, being your boyfriend and then your fiancé has been one of the greatest privileges I've ever been blessed with. When I met you, I didn't think I'd ever stand a chance. I was just the guy who slept with countless women to you, and I knew I'd never be good enough. But one day, I took advantage of your grieving heart and you let me kiss you and I was a goner. I knew that in that one moment, I'd love you and hoped you'd love me, too."

Clara's hand reached up and cupped Liam's cheek. It was an intimate moment that crushed Noel's heart.

"You have time to make a choice, an honest choice. I'm

going to be okay if you walk out of this church to him. When your heart is set on someone, you don't want to let them go, no matter how much it hurts. And right now, Clara, my heart won't let you go. You have to make a choice for yourself and not for me."

Clara let go of Liam's other hand and brought it to his face. Noel noticed the tears she cried and his heart tightened at the sight of them.

"One wise and heartbroken man gave me some advice. He told me that I should marry the one person I can't live without. But I realised that there's more to that one quote. When you love someone, you can't breathe without their love. You can't imagine the next second of your life without them. And I want to marry that one person who I can't spend the next seconds of my life without."

Noel wiped the tears that fell at Clara's heartfelt honesty. Her choice would be the right choice for her. He would accept that. Noel watched Liam's own tears fall. Clara wiped them away and smiled up at him.

"Close your eyes, Clara," Liam instructed, and Clara did what he asked. He looked over at Noel and gave him another sad smile. Liam then moved Clara's hands away from his face and he held her face in his hands. "I want you to imagine yourself getting married. I want you to imagine the life you live with the man you marry. Imagine your happiness. Who do you see, Clara?" Liam asked.

Noel recognised the brokenness and the hope in his voice. Liam's hands moved to Clara's hips. A smile appeared on Clara's face as she slowly opened her eyes. Her palms returned to Liam's cheeks. Then she brought his face towards her and pressed her lips against Liam. Noel felt the sudden stop of his heart and his breathing, the pain enveloping him.

One chaste kiss then she said, "I love you, Liam."

He stared at them. At the end of the altar, he could see them saying their vows and Clara becoming Liam's wife. Her thumb caressed Liam's cheek, the love and tenderness in her eyes broke his heart. But that smile on her face set his heart free.

She's finally made her choice.

Noel took one last look at Clara. She was happy with the choice she had made, and he was happy that she had made *her* choice. He smiled and quietly left the chapel of the church. He decided that he wouldn't look back. It was time he let her go. Walking out of church to the sun shining down on him, he was content. The chauffeur looked at him and Noel nodded.

"Back to The Hotel Windsor, please."

He got into the back seat. When the car started, he stared out the window and at the church. It was a new beginning for them all. And it was the ending of Noel and Clara.

She finally has her happily ever after.

The Final Act

Noel

Two months later

When Noel opened the email from his best friend a week ago, he couldn't believe it. The first thing he did was walk out of his Hong Kong office to his superior's and file the papers to return to Boston. His stay in Hong Kong was only meant to last a month, but he had offered to stay and help with the Asia expansion of G&MC. It wasn't as if he had anything tying him down, so he took the move without a second thought. The move had been a surprise considering he had left in the middle of an important meeting back in Boston months ago. When he asked, Gregson had said that he needed a manager who could stand up to him. As the yellow cab pulled away from the curb of J.F.K International Airport, he started to feel the anxious nerves start to invade his system.

I'm going to see her.

The thought had him gripping the door handle tighter. It had been two months since he'd walked out of Clara's wedding. Hearing her say she loved Liam when she was asked for a choice was too much for Noel. He'd promised he'd watch her marry Liam, but he couldn't. His heart finally accepted the fact that it was finally over for them. Noel finally lost the love of his life to the more deserving man. Liam would offer Clara the world; he just wished he were the one who could have provided it for her.

I left Hong Kong for Alex. I'll have to ignore her the best I can.

When he'd read the email, all he could think was *finally*. If anyone deserved to be getting married, it was Alex and Keira. Noel knew Alex was waiting until after Clara's wedding to propose to the love of his life. He might have lost at love, but he was happy that Alex had won. The cab pulled up in front of Crabtree's Kittle House and Noel looked out and whistled. Getting out of the cab, he took in the enormous pillars of the white building. Alex had gone all out for his engagement party. Noel heard the boot pop open, walked around to the back, and retrieved his bags. Before instructing his cab driver to Chappaqua, New York, Noel had him stop by a local gas station so he could change into his suit.

Closing the boot, he handed the fare and tip to the driver. The cold wind hit his skin and Noel gripped the handle of his bags tighter. After he made his way up the path, Noel walked through the white painted glass panel doors to hear the sound of the engagement party in full swing. A middle-aged woman holding a bottle of wine stopped him with a smile.

"Hello, sir. Welcome. Can I help you with anything?" she asked with a pleasant smile.

"I'm here for Alex and Keira's engagement party."

"Oh, yes. Let me just set this bottle of wine down and I'll take your bags." The server placed the bottle on the closest table and took his bags from him before he could argue. "If you follow the main hallway down to the function room, you'll find everyone."

Noel peered over her shoulder and thanked her for her directions. He followed her instructions and saw the bright lights at the end of the hallway. When he stepped into the white function room, he noticed fairy lights wrapped around the pillars and lit candles on every table. Scanning the room, he saw his best friends—Max, Rob, and Julian—chatting. They all stopped their conversation and nodded at him with excited smiles. Rob looked relieved to see him and the smile on his face had Noel grinning back. He had missed his friends. His nights were lonely in Hong Kong. The loneliness was not what he wanted, but it came with his heartbreak. Even though he was happy for her, he was still heartbroken.

Noel glanced around to see neither Clara nor her husband and he breathed out. His body relaxed the moment he spotted Alex and Keira towards the main table talking to guests. There was a bright smile on Alex's face as his arm wrapped around his fiancée. For a moment, Noel was jealous. He wanted that smile Alex had, but he would never have it. Noel shook his head and maneuvered through the crowd until he was face to face with the newly engaged couple.

"Noel, you made it!" Keira cheered and smiled brightly at her fiancé.

Alex nodded at Keira and smiled up at Noel. Ignoring their exchanges, he pulled Keira into a hug and congratulated them both on their engagement.

"You're here. Didn't think you'd show up," Alex said after they shared a quick hug.

"Where have you been?" Keira asked.

Noel dug his hands in his pockets and shrugged. He knew Alex didn't tell his fiancée where he was. Noel wanted to be alone. Didn't want to hear about Clara or the wedding. The emails he exchanged with his friends were vague, never detailed.

"Took the expansion role in Hong Kong."

"You've been in Hong Kong all this time?" Keira sounded astonished.

He let out a laugh and nodded.

"Hong Kong. I can't believe it!" She shook her head.

"Keira, why don't you go speak to your parents while I have a chat with Noel quickly."

Keira gave Alex a firm nod. She walked towards the other end of the room and over to her parents. Alex called over a server and handed him a beer. Noel wasn't one to drink, not after his binge shortly after his arrival in Hong Kong. Alcohol was cheap and easily accessible. But tonight was a celebration. His best friend got the girl. Then Alex's hand rested on his shoulder.

He wants to talk about Clara's wedding.

"I have a favour to ask of you," Alex asked.

Noel took a long pull from his beer before he nodded.

"I want you to be my best man."

Noel's eyes flashed in surprise as he placed his beer on the table next to him. "Me? You sure?" he asked.

Alex let out a laugh. "Best man belongs to my best mate. Can't have the other three idiots as a choice. I need the biggest idiot of them all taking up the honour. What do you say?"

"Shit. You really are getting married," Noel pointed out.

"I'm gonna take that as a yes."

"Hell, yeah. I won't let you down!" For the first time in two months, he was actually happy. He'd find a way to get over Clara. *One day.* It just took one day at a time. Unable to help himself, Noel turned and scanned the room.

"She's here, but Liam isn't."

Noel's jaw locked.

She's here.

"He's on a business trip in Ireland." Alex answered a question Noel had no intention of asking.

He simply nodded his head and tried to forget the burning in his chest. She had been married for two months. She was finally happy.

"I want you to meet someone," Alex said, bringing Noel back to reality.

He turned and frowned at his best friend. "Really? Look, it's nice that you want me to meet someone, but your sister ruined me. I don't think I could look at another woman for a long time. Just tell whoever it is that I'm good."

Noel reached for his beer only to have Alex grasp his arm.

"I want you to be my best man, Noel. All I ask is this one request. I see how hurt you are and let me help you. You walked out on Clara's wedding and I know it hurt you but let me make it better, please."

Noel sighed. It was Alex's big day after all. He never wanted to disappoint his best friend. "Fine. Lead the way."

The smile on Alex's face had Noel rolling his eyes. Alex led him towards the double doors. Following him down the stairs, Noel saw a woman towards the end of the garden. The first thing he noticed was her pale pink dress and how it was too cold to be out in such a short outfit. Her dress seemed so *familiar*. She faced the short hedges looking out at the darkening scenery. Their footsteps had the woman turning; Noel's throat dried and his heart stopped.

Clara.

"All you got to do is talk to her. You owe her an explanation for walking out on her wedding. It crushed her not to have you there."

I should have done the right thing and supported her decision, but I didn't. I couldn't.

"Okay, Alex," was all Noel said as he walked across the damp grass towards the waiting Clara.

It seemed she was always waiting. Noel's eyes remained on her face. She was still as beautiful as ever, and that smile had him closing his eyes briefly and wishing his heart would shrivel up. Her smile did wonders to him. Noel heard the doors shut behind him, and he knew they were alone. He stopped in front of Clara as her curls danced with the wind.

"Hey," he said carefully.

That smile of hers didn't fade as she looked at him. Those golden brown eyes were a reminder of what he once had with her. She looked relieved to see him. His heart was hopeful, but his brain reminded him that she was now married.

"Hey, yourself." Her voice was sweeter than his dreams had mimicked. "How are you?" she asked.

"Fine," he replied. Noel dug his hands in his dress pants pockets to stop himself from doing something stupid.

Clara blinked quickly as if to hide her tears.

God, why do I still love her? Why couldn't I just have gotten over her?

"I'm sorry I walked out on your wedding. I..." Noel stopped himself as Clara's eyes met his. He was sorry for many things when it came to her. It seemed like he had a never-ending list of apologies.

"You walked out on my wedding. You promised you'd stay." The hurt in Clara's eyes broke his heart. He promised her he'd be there, but it was too much. Watching the love of his life marry someone else wasn't high on his witness list.

"I know, Clara. I thought I could watch you marry him, but I couldn't. I couldn't be there and accept it. Knowing you chose him and married him—it made me hate the man that I am. I wanted to be good enough for you. To be the choice you made. Just know that I'm happy you married Liam. You deserve the best and I'm glad you chose him. He deserved you more than I ever could have."

His eyes stung. This was his final goodbye. *His final act.* Their story had finally reached its ending. Tears ran down Clara's face. He wanted to wipe them away, but she was now a married woman.

"You really have been gone for two months."

"What?"

"Never mind. You still owe me a dance, Nolan Parker." His name on her lips had him completely bound. No matter how much time would eventually pass, he would always want and love her.

"Clara, I don't think—"

She shook her head. "I don't want your excuses or explanations. Just one dance. Liam isn't here. You have nothing to worry about."

He couldn't deny her wants. He needed one more touch of her body. One more reason to hold her for the last time before their story ended.

If I weren't already going to hell, I would be.

"Okay." Noel stepped forward and kept his eyes on hers. He placed his right hand on her hip and brought her closer to his body. She let out a gasp he wished he'd never witnessed. Then he took her right hand in his and felt the tingles shoot straight to his broken heart, slowly mending him.

She was home, and he knew it. But she belonged to another man and he knew the wrongfulness of this one final dance. His eyes never left hers. If they did and he saw that wedding band, he'd die inside. He'd be a memory lost in the new ones she'd make with her husband.

"Noel," she said softly. "Why won't you look at my left hand?"

He stopped the swaying movement his body was making and looked at her. She squeezed his hand and his body tensed. Noel closed his eyes tightly as he concentrated on finding the ability to breathe. When he opened them, he gazed down at her plump lips and he was tempted. He loved her lips. Noel would never found another pair as heart-shattering as hers.

"Because if I look at it then it's real, Clara. Then I know that it's over for good between us. That wedding band is proof that

I will never get the chance to love you and be with you. That wedding band tells me that I lost you and it was evident that you found a better man than me. That wedding band signifies that you will never love me and never want to spend your life being *my* wife. Once I even glance at that wedding band, I know I'll never be yours."

Tears ran down her face and he was surprised to feel his own.

I will never get over you, Clara. I'll spend my days trying to find an impossible way to.

Clara squeezed his hand tighter and then she closed her eyes. When she opened them, the sadness in them consumed him. His heart was on its last beat, and he knew it was all ending.

"Please, Noel. You need to look at my left hand. I can't live the rest of my life if you walk away and not look at it. I need you to. That's all I ask. We'll walk away tonight, but please, I beg of you."

The want and need in her voice had him pulling away from her. "Okay," he whispered.

Clara gave him a sad smile that pierced his heart. At least he'd have that one last smile. "Close your eyes," she softly whispered, and he did just that.

He felt Clara's fingertips in the palm of his right hand. Her touch was one he missed and had consumed his thoughts. She placed her hand flat on his palm and said, "Open your eyes, Nolan Parker."

Oh, God.

His tears brimmed his eyes. The burning in his chest overwhelmed him as his breathing faltered. He held onto her left hand and finally breathed out.

"Clara." He looked up.

Her tears mirrored his own.

"Don't let this be a joke."

Clara shook her head. "It's real."

His heart expanded and he felt every inch of the pain, but it was a different sort. "You're separated? Divorced? Getting divorced?"

Clara smiled beautifully at him. Noel looked down at her left hand once more. There was *no* ring. Not her wedding band or engagement ring on her finger. He let go of her hand and cradled her face in his palms.

She isn't with him. There's no ring!

Clara's hands gripped his wrists as his thumb brushed the faint mole on her cheek. "I never married him, Noel. I couldn't marry him because I love you and I'll only ever love you."

Never. Married. Liam.

"You never? But the wedding…"

Clara let go of his wrists and wrapped her arms around his back. "I never married Liam. Annie and Jarred took our places at the altar. He asked me for my blessing days before the wedding. You left before I could tell you that the wedding was off. I've been waiting two months for you, Nolan Parker. I've been waiting for the day you'd come back and I could have a chance to redeem myself."

She waited two months for me.

"Say it again," he said.

She tilted her head and raised her eyebrow at him.

"Tell me you love me again, Clara."

A soft laugh escaped her lips. That sound mending his heart. "I love you, Nolan Parker. I have and will always love you. You are the love of *my* life. We can be together, if I'm not too late." The vulnerability in Clara's voice had him stroking her left cheek in reassurance.

She still loves me. She's finally free to be with me.

"You're not late, Clara. You'll never be because I'll never get over you. You'll always have my heart. I'm yours." His thumb then ran along her bottom lip.

"I'm yours, Noel. I've been yours the moment you gave me that tulip when I was four. I didn't know it then, but my heart was set on you. My heart will forever be set on you." The beautiful smile he'd always love was finally directed towards him. Clara's tears brimmed her eyes, and he knew for the first time they would be happy tears.

"But at the altar, Liam asked you to imagine your wedding and you said you loved him."

Stepping out of his hold on her, Clara took his hands and threaded her fingers through his. "I imagined marrying *you*. I imagined you at the end of the altar waiting for me to be *your* wife. If you had stayed, you would have heard me tell Liam that I loved him but that I was *in* love with you. If you had stayed a little bit longer, you'd know that I gave Liam back his engagement ring and that I came running back for you."

He remembered the moments after he got into the back of the black car. He hailed a taxi outside of The Hotel Windsor and returned to Max's apartment. He then packed up the little belongings he'd brought from Boston and visited his parents in the suburbs. Noel had turned off his phone once he booked his ticket back to the States and spent the rest of the night catching up with his mother and father. His brother had stopped by before Noel had left for his early morning flight.

"Why did you go?" she asked.

"I was actually happy with your choice. From where I stood, it looked like you chose him and I was honestly happy."

Letting go of his hands, Clara wrapped her arms back around his neck. "I couldn't possibly live another second without *your* love. These last two months I've just been hanging on. Alex told me to be patient. I didn't even know if you'd talk to me, so Alex had this plan to ambush you."

He wrapped his arms around her and he held her tight, afraid to let her go. "Now I wish I hadn't left and gone to Hong Kong."

Letting out a short laugh, Clara shook her head. "No, I think those two months between us was good. Waiting was hard, but I know I made the right choice. I spent my hours at the restaurant."

Restaurant?

Noel tensed at the thought of her waiting two months for him. "Wait. The bakery?" he asked.

Clara's shoulders drooped and her lips curved downwards and he knew then that she had lost it.

"I'll buy it back. I—"

"Not necessary. The greatest sacrifices are made for the greatest love. And losing the bakery was nothing compared to losing you. I have plans for the money I could have spent on buying it back. Liam insisted it was a gift for me to keep, but I couldn't. Is there any chance I can be with you? No Alex or Liam this time. Is there a chance we could have a life together?"

His heart ached at her request. One vulnerable question and he was in tears. There were no obstacles this time.

I can have a life with Clara. I can grow old with her. I can finally call her mine and I can finally be hers.

Suddenly, Clara started to sob and he realised he had been quiet for far too long. "Oh my God, you don't love me anymore. I am too late." She stepped back and her bottom lip quivered.

"Look at me," he instructed.

The sad gleam in her eyes told him how much she really did love him. He took that step forward and held her beautiful face in his hands. "It's impossible for me to ever stop loving you. I love you, Clara Louise Lawrence. I could never stop loving you. And I couldn't ask for anything more from this world than a life spent with you. I want the rest of my days spent with you because you, Clara, are the love of *my* life."

Clara breathed out and tears rolled off her face. "I love you, too," she whispered.

"Then love me forever," he mimicked the words she had said over a year ago. Clara nodded and he never asked for permission as his lips touched hers. His heart exploding in pain, but it was the type he enjoyed because he *finally* had the love of his life.

Her warm lips perfectly moulded around his as he kissed her with more love than he had ever felt for her or any other woman. In this one kiss, he hoped she believed the promises he hadn't voiced—a promise to marry her; a promise to love her; a promise to be her friend; a promise to be the best father for their children, if she'd let him.

Clara's fingers threaded his hair as she deepened their reunion kiss. A small moan had him exploring her mouth. His tongue touching hers and his heart expanding, knowing that they had a chance to be happy together. These lips stopped him breathing and halted his heart from beating.

"About fucking time!" Alex's voice boomed from behind him, ending their kiss.

Noel drew back as Clara laughed. He let his forehead rest against hers. "This is forever," he whispered to her. Then he turned around to see Alex, Keira, Julian, Max, and Rob on the steps, hollering and clapping. Keira was in tears, and Alex stood there proud and happy.

"Come on, you two! We're celebrating two things: my engagement and your reunion!" Keira shouted.

Noel's palms ran along Clara's arms until his hand found

hers. Her touch had always made his heart flutter. He then brought her hand to his lips and kissed the finger that would one day wear his ring. "I look forward to spending forever loving you, Clara."

There was no greater feeling than having Clara back in his life and having her love him so openly and freely. Watching her laugh and dance with her brother was one of his most favourite sights he had ever witnessed. It was perfect. Every so often, she'd looked over at him and the love in her eyes had him falling in love with her all over again.

Sitting in his chair, he was content with his life. He had forever with Clara and he couldn't help the smile on his face. Noel lifted his beer to his lips and took a drink as he watched Clara laugh at the words Alex spoke. They made it out of all that misery and pain with the one thing they had both wanted from the very start: Alex's blessing.

"Never thought I'd see that damn smile," Rob pointed out as he took the vacant seat next to him.

"Didn't think I'd get to keep her after everything." Noel turned away from Clara and looked at Rob.

There was a happy smile from Rob as he held his beer up at Noel. "I told you it'd all work out."

"We took the long and messy road it seems. But she found her way back to me."

Rob nodded his head with a satisfied grin. "Listen," he began to say. Then he set his beer on the table, reached into his pocket, and he pulled out a small velvet box.

Noel's heart stopped at the sight of it.

"I think it's time I stopped holding on to this. I told you you'd need it someday."

Glancing over at Clara, her attention was still on Alex. Noel took the small box from Rob and held it tightly in his hands. "Thank you for holding on to it." His fingers ran along the velvet, and he held it out of sight.

"Happy that I'm giving it back to you. Do us all a favour and marry her." Rob chuckled.

Noel took a deep breath and opened it. The sight of the ring made him smile. With the Celtic knots next to the large diamond, he knew the ring was still perfect. There was no other option. He was going to marry Clara Lawrence. Closing the ring box, Noel beamed up at Rob. "I've already got the plans to propose in motion."

Settling into his chair, he watched the smile on Clara's face as her eyes met his. The exact same eyes Noel would spend forever looking into.

The Final Step

Clara

"That's the tenth time you've looked over at Noel. He isn't going anywhere."

Clara looked at her brother and blushed. He had caught her staring before he began to chuckle.

"Don't laugh at me!" she whined poking at Alex's chest. She barely made him flinch, and she sighed in utter happiness.

"I told you he'd make it."

"I had every belief and every hope that he would," Clara replied with a smile. "I never thought about emailing him. I called him a million times, but they ended up going straight to voicemail. I stopped trying after you told me to. I'm happy you got him here. Thank you, Alex."

Alex beamed, proud of himself. "I'll do whatever it takes to make my little sister happy. Even if it means bringing the asshole back into her life."

Clara glared at her brother. "He's the good kind."

"Clara, he's the best asshole I know. I also know he's very much in love with you," Alex said, making her smile.

He swayed her along with the soft music and she giggled at

his attempts to make this dance special. Clara tilted her head to see Keira and her father dancing. The sight made her wish for her own dance. But she knew it would never be a reality. Her father didn't care enough.

"I'm sorry this couldn't be your daddy-daughter dance with Dad," Alex sadly said.

Shaking her head, she gazed up at her brother. "This—with you—means more than it would with him. Alex, you are more my father than Dad will ever be. Thank you," she said wholeheartedly. Alex was one of the two most important men in her life and, at this moment, she had them both in her heart and her life.

"Mind if I cut in?"

Clara instantly smiled at his voice.

Alex rolled his eyes at her and said, "I'd say yeah, but it'll probably upset my sister, so go on. I'll just go steal my fiancée from her old man."

The contented smile on her brother's face made Clara unbelievably happy. She had wanted this sight all those months ago: Alex giving them his blessing to be together.

However happy she was, the thought of Liam had always made her sick. Breaking his heart was the last thing she had wanted to do, but she finally set him free and that was the best for him. She had seen him less and less as the days passed until he left for Ireland. Packing up her things was the hardest part. He had tried once to convince her to stay, but she'd said no. After that one last attempt, Liam had stopped. Instead, he became her friend rather than her significant other.

The moment Noel's hand touched hers, Clara felt alive. There were no more secrets between them and staring into those green eyes, she knew forever was possible for them. His hand settled on the small of her back and brought her closer to him. Her body was always drawn to his, a feeling that she would never get over. He had a power over her. As 'How Long Will I Love You' by Ellie Goulding played, Clara knew how special this moment was for them, as her eyes never left his. Noel would never have to say those words again, not when his eyes spoke for him.

"When I caught that plane to come back to New York, I never imagined I'd be hearing you tell me you love me. I never thought I'd hear you say you wanted a life with me," Noel said and then he twirled her.

When she placed her hand back into his, the smile on his face had her feeling complete. "I didn't think you'd let me have a chance to say it."

Moving her to the soft music that played, Noel squeezed her hand. "Clara, it only takes one smile and you've got me. It wouldn't have taken much to get me to listen to you."

Clara had let out a laugh before she composed herself, the nerves ravishing her system. "Is dating me going to work?"

Noel stopped his movements and looked her in the eyes. "Dating isn't going to work for me."

"Oh," was all she managed, her head dropping.

Noel's hands had left her body before she felt his finger under her chin, lifting her eyes to meet his. "Honestly, I'd love to skip it and get to the part where you're *my* girlfriend. We've been through enough, don't you think?"

Her heart melted and she clenched her eyes shut for a moment. After opening them back up, she nodded at him. "I get to be your girlfriend?" she asked to confirm that they were on the same page.

"It's been a long time coming, but I wouldn't want any other woman claiming that title but you."

Clara didn't need any other words. Instead, she cupped his face in her hands and gave him a light yet lingering kiss on his lips.

"Question eleven," he announced.

She raised an eyebrow at him.

"How long are you in New York for?" Noel looked almost terrified to hear her answer. She was thankful that their questions game had gone unfinished until now.

Wrapping her arms around his neck, she answered, "Two weeks."

"Why just two weeks?" he asked sounding disappointed.

"I have my culinary school graduation. I finished my apprenticeship last week. I needed to complete two hundred and forty hours of kitchen work at a restaurant. That's what I've been up to while I waited for you," she replied. The idea that they'd have to have a long distance relationship made her heart sink. But it was more than she ever thought possible and accepted the idea with a smile.

"I'm so damn proud of you," Noel said as his hands returned to her hips. He bent down so that his lips almost touched her right ear. "Question twelve. Can I come back to Melbourne with you?" His hot breath touched her skin and her breathing heaved. Noel then pressed a kiss to her cheek and looked at her.

"You want to come back to Melbourne?"

"*My* girlfriend's graduating from culinary school, like I'd miss it! Plus, I have a lot of my annual left."

Just the words '*my girlfriend*' had Clara in tears. Noel brought her face closer to his, but the moment was lost when they heard the sound of a throat clearing. He let out a groan that she had internally mirrored.

"Way to hog Clara all night. We get it! You're back together. Now you go sit and talk to Max because that man is dying of guilt while I dance with the hottest thing that has ever kissed you!"

Clara blushed and let out a laugh.

Noel kissed cheek and gave her a smile. Then he placed her hands in Julian's. "Not too close now, Julian," he'd warned before leaving them on the dance floor.

"You've got him already protective over you." Julian laughed and rested his palm just on her hip.

"He's being an idiot," she said, shaking her head.

"No, he's in love with you. I wasn't lying when I said you were the hottest thing he's kissed." Julian winked.

Clara snorted at him. "You've seen Andrea and Valerie, right?"

He glared at her. "I've seen them both. They hold no candle to you, Clara. To me, you're beautiful in 'you're practically my little sister' way. But to Noel, you are beyond words. You never have to be worried about any other woman. He's too in love with you to see anyone else. He's lost you too many times to risk losing you again. I'm glad you found your way back to him."

Squeezing his hand, she glanced up at Julian and smiled thankfully for his influence in her choice. "I only found my way back to him because of you. I couldn't survive life without Noel. Liam was only holding me up for air for a short amount of time. If you took him away, I wasn't breathing anymore. You steered me in the right direction."

"Are you happy, Clara?" His question had her stopping their dance.

Looking around the room, she saw her brother and her sister-in-law-to-be dancing, she noticed Noel talking to Rob and Max, and in front of her was one of her oldest friends. Back home, Annie and Jarred were happily married, Stevie was still Stevie, Josie was still at the bakery, and Ally still claimed Clara as her sister.

Smiling, she knew the answer. "I've never been happier with my life than right now."

Julian wrapped his arms around her waist and held her up in the air.

"Julian!" she shrieked.

When he put her down, they both stopped their laughter. He beamed at her. "You've finally got *your* happily ever after, Clara. This one's yours to keep."

"And how about you?" Clara asked once she fixed her curls back into place.

Julian pursed his lips and raised his eyebrow. "What about me?"

"Still not over for you?"

"She's somewhere in this world, and if you and Noel are anything to go by, maybe I might find her someday. I'm not a man who believes in miracles, but until I see her, I won't start believing. Plus it's fun being single. I've had Italian models throwing themselves at me. When is that not ever fun?" He let out an unconvincing laugh that caused her to frown.

As if he sensed her doubts, Julian winked at her and said, "Prison guard's on his way. I better leave you alone tonight."

Turning to her right, she saw Noel walk towards her. His eyes only on her and she felt the universe accept their love. This time, she was done running. She'd savour and memorise each step they'd take together. Clara knew it wouldn't be smooth sailing. When his leave was over, they'd have to figure out how to make it work for them.

"Is it crazy that I don't want to leave your side?" he asked once he took her hand and led her to the tables.

"Not one little bit," she replied.

Noel held out a chair and then tucked her in. The smiles

from around the table had her blushing. She glanced at Noel the moment he sat next to her. Those green eyes had her heart racing. The smile on Noel's face had her left hand reaching for his, assuring him that she wasn't going anywhere. Peeking up, she noticed Rob staring at their linked hands. Rob then looked at Noel and grinned. Clara couldn't help but squint at them both. But before she could question their exchanges, Noel's lips grazed her cheek and instantly caught her attention.

*B*eing able to dance with Noel so freely was a blessing. He didn't give up; every song that had played he was on his feet, dragging her to the dance floor. Not that she minded. She loved the feel of his body pressed against hers. Every so often, he'd whisper in her ear of the life they'd live together and how much he loved her.

Each time he spoke those three words, he claimed her heart all over again. And each touch of his lips had her almost in tears. They slowly danced on the empty dance floor, the room almost void of guests. His eyes never left hers as they swayed along to a soft song she didn't recognise.

She took him in, and he was utterly beautiful. He wasn't perfect, but neither was she. Both imperfectly perfect together. His green eyes were the first thing she loved about him and then his heart. Clara smiled as she cradled his face in her hands.

"What time do you want to go back to Alex's?" Noel asked, his arms wrapped around her and brought her closer to him.

"Actually," Clara said as she let her fingers stroke the side of his face.

"Yeah?"

"I have a room here. The boys already shotgunned Alex's free rooms before I got to Scarsdale. And well, with the plan to get you back, I wanted us to be away from everyone. But if you want to stay at Alex's, I'm good with that." Clara bit her bottom lip, hoping that tonight she'd sleep in his arms. She yearned his touch and his body.

"I was going to suggest we find a hotel. I need you alone tonight."

Her heart skipped a beat and she released her lip, smiling at him. "Why would you need me alone, Noel?" she asked in a low voice.

"Because I want to make love to you, Clara. I'm going to need you tonight and I don't want any of the boys around, especially Alex."

She felt her cheeks heat up, and she swallowed hard.

"But if you're not ready for us to make love, I understand. Just let me hold you tonight and let me wake up to you tomorrow morning and every morning after that."

The love in his eyes completely struck her. She took his hand and leant closer to his ear before she whispered, "Please make love to me."

Her heart and body needed to feel him, to complete the love between them by consummating their relationship. And maybe one day, consummate a marriage between them. Because she saw it, she saw herself being Noel's wife. Maybe one day. For now, she was happy she had the opportunity to be his.

"You sure?" he asked.

The control was clear in his eyes, and she nodded. She watched his chest fall heavily; she had kissed him gently on the lips before she quickly grabbed her clutch from their table and led him out of the large function room.

Once they had walked up the stairs, they stood in front of the white door of her room. Letting go of Noel's hand, she opened her clutch and took out her room key. She placed the key in and unlocked the door. Before she even had time to return the key back in her clutch, Noel turned her around.

"I'm so in love with you. Tonight, I'll show you just how much I do," he softly whispered.

He placed his hands on her hips and lifted her up, her legs instinctively wrapping around him, and her arms locked around his neck, key and clutch still in her hands. Her heart pounded at the feel of his body and his hands holding her backside. Noel held her up as he opened and closed the door behind her. Taking a step inside of the room, his lips crashed into hers. Hot, demanding, and passionate. His lips perfect as they moved against hers. His tongue ran along her bottom lip until she let out a small moan that allowed him to explore her mouth. His tongue needing and wanting as it touched and moved against hers, leaving her panting.

"Baby, I need to put you down," he groaned against her mouth.

She smiled against his lips as he bent down, allowing her to unwrap her legs and put her feet on the floorboards. The room she had booked had a regal-inspired bed against a blue almost grey wall, a buffet against the wall next to the bed, and a small desk next to the window. When she had untangled her arms from around his neck, Clara walked over to the antique buffet table and placed her clutch and key on the wooden top. She had heard his footsteps before his hands covered hers — his mouth close to her ear and his body against hers.

"Are you sure you want this tonight?" he asked in a strangled voice. His hot breath touched her ear until she felt his lips graze the curve of her neck. She let out a sigh and closed her eyes tightly at the feel of his mouth on her skin.

"Please," she softly begged.

His hands pressed against hers as his lips trailed up her neck then they disappeared. She opened her eyes and looked down at their hands. They always fit so perfectly together, and she smiled at the sight. Noel's hands left hers as his fingers ran along the back of her neck. His touch sent shivers to roll down her spine and she realised how much she had missed the feel of him. Just the sheer pleasure of his touch made her heart ache and expand.

"I love you," he whispered in her ear. The emotion in his voice had her tearing. She felt the tug of the zipper of her dress and she bit down on her bottom lip. The anticipation had her breathless. When the zipper stopped, the dress had loosened before it fell on the floor. Noel then placed his hands on her hips and spun her to face him.

It hurt her to see those green eyes so sad, but the love and adoration mended that hurt. She swallowed hard. She finally had what she had dreamed of standing in front of her. Slightly feeling insecure about her white lacy underwear, Clara turned away from his stare.

Noel rested his palms on her cheeks. "I'm staring at you because you are the most beautiful woman I have ever laid my eyes on. You need to start believing that you are breathtakingly beautiful." He placed his hand over her cleavage, her heart racing at his touch. "I fell in love with your heart. This is what's so beautiful about you. Your laugh, your smile, and everything else is a bonus."

Tears brimmed her eyes at his words. The basic human function of breathing rendered difficult. He didn't let her reply. Instead, he bent down, scooped her into his arms, and walked her to the bed. Noel set her down on the cool sheets and her head settled on the pillows of the bed.

"You seem to have too many clothes on, Noel," she whispered, mimicking the words she had uttered when they were on that beach together, over a year ago.

A bright smile filled his face as he hovered over her body. "Before we go through with this…" he said sitting up.

His face tensed and Clara automatically sat up. She took Noel's hand in hers and gave him a reassuring squeeze.

"I don't have any protection, Clara. Are you still on the pill? I don't know if you and Liam were trying for a family."

Clara let out a short laugh, lifted her legs over his lap, and straddled him, ensuring that she gazed into his eyes. It was time she was honest about her sexual experiences. "Liam and I weren't trying for kids, far from it, and I'm still on the pill."

His hold of her hips was a feeling that consumed her, a feeling she wanted to keep. She wanted to hold on to him, to keep him simply forever. She wanted to be the woman who tied him down and he continued loving for the rest of time. She would be strong enough for him.

No more running.

"Clara, are you sure you want this to happen between us? I mean, I want to, but if you want to wait, we can."

The nervousness in his voice had her fingers trailing along the side of his face. "I love you and you are the only man I'll ever want. I want us to make love tonight. I want you to own my body as you did before. I want you to own my heart with each breath you take and each slip of my name. I want this because I love you. But… you need to go easy on me, Noel."

He flinched and brought his hands up to her face, pulling her back so he could look at her clearly. "What do you mean go *easy* on you?" The callousness of his palm was one she missed, his hands firm and strong as he held her face.

Breathing in deeply, she realised how happy she was

to confess this to him. "I've only ever had sex with *one* man before."

"What?" he breathed out utterly shocked.

"I've only ever made love to you, Noel. You are my one and only. It's only ever been you."

He turned them slightly before pushing her back onto the pillows and finding her lips. Her hands tangled in his hair as she held on to him. Breathless at each needy kiss he gave her. She loved him and now she was thankful Liam had asked to wait.

Breaking their kiss, he held himself up with his hand on the mattress near her head. Then Noel moved the messy curls out of her face. "How is that even possible?"

"Liam wanted us to wait and then he proposed and asked if we could wait until we got married. He's never touched me. I hope this isn't a problem. The only experience I've had is with you and that was a long time ago."

"I'm the only one who's…"

Clara nodded. The look in his eyes had her smiling and utterly thankful that she could claim him as her only. Noel had sat up and loosened his tie before he removed it and made quick work of his shirt.

His hands were on his buckle when Clara sat up and asked, "Can I do it?"

He didn't say anything, only nodding his answer. The look in his eyes told her that this between them was to show her his love, to claim her heart as his. Her trembling hands reached over and unbuckled his belt. Noel's lips kissed their way up and down her neck as she unsnapped his pants. The anticipation truly left her breathless.

"I can't wait to spend the rest of my life with you," he breathed against her neck as she slid the zipper down. Tears brimmed her eyes, as she tried to control her breathing. This moment and his love overwhelmed her.

"Stay with me, Clara. It's okay. We have each other now. I'm here, and I'm never going to leave you." His lips found her mouth as he gave her a quick open-mouth kiss and then he got off the bed.

Watching Noel shimmy out of his pants and underwear was breathtaking. Seeing him naked was truly beautiful. She swallowed the lump in her throat as he returned to the bed, pushing her into the mattress and hovering his body over hers. He was bulkier than she remembered—his shoulders broader and his muscles more defined.

They had a layer of her underwear between them but she felt how much he wanted her and the feeling was monumentally mutual. Looking into his eyes, the love burned right through her heart, his name marking every inch and ruining her for any other man. But she was happy; there was no other man she'd rather spend her days with than Nolan Parker.

Getting on her elbows, Noel unclasped her strapless white bra and pulled it off her body. He disposed of it on the floor and he took in her bare chest. He had seen her naked numerous times before and his expression of awe always captivated her.

"If Liam knew what making love to you was like, then he would have never let you go. You have no idea how it feels to hear that I'm the only man you've ever been with. I'm the one and only man you'll ever be with again, Clara. This is forever."

The promise in his eyes had her nodding. "I believe you," she whispered and kissed the tip of his nose.

Noel's hands slid down the side of her body. They both held their breaths as Noel's fingers dug into the sides of her lacy underwear. His chest heaved and he closed his eyes tightly before opening them. Clara lifted her hips off the bed as he pulled her underwear down her legs.

This was what she wanted. No barriers between them, just the two of them promising to love each other for the rest of their days. Shifting, Noel settled between her legs as he held her face in his hands. Her hands wrapped around his wrists as he held her. She wanted nothing more than to make love to him. Completely giving herself to him and promising every bit of her to the love of her life.

"Clara?" he whispered, sounding vulnerable as he fell silent.

"Yes, Noel," she answered. The nerves formed knots in the pit of her stomach. Her hands squeezing his wrist to indicate she was staying. How she walked away from him, she didn't know. Her intentions were selfless, but looking back, she was selfish for not accepting her heart's choice sooner.

"Promise me something."

Her heart ached at the fearful glint in his eyes. A fear she wanted to rid him of. "Anything." She smiled.

"Promise when I wake up tomorrow, you'll still be here."

Clara's mouth fell open at his request. So simple and yet he sounded so terrified. His thumb ran along her bottom lip as he opened his heart up to her.

"Promise me that when I wake up tomorrow, you'll still be in this bed. Promise that you won't leave me, and that this isn't all just some crazy dream. Promise me that I get to wake up to the sight of you every morning for the rest of our lives."

This time she didn't hold back the tears. They spilt down and she let out a sob. Letting go of his wrists, she covered her eyes with her hands and cried. Being naked with Noel and having him say those three words and wanting mornings together overwhelmed her. She needed a moment. She closed her eyes tightly and tried to push away the doubts in her head.

I'll be worthy of Nolan Parker. I will come out deserving him. For the rest of my life, I'll keep him loving me.

"I promise," she said into her hands. Taking a deep breath, she moved them from her face and placed them on his cheeks. His cheeks wet with his own tears. "God, I promise. I'm never leaving you. I'm never running. I love you and I am so sorry. It took hurting you and losing you so many times for me to realise that I can't live without you. I'm so in love with you."

Noel's sobs mirrored hers. He leant forward and kissed the tears away. Reaching up, her hands cupped his jaw and held him close to her.

"I wouldn't let you run alone. I'd run with you." He looked down at her and propped himself up on his hands, positioning himself.

"I love you," she whispered and then pressed her lips to his chin.

"And I love you, simply forever," he whispered back. His words reminded her of the ones she had written in his letter.

She held her breath and blinked the tears away as he slowly entered her. The slight pain couldn't take away from the pleasure she felt. This time there was no barrier, and as he sunk into her, they both let out a moan. Tears welled again as she realised just how much she missed him and how much her body and soul belonged to him.

His chest pressed against hers as he stilled. He breathed

heavily near her left ear, her breathing just the same. They didn't move as he stayed inside her, almost memorising the feel of their connection. "If I never say it enough, then just know how much I love you," he said softly. His words had her heart slamming against her chest. Making love to Noel only cemented a thought she had denied.

He's my home. Noel's where I belong.

The next morning she wasn't surprised to be sitting in Alex's car as they drove away from Chappaqua. When she saw the Scarsdale sign, she knew they were going back to her brother's. Clara didn't mind. Breakfast as an entire family sounded perfect. Things were finally how they were supposed to be.

The moment the car pulled into the driveway, Noel cut the engine and took her hand. Looking at her left hand, she saw the bareness of her ring finger. Sadness crept into her heart, but she pushed it away. This was the best for everyone, especially Liam.

"Do you trust me?" Noel asked.

Clara's eyes met his, and she nodded.

"Then close your eyes."

Following his instructions, she clenched her eyes shut and felt his hand leave hers. She heard the driver's side door open and then close. Her curiosity was getting the better of her as the urge to open her eyes intensified. Then the passenger side door opened and she instantly felt the cold air hit her skin. She was thankful that he had told her to dress warm.

The almost half an hour drive was catch up time. He had asked her a series of twenty-one questions and in total he had so far used seventeen out of twenty-one. His questions were basic: what she had been up to; culinary school; Annie and Jarred's wedding. She remembered the day Jarred gave her the letter; the smile on his face as he told her of his intentions on asking Annie to marry him and if he had Clara's blessing.

The moment news broke out that the wedding was off, Jarred's plans changed and he decided to be that spontaneous man. His proposal instead changed to, *"Will you marry me, today, Annie?"* It was a quick scramble to get Annie and Jarred's family to the church, but with the help of Liam and Jo, the wedding was breathtakingly beautiful. Although they couldn't legally get married without first submitting their Notice of Intended Marriage, they did however have the ceremony. A month later, Jarred and Annie had properly and legally exchanged vows and became man and wife.

Noel's lips grazed her cheek and she smiled. This man was finally hers. His hands touched her arms as he unbuckled the belt and took her hands, helping her out of the car. Then his palms covered her eyes as he began to lead her away from the car.

"Where are we going?" She laughed and her brows knitted. "I don't like surprises."

"Well, my love, this one you're going to have to."

She sighed. She remembered his surprise first date and grinned. It was a lie. She loved *his* surprises.

"Clara, I can feel your eyelashes as you blink. No peeking! Just trust me," he groaned. His want for such a surprise had her heart melting.

She could hear a gate open, and they continued to walk a little more.

"Careful," Noel warned as he helped her up a few steps. He stopped her and then moved his palms from over her eyes, running them along her arms before he held her hands.

The butterflies in her stomach had her feeling queasy as a million thoughts ran through her mind.

"Okay, open your eyes."

When she did, the first thing she saw were those eyes that left her mesmerised. Looking around, she realised where they were. They stood on her brother's porch and she saw the sun slowly start to rise.

"I know it's a stupid surprise but let me explain. I promised you in this spot that I did not intend to be platonic with you. I also told you here that I couldn't watch you walk away and this is the exact spot that I'm making you the same promises."

Smiling at him, she dropped one of his hands and placed her free hand on his cheek. "You want to make me promises in this exact spot?"

"Yes. This spot means the world to me. It got me closer to you and closer to being with you. The mornings we spent here are some of the best mornings of my life. I promise you, Clara, I never want to be just platonic with you. I want to be your best friend and your soul mate. I want to be the man you spend the rest of your life loving and I want to be the one you smile at every day. I promise never to watch you walk away again. Because when you walk, I will never let you. I will follow you and beg that crazy mind of yours to stay. I promise to love you and spend every morning watching sunrises with you. I want to grow old with you and I promise to do so."

Her heart stopped beating as his words mended every break she had. He wanted the things she had wanted for them and she was sure she'd never run. Stepping forward, she removed her hand from his cheek and circled her arms around his neck. Tilting her head to her right, she watched the sun rise.

Perfect.

The beautiful and simple surprise had her saying, "Question seven." He might have asked the questions in the car, but she had saved hers.

His hands were on her hips and pulled her close to his body. "Okay."

"Ask me to stay," she said.

The confusion and surprise filled his eyes. "What?"

"Noel, ask me to stay here in the States."

His mouth gaped. "Why?"

Letting out a short laugh, she replied, "Just ask."

He squinted at her for a moment, trying to read into her request. "Clara, will you stay with me in Boston?"

She didn't have to think. Saying it was as natural as breathing. "Yes."

"Yes?"

Clara nodded her head with a contented smile.

"B-but the bakery and your home?"

"I don't own the bakery. It was under Liam's name and he's already hired a new chef to run the business. I interviewed her and she'll do a fine job. I don't want to buy the bakery because I want a home and a future with you. And as for Melbourne, it's going to suck not seeing all my friends, but like I said, the greatest sacrifices occur for the greatest of loves. Melbourne is just a city. But you, Noel, you're *my* home. I don't care what city I'm in. As long as I get to be with you, I'm happy. I have nothing in Melbourne when you and my brother are here. Your career is here and I don't have much happening for me back home without you once I graduate from culinary school. What do you say?" She was hopeful he'd say yes, but she had to steel herself. She knew it was too soon, but they had been through so much that she didn't want to waste any more time apart.

"So you'll move to be with me? You'll live with me in Boston?" The excitement in his eyes had vanquished the queasy feeling she had felt moments before.

"You're *my* boyfriend, and I love you. I need to wake up in your arms every morning." Danny being a successful head chef in San Francisco opened doors for her in Boston. A recommendation from him and she could work in any restaurant in Massachusetts.

"There's kind of a slight problem," he stated with a frown.

She wasn't overly worried. They have had their share of problems, and she was sure they wouldn't be anywhere near as tough as her engagement had been.

"What kind of problem?"

"The 'I'm kind of homeless' problem. I sold my apartment and Camaro when I left for Hong Kong, but it's a good thing." Noel took her hand and sat them on the step. He wrapped his hands around one of hers and gently stroked her hand.

"How is it a good thing?" she asked.

"It means we can go house hunting together. We can make it *our* home and it'll be our safe haven. I'm done with apartments and the city. I want suburbia and a house with you. I want the life we imagined for each other."

She smiled and rested her head against his shoulder. "I want all of that with you," she said. Clara envisioned what it would be like to live with Noel and one day have little footsteps running along their floorboards. A house they could fill with memories for the rest of their lives.

He'll make a wonderful father.

"Question eighteen. What happened to your locket?" he asked, looking down at her.

Her fingers pressed on her bare neck as she looked up and sighed. "The clasp won't lock and the hinge is a little loose. I was scared it was going to break, so I haven't worn it as much. I couldn't live with myself if it broke or I lost your note."

"I understand," he said as he let go of her hand, wrapped his arm around her, and pulled her close to him.

"This is our first proper sunrise together," she noted. Clara squeezed his arm as she glanced back at the rising sun and then at his face.

Noel smiled, kissed her lips once, and said, "We have a lifetime of firsts ahead of us, Clara."

Closing her eyes tightly, she let his words consume the rest of her heart. "I believe you," she whispered, knowing they'd have a happy life together. This was a new chapter in their lives, and she would enjoy their first sunrise together.

The Final Dive

Noel

After taking in the sunlit room, Noel sighed. Clara's bedroom had hardly changed. The only thing that had changed was them. They had grown. They weren't the same couple that lay in the exact bed over a year ago. His love for her was stronger. They had done their fighting and now they had the chance to be together. This time nothing was in their way; this time a future was in their reach. Hugging Clara tighter, he reassured himself of his choices.

Clara's the one.

Arriving back in Melbourne a few days before her graduation, he never saw Liam. Noel had called the number that he had for him, but he didn't get an answer. Not that Noel was expecting him to, but he had to personally thank Liam. He was the reason for Clara sleeping in Noel's arms.

"What time is it?" Clara asked, her eyes heavy with sleep.

Ducking his head, Noel kissed her lips and whispered, "Just after nine."

She smiled and lay back down, her eyes fluttered. Clara's graduation wasn't until eleven. The afternoon after their sunrise on the steps, he had called his family and told them of his intentions to marry Clara before she moved to Boston with him. That meant he had two weeks to marry her before they left Australia for Christmas in New York. Looking down at her left hand, his heart expanded. His proposal plans were already in motion.

"Baby, my parents are going to be here soon. I'd love nothing more than to spend today in bed with you, but it's your big day."

Clara snuggled into his chest and held him tighter. "Argh! I'm sure they can send my certificate in the mail."

He laughed at her groan. "You know my gran won't be happy with that. Let's not forget Alex, Keira, and my mother. They want to see you graduate," he reasoned.

Clara sat herself up and looked down at him. "Fine!" She smiled. Everyone besides Julian had returned to Melbourne on the same flight. Julian went back to Milan to continue his consulting services with an advertisement company that paid him top dollar.

Noel sat up and brushed the hair out of her face. "That's my girl."

Clara leant forward and kissed him full on the lips. Pulling back, she raised her eyebrow at him. "Yours, huh?"

Her golden brown eyes shimmered beautifully in the sunlight. This room was one he'd always love. So many moments happened in this bed: their first time together and the moment he realised he wanted her as his wife.

"Unlucky for you, this is forever," he said as he pulled her onto his lap.

Her hands instantly cupped his face as his hands ran up her thighs. He stopped the moment he hit the hem of her nightdress.

Clara graced him with a beautiful smile before she whispered, "I love you," and proceeded to kiss him.

He'd never tire of her speaking those three words. Wrapping his hands around her waist, he pulled her forward to deepen their kiss. His heart pounded at each slow taste of her lips she allowed. He broke away and then trailed kisses along her jaw and down her smooth neck, her skin soft against his mouth. Clara softly moaned and sank further into his lap, causing Noel to let out a groan.

He felt her breath hit his right ear. "Either you need to stop this or I'm going to miss my graduation."

He smiled against her neck then he pulled away and looked into her eyes. "You better get in the shower before everyone gets here."

The only moment he was able to get her alone for them to be intimate was when Alex and Keira went away to Philip Island for the day. He wasn't going to let Alex hear his and Clara's lovemaking.

"Good idea," Clara said as she quickly kissed him and sashayed to the bathroom, intentionally torturing him with each sway of her hips.

"Where's Clara?" Noel's brother, George, asked. Noel handed him the cold can of Coke. It was just after ten when his family had arrived at the apartment for pre-celebrations. Grabbing a can for himself, he nodded towards Clara's bedroom. "Ironing her chef's jacket. She'll be out in a minute."

"You look happy," George stated as he opened his can and took a sip.

"I don't think happy truly defines how I feel." A contented smile plastered Noel's face as they stepped onto the balcony. "I'm proposing tonight," he had softly stated before they reach their parents.

George settled a hand on Noel's shoulder and grinned. "Got the big brother's blessing?"

Noel nodded his head and remembered pulling Alex aside after dinner the night before. For a second, the blank expression on Alex's face had Noel worried, but then Alex had smiled and gave him permission.

"Yeah, I have Alex's blessing," Noel beamed as his eyes met Clara's brother. The approving nod from Alex settled his nerves. All he had to do was propose and hope to God Clara says yes.

"Nolan, you come here," his grandmother called, waving her hand at him.

Noel approached his grandmother and hugged her. Then

he kissed her cheek and set his can on the patio table.

"You've got that ring ready, son?" his father asked.

Noel patted his pocket and nodded.

"You better treat that girl right," his mother warned.

Noel chuckled. "Yes, Mum."

Before he could say anything else, his father had cleared his throat and signalled for him to hush. Turning around, he saw Clara in her chef's jacket, checked pants, and a blue scarf around her neck.

She bit her bottom lip and held out her arms. Releasing her lip, she asked, "How do I look?"

She truly looks beautiful in white.

Her question was directed at him. He closed the distance between them and gently placed his hands on the back of her neck. "Utterly beautiful."

His lips pressed to hers and he kissed her deeply.

Clara smiled against him. "Your parents and gran are looking."

"We don't care. If you kids need a minute..."

Opening his eyes, he watched Clara's cheeks turn that beautiful red colour. "Gran!" he whined, staring at his fiancée-to-be, hopefully. "Ready to be a graduate of the culinary arts?"

The excitement reached Clara's eyes as they shone brightly. "Yes. It means I'm one step closer to living in Boston with you."

"We can honestly live here. I don't want you to give up those restaurant offers."

Clara poked at his chest and then shook her head. "Stop trying to change my mind. I want to live in Boston with you. Why wouldn't I turn down those offers when I get to live with the love of my life and be a three-hour drive away from my brother?" She raised her brow at him.

He knew she was sacrificing a lot for them, but she was sure of her choice and he wasn't going to change her mind again. He had a stable and secure job and could offer her a happy life in Boston.

Turning around, he walked Clara onto the balcony and to their family. The smiles on their faces were ones he enjoyed. Looking at Clara, he could see the realisation that for all her life she had her own family. The proud smile on his father and mother's face told him they were happy to call her their daughter, too, if she gave him the chance at marriage.

*N*oel and Clara rode in Alex's Mustang to Le Cordon Bleu Culinary School. The moment Alex had parked on the school grounds, Clara gave Noel a kiss and went off to join the other graduates-to-be.

"I've missed driving this baby," Alex noted once he'd locked the car.

Leaning on the car, Noel peeked over at Keira, knowing the secret she had kept from her fiancé.

She glanced at the red Mustang and smiled. "Merry Christmas, Alex!"

"What?" Alex leant over the roof of the car and stared at Keira.

She laughed. "I was going to surprise you. Last time we were here, you said the exact same thing about this car. So I'm going to get it shipped to New York in the New Year."

"No way! Darling, are you serious?" Alex gaped.

"Alex, I wouldn't lie about your beloved Mustang. I'm just scared that you'll love this car more than you love me."

Alex's eyes widened. He stalked around the car and took Keira's hands in his. "Never, ever, darling. Never. It's just a car. You know how much I love you."

Noel felt someone loop an arm around his. He craned his neck to see his gran smiling up at him.

"Ready to see your fiancée graduate, Nolan?" Gran smiled.

"She's not my fiancée, yet. You know, she could say no."

Alex's loud belt of laughter caught his attention. "My sister is not going to say no to you. She broke off her engagement to Liam for you and is moving to Boston to be with you. My sister is in love with you. Now don't be a little shit tonight and just ask her!"

The playful tease didn't mask Alex's impatience with him. There were times during their two-week stay in New York that had him almost proposing, impatience almost getting the better of him. But he wanted his proposal to be special.

Gran's hold of his arm tightened, and his brows furrowed at

her sullen face. "It's a shame that your family couldn't be here today, Alex."

Noel's heart sank. That was one thing he couldn't do for Clara. He couldn't get her parents to her graduation. He also hadn't heard back from Liam either. Giving his gran a reassuring smile, he led her up to the hall doors.

Relief filled his body when he saw the man he'd been waiting for next to a woman and a little girl. Releasing his gran's arm, Noel walked over and shook his hand.

"I'm glad you made it. You have no idea how much she'll appreciate it," Noel said. When they finished shaking hands, a smile plastered his face and Noel was pleased.

"It's her graduation day. I wouldn't miss it for the world. Sorry I didn't get back to your calls. Only got back from Ireland a few days ago and was up in Sydney," Liam explained.

Before Noel could say anything else, he heard a small girl's voice speak. "Li, is this prince charming?"

Noel noticed the little blonde girl smile at him, her hand clutching Liam's. Crouching down, Noel's eyes met the big blue eyes that Clara helplessly loved.

"Yes, CeCe. This is Clara's prince charming," Liam confirmed.

Peeking up, Noel could see the sadness in Liam's eyes.

"We had to explain why the wedding was called off and well, this was the only way Liam could get her to understand. I'm Ally, by the way."

Noel flinched as he remembered those sad hazel eyes and ash blonde hair from the wedding months before. She had Liam's eyes and she was beautiful. Not as beautiful as Clara was, but Ally O'Connor was stunning.

"Where's Clara?" he heard Rob say behind him.

Noel watched as those hazel eyes flashed, the hope that consumed Ally's face had Noel realising the attraction she had for his best friend. He smiled as Ally's gaze met Rob. Turning his head, Noel saw the surprise of seeing her register on Rob's face. His best friend tensed and then he looked down at Noel.

"She's waiting with the other graduates. We'll see her inside," Noel replied.

He felt the tension between Rob and Ally. Rob's tough nature had her frowning and looking away. She appeared almost dejected at his dislike for her.

"Are you a nice prince?" CeCe asked innocently.

Noel stared at those big blue eyes and the little girl had already pulled him in. "I hope I am. I'm Noel," he introduced himself and held out his hand.

CeCe smiled at him and placed her small hand in his. She let out a giggle as they shook hands. He understood why Clara found it hard to let them go. They were a family who had loved her unconditionally.

Standing up, he gave CeCe a wink and then faced Ally. "It's nice to meet you, Ally. I'm Noel."

She seemed apprehensive but after a quick glance at Liam, Ally gave him a sincere smile. "It's good to finally meet you."

"Noel." He heard the familiar voice behind him. It was Stevie. He turned to see Stevie, Annie, and Jarred walk up the path to the group. They stood next to his parents, and his mother held Clara's bouquet. There was a painful expression on Rob's face as he stared at Stevie. The sorrow in her eyes had told Noel they had ended. For some reason, Noel didn't believe they were right for each other. It seemed they were both trying to make something out of nothing, but he wasn't sure. He just didn't see Rob being the one for Stevie.

Pulling Annie in for a hug, he held her tight until she laughed. "Congratulations are in order, Mrs Harper."

Annie beamed up at him, her smile honest and filled with joy. "You, too, Noel." He could tell she was holding back her joy for him and Clara. She was respecting Liam's feelings.

"Look, I'd love to continue this catch up, but my sister is about to graduate. Can we get going? I don't want to miss it," Alex moaned as he started ushering everyone towards the entrance of Le Cordon Bleu's graduation hall. Today was Alex's day to be a proud big brother.

Clara's brother grasped Noel's shoulder, stopping him from going into the hall. Noel looked up at his best friend and gave him a smile.

Alex arched a brow at him and whispered, "Not getting cold feet, are you?"

He shook his head. "Nope. Tonight's the night."

"Ahh, Nolan," his mother said, gaining their attention. Noel turned to see her holding up the tulips.

"Oh, right!" Noel approached her and gave his mother a kiss on the cheek. Then he took the purple tulips, staring at them with a smile.

It all started with a purple tulip.

Clara

*T*he moment she received her certificate, Clara was ecstatic. Leaving her bachelor was a tough and risky move, but hard work and the love of cooking got her the certificate in her hands. After countless photos with her fellow graduates and her chef mentors, Clara walked out of the hall with a large smile on her face. The final step before she took the final dive and moved to Boston. By the end of the night, she would tell him that she was offered a job at a French-Mediterranean restaurant on Columbus Ave in the South End, seven minutes from Noel's old apartment.

Getting into contact with Danny and his networks, Clara had several Skype interviews the day after she got off the phone with her mentor. Danny was now an established and well-respected chef in San Francisco; his recommendation got Clara a dessert and pastry intern position at Mistral. It was only an entry position that paid less than what she'd made at the bakery, but this time she'd be working in a real kitchen and learning from Boston's best dessert and pastry chefs.

The first thing she saw was her boyfriend holding a bouquet of purple tulips and a smile on his face, his eyes filled with pride. She looked over at his light green dress shirt and his black dress pants. He'd dressed for the occasion, and she truly did love him in green. Two weeks together and it was perfect. She couldn't wait to start a life with him. She took off her white top hat and ran up to him, her hands wrapping around his neck and she kissed him hard and passionately.

"Congratulations, baby," Noel mumbled against her lips.

Clara smiled as she drew back. She stared into those green eyes that put her in a trance most of the time. She was unbelievably in love with all of him.

"These are for you," he said once they untangled.

Her smile grew larger at the sight of the purple tulips. Clara handed him her certificate and hat, holding the bouquet up and taking in the fresh smell of her favourite flower.

"Clary!"

Turning around, her heart stopped at the little girl she loved so hopelessly. Clara had handed Noel the tulips before she bent down and held her arms open for CeCe to ran into them.

"How have you been, pretty girl?" Clara asked as she held CeCe in her arms. Tears escaped; she was happy that she didn't lose any of the O'Connors in her life. Peeking up, she saw her former fiancé walk up to her.

"You came." She smiled.

"Of course, sweetheart. It's your big day." Liam grinned.

He didn't drop the 'sweetheart,' and she didn't mind. Noel owned her heart. One nickname wouldn't send her running back to Liam. A smile on Ally's face told her that they could all be happy, could still be in each other's lives considering the mess she had put everyone through. CeCe held on tight; she had grown so much since the first day Clara had met her.

"You ready to go eat lots and lots of cupcakes?" she softly asked in CeCe's ear.

"Yes! I want the pink ones!" she said excitedly.

Clara handed her back to Liam. He put her down but didn't let go of her hand. She shifted her gaze to see that Stevie and Rob had distance between them. She frowned at the sight. Stevie let Rob go; she couldn't move on with him and it broke Clara's heart to see them so apart. But Clara knew Stevie's pain. If only she knew who it was that Stevie fell in love with, she could track him down. But Clara had decided to put it to rest. She'd let Fate take charge for them all.

"Photo time!" Noel's mother, Louise, said.

Clara's shoulders sagged. Looking around, everyone was dressed stunningly, and she was in her chef's jacket and pants.

"Mum," Noel whined next to her.

"Come on. I want photos of you both before Clara moves to Boston with you!"

Clara froze then she spun around to see the shocked and hurt expressions on both Ally and Liam's faces.

"I'm so sorry," Louise quickly apologised. Clara swallowed the lump in her throat.

"Boston?" Liam breathed out in disbelief.

"Liam," Clara cautiously said.

"No. I let you be with him, and he takes you away?" Liam's voice pitched higher.

She heard Noel's voice behind her, but she tuned him out. She hated herself for the hurt in Liam's eyes. "I'm moving to Boston to be with him."

Liam shook his head. "I don't understand. Why can't he move here to be with you? Why does he have to take you all the way to America? I'm okay with seeing you both together."

"I'm the one who wants to move, Liam. Noel's tried to get me to stay here, but I won't budge. I want to move to America to be with him and Alex."

"If you go, then we'll never see you," Liam said, dejected.

Clara glanced up at the cloudless sky and took a deep breath. She didn't think it would be this hard, but it was. Liam being away and not answering her calls gave her no opportunity to tell him of her decision. "Liam, I'm moving to be with Noel. I love him."

Liam gave CeCe to Ally, took a step forward, and looked down at her. "And what about us, Clara? You're just going to leave us behind?"

Her lips parted and the shock entered her body from his words. She didn't know what to say.

"Okay," Liam breathed out before he turned around and walked towards the car park.

"Liam," she called out, but he kept walking.

Ally offered Clara an apologetic smile and said, "I'll see you at the bakery," and chased after her brother, CeCe holding her hand.

Clara took a step towards them, but Noel's hand on her arm held her back.

"Let me," he said.

She was too speechless to say anything to him. Clara nodded and forced a smile. The hurt in Liam's eyes was her fault and all she wanted to do was make him happy, but not at the expense of Noel.

"Rob, mind coming with me?"

She heard Rob take two steps next to them.

"I'm sorry, Nolan," Louise apologised once again.

"It's all right, Mum. Not your fault. Let's take a quick photo before I go talk to him." Noel's sad eyes met hers as he blocked the vision of Liam walking away. "Baby, it's okay. I'll talk to him."

She shook her head and smiled up at him. She wasn't going to leave Noel. Not ever again. Then she faced their family.

Noel wrapped his arm around her waist and pulled her close. "I'm so proud of you, Clara," he whispered, and she smiled in time for the photo.

Once she'd taken a photo with Rob, Noel gave her a quick kiss and said, "I'll see you at the bakery." He handed her white top hat, bouquet, and certificate to Alex and went after Liam.

Clara stood there watching Noel and Rob walk away. She felt a hand on her shoulder, and she turned to see the tight smile on her brother's face.

"Noel will work this out. You're not changing your mind about him and Boston, are you?"

Clara frowned. Though she was insulted by the question her brother asked, she knew he was only asking. "I'm moving to Boston. I want a life with Noel."

The tight smile on Alex's face broke into a large grin. Her eyes met with Noel's family. The smiles on their faces had Clara mirroring theirs. The tears in Louise and Granny Parker's eyes had her heart filling with warmth. When Clara was a little girl, she had always loved Louise and Granny Parker; they had showed her a maternal love her mother didn't.

"Forget that happened. Let's take photos," she reassured her family and friends. They all seemed to relax at the smile she gave. However, in the back of her mind, she was dreading the outcome of Noel and Liam's talk.

*O*nce Alex parked the car, Clara went into the bakery bathroom and changed out of her chef jacket and pants and into a pale purple dress. She returned to the party to see familiar faces and the bakery she would be telling goodbye.

"Congratulations, Clara."

She smiled at Nadia, the new head baker of The Little Bakery. Having heard of the plans, the bakery would be a dessert restaurant, serving a three-course dessert-based menu. Nadia was instrumental in the change in business direction. Her Italian upbringing and speciality would certainly make The Little Bakery one of the best restaurants in the city.

"Thank you, Nadia. I saw the menu, and it's impressive."

Nadia blushed and shook her head. "I have some pretty big shoes to fill."

She let out a laugh. "No, you don't. I made cupcakes and that's it. You are turning this place into a restaurant."

Clara saw the pride in her chocolate eyes. Nadia smiled and excused herself to go speak with Josie. Stevie was by Clara's side instantly. Clara took in the guests who came to celebrate her graduation. In a corner were Annie, Jarred, Alex, and Keira talking and towards the table of finger foods was Noel's family: Marcus, Louise, George, and Granny Parker. Penelope couldn't make it as she was visiting family in New South Wales. George would be flying out to meet her later in the evening.

Sienna sat on a stool as she tapped her foot along with the soft music. Their eyes met and Sienna smiled at her, holding no resentment towards Clara for breaking her best friend's heart. The moment the familiar bakery doorbell rang, she quickly turned to see Max walk through the door, and Clara's brother met him halfway. Max glanced over at her, giving her a controlled smile before it faded and he walked over to George.

"He's sorry, you know?" Stevie pointed out.

Sighing, Clara faced her best friend. "I know. I tried so many times to talk to him in New York but he just kept saying 'I'm sorry' and walking off. It's not his fault I believed Sarah and let her get to me."

Stevie nodded her head. "You were pretty stupid for believing that bitch. If I had known that was what broke you two up, I wouldn't have let Noel go to Boston."

"I know. I was looking for a way out. But I'm not going through that all again. I can't lose him anymore. Noel keeps apologising for even going to Valerie's that night. What's going on with you and Rob?"

There was a huff from Stevie and she took a long drink from her wine glass. "I told him I couldn't do it. I told him to go back to Jewel. We got her jealous enough."

"Still not over Thailand guy?"

Stevie stared into her glass. "Guess not. Rob was bringing back too many memories, and I couldn't do it again. It was nice having him care and everything, but with his rowing career and my marketing internship, there was just no time to try."

She placed her hand on Stevie's shoulder and offered a smile.

"Plus, I saw the way he looked at Ally during Annie and Jarred's wedding. She has his attention. I'm kind of glad that she has because it means a quicker escape for me. I just wish he'd shown his interest so openly. She thinks he hates her."

"For a long time, I thought Rob hated me, too. He's like that though—" Before she could continue, the bell rang and she saw Noel walk through the newly painted blue door. She pushed off the counter and ran up to him, inspecting every inch of him. His face clear of any bruises and marks.

"Thank God," she breathed out, grabbed him by the shirt, and kissed him. Relief poured into her heart once he had composed himself enough to kiss her back. It was desperate and full of desire. It wasn't the slow kisses she loved but a kiss that marked her as his. When Clara pulled back, she panted. He had a way with her, but right now, she was thankful he wasn't hurt. She lightly touched his cheek and breathed out.

"Clara," Liam said gaining her attention. "I'm sorry about back there. I just didn't expect you to move so quickly. I'm happy for you, I really am. You have my blessing and my support."

Clara's heart finally relaxed. She had his support. She saw the genuine happiness in Liam's eyes, and she smiled up at him. He was going to find 'The One' soon enough. "Thank you, Liam. I appreciate your support more than anything."

Liam nodded and excused himself, walking up to the table of food. Ally, CeCe, and Rob then entered the bakery, smiled at Clara and joined in on the party.

She felt Noel's body relax next to her. It must have been some talk between them. He wrapped his arm around her waist and held her close as they looked over at the long table of food at the end of the bakery. His touch was one she'd never want to run from again.

"They could be happy with each other," Noel stated.

She took her eyes off Liam and met Noel's before she shook her head. "No."

"No?" Noel frowned and looked at Sienna and Liam again.

"Not Sienna. When Liam asked me to imagine myself getting married, I did imagine you, but I also imagined him getting married. It wasn't to me, and it wasn't to Sienna." Clara glanced at her ex-fiancé. "I'm the woman who ruins him," she uttered.

"Don't say that!" Noel defended.

Clara let out a laugh. "No, I am. I'm the woman who messes him up. I'm the one he's with last before he meets 'The One.' I'm the one who leaves him broken for the next woman. I make him hate and lose faith in love so that she can come and make him believe all over again. Liam saved me, but this time, he's the one who needs to be saved and that woman will do it. She'll show him what love is really like. She'll love him the right way. It's time someone showed Liam that he's truly worth being rescued."

Noel stepped in front of her and focused on her. "Don't do that to yourself, Clara. You saved Liam and showed him that all it takes is one woman to make you fall in love. You showed *me* that."

She smiled instantly at his loving words. In two weeks, they'd be off to New York for Christmas. Back when they were in the States, they went to Boston for the weekend and she instantly fell in love with Brookline. The streetcars reminded her of the trams back in Melbourne and her heart was set. Washington Square was her favourite. It reminded her of the old village centre that she grew up in back in the suburbs. For now, they'd rent an apartment until they found a house together. She did spot a house she loved that was on sale, but Clara would wait until she officially moved to Boston to decide on a house.

"I got a job offer," she said before he could say anything else.

"Take it! I'll call Gregson and we'll stay here."

Clara laughed and shook her head. "No, I got a job offer in the South End."

"In Boston?" His eyes were wide in disbelief.

"Danny got me a few interviews, and Mistral wanted to hire me for the dessert intern position." The utter joy in his eyes made her heart leap.

"So we're *really* doing this? We're really going to have a life together in Boston?" he asked.

Clara squinted at him. "Don't you dare back out, Nolan Parker. We are in this together."

He let out a heart-warming chuckle and his eyes sparkled. "I have some news, too."

"Go on," she urged.

"That house you like in Brookline... it's *ours*."

"Ours?" she breathed out.

"Working for G&MC and my promotion put me in a good position with the bank for a loan."

She knew how expensive that house was but she didn't care. The moment she turned twenty-one, she would pay it off in one transaction. She would use her trust funds on the house they'd own together.

We have a house and a life together.

"Question nineteen," he said, pulling her out of the daydream she had of their lives together. "Would you come for a drive with me?"

She raised her eyebrows at him. If it was to get her alone and to be intimate, then she was all in. Looking up at her brother, she saw him shrug. Her eyes met Liam's and she saw right through the forced smile he gave her.

"Okay," she agreed.

"It's a long drive. We're going to a few places."

lex's Mustang stopped outside of a home she knew so well. It was a long drive from the city to their childhood suburb. The bricked house was one she'd frequently visited as a child, and she smiled at the memories. Her side door opened and Noel held out his hand. Taking it, she stepped out of the car and looked over the Parker family home.

"Where are you taking me?" she asked as he led her to the side gate.

"Just wait and see." Noel reached up and unlocked the wooden gate. He led her into the garden, and she could see their childhood play out in front of her.

Walking past the deck, she remembered the little boy in his baseball cap and she smiled. He stopped her at the edge of the garden and she gazed at the very spot they stood over sixteen years ago.

"I want you to see some of *our* spots before you move to Boston." Noel dug his hand into his pocket and took out a small card.

He handed it to her and she opened it.

> This is the spot where one tulip started it all for us. Little did I know that, years later, I would fall madly in love with you. This is the spot where I helped a little girl smile with just one purple tulip. This spot started our story.

Her heart melted at this one card. Her eyes prickled at the thought of this very spot. Noel bent down and pulled out one of his mother's tulips. Like he did over sixteen years ago, he shook the dirt off and broke off the roots before handing it to her. He didn't let her say a word as he kissed her softly then took her hand and led her away from that one memorable spot.

"Where are we going now?" she asked curiously, clutching the single tulip and card in her hand.

"We have two more stops."

Clara took in the smell of the salty air and the cool breeze. It was just after two p.m. when they had made it to Chelsea Beach. Being a Wednesday, there weren't many people on the beach. She turned her head to see a contented smile on Noel's face.

She remembered the day they'd spent at Chelsea. It was the day after she gave him her virginity. The day they took pictures she wished she hadn't burned. But, at the time, it was necessary. Taking her hand, he walked her down a sand dune and towards the shoreline. Then he wrapped his arms around her and they stared out at the ocean.

Resting her cheek against his chest, she closed her eyes and got lost in the moment. His heart beat strongly. She peeked up to see the love in his eyes and she felt content with her choices.

"What did you say to Liam?"

The smile on his face quickly vanished, and she knew she had ruined the moment.

"I told him of the life I wanted with you, and that I'd spend the rest of my life trying to make you happy. I told him that I wouldn't hurt you again and that I could provide for you." The honesty in his voice was clear, and at that moment, he sounded like he was promising her, too. His arms tightened around her once then he stepped back. Noel reached into the other pocket of his dress pants and handed her another card.

Clara opened it.

> This is the beach where you told me for the first time that you believed me. The same beach we spent a flawless day together. The same beach where I promised I intended to make you happy for the rest of your days. It's a promise I'm never going to break. I want to make you happy, simply forever.

"Noel," she whispered. This time tears slid down her face. She remembered him promising to count every grain of sand on the beach if it would make her happy. She held the card against her chest and he kissed the top of her head.

"We have one more stop left." The nervous smile on his face made him look vulnerable.

She nodded at him. These spots were ones she'd miss in Boston, but seeing them one last time made her heart melt at his effort.

The car ride from Chelsea Beach to Eastern Beach took almost two hours. By the time they arrived, it was late afternoon and hardly anyone was on the boardwalk except for some joggers. During the car ride, Noel had said little as he focused on driving. Clara didn't mind. She held the two cards and the tulip. She reread the cards and felt herself love him more for each word he wrote.

"Last stop, Clara."

He held out his hand, and she threaded her fingers through his. She pressed her body close to his as they walked on the boardwalk. The sun was still high and wouldn't set for a while. But, at this moment, she was ridiculously happy. Though she'd miss these spots around Victoria, she'd happily give them up for him.

The wind blew and she snuggled into his arm. "I love you, Noel," she said as her right hand wrapped around his arm.

He squeezed her hand. "I love you, too, Clara."

When they reached the white diving tower, she smiled at the sight of it. She was no longer scared of it because of him. One of her favourite memories was of him jumping off with her. Noel led her up the white steps and she smiled when she reached the top. Letting go of Noel's hand, she looked around at the beauty that surrounded her. The view of Geelong was breathtaking. She took a step forward and looked over the edge.

Clara could see it as if it were a projection in front of her. Noel never letting her hand go as they jumped off the platform and entered the water. Their embrace afterwards was one she had often remembered. Her eyes welled up at the happy moments they'd shared. Noel had taken her to three of her favourite spots in the world. She couldn't wait to start a life with him in a new city. Then she felt his hands on her shoulders and his warm breath touched her left ear.

"Question twenty."

She held her breath knowing that their game was about to end. She would ask him for more questions; she didn't want to let their game end. "Yes," she said as her eyes focused on the sight of Geelong.

"Will you wear something for me?"

Her eyebrows furrowed. But, instead of questioning him, she trusted him. "Yes."

Noel swiped her hair over her right shoulder. His body close as her heart started to beat erratically; completely unaware of what he had planned. Suddenly, something silver caught her eye. She smiled at the heart locket that Noel fastened around her neck.

"You fixed it," she said as she turned her head to the left and noticed his smile from the corner of her eye.

"Yeah. Now open it," he instructed.

She felt the warmth of his body leave her. Her fingers held the silver locket, and she gazed at the Celtic knot. No end or beginning, just an endless nature of time, a symbol of their love. Clara unclasped the locket, the hinge secure, and she was relieved that she could now wear it. Inside she saw a piece of folded paper. She knew that paper from when he gave her back the locket on her supposed wedding day.

His words of love were on this one piece of paper. She took it out and noticed that it wasn't as worn as she had remembered. It looked new. She frowned. Clara closed the locket and let it rest against her chest. Unfolding the piece of paper, she didn't see the words that he wrote. It was new. She read it out loud.

Question twenty-one. Clara Louise Lawrence...

Her heart stopped and her breath left her. Quickly turning around, she watched Noel dig into his pocket, take out a small velvet box, and kneel down on one knee. She stared at him in utter disbelief, forgetting to breathe as he opened the box. He held a beautiful diamond ring with two Celtic knots before her.

"This is the spot I knew I was falling in love with you. This is my favourite spot in the world because it got me closer to you and it got you to trust me. This spot is where I saw you for who you are and not just Alex's little sister. This spot made me forget about everything else in the world but you. And this is the spot I'm asking you my *final* question."

Tears filled Clara's eyes as she placed one hand on her chest, clutching her locket.

"Question twenty-one. Clara Louise Lawrence, would you make me the happiest man in the world by being my wife? *Will you marry me?*"

She kept her focus on those beautiful, green, loving eyes of his as her tears ran. It was the most heartfelt and meaningful proposal she had ever witnessed. It was made for them. It was perfect. He was perfect. He was her world. The perfect moments in their lives would never live up to this moment.

Clara nodded her head and choked out, "Yes."

"Yes?" he asked one more time.

"Yes, I'll marry you," she confirmed.

He took out the ring out and balanced the box on his knee. The large smile on his face made her heart leap. Noel took her left hand and said, "I love you, Clara Louise Lawrence. For all my life I will," as he slid the Celtic knot diamond engagement ring on her finger.

Her life felt complete the moment she said *yes*. This was what she wanted for the rest of her life — Noel as her husband.

Noel quickly got up as the ring box fell to the ground and slowly kissed her. Tears of joy ran down her cheeks. She was engaged to the right man.

He pulled back and smiled at her. "I've been waiting over a year to ask you."

"What?"

His thumbs wiped away her tears. "The day of Max's cousin's party, I had spent the day getting your ring resized. I was going to propose to you that night once I got your brother's blessing."

Clara tensed in his hold. "Oh, my God. You were going to… and I ended it. I'm so sorry. Noel, I'm so sorry I believed her and didn't let you explain," she apologised profusely.

"Hey, it's okay. It was too soon back then. We know now that we are meant to be with each other. We don't ever have to think about her or anyone else again. It's you and me, Clara. We're perfect together, even if we're messy and clueless at times."

"We're perfectly imperfect together," she agreed. "Did you ask Alex this time round?"

Noel kissed her forehead and nodded. "I asked him and Liam for their blessing to marry you."

She was stunned at his effort. That was when Clara understood Liam's words to her at the bakery. He was letting her go, and she was free to marry Noel.

"Thank you for asking them for their blessing. Especially Liam," she said gratefully.

"I needed his blessing so I'd know that when I married you there would be no hard feelings and we could live happily together in Boston. But I do have another question."

She looked down at her hands on his chest and the

engagement ring on her finger. This was where her heart belonged. The ring was perfect. The Celtic knot was theirs.

"Will you marry me before we leave Australia? Will you be *Mrs Nolan Parker* before we go to Boston?"

Her heart stopped at the thought of her last name being his. *Clara Louise Parker.*

"Yes, I'll marry you before we leave. I want nothing more in this world than to be *your* wife."

The Final Vow

Noel

One month later

The moment they had returned to the bakery, his life changed. His mother and gran, along with his fiancée's friends, changed the bakery from Clara's graduation celebration to their engagement party. A quick message to Alex, and their family and friends knew of their engagement. The first thing Clara feared was Liam's reaction, but he had to reassure her of Liam's blessing. Liam was the first person Clara had walked to when they'd returned to the bakery.

With his impatience to marry Clara as quickly as possible, their plans for Christmas in New York were changed. His wait to propose meant they wouldn't make the one-month requirement to submit their Notice of Intended Marriage form to their celebrant. But there was nothing like spending Christmas and New Year with his family and his bride-to-be. His life was perfect. His mother, father, gran, and brother welcomed Clara into the family with open arms as they had all her life.

Alex and Keira stayed in Melbourne, deciding that Christmas and New Year was a family affair that they wanted to share with Noel and Clara. Each time he woke up, he had to look at Clara's finger to reassure himself that it wasn't a dream. That extra two weeks meant he was able to plan the perfect wedding with Clara. The only thing she was secretive about was her wedding dress; she wanted something new and wanted something just for him.

"Bad news," he heard Rob say behind him. His nerves were getting the better of him. He wasn't sure how to deal with bad news. Turning away from the sight of the golf course, Noel looked at his groomsman.

"Tell me she didn't run?" There was desperation in his voice, but he hadn't seen Clara in a day as they stuck to tradition. That would be the worst news he'd ever hear on his wedding day.

Rob let out an honest chuckle and shook his head. "Nope, she's in her bridal suite. Spoke to Annie and Clara's there. The bad news is the delay of Julian's connecting flight from Sydney. He's landing later than we thought. You have one fewer groomsman to walk one of Clara's bridesmaids."

Reaching for his dark purple tie, Noel thought about the options he had. One fewer groomsman meant one less bridesmaid, and he didn't want Clara with one less. "Is Jarred around? You mind asking him if he'd like to walk Annie down. I owe him a lot and no doubt he'd love nothing more than to be in the wedding."

"Right, good choice. Have you got the other surprise in motion?"

Noel nodded proudly. His other surprise was moments away from happening. He just wished he were there to see it happen.

Rob grinned and said, "I'll see you in a sec. I'll go find Jarred and ask," before he slipped out of the groom's retreat.

He remembered the times his and Clara's families had come up to Eagle Ridge golf course on the Mornington Peninsula. He had wanted to give Clara a memorable wedding and Eagle Ridge was one of many of their memories together. He suggested the golf course because he knew Clara would prefer an outdoor wedding and Eagle Ridge was a stunning location.

"Here, let me get that for you, Nolan."

Lifting his chin, he watched his mother enter the room with a smile he had never seen and close the door behind her. She looked beyond happy to see him getting ready to marry the love of his life. Given her age, his mother was still as beautiful as she had always been.

Stepping in front of him, his mother popped up his collar and adjusted the length of his tie. The sparkle in her eyes didn't disappear as she transformed the tie into a Windsor knot.

"I remember the day you gave Clara that flower," she said softly as she adjusted the knot into place.

"You do?" he breathed out.

When the tie was to his mother's satisfaction, she looked up and nodded with a tear in her eye. "I'm your mother, Nolan. I don't miss a thing. And I definitely didn't miss a thing when you thought you were secretive the first time you came back to Melbourne. I knew something was going on with Clara when you didn't visit your father and me as much after our cruise. Who can blame you for falling in love with her? Clara's beautiful. You were too young, but I saw the love you had for her in your eyes. Maybe it was a friendship at first, but I'm happy that it flourished. I'm proud of you, and I'm happy that you're marrying her. I've always loved Clara like my own daughter and you know your grandmother wanted to take her away with her."

Placing his hands on his mother's bare arms, Noel pulled her in and kissed her cheek. "All my life, I've unknowingly loved her. I'm not hiding my love for her anymore, Mum. I'm going to be the best husband I can be for her."

His mother placed her hand on his cheek and smiled. "Honey, you *are* going to be the best husband for her."

"How does she look, Mum?"

"Beautiful beyond words. Now, I better go make sure your grandmother gives Clara her something borrowed."

He raised a brow at her. "What is Gran giving her?"

His mother moved her hand from his face and adjusted the small purple tulip on his suit properly. "She's letting Clara borrow her lasagne recipe."

He breathed out and stared at his mother in surprise. "What? Gran is really doing that?"

"She's about to be a Parker," his mother said with such excitement.

The burst of the doors had him turning and his mother

stopping.

"You!" Alex pointed.

His mother's eyes widened and he knew his surprise had backfired on him. Giving his mother a reassuring squeeze of the arm, he ushered her towards the direction of the door. The fear in her eyes intensified when she walked past Alex.

"Listen, I can explain," Noel offered as Alex quickly stalked towards him.

If Alex was going to stop the wedding, Noel wasn't going to have any of it. He already had the headache of Clara's visa papers, Alex's dislike for the surprise was stress he didn't need. Before going to Hong Kong, Noel had applied and was granted a dual-citizenship, making him both a citizen of Australia and the U.S. He was thankful he became a dual citizen; it made Clara's stay in the U.S. permanent and avoided work visa papers.

Before Noel could explain himself, Alex wrapped his arms tightly around him. Noel stilled, surprised by Alex's actions.

"Thank you. Thank you so much," Alex cried. His best friend wasn't one to be overly emotional.

"Uhh, you're ruining my suit. I'm marrying your sister and I want to look decent," he playfully teased.

Alex untangled himself from Noel and wiped away a tear. Alex shedding tears was an unfamiliar sight for Noel. "How did you manage that? I've tried all my life," Alex said, shaking his head.

Breathing out and relaxing the nerves that his best friend had induced, Noel straightened his suit jacket as Alex sat in the armchair to his left. Following his best man's lead, Noel sat in the chair next to him.

"Simple. I asked your father for his blessing as well as yours and Liam's. I invited him to the wedding to walk her down the aisle if she wishes."

"But how did you manage that? He's divorcing my mother!"

The disbelief on Alex's face made Noel let out a short laugh. "When you were in the hospital, I confessed my love for Clara to him. When I asked for his blessing, he said he realised when they got back to Melbourne that he put Gillian first for far too long and that he was sick of being in a loveless marriage. He was over the moon to hear that Clara and I got back together. I hope you're not offended that I invited him but having your

317

dad walk her down the aisle is something Clara longs for," Noel explained.

"Honestly, man, I would love nothing more than to see the sight of my dad walking my sister down the aisle. It's something I've wanted for a long time. You truly are a good man. I'm glad you're marrying Clara. I'm proud to have you as my brother-in-law."

Noel grinned at his best man and soon to be brother-in-law. He wanted this from the moment he wanted Clara forever. It was something he thought he'd never have.

"I'm happy she chose me," Noel confessed.

Alex proudly smiled and then he breathed out. "Listen, I have to ask you something."

Noel noticed the vulnerable gleam in Alex's eyes and tapped his fingers on his leg to try to calm himself. "Okay?"

Alex had glanced down at his hands for a moment before looking back up at him. "You promise to look after her, right? I've spent my entire life looking after her and now I'm letting her go. I know she's in good hands, but I need to hear you say it. Clara's been my responsibility, and I want to know that when I let her go, she's gonna be okay."

Noel reached over and set his hand on Alex's back. "I'm gonna look after her, Alex. It's my turn to look out for Clara and provide for her. I'm about to make her my wife. The privilege is all mine. I'll spend my life making sure she's happy. I'm promising the world that today. But I promise you more than anyone that I'm never going to let her down. I'm never going to let her go, and I'm never going to let her feel unloved ever again. I promise you, Clara's my life."

With a satisfied smile, Alex stood up and adjusted his suit. "Thanks. I needed to hear that. I'm just happy that I know she's going to be safe and happy. I get to see her for all the holidays and know that she's only in Massachusetts. I had better go see her and get her ready for her surprise. You let me know what it's like on the other side."

Letting out a chuckle, Noel too stood up from the chair. "I'll let you know what married life is like. Get you prepared for when you marry Keira in June."

"First, let's make sure that you and my sister finally get married. I think we'll all relax as soon as she becomes Mrs

Nolan Parker."

With a grin, Alex exited the room leaving Noel to himself. He walked over to the full-length mirror and adjusted his attire to ensure nothing was short of perfection. Adjusting his suit jacket, he heard the knock on the door. Turning around, he watched as Max entered the retreat.

"Hey," Noel greeted. Things between them had been tense and Max continued to blame himself. He had avoided Clara more than Noel would have liked, but there was no way to remove Max of his guilt.

"Annie will be here to tell you when they're ready to start. She's just dropping off her husband at the doors." Max averted Noel's stare as he spun for the door.

"Max," Noel called out and walked towards him.

Max faced him and the guilt consumed his eyes. "Yeah?" Max's voice was so low that Noel almost didn't hear it.

"We don't blame you. It wasn't your fault. It was ours. But we're okay now. Please stop blaming yourself, okay? Clara thinks you won't ever talk to her again, and it upsets her. She doesn't hate you for Sarah's actions."

Max lifted his chin. "So you guys forgive me?"

The hope laced in Max's voice had Noel smirking. "No. Want to know why? Because there's nothing to forgive. You did nothing wrong, Max." Not letting the guilt consume Max again, Noel brought him in for a quick hug.

Once they separated, he saw the relief in Max's eyes. Another knock on the door had them both turning.

"Sorry to interrupt but Mr Parker is needed at the altar to marry his bride," Annie said as she entered the room; her blue eyes twinkled.

"Mrs Harper, you look quite beautiful. Jarred is one lucky man."

Annie blushed. "And Clara's a lucky woman. Now, let's not keep her waiting. Max, you'll be with Josie."

Taking two steps forward, Noel wrapped his arms around Annie. "Thank you... for everything," he whispered in her ear.

She made a small giggle as he unwrapped his arms from her.

"I'm sorry I wasn't there for your wedding."

Annie shook her head. "Don't be. I can always send you a

DVD. Now, shall we?"

He nodded. "I'm about to *finally* marry the love of my life."

Clara

"It's time, Clara."

She turned away from the mirror to see her maid of honour holding up a bouquet of tulips. Clara looked up at Stevie and gave her a reassuring smile. They had both heard the sound of a soft knock before her brother, Alex, walked into the bridal room.

"I've never seen such a beautiful bride in all my life, Clara. He's one lucky man," Alex said as he walked over to Clara and placed a kiss on her cheek.

Her heart tugged slightly, and she looked at the tulips. Even when she was a little girl, she had imagined these flowers at her wedding.

"Do you think I made the right choice?" she asked as she looked up at her brother.

A slight frown had appeared before Alex smiled and placed his hands on Clara's shoulders.

"Clara, you know I'm not impartial. I'm just happy that you're happy." After everything they had been through, she was happy. Her life was complete the moment she had said *yes.*

"*He's* there, right, Alex?" Clara asked. She needed to know that he would be there the moment she stepped on to the aisle.

"Clara, Liam isn't doing a runner. It's *you,* we're all worried about."

She closed her eyes and took a deep breath. With her brother walking her down the aisle to the person she would and could love forever, Clara knew she'd made the right choice.

"I'm not running, Alex. I'm staying. It was always him. He's the reason for this all."

In a matter of moments, she'd be walking down the aisle towards becoming Noel's wife.

"He's there in the front row with a smile on his face. He's happy to see you marry Noel!."

Another knock had her raising her eyebrow at him. The door slowly opened to Granny Parker dressed in a lovely salmon-coloured dress and matching jacket. Clara smiled at the grandmother she would be able to finally call hers.

"Oh, Clara." Granny's eyes roamed the wedding dress Clara wore and tears started to pool her eyes.

Alex took a step to the right as Stevie closed the door behind Granny Parker.

"Granny Parker, is it okay out there?"

"Honey, you shouldn't worry about chairs and tables. Let the others worry about that."

Smiling, Clara walked up to and hugged her fiancé's grandmother. She smelt of apples, a smell she remembered from her childhood.

"I have something for you."

"You do?" Clara asked as she untangled her arms from Granny Parker.

"I have your something borrowed." The wrinkles around her eyes deepened as she smiled at Clara.

"Oh, Granny Parker, I can't take anything from you." Clara raised her hands and shook her head.

"Nonsense. You are about to be my granddaughter, and I want to give you this." Granny Parker claiming her made Clara's heart burn. She was happy a family loved her. Her own biological parents wouldn't be here, but at least the family she'd be marrying into was in attendance.

"Here," Granny said as she pulled out a folded piece of paper.

Clara moved back a loose curl, took the piece of paper, and started to unfold it. Her mouth dropped. "Granny, I can't take this," Clara breathed as she gazed at the recipe for the Parker family lasagne.

"Don't be silly, Clara. You are about to be a Parker, too. And it's yours to borrow and feed that grandson of mine."

"Thank you so much," Clara said and then kissed her grandmother-in-law on the cheek.

"Have you got everything else?" Alex asked once he gave Granny a hug.

Adjusting the sleeve caps of her tulle wedding dress, Clara nodded. "I have my something old, which is my locket. Something new is my engagement ring. Something borrowed is Granny's recipe. Something blue is the earrings my bridesmaids got me, and I have the silver sixpence in my shoe from Noel."

Clara smiled at the memory of Noel showing her the sixpence the day before. He had her close her eyes and after his countdown from three, she saw him holding it up to her, grinning. A 1943 British sixpence coin completed the wedding tradition. The reason why Noel had purchased the 1943 sixpence coin was due to her love of King George VI and the story of *The King's Speech*.

Seeing the sixpence coin he held before him, she was utterly in awe of how much she truly loved him. Though it was uncomfortable at first, she loved the idea of the coin in her shoe. But the one thing she cared about more than anything was the silver locket around her neck. Inside it still held the note that had asked for question twenty-one. The one question she had never hesitated answering.

Looking at her engagement ring, she smiled to herself. The Celtic knots melted her heart, and soon, she'd have a wedding band. A symbol that Noel forever owned her heart. The door to her bridal suite opened and Clara peeked up to see Annie enter the room with a joyous smile on her face.

"The boys are ready!"

Alex linked his arms around hers. "Showtime, Clara Louise Lawrence... for the last time."

Clara placed her hand over brother's arm. "I'm always going to be your little sister."

Alex looked down at her fondly. "Now that you're going to be a Parker, I don't want the same pain-in-the-ass attitude I get from your damn husband!"

Granny Parker let out a snort. "Alex, we Parkers are known for our ways. Can't say we won't corrupt Clara. I had better go find my son and Louise. I'll see you all at the gazebo."

Granny Parker had given everyone in the room a hug and a kiss before she slipped out. The gazebo they'd say 'I do' under was breathtakingly beautiful. It sat on the small island on the golf course lake and had a bridge that connected it to the main course. When Noel had suggested Eagle Ridge course, Clara laughed. The first thing she remembered of the golf course was Julian and Noel chasing her with their golf cart when Clara was eight. Seeing the gazebo for the first time in years instantly changed her mind. She wanted to marry Noel at that spot.

"Keira, Josie, and Ally are at the door. Ready to go?" Stevie asked as she placed the bouquet of purple tulips in Clara's hand.

Alex gently squeezed her arm. She turned her head and looked up at him.

Letting out a blissful sigh, she nodded her head. "Let's put that poor man out of his misery before he thinks I got cold feet."

The anxiousness had her on edge. She was impatient to be Noel's wife. Alex led her out of the bridal suit and towards the glass doors that opened to the golf course. She felt the fast beats of her heart as she took the steps that would lead her closer to becoming Clara Parker.

Alex whispered jokes to calm her and Clara laughed as they rounded the corner. She noticed her bridesmaids standing on the other side of the glass door with their groomsmen. But Clara's eyes met with a tall man in a black suit. She instantly stilled, holding Alex back.

"Daddy?" she breathed out unbelievably shocked.

He turned around and she saw a loving smile on her father's face. She didn't bother to invite her father or mother to her and Noel's wedding. She didn't want any trouble that involved her parents.

"What are you—"

Alex untangled their arms, and he hugged their father. When Alex turned around, he had a relieved smile on his face.

"Noel asked for my blessing and asked if I'd walk you down the aisle. If that's okay with you and Alex?"

The hope in his eyes was one she had never thought he'd have towards her. Clara closed her eyes tightly, took a deep breath, and then opened them. Noel had asked her father for his blessing and surprised her with her father's presence at their wedding.

"Alex?" she asked for his permission.

"I would love nothing more than for Dad to walk you down. I couldn't let Stevie walk down the aisle by herself."

"Okay, Daddy." Clara took a step towards her father. She vowed she wouldn't speak to him again, but this time he sought her love and affection, and he broke her resolve and won. She wrapped her arms around the man who had been blinded by love. Clara knew her veil shifted out of place as they hugged, but she didn't care. Today was perfect.

"I love you, Clara," he said in her ear.

Clara fought hard to stop the tears from falling. Untangling from their long and overdue embrace, her father kept his hands on her arms.

"I'm sorry I've been a terrible father to the both of you. I did it because I didn't want your mother to hurt you further. I'm sorry, Clara. I was wrong to choose Gillian over my daughter. I'm divorcing her. I'm sorry I couldn't get her to attend your wedding."

"I don't care that she's not here. I'm just happy that you're here, Daddy. I've always dreamed of this moment."

Clara turned and faced the glass doors as her father linked his arms around hers. The smile on Alex's face had her content. Alex nodded at the golf club workers who held the doors for them, and Clara instantly felt the warm air hit her skin.

Alex winked as he walked to the front of the line. Clara could just see CeCe holding her basket of white rose petals. Turning around, Jarred smiled at her, and she felt the surprise creep on her face.

"How?" she mouthed at him.

Annie turned and smiled at Clara.

"Rob's brother's flight was delayed. I'm filling in," he replied in a whisper.

Clara heard the sounds of the violins, and she could just see Noel lift his head up in her direction.

"Ready?" her father asked.

Clara tore her eyes away from the gazebo and looked up at him. With a nod of her head, the bridal party started to walk towards the bridge that acted as the aisle. She watched as they all walked in sync with the violins. The golf club events manager signalled at Clara that it was time.

The violins changed its tune to the bridal march, and she watched as her guests stood up from the chairs that circled around the gazebo. Her gaze landed on the man she would call her husband.

As she walked closer to Noel, her eyes never left his. Jane from *27 Dresses* had dreamt of this moment. The way Noel looked at her as if she was the only woman in the world. The way he held his breath at the sight of her made her smile. The way he looked at her confirmed that no one would love her the way Nolan Parker did.

She couldn't wipe the smile off her face as she crossed the bridge with her father. Her bridesmaids and Noel's groomsmen stood against the railings of the bridge. Passing Alex, she noticed his wink from the corner of her eye. Just before she got to the end of the bridge, Clara handed her bouquet to Stevie. When she reached the gazebo, Noel stepped towards her. She turned to her father as he produced a proud smile.

"Thank you, Daddy," she whispered once he'd kissed her cheek and offered her hands to Noel.

"You take care of my girl, now."

Noel didn't take his eyes off her. "For all my life, I will," he promised. "You look beautiful," Noel whispered for only her to hear as they looked at their celebrant.

Noel took both her hands and faced her. Those green eyes pierced her heart and she couldn't wait to hear the proclamation that she was his wife. Her eyes never left his as the celebrant began their wedding ceremony.

"Nolan and Clara have decided to write their own vows. Nolan," their male celebrant said.

Noel breathed out, and she smiled largely at him. "Clara, there is not a day that goes by that I don't think of you. Today, in front of all our friends and family, I take you to be my wife. I vow to eat every cupcake you make me, I vow to make you smile when all you want to do is cry, and I vow for the rest of my days that I will love you without a fault and without a doubt. Falling in love with you was easy and being in love with you makes forever seem as if it's not long enough. We've had our troubles and our journeys, but I thank God every day that we found a way back to each other.

"I was asked my reasons for loving you and I would need an endless supply of paper. Because every reason is purposeful and every reason is valid when it comes to my love for you. My life reason is you. You are what makes me valid and you are what makes me purposeful. I don't need thirty-eight reasons. I just have one: my reason for loving is you. Clara Louise Lawrence, I will only ever need you in my life. You are my reason."

She sniffed at his words. Beautiful and honest. She promised herself she wouldn't cry, but his vows were perfect beyond words. Taking a breath, she knew it was time for her vows.

"Nolan James Parker, you are the most infuriating man I have ever met, but you are also the greatest man, too. Being in love, I found it to be unexpected and messy as well as completely and utterly liberating. And that sums us up. I've never been perfect, but with you, we're perfectly imperfect together. I have flaws and I have faults, which you see past and still love me. All I ever wanted was a little bit of you and you gave me all and everything.

"Your love makes me a better person. Your love makes me feel beautiful. And your love makes me feel loved. I fall in love with you more and more every day, more so than the day before. I vow to always be madly in love with you. I vow to always be your friend and your soul mate. I vow to be the best wife I can be. I vow to give you the happily ever after that you deserve. And I vow that our love will be timeless and without a concept of any forms of limits, like a Celtic knot. I've known you all my life, but it took you standing at my doorstep for me to fall madly in love with you. In front of all the people I love, I promise to wake up to every sunrise with you for the rest of our days because I love you and I will never stop being in love with you, Nolan James Parker."

A tear ran down Noel's face and he mouthed 'I love you' to her. The happiness that engulfed her completely fuelled her body. She squeezed his hands and reassured him that this was all she ever wanted.

"Nolan James Parker, do you take Clara Louise Lawrence to be your lawfully wedded wife? Will you love her, comfort her, honour, and respect her? Do you promise to share all life has to offer you both, the hopes and dreams you both have as well as your achievements and disappointments with her from this day onwards?"

Noel didn't blink as he said, "I do."

"And do you, Clara Louise Lawrence, take Nolan James Parker to be your lawfully wedded husband? Will you love him, comfort him, honour and respect him? Do you promise to share all life has to offer you both, the hopes and dreams you both have, as well as your achievements and disappointments with him from this day onwards?"

Her thumbs gently ran along the back of his hands and without a single hint of hesitation, Clara said, "I do."

The relief that filled his eyes almost had her giggling. She closed her eyes and allowed this moment with him to consume her. They had both just promised, in front of their witnesses, to love each other for all of their days.

When she opened her eyes, Alex handed Noel the ring.

"With this ring, I marry you, Clara, and offer a symbol of my everlasting love for the rest of our days." His thumb had stroked her ring finger before he slid the wedding band on. The burst of her heart had her almost breathless.

Then she took Noel's ring from Stevie with a smile. "With this ring, I marry you, Nolan, and offer a symbol of my everlasting love for the rest of our days." She took his hand and placed his wedding ring on his finger. The sight of it made the tears brim her eyes. Noel was finally and legally hers. She glanced at their hands and loved the sight of their wedding rings.

"Friends and family, Nolan and Clara have declared before you all this day that they will live together in marriage. They have symbolised their everlasting love by joining hands, taking vows and exchanging rings. I, therefore, declare Nolan James Parker and Clara Louise Parker to be husband and wife."

I'm now Clara Louise Parker, wife of Nolan James Parker.

The thought made her breathless and she saw Noel hold his breath as he waited for the words she knew he had been eagerly awaiting.

"Nolan James Parker, you may now kiss your bride," the celebrant said with much happiness in his voice.

"Finally," Noel breathed out.

She couldn't contain her smile as he brought her into his arms.

"I love you, Mrs Parker," he whispered with so much love then his lips found hers as their first kiss as man and wife. It was perfect. His lips caused another burst of her heart and she smiled as she heard the increase of hollers, claps and cheers.

The moment their first kiss had ended, she placed her hand on his cheek and gently stroked it. "And I love you, Mr Parker, simply forever."

Epilogue

Noel

y wife.

    Noel stared at the woman he had just married as she gave their flower girl a kiss on the cheek. She was breathtakingly beautiful and she was his. Clara Louise Lawrence was now Clara Louise Parker, his wife. She looked his way and a smile slowly touched her lips. The love and happiness in her eyes caused his heart to skip a beat. She brushed her brown curls out of her face and she slowly walked towards him. He held his breath as she took each step to him, just like when she had walked down the aisle. Noel didn't take his eyes off her.

I love my wife.

His heart throbbed, agreeing with his thoughts. He was madly in love with the woman who stopped in front of him and placed her hands on his hips. His hands cupped her face as he stared into those brown eyes of hers. The same pair that had looked back at him when she had discovered him at her doorstep the first time they met again.

"Thank you," he said, brushing his thumb across the faint mole on her cheek.

She tilted her head and asked, "For?"

Noel smiled and placed a chaste kiss on her lips. "For letting me love you," he said.

Then he placed another. "For letting me marry you."

Then another. "For letting me have a life with you."

And another. Clara smiled against his lips and he pulled back. He brushed her loose curls away and smiled at her. Everything he ever wanted and would ever want was in his hands. She wore his ring and had his name.

Her eyes never left his as her fingers squeezed the side of his waist. He ignored the photographer calling their names and grazed the pad of his thumb along the bottom of her lip.

"For finding your way back to me." This time he kissed her forehead. "And finally…"

He pulled back and placed his hands on hers, pulling them off his body. Noel clutched her left hand and his fingers trailed over her wedding band. His heart throbbed, sending warmth throughout his body. He let go of her left and held her right. His fingers rested on the Celtic knot engagement ring and he smiled, remembering the first time he placed it on her.

Noel's thumb and index finger pulled off the engagement ring and he took hold of her left hand on his right. His eyes met hers and the smile she gave him was one he looked forward to seeing for the rest of his life.

"For loving me," Noel said as he slid the engagement ring on her finger, resting on her wedding band.

Clara pulled her hands away from his and placed them on the back of his neck, bringing his mouth closer to hers. Just shy of contact, Clara stopped and said, "Thank you for loving me the way you do. For believing in me and for us. Thank you for us, Noel."

"Thirty-eight," he whispered, looking down at her. Noel placed his hands on her hips, loving the feel of her wedding dress beneath his fingers.

"Thirty-eight. You said that in your vows," his wife said as her hands moved to his shoulders.

"When we first ended, we were apart for thirty-eight days. And every day for thirty-eight days, I wrote a reason why I love you," he revealed, and Clara's lips slowly parted.

"You wrote me thirty-eight reasons," she said softly.

He nodded. "The only reason that matters is that you, Clara

Louise Parker, are my reason for loving. Those reasons are all about you. I love all of you. You are my life reason."

"And you, Nolan James Parker, make me valid and purposeful," Clara said, reciting his vows.

She removed her hands from his shoulders and Noel reached inside his jacket pocket and pulled out a folded piece of paper, handing it to his wife.

"I love you for more than just these thirty-eight reasons. I have a lifetime of reasons for loving you. And I can't wait until the day I get to say to you that one of my reasons for loving you is that you're the mother of my child."

She had blinked twice before her hands cupped his face and said, "That will be my favourite reason for you loving me. I love you, Noel. Simply forever."

I love my wife for wanting to have my child. I love my wife for wanting a life with me. I am in love with my wife, for more than thirty-eight days and more than thirty-eight reasons.

The End.

What You
LEFT BEHIND

No amount of white sand or distance could bury their past.

Some things are just never meant to be forgotten.

When Julian Moors returned from Thailand he left behind all his belongings, his father and only brother in Melbourne and moved to Sydney. One girl shattered his world and left him with more questions than answers.

Behind the persona, Stevie Appleton tries to outrun her past. Nightmares and memories have started to collide, putting her future and her heart at risk. No one can know the secrets she tries to keep locked away, even if it means betraying the people she loves the most.

Everyone has a story but not everyone has a past quite like Stevie and Julian.

When they meet years later, don't expect a happy ending. The past holds skeletons and not even these skeletons can be buried.

Available now.

Read on for an excerpt of Stevie and Julian's novel.

Prologue

Stevie

Four Years Ago

Stopping by one of the small drink vendors across from Karon Beach, Stevie bought a bottle of cold water. Once she had crossed the road, she placed the hat over her blonde hair and looked out at the crystal clear blue water. She was in awe.

They don't have beaches like this back home.

Stevie slipped off her thongs and her bare feet instantly felt the hot sand. Although she had been here not too long ago, she couldn't help but smile at the fact that she was miles away from home. Life at home hadn't been horrible. She had felt suffocated and needed to find herself before she started university. That had been one thing she wasn't looking forward to — finding out whether or not she had been accepted into the university of her dreams.

Instead of trying to pass tourists to get to the water, Stevie decided to sit on the white sand and enjoy the peace offered by the beach for now. She knew that tonight would be one of the beach's moonlight beach parties. She wasn't sure who organised them, but the alcohol was cheap and every young foreigner attended.

Just as she was about to sit down, she noticed a pair of pale blue eyes on her. His brown hair was damp, and his wet body glimmered in the sunlight. Those eyes glared at her as if she was holding a secret and he was trying to decipher it. Stevie felt the air in her lungs flee, as he didn't break eye contact. She neither smiled nor frowned. Instead, Stevie directed her attention back to the clear water and sat on the hot sand. Then she set her beach bag and thongs down. She fought an internal battle to resist the temptation to

glance back at him. To discover if his eyes had been focused on her or not. But she heavily doubted it. However, there was no denying the fact that he was beautiful. His eyes were what lured her into a sense of curiosity towards him. They were so pale that she filed them as unique. Her eyes, however, were bright blue as the sky on a cloudless day — or so her last boyfriend had said. No way did hers match this man's beauties.

Ignoring her roommate predicament and the attractiveness of that guy's light blue eyes, Stevie reached into her bag until she found her copy of *To Kill a Mockingbird*. The same copy that her father had given to her when she was ten. The cover was worn with creases and spill marks, but that was what she loved about the book. It had lasted through the years she'd spent in Melbourne and Paris. After flipping through the novel, she landed on the page marked by the same gift tag her father had written her name on. She smoothed out the page and continued to read.

"Tell me you're a local and that you do this every day when you come to the beach," she heard a smooth voice say when she had almost finished the chapter.

Heart stopped. Breathing ceased. *Oh.* Slowly — as she tried to process the unnatural movements

that her body made — Stevie placed the book on her lap. Then she turned to see those pale blue eyes staring at the pages of her book. At first, his closeness startled her as he peered over her shoulder, but she had managed to hide her flinch. Then she felt a cold drop of seawater hit her exposed shoulder, and she shivered.

"Excuse me?" she asked.

"You've got to be a local. There is no way a tourist comes to

Phuket to read Harper Lee's classic."

Stevie blinked as he took the book from her lap. His wet fingers moistened the pages as he flicked through them. Suddenly, he stopped going through the book and ran a finger down the page.

That was when Stevie felt her jaw drop. This stranger picked out and read out loud one of her favourite quotes from her favourite novel. He smiled and closed the book before handing it back to her. After a few blinks, Stevie quickly took the book back and returned it to her lap.

"I like your choice in classics. I think we'll be good friends," he stated with a hint of excitement in his voice. He gave a genuine smile, and she couldn't refrain from staring into his eyes. More grey than blue. But then more blue than grey. They were beautiful. Alluring, even.

"What's your name?" he asked.

The ability to voice her name had become a struggle with her dried up throat.

You don't just tell random strangers your name, right?

"Blondie, what's your name?" His nickname for her snapped her out of her thoughts. "It's not Blondie, that's for sure. And I'm not here to make

friends," she retorted.

Those goddamn eyes. Seriously? I need to get out of here. I can hide out near the pool... Yeah. I'll do that. Stevie leant forward and grabbed her beach bag. Those eyes

and that smile had her alarm bells ringing. And she was sure that he was Australian. His accent wasn't strong, but she knew he couldn't be from up north.

"Whoa, whoa, whoa, Blondie. Need to be somewhere?" he asked as he gently wrapped his hand around her arm, stopping her. Stevie looked down at his hand and then up at him, his eyebrow raised at her.

"It's not 'Blondie.' Okay?" Her body remained tense under his grasp.

"Come on. I have to know the girl behind the mockingbird. You intrigue me," he explained then released her arm as he sat back.

Stevie turned to see him still staring at her. She sighed. "You aren't going to leave me alone, are you?" she asked, already knowing the answer.

He pulled a boyish grin that disarmed her immediately.

Kill. Me.

"Julian," he said as he sat forward and held out his hand.

Stevie tensed as she hesitantly glanced down at the hand he offered.

Julian shook his head and chuckled. "Here's what we'll do, Blondie. We'll be one of those types of friends, the holiday kind. No last names, no pasts or where we come from. We'll just hang out on this beach. What do you say?"

He seemed so open and friendly. But Stevie had to be cautious. If they were just going to be friends, then he wouldn't have to know a whole lot about her. This beach would be all that they had, and then they'd leave it behind and let it wash away with the water.

He doesn't have to know who I really am. He'd never look for me. I won't give him a reason to.

"Stephanie."

AVAILABLE NOW

Acknowledgements

As always, I'd like to thank my ever-so-loving family for their unconditional love and support. You can't pick your family but I am so glad we got stuck with each other.

Thank you to my friends for having to deal with my constant complaining over my workload... you know who you all are and I'm sorry!

My favourite authors in the world, Jaycee Ford and Alex Rosa. Thank you for being by my side and for listening to every concern I've had. I couldn't have done any of this without you both.

I can never thank Najla Qamber from Najla Qamber Designs enough for the amazing cover for this book. You are a privilege to work with and I am so happy to have worked with you. Don't think our working relationship is done just yet. I'm writing books just for you to make me covers!

Jenny Sims, my brilliant editor and proofreader. Thank you for everything you do. My books are better because of you. I am a better author because of you and every book we write together.

My beta readers, Danielle Woodside and Michal Sue Walker. Every failed attempt at writing you've read first. Thank you for reading the very worst of my work. You both deserve a gazillion pardons from the universe.

My Lenatics, you have rallied into the hundreds. When the group started I wanted twelve members now look at us! We are mighty! Thank you for supporting me when you could have supported someone more deserving of your love!

My readers, I am what I am because of you. Thank you for putting up with my bachelor to get this book. I have never felt more privileged in my life than when I get your messages.

Thank you so much for being part of the journey.

Remember, if anything, love is never easy.
xoxo

P.S. Thank you for trusting me with Noel and Clara's story.

About the Author

Len Webster is a romance-loving Melburnian with dreams of finding her version of 'The One.' But until that moment happens, she writes. Having just graduated with her BBusCom from Monash University, Len is now busy writing her next romance about how a boy met a girl, and how they fell completely and hopelessly in love.

Connect with Len

Website: www.lenwebster.com
Facebook: www.facebook.com/lennwebster
Twitter: twitter.com/lennwebster
Goodreads: www.goodreads.com/author/show/7502135.
Len_Webster
Amazon: www.amazon.com/Len- Webster/e/B00HIFA2GM/
ref=ntt_athr_dp_pel_14
Instagram: instagram.com/lennwebster

Made in the USA
Charleston, SC
21 June 2016